SLAVE

Also by William Malliol

A SENSE OF DARK

SLAVE

WILLIAM MALLIOL

W · W · NORTON & COMPANY

New York   London

Published simultaneously in Canada by Penguin Books Canada Ltd,
2801 John Street, Markham, Ontario L3R 1B4
Printed in the United States of America.

The text of this book is composed in Times Roman, with
display type set in Neuland. Composition and
manufacturing by The Haddon Craftsmen Inc.
Book design by Jacques Chazaud.
First Edition

ISBN 0-393-02268-4

W. W. Norton & Company, Inc., 500 Fifth Avenue, New York, N. Y. 10110
W. W. Norton & Company Ltd., 37 Great Russell Street, London WC1B 3NU

1 2 3 4 5 6 7 8 9 0

DEDICATION

In Memoriam
JEAN-CLAUDE QUINTIN
Captain
1st Bn. 1st Regiment
French Foreign Legion

M. MOODY WHITE
de furtivis literarum
notis
de cryptomenysis patefacta
negotium perambulams
in
tenebris

A. B. RACHIELE

C. A. JOSEPH DING

STARLING R. LAWRENCE

COL. L. S. L. WESTERHOFF

SLAVE

How do I know when I was born? Aoi-yo. To reach my age being a slave takes much effort of the body and the head you must understand. But—puh!—you do not. However, we black men cannot today remember the number of years that we have lived. Perhaps it was sixty years ago—I do not know; I do not care. I am alive and still full of life, and I am not an old man yet, am I? My muscles are strong, look, and firm. My teeth are sound and do not wobble in my mouth. My skin is smooth, look, and shining and not puckered and scaly as it is with old men. And I know that I am not that young because I have left my country in the south land of the blacks for a long time. But I recall when I was first caught by the slavers, I was a strong full-grown man already married. What curious people you Europeans are. You ask so many questions and you want to know so much about things that do not concern you. Why should you care about slaves from Bornu, Sokoto, Yariba, and Kano and how they live and what languages they speak? See, you have written many words already that I have spoken of, and yes, I can speak Marghi and Fulde and Popo and Batta and the other tongues of barbarians and pagans, who know not God and reject the teaching of His Prophet. I too was like them once.

The country where my mother bore me is far away—far, far away below the desert, beyond the Great River, beyond the kingdoms of the Muselmin Fullani and Hausa and in a land of Kufar unbelievers where the people, my village brothers, went naked and knew not shame. It is a country so far, that though you may love traveling, I doubt if you would ever reach it. Yet once or twice I have heard that you white men have been near my motherland. They came —I have heard it said—to spy out the country and the chiefs of the Fullani people and the Vizeer of Bornu afforded them protection. Then too, I have heard that the great rushing river which was distant a month's walk from my home, toward the north—the river that the Fullani call Mayo Fumbina, and the Batta call the Benue—that this water flowed towards the setting sun where it joined the Kwara which comes from Timbuktu, and up this Kwara they used to say that men of the white tribes Dano, Germani, Nederlandi, Francswari, and Porto-Kee came in big ships to buy slaves. All these white men, I heard, would come to the city of Iddah, and sometimes the Arabs have told me they were mostly English and sometimes they said they were yet another kind of Englishmen, called Merakani. And once too, some white men of the Swenski tribe came up the Benue River in a steamer. Now the Swenskis have got houses on the Benue where they trade with the Fullani people. It may be lying, it may be true. I do not know. But you white men are at one wonderful, and at two, terrible, and so are the things you do.

Are you going to write my history in a book? Yauri, my headman, said you wished to do so, and as he likes you and wishes to please you because you have given him favors, he has asked me to come here, and being I am, I am to do your bidding. If you wish me to be silent, I am to be silent. If you wish me to talk, I am to tell you all that I know even if it be words of the jargon of the savage language of the pagans, or if it be of all the things that I have seen and done, in all my life since I was born. Oh yes, I will tell you truth—by God I will not lie—why should I? You white men know everything, and if you found I was deceiving you, you would send me away and not hear things you would otherwise have no knowledge of.

And I like coming to see you. It makes me bigger in the eyes of my people to talk to a white man—all my friends will say:

"See, Hadi Abbabba Guwah, the strong and the lusty, must be a man with something in him or the Englishman would not send for him every day and write down in a book the words that he speaks."

The name they called my mother country was Popo. It was a land of forests and mountains—a land where water never failed, because in all directions there were brooks and rivers and my country people never thought of digging wells.

When I can first remember, I was a small, small boy, of perhaps eight hands high, and I lived in a large village of perhaps five hundred people, of this district called Bahom. My mother, who was called Teeta, was a young woman who had a pleasant face, although after the manner of these pagans it was, by custom, scarred and tattooed on the forehead and cheeks and chin. My mother, Teeta, was one of

the five wives of a man called Asho-eso, who was the chief of the
village and also ruled over three other neighboring towns. We lived
in a type of walled compound, the four sides of which were houses
built of wood posts with palm thatch roofs. In the middle of the
compound, or yard, was a small tree growing. And on this tree were
hung the skulls of people whom my father, the old chief, had killed.
And there were also a lot of charms and gri-gris such as these pagans
believe in, tied round the trunk of this tree. And every now and then
when the men of the village killed a man that had been made a slave,
or a war prisoner whom they had captured when they fought with
the Bakuba—the Bakuba were a tribe who lived on a high mountain
two days' journey from our village, and who used sometimes to, for
excitement, fight with us. Those we had killed we roasted. When I
say the fighting men of our town killed someone and roasted his flesh
for a feast, it is because it was the custom, for my people were
maneaters like the Ghuls of the desert. The bones once clean of the
men they had eaten were carried into the compound, and by my
father the chief's command, were laid round the base of this my
father's tree. I do not know why.

The first thing I remember clearly was playing with the skull of
one of these Bakuba people whom the young men of the town had
eaten. I used to roll it about on the ground of the compound and
amuse myself by filling it with sand and then holding it up to let the
sand run out from the eyes and nose. There were a number of other
boys, my compound brothers—perhaps eight or ten, living with me
in the yard, who were said to be my father's children. My true
mother was the youngest of his wives. And strong and with good
skin, good teeth, and laughing all the time. And the name of the
Head-Wife was Ndeba. I liked Ndeba because of the way she danced
but she did not like me because she was jealous of my true young
mother and besides, Ndeba's own children all had died. The old
chief, my father, the fighting men said, had been a strong man when
he was young, and they had made him chief because he had fought
very bravely against the Bakuba and had captured many prisoners
and women and goats and sheep and as he was very generous in the
giving of these to our warriors. They made him chief in place of
another man more in favor with the village and of mothers of people
who had been killed in the fighting. But, when I remember him, my
father, he was old and his eyes were dim and he had a short gray
beard and the hair of his head was gray. He had lost most all of his

teeth. His knees were swollen and large, and he could only walk slowly and with a stick and bent way over. For hours I would look at him as he would sit on his haunches over the fire in his own big hut and do nothing but take snuff occasionally out of a small antelope horn which hung round his thin neck. Only when the women wrangled too loud would he raise himself and find his voice. And when they had made him so angry to cause him to shout, the brightness came back to his eyes and his voice was strong, and it made us tremble because it was told that once in his younger days when a wife had refused to stop yelling because the Head-Wife had taken her portion of peppers, he struck her on the head with his ebony stick and she died because of it and instantly.

Sometimes because I liked him so, I used to creep into my father's hut and watch him as he sat over the fire. He never spoke much to me, and much of what he tried to say seemed to be nonsense. A few sentences of his talk I still remember; he said them over and over again, like a kind of song:

"The elephants came down from the mountains—two—three elephants came. They wasted terrible my farm, they dragged down terrible my plantain trees and my plantain foods, and they trampled my tall maize stalks and I, Eso, I, Eso the chief, did a cunning thing against them. For I, Eso, dug a big, big, pit and I overlayed its wide mouth with thin sticks and on these thin sticks I reared all the maize stalks upright as though they were truly growing and I scattered grass about in between them so that none might know that the sticks hid the wide mouth of the pit. When the elephants came at night to eat my plantains they pressed on the sticks and one, the biggest, their chief, fell into the pit and there, I, Eso, found him. And I jumped into the pit and I cut the tendons of his feet with my short knife so that he could not stand but fell, then I, running round in the pit and my men running round the mouth, struck him in many good places with our long spears so that he bled to death. For many days we feasted on his flesh till our bellies ached with food. And his tusks, one I sold to a Fullani trader, and the other, I made into bracelets for my wives of that time and that is why they call me Asho-eso, the elephant killer."

And this tale he would tell many times until I wearied of it. And little else he would say, except when the women quarreled and he could not sleep, then he would yell and throw cooking pots at the women.

My eldest brother was a tall and wide man named Nkobub. He was the son of the second wife. I liked him because he was kind to me. He also hated the eldest wife, Ndeba, and because he was bigger than I, and he did hate her and I did not, I thought it wise to pretend to him I too hated her. When she quarreled with my mother Teeta, Nkobub took my mother's part. His own mother we all laughed at because she had once broken her leg and when it mended the bone stuck out in a lump, and one leg was shorter than the other, so that when she walked, she walked with a hop. We called her "The Jackal" because her gait was limping and in our language we called the jackal the "limping leopard." But my big and wide eldest compound brother was good to me and would play with me for hours under the palm trees down by the lagoon and when he took part in these raids to get Bakuba men for these pagan feasts where they roasted them and ate them he would bring me half a handful of some man's heart he had eaten, so that I might taste it and grow brave for our village. Yes, I once liked much being a pagan and a maneater also. I knew no better and I was a brute and an infidel because none had told me at all of Allah and his Prophet, Mohammed. I would in a day distant know of His Blessed Path.

My eldest brother Nkobub taught me to make bows and arrows —the bow out of the springy wood of the climbing palm, and the string too, of palm fiber or the twisted gut of a goat. And our arrows were made out of stout grass stems and notched to let the blood out. Sometimes the blacksmith of the village would beat me out a small barb of iron which I would fasten with goat gut onto the end of my arrow. With these bows and arrows I soon learned to kill small birds, which I took home to roast and eat. I always shared the birds with my true brothers as was our custom, for we shared everything, we boys. But if any of the women tried to take something of what I had killed to put it in their own pots, I made a great noise, and picking up rocks, stoned them. My true mother would also scream and shout at the other women if they tried to take away the things I had killed. I am happy to say my own mother set much store by me, and would let no one do me hurt if she could prevent them.

And I learned from Nkobub to fish in the brooks, where we made weirs of reeds and bush creepers, and once I remember when I jumped into the deep water of one of these pools which we had dammed up, in order to catch in my arms a large fish that was entrapped there, a big lizard such as the Arabs call "Waran" attacked me, for he too was after the fish. And with his long sharp-edged tail cut the skin all down my right thigh. I thought I should have died because so much blood ran out and all down me. I could hardly drag myself home where then my mother wailed over me because she did not know what to do. Yet the Head-Wife, Ndeba, was learned in medicine and knew the best way to stop the flowing of blood and heal the wound. For this my mother had to give her a large present. I think she gave her a goat so that Ndeba would apply her skill to close up the wound in my thigh, and this she did, as I remember, by washing it and putting on it the red paste of a wood that was bitter to the taste. Then she strapped up the whole thigh in plantain leaves and in a few days, I was well. Aoi-yo.

About this time a great trouble came on us, for my elder brother Nkobub went out to show to all he was brave and hunt the elephant with some young hunting men of our village. They would follow the elephants till they came to a great marsh which was a long day's journey from the village and here, hiding among the reeds where the elephants came to drink and bathe, they would let fly at them with spears and poisoned arrows. Then by making much noise and by gradually coming in a circle round them to drive the elephants out of the clear water into the thick mud where they would stick in it, and where the men could get close to them and kill them without the elephants having the power to escape or run at the men. But one elephant that was stronger and more cunning than the others would not fly before the shouting. This elephant turned round and made straight at my brother, whom he seized with his trunk and carried to the firm land among the bushes and here, though this angry elephant was looking like a porcupine for the lances and darts that stuck in his hide, he was stopped not from his purpose. Slamming Nkobub on the ground with his trunk, he knelt down and drove one of his great tusks through my brother's body. Then he broke away and ran from the young men so swiftly that none saw in what direction he escaped through the forest; he bearing all the time my brother's body spitted on his tusk. And when the news was brought back to the Limping Leopard, she commenced to say everywhere and in every compound that it was witchcraft. That some enemy of my brother Nkobub had entered into the elephant's heart as a devil, so that he might bring about my brother's death. I heard the Head-Wife whisper to the third wife, Maleki, that the enemy who had done this was my father's youngest wife, Teeta, and The Jackal, my brother's mother, was mad for rage and threw herself on my poor true mother Teeta biting and striking her until my father roared in his angry voice and swung his ebony stick knocking the first wife and the third wife down and the remaining women pulled The Jackal off, and dragging her out yelling tied her to her hut pole with bush rope. And then for two days there was quiet.

But in the huts and over the fires the other wives of my father still whispered. He had also listened and taking a minute to be angry he did say to them that if they would continue with their talk and make more trouble about Teeta he would take away all their goats and make his young fifth wife his first wife. And this caused my mother to walk with a chin high and with a glance always looking down on the other wives. At this time also the Epfumo, or, as you name him, the witch doctor, did visit our compound to tell my father that Teeta had been seen speaking with a Fullani Muselmin Holy Man and between them one to the other my father and the Epfumo dispersed loud words one at the other lasting an overlong time till it became only noise. Then the young hunting men had found part of my brother's body in the forest, and brought it back to the town. Then I heard it said that the Epfumo was out to find who had bewitched Nkobub and entered the elephant so that he might kill my brother.

When I heard the great "bong, bong" of the Etum, which is a kind of drum made of a hollow-sounding wood that gives out a noise almost like a bell, I was frightened being only eight hands then, and ran to my true mother Teeta, she everywhere looking for me to hide me with herself in the house, for you must know our custom was, when this Epfumo was out after the beating of the Etum drum, that he could slay all women and children and all youths who were uninitiated whom he met in his path about the village. And the reason of this was that these pagans believe that the Epfumo is a "shaitan," a great devil, who is able to search out the truth.

He appears like a man dressed in a great mantle made of palm fronds, a mantle which descends from his shoulders to his knees and is very broad, and constructed somewhat like a cage, but there are holes to let the arms pass out through. And onto his fingernails are fastened leopard's claws. In one old hand he holds a great cutlass, and in the other a pierced antelope horn, with which he blows a strong blast at times to warn people out of his way. On his head is a hideous mask of painted wood from the top of which hangs down behind a black and white monkey skin.

When I was a child I thought that the Epfumo was a real devil but now I know it is only a man dressed up and generally known as the "doctor," who is nonetheless a pagan priest of a village.

This Epfumo that had come out to find the person who bewitched the elephant must have been an old man named Ashontshon, which means in our language "kill-thief." And all this time that the Epfumo was searching through the town for the bewitcher of the elephant, the drum in the fetish-bone house was going bong-bong-bong and there was no other sound in the town but the noise of the drum except when a dog howled or the fowls cackled and I hid myself in the darkness of my mother's hut, fearing to let go of her hand. And she too was frightened, and this fright had made her put the screen of strong crossed lattice palm stems against the doorway of her hut. But presently we heard quite close to the entrance to our compound a blast from the Epfumo's horn.

My mother started up and trembled all over.

"He is coming in here," she said, "I know it. It is the Head-Wife that has bewitched the elephant."

And although I was very frightened, I was very curious to see what the Epfumo would do, so I crept close to the doorway and peeped through the cracks of palm lattice. And for the first time I saw in the morn light the terrible Epfumo. He came into our compound walking at the head of a troop of other devils, dressed somewhat like himself, but with long white staves in their hands and none had cutlasses. And the Epfumo cried out in a loud voice:

"I smell the one who bewitched the elephant."

At these words I saw my father come out of the house walking very slowly and painfully, and helping himself with his stick he said:

"What do you seek here Epfumo?"

And this devil said:

"I seek the bewitcher of the elephant who killed Nkobub. And I know I am near."

The Epfumo walked towards our house, or rather, he danced towards us with what you English call a curious mincing step and again I shut my eyes with fright, for I saw he was coming to our door. All this time my true mother was crouching on the ground putting her hands before her eyes and crying and when I looked out again the Epfumo had passed on and he went very near the next house and the next, but stopped at none. Then he came back to the house of us, and here he danced in; and then I heard a fearsome yell and when I had opened my eyes, the Epfumo was going out, dragging my true mother Teeta by the wrists and she in her scare set both feet together and bent her body so that he might fail to move her from the threshold of our hut. But it was of no use, for my father pointed his hand holding the ebony stick and said:

"Bind her."

And the other dressed-up men that accompanied the Epfumo took coils of bush-rope vine from underneath their mantles of palm leaves and bound my father's fifth wife round and round so that she was stiff and could move nothing about her but her head. And all the while she screamed, I screamed, and screamed until our screams became like the hoarse cry of an angry leopard and then when she was bound they lifted her up and carried her out of the compound. And then after some little time the tum-tum-tum of the fetish drum was stopped for the witch, it said, was found. And the village came to life again.

Then my father's other wives, Ndeba, The Jackal, Maleki, Lete, all rose up and lifted away the doors from the entrances to their huts, made up the embers of their fires, and then rushed out into the compound to meet the other rushing round women who were already raising a mighty clamor with their tongues. They were all shouting to each other and to my father's wives:

"Did I not tell you so—did I not say the youngest wife had bewitched the elephant that has killed Nkobub? Were not her ways always the ways of a witch? Aha, now she will be punished as she deserves."

My other compound mothers screamed about her the loudest of all. I did not know then they would be glad and hated my true young mother. As I still screamed, the other boys and the small girls beat with sticks on the wooden drums and the goats baaed and the fowls crackled and there was great noise. Only my father sat quiet on his haunches and seemed sad. He said once or twice:

"But who will tend me as she did now that she is soon to be gone?"

Then some young men came rushing into the compound and said the trial would take place upon the rising of the moon.

And all that hot wet day was hard to pass. I longed so to see what they would do to my true mother who now they all said had bewitched that elephant that killed my brother. And at last the evening meal was over and it was dark and lighting a bundle of palm shreds, which we use as torches, Lete, the fourth wife, took me by the hand and led me out of the compound, and the other wives and women going along too. But as we passed the open door of my father's hut, his fire flickering up, I saw him sitting there alone, staring over the hearth, his chin resting on his hand, while the other held his ebony staff. And I said to Lete, my compound mother:

"Is he not going too?"

And she said:

"He is too feeble to walk so far and besides, he is too old to care for anything now but his soup and his snuff," and she laughed.

But The Jackal, the second wife, as she passed said to Lete:

"It is not well to laugh, for Asho-eso was a strong man once and it is you young women who have taken his strength from him."

So we passed out into the damp darkness and Lete separated herself from the other wives and here and there we saw the flare of the other torches, for many people were wending their way to the place of trial. But Lete now walked not with the other wives, saying to me before that she did not like their company. And as we passed a big new house that had been built in the village, a young man, a fine tall handsome fellow—his name was Neekwi, the leopard—came out from under the eaves of the house and looked in Lete's face as she held up her torch, and Lete nodded to him and let go my hand, taking and holding Neekwi's instead while she still held up her torch to light the way. Then presently she saw the other wives of my father a little way in advance and she told me to get away and go with my compound brothers for there was something she must say to Neekwi first. I asked if she would speak to him of my true mother but she slapped me hard, and so I ran on and joined myself to The Jackal, who was very sad and sobbed and cried still, to think of the death of her son, my eldest brother.

And when we arrived at the place of trial, I found it was a large open space in the forest where the ground was smooth and had been beaten hard by men's feet and all vegetation was removed except for one great tree, with spreading branches, which grew in the middle of the clearing and all round the border of this maidan, or square, there were great fires burning so that the place was full of light. And round these fires were squatting or standing all the old men and all the young men of the village. The young men, drunk with palm wine for these pagans defy Allah and take spirits, kept shouting and singing without any sense. Close to the base of the big tree there lay my mother still in her bonds. She could only move her head a very little from side to side and her eyes rolled horribly like frightened animals Nkobub had trapped and there was another thing close beside her which made me feel very sad and sick—it was the remains they had found of my brother Nkobub. Only the torn head and the crushed trunk and part of his thighs were there.

Then presently there was a blowing of horns and into the square came Asho-ntshon, the old "Nganga," or medicine man of the village, who before had dressed up as the Epfumo, but this time he was not the Epfumo at all or the women and children would not have been there. This time the old Nganga had painted a strange pattern of white lines over his body and he had a lot of charms hung about his neck, a tall plaited hat on his head, which I much admired, and ruffs of white goat's fur round his ankles. He blew a loud blast on his antelope horn and all the noise and talking ceased. Then into the midst of silence he said:

"The Epfumo has found the witch who brought about the death of Nkobub. It is Teeta, the fifth wife of Asho-eso, the chief."

At these words the other wives of my father—except Lete who had not come—all said, "Aya, Aya, it is true." But the Nganga quickly blew another blast on his horn to silence them and went on:

"Teeta says no that she bewitched the elephant, so it shall be put to the test and we will see if the Epfumo was wrong."

Then after saying these words he took his short knife and cut off a piece—a large mouthful—of the flesh of my dead brother and called to one of his attendants, who brought a small wooden box in which was kept a red sauce. Into this sauce he dipped the morsel of my brother's flesh and turned it round two or three times. Then he bade them hoist up Teeta, and while they held her upright he said to her:

"Open your mouth and swallow this piece of the flesh of the man whom the Epfumo says you caused the death of. If it stays in your stomach, you will be set free and the Epfumo will have told a lie, for all men will see that you could not have bewitched the elephant if Nkobub's substance will unite with yours. But if you vomit up this piece of his body, the Epfumo will have shown truly that you are a witch."

Then my true mother opened her mouth and received the morsel of my brother's flesh and I saw the muscles of her face and throat working as though trying to swallow it, but perhaps the sauce in which it was dipped made her retch or perhaps, after all, she was a witch. How do I know? I cannot now know. It has been too long a time ago and too far a place from where you sit here. Perhaps there is some truth in what those pagans told. How it was I know not, but my mother shook all over and vomited forth the piece of flesh that had been put into her mouth.

Then a great cry went up from among the people; they all shouted:

"It is she, Teeta is the witch. Teeta. The Epfumo never tells a lie."

And the young men beat on their Milupa drums and blew their antelope horns and The Jackal, Nkobub's mother, gave a sob and a scream and rushed forward at my mother who had fallen down on the ground for the young men had ceased holding her up. The Jackal tore Teeta's face with her nails and smashed in her nose with her fist and would perhaps have killed her in her rage only the Nganga yelled and kicked and cuffed The Jackal and dragged her off and said it was not thus my mother was to die. Then the Nganga called upon the drunk young men and they came up and took hold of my mother and while some unwound the bush-rope that had bound her, others roughly tied fresh ropes round her neck, ankles, and wrists and with the ends of these ropes they lashed her round the trunk of the big tree.

"And is that all?" I forced myself to ask of the Head-Wife Ndeba, for I could not find Lete. "Are they to kill her?"

"I do not know," she replied. "It is the Epfumo who will speak of that."

And all this time my mother said nothing, she was quite dumb, and did not seem to know what had happened. And after she was tied to the tree everyone of the village seemed to forget her and the men and women had a big dance around the fire. The Jackal had in truth split her face. And I thought this might satisfy the other wives for no longer was my mother of great beauty and likely to receive favors.

Presently Lete came up to me and took me home and I asked where she had been all the time and if she had seen what had been done to my true mother, and she said yes, she had seen all. It was a lie to me. I did not believe that she was there.

And next morning there was another great roaring among the wives in my father's compound and Ndeba, still being the Head-Wife, took Lete by the hair and reproached her for her love for Neekwi, and threatened she would tell everything to my father. But Lete soothed her and hushed her and promised presents, and pointing to me reminded her that the dead Nkobub had been such a good friend to me and when Lete mentioned Nkobub's name, The Jackal gave out crying and then Ndeba promised not to say anything about Neekwi. And that day Neekwi sent Lete two large fish which he had caught in the river, and she gave one to Ndeba then divided the remaining fish among all the other wives and they seemed to be great friends.

The next day I was sent out by Ndeba with some of my village brothers to snare birds in the forest. When we were coming back in the evening we passed through the square where the people danced and where the sacrifices took place and there was my true mother still tied to the tree. I went up to her. Her eyes opened and she looked at me. She did not speak. She could not speak because someone had made her open her mouth, then driven a stake through one cheek with the point of it coming out the other. Just above her head someone had suspended a bundle of red parrot feathers. These I knew were from the basket of the Epfumo. These meant that my true mother was "fetish," that no one must touch her or have anything to do with her or the Epfumo would kill them. So the other boys dragged me away from staring at her and they made me wend my way home with the birds I had caught for Ndeba.

And three days after that there was a big market held in the square of which I was permitted to go to because of my mother Teeta. It was a market that took place in our village every ten days and I was told that people came to this market from great distances when there was not war with the Bornu people or the Sokoto people. And here, for the first time ever, I saw a Fullani merchant, a Mohammedan, who had come from the north to buy ivory and slaves.

He had with him one or two people from a country near ours called Yariba, who had become the war allies with the merchant servants of the Mohammedan Fullani, and who actually dressed in long blue robes and white turbans and capes and who carried curved daggers, and although I was frightened at first, and held on tight to Lete's hand, still I looked at this man with a beard and metal bands round his fingers with wonder and curiosity, and I being then an ignorant pagan and one of the brutes of the field, at this time wondered that this man should cover his body with cloth, for all the people of our town and country went naked except for their bracelets of ivory or their neck ornaments. And when I looked not at the Fullani but at the tree where my true mother was bound, I saw that she was still alive—that is to say, her eyes opened and shut as she watched the coming and going of the people of the village. But they all took no notice of her and none offered to give her food or water or loose her bonds.

Once the Fullani merchant asked about her, but the young fighting men of the town said to him:

"It is our law. Meddle not with her."

And he nodded, looked at me who was now staring at him, and turned away.

The next day I sobbed and thought much about my mother and wondered whether she still lived and whether her eyes could still open and shut. So without telling Lete, who I knew would scold me, I slipped away from the yard alone and stole to the square in the forest. Round the base of the tree were walking two or three brown vultures of a kind that were tame in our town like fowls, for we allowed them to eat the offal and it was decreed no man might disturb them.

When I stepped as close as I might to my mother, I saw that her eyelids had dropped. But when I said in a soft voice, "Mother!" her eyes opened and she looked hard at me.

Here she had been tied to the tree for six days and was not dead yet. But I sadly knew to myself as I ran back home, "She will surely die soon or the vultures would not be walking about her as they are doing."

And still again the next day I thought about my true mother and wondered whether she was yet dead. But I feared much to leave our compound early the next morning because Lete had asked me many questions about where I had been the day before, and had told me in great anger that if I went anywhere near to my mother she would hand me over to the Epfumo. However, soon there arose a clamor in the yard because The Jackal rushed out of my father's house where she had been taking his morning food and said he was not there, and that he had disappeared for some hours because the fire was out. They sought for him everywhere in the compound but none could find him.

Lete laughed and said:

"Puh! He has found his strength again, that is all. Perhaps it was Teeta that bewitched him and now he is our old chief again and he has gone off to hunt or trade."

And then all the other wives began shouting and throwing sharp stones at Lete, saying she had hidden him, or killed him, lest he should find out about Neekwi, and while they were making all this to-do, I slipped out of our compound and ran off to the forest to see whether my true mother was living still.

And when I got to the square, to my surprise, I saw my father sitting down near my mother's feet and leaning against the trunk of the tree. But also a vulture was perched on my true mother's shoulder tearing the flesh off her cheeks; and so it was I knew her to be dead.

When I touched my father's body to awaken him, for I thought he was asleep, he rolled over onto the ground. And what do you think? My father was dead too. I was so frightened at this, fearing lest they should say I had killed him, that I ran right into the forest and hid there the rest of the day. And at nightfall I returned home hoping they would not notice my absence or, if so, would believe that I had been out under the trees to snare birds.

But long before I reached our compound I heard the wailing of women crying out my father's death, for his body had been found in the marketplace and brought back to our home. And Lete told me that the Epfumo had killed my father because he had been to say goodbye to my mother and had violated the fetish.

The next morning, quite early, my compound mother caught her largest she-goat, one that had a little one running by her side, and a duck which she had bought from a Fullani trader and cut a big bunch of plantains out of her garden. She set the large bunch of plantains on my head and with a stick hitting my buttocks, made me carry the duck under one arm, then lead the goat by a rope in the other hand. And she told me to go to the compound of the Nganga and say:

"This is a present from Lete, fourth wife of Asho-eso."

That only I was to say and nothing more and then to return as quickly as possible.

When I reached the Nganga's compound there too was Neekwi, the young man that was Lete's friend and he had with him two goats and a bag of Kauri shells. He went into the hut before me and gave these things to Nganga, with whom he had a long talk which I could not hear. I was tired of waiting, so to amuse myself I began to rummage among the rubbish which lay in the Nganga's courtyard. And in one of the heaps of rubbish I remember I picked up part of a man's jaw which had the teeth still in it, although they were loose. I pulled all the teeth out to make myself a necklace as most of the fighting men had, but while I was doing this, the Nganga came up and cuffed me hard on the head for meddling with his treasures.

Then he asked my business and I gave him Lete's message and the presents she had sent. He bade me wait while he went back into his house. Then he came out again with the red feathers of a parrot that had hung above my true mother's head and some string made of human gut which he told me to give to Lete, who was to now hang the feathers round her neck with the piece of string. When I returned to our compound Lete was waiting for me near the gate, and took me aside and under the trees asked in a whisper what the Nganga had said. I gave her the string and the parrot feathers and told her what she was to do, at which she clapped her hands quickly and seemed very pleased. When I stepped forward with her into the courtyard I saw The Jackal, who was still sad since Nkobub's death, sitting on one of our native stools while other women were painting her all over with camwood dye and then drawing lines of white in a kind of pattern round her eyes, down the sides of her neck, and along the outer part of her arms. I ran to Lete to know what they were decking The Jackal for and she said with a laugh that she was making herself smart for her journey to the Underworld.

"Why The Jackal?"

"Your father has gone there since the Epfumo has killed him. Now The Jackal must go too, to tend upon him. Ndeba is too old, and soon The Jackal will not be able to bear sons."

That same day some of the young men from the village came to prepare my father to be put down into the earth. With their fighting knives they opened his body and took out his bowels which they buried in the ground in the middle of the compound. Then they made a big fire in the hut where my father had lived and after they had sewn up the body, they smoked it on a frame of sticks above the fire. There it lay all the rest of the day and the whole night till he was quite dry and he had got so small, so shrunken, that it was not like my father at all. I laughed to see it. The next morning they took him down off the sticks and rubbed the smoke black off with the husks of bananas and with corn cobs so that the body was shiny like leather. After this they got the red dye and the white ashes and painted the face of the corpse red and white. They put on the ivory bracelets and the charms that my father had worn round his neck when he was alive. Then they got the grass cloth which our people used to weave and dye red and black and they wound these cloths round and round his body so that it was like a bundle. Only the head was free. But before they wound this cloth round him, they bent the legs up so that my father was sitting with his knees close to his chest, just as he sat when he was alive. Then they dug a big, big hole in the floor of my father's hut.

And while this was going on, all that day The Jackal had been led round about the village painted up in the way I have told you; she was led by the three other remaining wives of my father, and she went to all the people in the town to say goodbye and each gave her greetings and many gave her presents to take with her. And when all was ready, the grave dug, and the corpse of my father prepared, they sent for the Nganga and all the people began to come to our compound carrying torches, for it was night. Then some of my other compound brothers brought three white goats from my father's flock and three white fowls and baskets of ground nuts and maize. And the Nganga, who was painted all over in different colors and had a monkey skin cap upon his head, began to dance round the grave and said a lot of silly words which I did not understand. After this he called in a loud voice to my father, "Asho-eso are you ready to meet your fathers?" And though no one answered, he pretended to listen at the lips of the corpse whom they had seated at the edge of the grave, and then he turned to the other people and said, "I hear him say 'yes.'" So the young men got bush-rope and tied it round the corpse and lowered it into the grave.

Then someone led up The Jackal and I could see that she was trembling very much, but she did not speak, and the Nganga bade her lie on the ground by the side of the grave. She lay down slowly onto her back, and then he kneeled on her chest, got her neck in his skinny hands, and squeezed it so that she was strangled and died.

Then they laid her body in the grave at the feet of my father. And after this they brought the three white goats and the three white fowls and cut their throats one after another over the grave so that the blood fell on the two corpses, but the bodies of the goats and fowls were not dropped into the grave but were taken away to be eaten at the funeral feast. The Nganga scattered a few of the ground nuts and some maize into the grave and they put in a horn of snuff and a wisp of salt in a banana leaf, and a gourd of water, some red peppers and some wooden dishes and then the earth was all heaped back into the grave and trampled down by the young men. After this they had a big feast and Lete gave me a large piece of meat. All the night they stayed singing and shouting and drinking palm wine until they were, most of them, drunk.

The next day all the important men met in the Epfumo house, who was absent, to say who should be the next chief, and some said one man and some said another and while they were quarreling the silly Nganga came dancing in blowing his horn and shouting out that he had a big message from the Epfumo and the message was that Neekwi was to be the new chief.

Some grumbled at this and said he was young, but no one thought of disputing the order of the Epfumo. So the next day the Nganga gave to Neekwi my father's ebony staff and Neekwi came down and took possession of our compound and all that was in it, and the three remaining wives of my father became the wives of Neekwi and Neekwi made my father's fourth wife Lete the Head-Wife over the first wife Ndeba and the third wife, Maleki, so that Lete had all the other wives as her servants. And so, Neekwi became my compound father.

And Neekwi killed ten of my true father's goats and tapped many palm trees so that there were great jars of palm wine. And he dug up many yams and ground nuts and prepared a big feast to which all the men of the village came. They were all pleased at this and said Neekwi would make a good chief after all, because he was generous and fed the hungry. And I liked Neekwi, because he was kind to me and gave me a big ivory bracelet.

After my true father's death, several years went by and all was prosperous in our village. Neekwi was seen by all to be a brave man in war, and three times defeated the Bussang people of the mountain, bringing back with him many slaves and goats and sheep. He made several new plantations and dug cunning pitfalls for the animals and the elephants so that our bellies were full and our store of ivory increased. And he took four new wives and begat children with them all. I learned to shoot very well with bow and arrow and to hurl the dart with a good aim and Neekwi, still being my compound father, promised me that when I should be made a man he would give me a long gun, for at this time our people the Popo had begun to get long guns from the Fullani traders.

As I grew older I saw less of my compound mother, Lete, and as she had another child by Neekwi, she cared less for me and would often drive me out of her hut impatiently when I came to her for sauce food, and besides, I liked now to give my attentions to my compound sisters, Tutu, who was ten hands high, and Ejoka, who was eleven hands high. To these I would bring my birds that I had snared and the small animals I would kill with my arrows. Also I liked more to go out with the bigger boys fishing or scouting out the big animals or pretending to play at war with blunt arrows and wooden spears, which we used to aim at each other. They did not do much harm as they had no sharp points. But one day I shot an arrow into a boy's eye and put out part of his sight. I was very proud of my good aim and Neekwi praised me and my compound sisters Tutu and Ejoka and said that I should make a good warrior. But Neekwi, he had to pay a goat in compensation to the father of the boy who was half blind.

Neekwi was very good to me still, and used to, among many things, take me with him sometimes when he went on a trading expedition to a Fullani settlement two or three days distant from the village. Here I used to see the Mohammedans riding on horses and asses, animals that were new to our people, who always called them "the white man's cows," for as the Fullani were so much lighter than we in color, we used to call them white men.

One day Neekwi looked at me attentively and said I was getting big enough to be made into a man, and soon after that the old Nganga came to our compound and told me I must go away with him, also for me away from Tutu and Ejoka. At the same time Neekwi had to pay him a goat and my compound mother gave him a small present too. Neekwi gave the goat because, as he had taken our house and Lete, he was looked upon now as my real father. The Nganga made me follow him to a place about an hour's walk from the village in the middle of the woods. It was a large enclosure surrounded by a hedge of spikey-leaved plants called Ngonje. Inside were a number of huts with a large Epfumo house in the middle of the enclosure. As we went in, a number of big boys as big and bigger than myself rushed out of the little houses making a curious noise like "Drrr" and speaking to me in a strange language which I did not understand.

To my surprise they were all clothed in a large skirt made of palm leaves which was attached to their waists. Their bodies were covered with red paint and a lot of white marks were drawn about their faces. When I had looked carefully into their eyes I recognized first one and then another as my old playfellows who had disappeared from our village recently. And at the time I had asked about their disappearance, I was told that they were sent away to be made into men. When I called them by their names they were very angry and beat me with sticks and their fists and the old Nganga told me that I must not call them by their old names any more as they had changed them for new ones, and also that I must not speak to them until I had learned the Sacred Language and that every time I spoke in the old tongue, the boys would beat me; that I must not eat this or this or this until I was made a man, or it would kill me. The things that we were allowed to have for our food were certain roots and fruits which we had to search for in the woods and flesh of monkeys and lizards and snakes and any larger wild creatures which we could kill with our bows and arrows. But goat's flesh and fowl's flesh and fish meat were forbidden to us. But having a great hunger one day, I speared a small luwumpum fish and, finding I did not die upon the eating of it, caught a second. This discovery I kept a secret from the other boys in fear they would inform the Nganga in which case I should surely be sold away as a slave and never return to see my compound sisters again.

At first I was told that I must be a servant to the elder boys, and together with others who like myself had just been admitted, we had to prepare the food and cook for the bigger boys and often, too often, these elder ones beat us for very little reason and the Nganga seldom interfered, saying that beating was good for the young. Puh!

Once when I forgot the rule about speaking in the Common Language, one of my companions hit me such a blow on the head with his club that for some time I did not know where I was. But the next day when we were out hunting, I shot him in the back with an arrow so that he was long afterward unable to stir from his hut and this I said I would do to anyone who struck me again. After this the bigger boys did not treat me so harshly—Wallah! When I had been eight days in this place, the medicine man took me and some other young boys who had entered the enclosure about the same time as myself and circumcised us.

After this we who had run naked hitherto were told to make ourselves skirts of palm fronds and to paint ourselves red and white like the other boys. Now we were considered to be men and we each received a new name. I, who had been called M'uu, was renamed Mitwo, which means "The Big Head." And like the others, I began to learn the new Brotherhood Language, which was different from the one we commonly talked, though it was made chiefly by turning the words the wrong way, thus instead of "ugno" we said "ongu" for stone. Sometimes in our walks abroad we met people of our village and were told that if we spoke to anyone who did not belong to the "Ndage"—as our brotherhood was called—the Epfumo would kill us; moreover, we had the power to beat and wound any women who got in our way and also whenever we heard people approaching we always made the noise "Drrr," so that they might get out of our way. All this time the Nganga would visit us once a day and tell us many things and hold with us much tribe conversation that I may not repeat to you. Every now and then the bigger boys were leaving our enclosure and coming not back. When I asked where they were gone I was told by the other boys that they had left for another place where they must learn the last things the Nganga had to teach them.

And when it came my turn to go, the Nganga had a piece of goat skin tied over my face so that I could not see, then he led me by the hand for some distance through the bush telling me always that if I pushed aside the skin of the goat and looked at the road I was going, the Epfumo would kill me. At last we stopped, and he bade me go down on my hands and knees and then pushed me through a narrow place between some branches. When I got through, he made me stand up and took the goat's skin off my eyes. Then I heard loud voices and girls' laughter and when I looked round I saw many young girls painted with red and white and with the palm leaf skirts, and with them were some of the older boys who had left our enclosure. At first I felt silly for the girls laughed and jeered at me in my new appearance but the medicine man bade me be of good courage, and heed not what they said as I was now a man. And in this place

I sojourned some twenty days. When this time was over, the Nganga again put the goat's skin over my face and led me away along devious paths for about the space of an hour. And then when we had stopped, he removed the goat's skin from my face and said to me:

"Now go to this brook and wash all the red and white paint from your body and cast away your skirt of palm leaves. Then follow this path and it will take you back to the village, where you can return to your father's house. Tell all that you meet that your new name is 'Mitwo.' Speak no word of all that you have seen and done during these months that you have been in the Ndage or assuredly the Epfumo will kill you. And suffer that no man call you by the name of your childhood or it will bring you misfortune."

And after this I returned to the village and entered my father's compound where Lete and Neekwi rejoiced greatly to see me back; and gave me a living goat and a large basket of plantains and a gourd of ground nuts wherewith to make a feast with my friends.

Allah! How I have talked to you today. See, you are weary after writing much. You squeeze your hand and I think in it you have pain. I have said enough today. Let me go my way about my business and I will come to you again in the morning.

When I had returned from the Ndage I was not allowed to live any longer in my father Neekwi's compound, for it was not considered seemly for a young unmarried man to live among his father's wives, or among his compound sisters. I do not know why. Now I had to take up my abode with the other young men of the village who were bachelors. We had a big compound to ourselves, but we were obliged to hunt and fish and make plantations to supply ourselves with food.

And it was about this time that the Nganga instructed me as to the Epfumo Society, to which nearly all the young free men of the village belonged. It was there that I truly learned—as I had suspected, English—that the Epfumo was really a man dressed up and not a devil. Aoi-yo. We were sworn a solemn oath not to reveal this secret so that the women and children and the men we had captured from other villages and made slaves might still be kept in awe of the Epfumo, whom they had to think always to be a strong devil that would be able to find out all secrets. And several times—I knew no better than these other pagans, and did as they did—have I dressed up myself as an Epfumo with the other young men of the Society and lain in wait to catch wives and unmarried women who were out of their houses at night after the Epfumo gong had sounded and these skulking wives and unmarried women, who wanted to be laid upon, we could do with as we pleased and no one could say us nay, and indeed, some of us hid these women that we so captured for a long time in the forest, and to them we always threatened that they would be surely killed by the Epfumo if they should at any time reveal the names of those who had carried them off and laid upon them, and when we had tired of the women, we would let them return to their compounds, and knowing that they had been captured by the Ep-fumo, no one dared to ask them questions or rebuke them for their absence, or what had been done to them in that time.

And once we caught a village slave, a Bakuba on the road who had not hidden himself at the sounding of our drum, and him I and my Society brothers killed and ate—Wallah! I remember we were but as the brutes, English. An hour afterwards, I thought it would have been more profitable for us to have sold him than eat him. In the Epfumo house that same night, the old Nganga man praised us for our dexterity in our treatment of the slave. Witless!

Twice while I was living with the older young men of the village we were called upon to go to war with these Bakuba people of the mountain, a few days distant from us. The first time we fought them hard because they had carried off a woman belonging to our village and killed her husband, having surprised them on their way to trade with the Fullani. But the second time it was Neekwi who said we must attack the mountain Bakuba people by stealth and try to capture some of the people to make and then sell as slaves to the Moslems. To me this was better than eating them and Neekwi was using his wit.

The first time I had to go to war I truly feared and greatly. Although my village people called me "The Big Head" because they thought in their own heads I was strong and I was courageous, but truly I was not. I was new to war. I feared to be killed and eaten by the mountain people. And so of this reason I did not adventure myself in the front of the party that attacked the Bakuba. But while I was skulking in the rear, I spotted a Bakuba man and woman who had been out cutting grass for their goats and whom our attack had cut off from their village. They sought to escape our notice by crawling on their stomachs through the grass like snakes and winding behind every rock· and stump till they should arrive close to the Bakuba stronghold. Seeing they were unarmed save for the small cutlass which the man had, I attacked both of them suddenly as they were lying on the ground, drove my spear right through the man's body and pinned him to the ground and knocked the woman with my club. Then my head grew big and I shouted loudly to my comrades to tell them what I had done, and some of them came running up and one of them cut off the head of the man through whom I had run my spear. Then another, an older man who liked me, called Kangtuma, helped me to tie the arms and ankles of the woman before she awoke.

The rest of our war party did not do much against the Bakuba because they found the village well defended and too few of its fighting men were absent. So after our warriors had shouted much at them and shot many arrows and called the Bakuba as many foul names as they could think of to draw them from their stockade, Neekwi and some older fighting men then decided to retreat. So we returned to our village with the body of the man I had killed and the woman I had captured and my compound mother Lete shrieked loudly with joy when they told her what a brave man her son had become. The body of the man I and the other warriors ate in the Epfumo house, and good and sweet was the flesh said the Nganga, my companions, and some others. It is with great shame that I say such things now, but Alhamdu'lillah! I am no longer a pagan and an eater of man's flesh. The woman I had captured I decided to keep and look at to see if she was a good woman. So I made her work in my plantations. My compound mother said to me about this woman:

"Treat her well and she will remain with you. But if you have the heart to use her badly, it were better to sell her to the Fullani than to let her remain in our village, for if she is unhappy she will surely find a way to escape back to her country."

So then I thought to say to the woman who had as great a beauty as had my true mother Teeta:

"Will you swear by the Epfumo to stay with me, and if I see you are a good woman, I will make you a true wife to me?"

And she replied:

"My heart is sad for having left my country, and you have proved to be the strongest. You have killed my man. What other man have I now to love besides you? Also, if I am not good to you and do not work well in your plantation and on your mat, you will sell

me, what can come then? It is only wise to stay with you. So I will
swear by the Epfumo not to leave you, to work much, if you treat
me kindly."

Her name was Nijina. I decided to make her my wife. I sent for
the Nganga and by and by he brought the ju-ju mixture, which is
made of man's flesh and the flesh from his own last finger and drugs
he knows from the woods. He put some of this on the tongue of the
woman I had captured, and she putting one hand on her head, and
the other hand into mine swore that she would remain with me and
become one of our people. And in such manner was I married. After
this I got Kangtuma and many of my friends to help me and we all
built a house and made a compound for me to live in, for I was now
a married man and dressed my hair in the fashion of those who were
married men.

The second time I went to war with the Bakuba, as I have said,
was because of Neekwi's plan to capture people to sell to the traders
Fullani. It was because of Nijina. For when my wife had grown to
know me, and very much like me, and to help me, she told me one
day that, about the night when it should be the full moon, it was the
custom of the best hunting men among her people to leave the village
and surround the plantations where the elephants came to rob them,
and that they, the Bakuba, had fashioned two great hedges of sticks
and thorns which narrowed to a small lane, at the end of which was
a big, big pit, and that when they had surrounded the plantations that
the elephants were robbing, they began with great shoutings and
using the flames of their torches to try to drive the elephants into the
space between the two hedges that led to the pit and so were at the
men's mercy. The elephant in some things is a foolish beast and has
not the wit to turn aside and break through the fence of thorns, but
presses on towards the outlet where the pit awaits him.

And when I told all this to Neekwi, he considered a while and
said:

"I have a good plan in my head. Let us select all the strong and
valiant among the men of this village two days before the moon is
full. And let us journey secretly through the bush until we are close
to the Bakuba town on the mountain. Then we will lie concealed in
the woods among the stones and trees and await the time when we
shall see the men of the town issuing forth with their torches to hunt
the elephants. And when they are away in the plantations, we will
take the town by surprise and capture as many of the women and

remaining men as we can secure quickly, and having done this we will return to our town with what speed we can."

This we did, and brought back with us, it might be thirty, it might be forty women and men and a few young children. We had captured many more but the elephant-hunting Bakuba men were warned and pursued us and harried us on our return and recovered some of their people, although in their fighting they themselves lost nine or ten men, whose bodies we carried back tied to poles and ate on our return. And of our village four men only were killed in battle, for my father Neekwi was cunning and knew how to skillfully direct the fighting. And as the bodies of our four valiant warriors were carried off by the Bakuba warriors, and therefore could not be buried, the Nganga nicely said that none of their best wives need follow them to the Underworld, inasmuch as the bodies of their husbands rested doubtless in the stomachs of the Bakuba. This was said to be a wise word, and the men of the town applauded when the Nganga divided the wives of our slain warriors among those who had been bravest in battle.

And as I succeeded in pleasing much the Nganga by my prowess in battle, I received one of these women by his hand so that I might have her as a slave, and moreover, O'Aoi-yo, I had kept back for myself, O Foyo, a young girl of fifteen hands high whom I had captured in the Bakuba country so that I had now by war one wife and two women slaves and I, Big Head, became by this a big man in the village.

But what we had done against the Bakuba was surely bad in Allah's sight, for He made it a means of bringing about our punishment, I think.

When the day came round for the next big market to be held in our town—the market we used to have every ten days—there were more of the Mohammedan Fullani and Hausa traders there than we had ever seen before. Perhaps fifty or sixty of them altogether. They had heard that we had captured and made some new and good slaves to sell. About this time too, from the number of elephants that our young hunting men began to kill, we had a large store of perhaps one hundred or more of ivory teeth to trade with, all of which wise Neekwi made us sell for guns and gunpowder, for he was determined that we should become so strong that the Bakuba people should no longer be able to fight with us, and should come under our power altogether.

One of these Mohammedan traders, a Hausa, whose name was Rashidu, gave his time kindly to me to talk to me much about the power and wealth of the Sultan of Kashka, then asked me how our people, the Popo, would like to become Mohammedans and live under the Sultan of Kashka's rule. I told him, foolish pagan that I was, that we liked best to worship the spirits of our fathers like my wise Neekwi and to follow in their cunning ways. And that although His Excellency the Sultan of Kashka might be a strong and just man, we would sooner live under our own chiefs.

This Hausa Rashidu asked me many questions about our country and the countries beyond us to the West, and he told me if we Popo all went many days' journey towards the setting sun, we should come to the great water where the white Francswari people ruled. He also said he liked so much the slaves he had bought at this market that we must wage more wars on our neighbors and get more and more slaves so that when he came again, in three months' time, he would find a good number of slaves ready for sale to him and other Mohammedan traders. He talked to me in the Juku language, which I partly understood from the trading journeys which I had made with Neekwi.

When the market was over and the Muselmin traders had left our village with their many slaves and asses and the ivory they had bought, I reported to wise Neekwi all that the Hausa Rashidu had said to me. When he heard these words, he shook his head and said he liked them not, for he had heard that a town not far away from us called Banyo had lately been ravaged by this same Sultan of Kashka and many of its people carried off into slavery. What if the Hausa of Kashka should do the same to us?

But I, not knowing the strength of the people beyond our borders, laughed for the first time at Neekwi's words and said:

"And if they do come and fight have we not also guns now, and would we not fight for our homes and our women?"

"How long did it take you, Mitwo," he answered, "to use well the bow, the spear, and the knife? You think the gun is easier?"

His rebuke was true. Pride and my accomplishments and my women had made me drunk in my head. To have good women is sometimes bad. Nay it is terrible. I said in the humblest voice to my wise father Neekwi that I had been foolish and that we must now start practice using the guns for our hunting, and on the elephants for the ivory.

A matter of some three months slipped by and nothing troubled us, but we had not got the number of slaves we had hoped to obtain because Neekwi had gone over and made friends with the Bakuba people of the mountain, Aya!

It was such Bakuba people as we had among us, all round as slaves and wives to us, that urged Neekwi to do this settlement and Neekwi told us he was of the one opinion that it was foolish for this fighting between the Bakuba and the Popo always to go on. Moreover, the Bakuba people agreed that, if we swore an oath not to attack them any more, they would consent to accept wise Neekwi as their Head Chief, and many of the elders in both Bahom, my land and Bakuba, were of the opinion that it was time we made up and became as brothers. And we Popo would save our guns and powder and shot for the elephants and not hurt the Bakuba or anyone. Yes, English, it is not that the Bakuba loved us or loved Neekwi. They feared the Fullani more.

Then their Bakuba elder said:

"We hear news from the north that the Fulbe Fullani chiefs who worship Allah are establishing their rule in all directions and are enslaving all of the black men who are all of this land. It is time therefore we black people were united against them."

And when we were all agreed upon this we sent messages to the Dokaka and Jetem peoples to the east and south of us telling them what we had done and asking them to join us in resisting the Fullani slavers. And they consented to do this. And the chief of the Bakuba sent one of his comely daughters to wed with Neekwi so that the two peoples might become more surely friends. Now Neekwi had another wife, O Foyo! But all this treaty-making and friendship availed us nothing against the solemn decrees of Allah, as I will further relate to you.

After, as I think, some six months had passed since the Muselmin traders had come to buy our Bakuba slaves and found none, our great trouble came upon us.

One day some of our older men, who had been two days' journey to the East to trade with our new friends the Dokaka, came back to our village breathless with much running and exhausted with want of food. When they had got their speech, they told us that the Sultan of Kashka had sent a great army, some on foot and many riding on horses and asses, which had suddenly entered the Dokaka country and wasted it in all directions, burning the town, shooting the fighting men, and catching the young women and children for to make them slaves, and added that having destroyed the Dokaka, it was likely that the Kashka warriors would now attack us and the Bakuba.

At these words we were filled with great fear. Neekwi, using haste, sent some of the young men to creep stealthily through the grass under the forest till they reached the High Hill, which was a short distance from our village in the direction of the Dokaka, and he told them to climb to the top of this hill and to look out in the direction whence the other young men had come, and to report whether they saw anything to bear out the statements of the men who had just returned. At eventide these spies too returned and terror was in their faces, for they said that along the horizon in the direction of Dokaka they saw the smoke of burning towns and one whose eyes were sharper than the rest thought he could distinguish men dressed in turbans and in long clothes and with flowing capes riding on horseback across the distant plain. Then Neekwi said that we must lay our heads together all that night so that we might make preparations for defense. The women and children were now told to all go to Bakuba, as being a place more easy to defend, and we men remained in the village sending our spies out into the black forest and on to the hills in all directions to keep us apprised of the advance of the Fullani.

But we had begun our precautions too late. The women who feared to start at night, on account of the wild beasts and ghosts, left the village to escape to Bakuba just before dawn. But before the sun was up they came running back into the village shrieking out that the men riding upon horses were upon us, and then our scouts, among them my friend Kangtuma, came back in terror one after another, some wounded by the enemy's bullets, among who was Kangtuma, and his comrades shrieked.

"It is the Fullani! The Fullani are upon us. There is no time to escape."

And all was hubbub then and confusion. Unheard were the words of Neekwi to the men. Some went and hid themselves. Some began to load their guns and get ready their spears and arrows, others cut down branches from the trees and tried to block the doorways of all the different compounds, but there was great panic and confusion everywhere, and although Neekwi and Kangtuma shouted more and much and tried to assemble the fighting men together, everyone seemed to go his own way and to think only of securing his own property in their compounds.

In the middle of all this turmoil, we heard suddenly the firing of guns and distant shouting of "Allah Akbaru," the war cry of the Fullani, and then, as it were, all at once from out of the forest the village was full of Mohammedans, some running on foot and shooting their long guns at us, and some crashing through our plantain plantations on horseback swinging their swords yelling "Allah Akbaru." And our people ran hither and thither and some in four square circles like frightened sheep. There was no escape, for the Fullani, and now also I saw there were Hausa, had surrounded the village and any who tried to slip past our enemies into the bush were cut down with cutlasses and shot down with long guns. Six of the Fullani with guns and cutlasses, four on foot and two on horseback, came into my new compound and I was afraid to resist them, for I saw it was useless to fight. But a little slave boy eight hands high, whom I had grabbed and carried away from the Bakuba and who I called Bignose, aimed at one of the Fullani on horseback an arrow from his little bow, and two on foot in rage seized Bignose and as each held an arm of him the Fullani on horseback came up to the little boy and blew out his brains. And then telling us that if we moved we should be likewise slain, they proceeded to bind my wife Nijina and my two women slaves and myself by roping our ankles together and fastening us one to the other round the neck with other ropes and tying our hands behind us. When this was done, five of them marched us out of the compound into the open space in front where we saw others of my village people also roped and fettered and some standing and some sitting or some lying in groups on the ground.

Round us, now captives, were standing a ring of Fullani and Hausa warriors, with their long guns loaded and ready to shoot any who might try to escape or resist. There was an incessant wailing of all our women and children. Among these I saw my compound mother Lete, who in between her cries told me that the father I did love, Neekwi, was killed, that he had in a wonder of foolishness fought desperately and had killed twelve of the Mohammedans, after

which they had at length managed to knock him down with a club
and then, with a cutlass, one of them had cut his head off. And when
I heard this, English, the thought that I first had was that if I were
not captured, I would now be chief or call myself chief. Aya!

While half of the Mohammedans guarded us whom they had
roped, the other part of their army was ranging through the village.
Some of these soldiers were searching for hiding villagers and others
were laying their hands on all the goats and ivory they could find,
and others were being sent to prevent any of our people from lurking
concealed.

Presently a great cry arose from among the Fullani and the
Hausa that were standing guard over us and now they all struck us
brutely about our heads and shoulders with the ends of their long
guns and the flat of their cutlasses. I could not understand what they
were saying because they spoke in their own language, which I did
not then at the time know. But it appeared, as I afterwards learnt,
that some of our people who at the first alarm had escaped into the
bush had set on two of the Hausa men whom they had found separated from their companions and looting some plantations, and had
killed them, and this aroused the wrath of the other Hausa men to
such an extent that we feared they would kill us all. They captured
most of the runaway party who had been concerned in the death of
their brothers, and brought them into the open place where we were
lying roped. A few of these runaways were poor women and little
children who could not have had anything to do at all with the death
of the two Hausa soldiers, but nevertheless, on the women as well
as on the husbands and their true brothers and sisters, the Mohammedans would wreak their anger.

They tied by the chest and hips the men down to stakes and
round tree trunks. They lopped their arms off one by one and waited
many minutes so that they could listen to their agonies. Then their
legs were severed off one by one and all the while they laughed at
our villagers' screams. Then they beheaded them. They ripped up the
women in the front and lifting up the little children by the feet they
swung them round and dashed their heads on the stone seats in the
open square where our elders used to sit under the shade of the big
trees. Then their leader, a Fullani, spoke to us in the language of
M'bum, which most of us understood, for it was a language of trade,
and told us that if any of us attempted to stir hand or foot from where
we were laid, the same punishment we had just seen should be meted

out to us. While these things were being said, a small body of Fullani were busy burning the village and cutting down the plantations of bananas and setting fire to the dry bush we kept outside the town so that the whole place might be laid bare and afford no hiding place to such of our people as might have escaped and think of lurking near the Fullani and Hausa camp.

All through that long day, some in the burning sun and some in the damp shade, we lay roped together in the wide square of our village, now collapsed and smoking. One or two of the women, who were far gone with child, died from the fright and the anguish of seeing their premature delivery. We lay all through the night while the Mohammedans made big bonfires and cut up and roasted our goats.

In the wetness and the cold of that early next morning, the Fullani and Hausa passed in review of all of us whom they had captured, which I supposed amounted to one-half of our townspeople—perhaps some three hundred. They made us stand up in our ropes—men, women, and children; the little children were not roped, because the Fullani-Hausa knew they would not leave their mothers. We were carefully examined by the leader of the Fullani soldiers. All such as were aged or deformed or weakly were separated from the others and put across one side of the square. Their ropes were undone and they were told jestingly by a Fullani captain on horseback that they might go where they pleased. But when the poor simpletons began to slink off towards the forest, the Fullani soldiers on foot, with shouts of laughter, began firing at them with their guns, and then those up on the horses began riding and the soldiers on foot began running. Some of the Fullani horsemen would stop for a moment and let a soldier tie a rope round the ankle of one of these fugitives who had fallen down, and after a second give the other end of this rope to the horsemen who would fasten it to his stirrup and then ride round and round the square at full gallop raising the dust till the man he had dragged with him was simply a shapeless lump of blood and bone.

At length their leader recalled all his men by having a drum beaten and orders were given to get ready for a start.

All we who had become slaves whom they had selected to take away with them were made to march in twos and threes to the river, where we were told to wash and drink. Here several who were mad with grief jumped into the river, though they were roped together,

and tried to swim down the stream but they all sank to the bottom
and were seen no more.

One woman who had been incessantly howling all the morning
because her son had been killed by a Hausa was ordered several times
by those who were guarding us to cease her noise, and as she paid
no heed to their warning, she was shot. After we had been made to
drink at the river, we were ranged in a row on the bank of this water
and the Fullani distributed among us bananas from our own plantations. This we were ordered to eat and threatened with immediate
death if we refused.

About midday the small party that were Batibari soldiers left
and went westwards while the Fullani-Hausa army got itself into
order to depart. We slaves were told we must march in the center
of the caravan and there would be soldiers in front and behind and
many of them widening the road as we went along—that is to say,
cutting down the bush to prevent any of their enemies concealing
themselves on the line of route. All of us who had been made slaves
who were men had our front fetters undone and now our hands were
securely tied behind our backs with the coils of bush rope and round
our necks were fastened slave sticks, linking every two slaves together. The young women's hands were free so that they might more
easily take their children with them, either by holding their hands
or by carrying them slung round their back. In this fashion we
walked up and down through the forest all the rest of that day and
by and by slept at night in a Fullani camp where we found a lot more
Mohammedan soldiers of the Sultan of Kashka, who had been slave
raiding at Bakuba and had brought back with them a great number
of Bakuba people, perhaps a hundred, whom they had captured.

The next day the whole force set out with all these soldiers to
travel to a large town called Banyo, which we reached in four days'
time. Any slave that could not keep up with the march of the caravan
was taken aside to be unbound then have his two arms lopped off
with a cutlass and then left behind. The fear of this sort of slow bad
death made us walk and forget the pain of our back and fight the
bush of the forest as we had never walked and pushed away the bush
before. But with some of the women that were young and comely,
the Fullani and Hausa soldiers were not so harsh, and would occasionally mount them on the asses that carried the camp luggage. In
this way I saw that my wife Nijina and my two compound sisters
Ejoka and Tutu had already made friends with their guardians and

one of them, Ejoka, was even laughing when the soldiers jested—so soon do these poor pagan women have now to think of having the best. On the road every night we stopped to camp. The Fullani gave us just as much food as would keep us from starving. And we who were young and well made got a little more than those who were somewhat old and ungainly and who had become sick and ill on our march. Thus my father Asho-eso's Head-Wife Ndeba, who had been stung by a palm spider, and fallen to looking yellow, and I believed she would be worth little as a slave, and did receive such scant food from the Fullani that the little of it caused her to die of weakness soon after we got to Banyo.

As I lay joined to another man in that marketplace that night, I saw her body released from its bonds by the soldiers and dragged away from us and cast out into the street, where the hyenas which wander through the town at night came and tore it to pieces.

Banyo is a big town belonging to the Sultan of Kashka. It is a place where the pagans of many nations who are now in most ways under the Fullani rule bring their ivory and slaves for sale. I saw men here from many far countries whose speech I could not understand. When we had rested several days at the marketplace in Banyo, we again set out for Kashka, which we reached after about two days' journey, passing a big mountain on the way. Along this road not a few of the slaves sank down from weariness and were killed with clubs by the foot soldiers, for the road we followed was very arduous, going up among tall hills and then going down into deep valleys and past great sharp rocks. When we reached Kashka I had become so tired that I cared not whether I saw the look of the town, or I lived or I died. But here, since we had arrived, we were to be a little better treated by the Fullani said the captain of this caravan. Before we could march into the town, this Sultan came out surrounded by a lot of his soldiers on horseback to meet this army which he had sent slave-raiding, and he was mightily pleased at the number of slaves they had obtained. There was a great firing of long guns and shouting and blowing of horns, and lalilu-ing on the part of the Fullani women who shrieked out all manner of jests at us as we were walking into the town, calling out many words about our nakedness which caused them to laugh. When we got into the center town, we slaves were divided into small companies of twenty or more and distributed among the principal men of the town who were to keep us in watch and ward till the Sultan should decide what to do with us. By great good fortune, I found myself with my wife Nijina and my friend who liked me, Kangtuma, and five other people of our village. Where Tutu and Ejoka were I do not know. Nijina and Kangtuma did not know. Much we wept together for the sorrows that had overtaken us.

The man to whom we were entrusted was none other than the commander of the expedition and him we found a not unkindly master. We were taken to his house and into his large courtyard and he explained to us in the Juku language that he would take off our fetters so that we should be free to walk about his compound. But if we attempted to escape we should be killed at once and, moreover, if we did get outside the town where were we to go? He said we were now many days' journey from our country Boham, which had been laid waste, and wherever we might wander, we should find the Fullani or Hausa there ready to recapture us. Then according to our country fashion, he made us take a pinch of soil between our fingers and swear not to run away, and thus, seeing no help for it, we did, and after so doing our lot was less hard, for we were allowed to wash ourselves and could eat and drink in plenty.

After we had stayed in Kashka perhaps ten or twelve days, a big slave market was held there at which nearly all the slaves which the Fullani had captured in their recent raids were exposed for sale. A Fullani slave merchant from the town of Yola, after closely examining me, bought me for two thousand Kauri shells. He also purchased five other of our people among whom were Nijina and Kangtuma. Our new master joined himself to a big Fullani caravan with which we would travel to Yola, taking many days to cross terrible mountainous country that was inhabited by the Kotofo people, who were friends of the Fullani. On our way we passed on the west of a big, big mountain, bigger than any I had yet seen and then we reached Yola after spending twenty days on the march. When I beheld this place, I was filled with wonder, for I had seen and heard of no town like it. It is not worthy to be compared to Katsena nor with Kano or Murzuk, or the great cities of the Sultan of Tibesti. But it far surpassed anything I had seen in my own country Popo and I began to think that, after all, we pagans were as monkeys compared to the Fullani-Hausa, and I felt ashamed that I was naked and had no clothes to make me look like a Mohammedan. On our journey to

Yola, I had taken much time and thinking to win the favor of my Fullani master, who now accepted I was strong and active and good-tempered, so when we arrived at Yola—Aoi-yo—he gave me an old blue and long cotton shirt to wear, with which I was greatly pleased, though he and his friends clapped their hands and laughed much to see the way in which I at first wore it, for we pagans reeking little of decency would have it that clothes should be worn to make a man look smart, and not to cover his body, so that when I first got this shirt, I wound it round my neck and shoulders until I was taught its proper use.

While I stayed in Yola I began to learn the Fullani language, or as these people call it, the "Fulful-de," and when my master old Nyebbu, the Fullani merchant, found that I was of a mind to learn, he began to show me favor, and entrusted me with matters of trade rather than with the hard labor in the palm groves such as the other slaves including Nijina and Kangtuma were put to. And as I had succeeded in pleasing this master with my ambition displayed, I resolved that I could also enhance my value, and therefore receive more favors, if I attempted to learn to make the numbers that the scribes used to tally the goods sold and purchased. It would be a considerable effort for me every eventide, but since I did learn well to throw the dart I did feel I could learn to hold and guide the pen that made numbers. And seeing that I was versed in the knowledge of the ivory traffic, I went with him on several small journeys into the Batta country and to the great Fullani town of Ribago, and he employed me to choose out and buy tusks from the people round the big mountain—I think its name was Alantika—and once I went as far as Ngaundere, where we bought much ivory and where my master gathered in many more slaves from the pagan countries round. Many of these were wild people like the Mdubikum, wilder than we had been in Popo. Most of them were stark naked but some wore leaves and I, who was now used to clothes, had forgotten the day when I also was a pagan. I laughed at and rebuked these M'bum bushmen I am sorry to say, and when they were handed over to my charge to carry the heavy ivory, I treated them as the slaves of slaves and beat them gladly when they did not understand my orders.

When my master of that time had at last collected a good supply of ivory and corn seeds and bags of the grains of Paradise, which

were the seeds of the aframomum plant, which your people call
pepper, and also slaves, his intention as he told it to me was to set
out from Yola and proceed to a great city of the Fullani called
Yakuba, which was in the country of Bantshi. This, he told me in
his own courtyard, was his home, and there he had a big house and
many wives. He had also resolved to dispose of his slaves and ivory
and other trade goods and to settle down with his women and
children and his hunting falcons for the rest of his days. So when he
had finished all his business in this town of Yola, even though he had
been made to tarry, and had as is the custom given a handsome
present to the Fullani governor of that place, he then trafficked with
the Batta people in their part of town and bought many canoes, all
of which, as in the fashion of these countries, were hollowed out of
a single tree, and not put together with boards and nails as are the
ships of the Arabs and the whiter Christians or even the league boats
of the great fishing people, the Kroo that live round the Eyhi water,
which you English call Avon lagoon. And we loaded these canoes
with all the private precious trade goods which my master had
collected.

In charge of each canoe was put me and other trustworthy head
slaves. The bags of corn seeds and pepper seeds were first weighed
and then the ivory and the bags were counted and all the numbers
written in a book, so that if any tusks or bags were lost, or stolen,
my master would surely find out and punish the slave who had been
in charge of the canoe. And in the biggest canoe, a league canoe, we
put together and lashed up a little house of palm thatch, which
should be a place for my master Nyebbu to sit in and be protected
from the sun and rain. Then the canoes, perhaps twenty in all, were
all put into the water and tied together and stowed away in them all
the precious goods, and we started on our journey from Yola down
the great river Benue to reach the place called Wuzu, or as you
English call it, Wukari.

Now it was the season of the heavy walls of rain and the river
Benue beyond Zeeri was greatly risen in volume and had overflowed
its banks for a considerable distance on either side so that the rushing
water seemed like a great white sea without limits except for the
deleb palms which rose above the flood and marked where the borders of the stream should be in the dry season. Here and there, I
could see distant hills which looked like islands in a great lake. Many
difficulties encompassed us in this journey and often I and the other

head slaves were near to destruction, for the floods of the river having extended so far, it was exceedingly difficult for us to know which should be the true channel of the tormented river and hard to know how we should avoid the great roots of the fallen-in trees which lay concealed so near the surface of the water and against which the canoes would often bump, so that we were near capsizing.

And worse than this were the river horses who live below the water and have too big mouths stuck with spear teeth, and these horses are of a bold and bad temper in the rainy season, for it was the time of year when they were breeding in the new waters and whenever they, who numbered near to one hundred, could find canoes in the shallow river, five or ten of the males of their family would often make for it and endeavor to upset it either by bumping the canoe underneath with their big heads, and at times they would stove a hole in the bottom, or else seizing the gunwale with their curved spear teeth and dragging the entire canoe and the goods therein over to one side and so capsizing it. And although my master gave orders that we should fire every long gun at these river horses and hurl iron tipped spears at them, this did not secure us altogether from their angry pursuit, and indeed, it caused them sometimes to wax more fierce and troublesome and in this way we lost five other canoes and thirty-five slaves and much over fifty bags of corn and pepper seed and much ivory, for one river horse ceased to attack one canoe, and now two or four would attack it and with their long teeth the river horses broke the canoe in half or pulled the sides off with their teeth and caused the ivory and the seed bags to drop into the river mud, where most of it was buried and hence lost. The slaves that were in these canoes, being thrown into the water, had to swim over the river horses. Aoi-yo, twenty of them were killed by these terrible river animals, who bit all their bodies in two or three pieces and then six others, as they were swimming, were then taken hold of and dragged around in the water by crocodiles, including Nijina, and with the crocodiles going under we saw them no more. Two of them who remained from these canoes, who were women, my master old Nyebbu took into his own house canoe. But the others of the men he would not stay to help because the other canoes were already overcrowded, and these slaves in the water being of little value now because of only one leg or one arm or none of both, he cared not to run any further risk by picking them up. So what became of them I know not. Perchance they swam on until they touched the water's edge and were able to drag their bodies up onto the wet ground or it may be the young crocodiles waiting on the edges caught them all and with their teeth and with their legs and tails dragged them back into the water so that they could put them into the mud to rot so that they could eat them at a later time, as is their custom.

Also for some fearful time as we paddled down the river, we could see lumpy heads bobbing like black points on the waste of waters and the others laughed much when every now and then they heard a scream and guessed that a crocodile had seized another slave. I did not laugh. But I was struck and jeered by them and so I thought it wise at these moments to laugh also. And all these slaves who cared little for the loss of the ivory or the corn and pepper, for all of it was not theirs, began to hold their bellies and make many merry jests about the lumpy crocodiles saying that they would thank Allah The All Merciful for the feast He had given the crocodiles. But our master, who was all sad for the loss of all his many and different trade goods, bade them quick to be silent, or he would throw us, all of us, to the crocodiles too. Puh!

In some places that we passed by there had been great floods and yes, owing to the heavy downpour rains in the country of Basama, the villagers were all on little islands in the water coming close up to the houses, and only the tops of the plantain trees showing here and there where the plantations were covered. And on one of these islands where the village had been deserted by the inhabitants, who had fled safely away in canoes, I think, we saw a strange sight. There was an old lion, due to his mane was black, seated on his haunches. There was a company of baboons on the roofs of the houses. There were some hogs, of a kind whose name is Nok in Popo and which the Fullani call Modondi, and called Ngena in our country language. There were two bush deer of a sort which we name Ngaba, which are red coated with white stripes, and also a large black snake of a kind whose name is Puk in Popo and which the Fullani call Dimobi. And all these creatures which are wont to disagree in the rain forest —the lion to eat the bush deer and the snake to eat the baboons and the hog to kill the snake—were now so scared by the flood which had driven them for refuge to this small village on a little mound that they looked not at each other but steadily watched the water only as it mounted higher and higher and ate up the ground as it rose and our witless master bade us shoot our long guns and hurl our lances at the lion. I told the slaves with guns to do so. But according to my mind it was a matter of foolishness to kill a hapless lion, and waste our strength in doing so. It was this occasion which made me think a master cannot always be wise and a slave sometimes can be. But whether my slaves killed him or not I cannot say, for the flood was so strong that we dared not turn the canoes broadside and stop lest they should be overwhelmed. And as we got nearer towards the district of Muri the great expanse of turmoiled water grew less in breadth, for the mountains closed in nearer to the course of the stream, but on this account, the force of the current now grew even stronger.

At length a Fullani soldier, who was one of my master's employed servants, called out to the steersman of the canoe that was leading to enter a small branch of the river, which appeared on our right hand, and here the water was quieter. Soon after we had entered this narrow branch, we stopped at the riverside town the Fullani called Wuzu, and which was our destination. Here all the remaining slaves and the left ivory and bags of all seeds were disembarked and we all left the canoes which were afterwards sold by my master to a Fullani who lived at Muri.

At Wuzu, or if you wish in English, Wukari, my master only stayed sufficient time to get all of a caravan in order, and then set out for Muri, or if you wish in English, Darorro, which was a day's journey from Wuzu. Muri was a big town of the Fullani in which every house belonged to the Sultan of Yakuba and here after traveling, my lion-killer master had many friends and abode with them for several days, and conversing with them for days the end of which it was here he bought many Ahaggar pack camels and Egyptian donkeys and Nubian horses with only some of his ivory and seeds, and the rest of the teeth tusks he packed onto the Ahaggar camels and the Egypt asses and he told me he resolved to sell them all at Muri, where there was a great market. Most of his slaves, for he desired to proceed quickly to Yakuba, he told me he no longer needed; he needed not slaves to carry anything he possessed. I feared greatly that he would sell me here, for several Fullani merchants had looked at me, and pinched my muscles all over my body and said they liked the look of me and the work I could probably do. But my master said to them angrily that he would keep me for his own household, as I had a good head for trade, and a manner of saying things which caused him to laugh, and that not only did I, a slave, pursue to learn to write trade numbers, but also I endeavored nightly to write the tongue of Allah who was All Merciful.

So when all was ready on the backs of the camels in huge reed baskets for our journey to Yakuba, my master bade me in a kind and generous manner to seat myself on one of those Egyptian asses which altogether had a load of ivory on its back. At first I was greatly afraid, for I had never ridden any beast ever before, and as the ass seemed to already know that I was a pagan because when I tried to mount him he would rear up his hindquarters and throw off all of the ivory and also me. Would I succeed in riding the ass? At length and through error I managed to get onto the ass, and although I slipped off onto my back and head over the ass's tail into the dust several times repeatedly, I got vexed when my master laughed and jeered at me due to not being able to sit on an ass. And so I resolved to do it. Then I clung on with one hand clutching the ass's mane, and with the other holding one of his ears, and every time this silly beast would rear up before me or behind I would put the tip of his big ear in my mouth and bite it. And soon he gave over trying to unseat me, and by the time we reached near to Yakuba, I could ride without fear and would even at times grab tufts of hair and ascend and mount up upon one of the huge Ahaggar pack camels, which were strange beasts in my knowledge, for there was nothing of their kind in our country.

When we had got within one day's journey of Yakuba, we saw the great mountains behind and below where the town lay, and my master with some of his well-clothed merchant friends and the guards he had employed rode on in front and in much haste of the caravan, carrying with him a present for the Sultan of the country, and bidding his own chosen head-man, or Overseer of Slaves, to lead us other head slaves and common slaves all by other roads to his private plantations outside the town, so that his wealth of ivory and slaves and bags of seeds might not be shown to the Muselmin people or the white Christian people of Yakuba. It was said that the Sultan of Yakuba was a very greedy man, and harassed those whom he knew to be rich, and so with precaution I was told to abide several days at the plantations where the ivory and other trade goods were to be secretly stored. Then one day my master came riding out from the town to see that everything was safely stowed away. Then he chose out such slaves among us as he wanted, myself among the number, and mounted on asses, took us back with him into the town.

And here I was amazed at what I saw, for although Yola was a big town and the governor of it had a great house and there were one or two large mosques, there was nothing there that could be like what was in Yakuba. The people of that place are more in number than even those of Gando or Murzuk, and perhaps it is only surpassed in populousness by Kano, though I have heard the city Sokoto is a vast place inhabited by many people. But to me, who was then ignorant and just away from being a bushman, Yakuba seemed the grandest of cities, with its fine two-level houses of clay and their wooden doors and decorated arches and window frames and its market souks, the like of which I had never seen before. Here were merchants from as far away as the Great Desert and even further north like Ghadames, and people from Bornu and Sokoto and Nufe. Some were selling the cloth made by the Europeans which I had seen and the pieces of which had sometimes reached even our country of Popo but from the lands of Diwala and the Great Sea. Others trafficked in the blue cloth of Nufe or the long taubs of Kano or sold leather sandals finely embroidered, or saddles and horse gear from the Hausa lands, or the white salt brought up the Kwara River in big ships by the Christians, and wonderful things of glass and plates of earthenware and brass. And I tapped my mouth with amazement to think that the hands of men could fashion such things. And in one souk they were selling paper to write on and reed pens and ink, and the Koran bound in dyed leather—the book of Our Lord Mohammed, Salaam "ala Rasulna wa Nabina"—peace be upon our Apostle and Prophet! When I first saw the sale of these books I reckoned not of their value, for I was still a pagan and I wondered to myself that men should give for them many Kauri shells or the great silver riyalat, or a small tusk of ivory, seeing that these books were to my ignorance but made of leather and paper and could neither be eaten nor burned for perfume nor used for any purpose for a man's body. And in another shop was an old Fullani "m'alam" who was selling small pieces of sheepskin on which he had written something with a reed pen. And as my master old Nyebbu stopped and got down from his horse to buy one of these, I asked him of what was their purpose? He said they were charms to be folded up and put in a small case which was made out of a shell of a nut and to be hung round a man's neck to avert any harm that might happen to him by evil spirits, or to cure him of some malady. And if perchance a man was sick, there was no better medicine for him than to soften one of these pieces of sheepskin in water when it had been written on by the m'alam and to swallow it for the healing of both body and soul. Afterwards, I came to know these things well, and many a time and wallah! have my bodily ailments been cured by swallowing these charms. Alhamdu-lillah! And yet other market souks sold sweet perfumes-pastilles to burn in the house and to make a grateful odor, or ointments where a man's skin should be rubbed so that it glistened and was sweet and pleasing in the nostrils of his friends. And so passing through this great bazaar we arrived at the courtyard of my master's in-town house.

And what happened after this I must tell you on another occasion, for my tongue has wagged too much today. Besides, yesterday I had trouble with one of my superiors after I had remained so long with you. He was vexed and told me that his business with the Francswari suffered by my useless talking with you, an Englishman. Is it useless? I see. Then if you want me again you must first make it all right with Si Abd-al-Ghirha, so that he may not be annoyed by my coming to you. Insh'Allah ushufka al-ghodwa—God grant I see you tomorrow. If you give me fifteen silver riyals, I should return with a glad heart and a new turban, for it is not fitting that I should talk to a great Nusrani, a Christian, with an old, old dirty head-cloth like this. Allah yasalink!

Aya! And must I go on telling you still the events of my life? Are you not, Englishman, weary of all this talk, talk, talk? It is difficult to talk, talk, talk. Easier to think, is it not so? Yes, it is strange how all the little things I, Hadi Abbabba Guwah, have seen and done come back to my memory as I sit here and converse with you. Think not that I am telling you lies. I speak the truth. Allah yashud!—may God bear witness! Of what were my last words of yesterday? Was I telling you about my Fullani master, old Nyebbu? Yes, now I remember, I was speaking of his house.

It was a place built in the fashion of the Arabs in Murzuk or in Gando, only not so fine because it was too near to the land of the pagans and hence dangerous to make a finer house, and moreover, unlike all our houses of thatch in the blacks' country, it was built of piled rocks with clay covering them and not fine stone as in Murzuk. We passed from the street through a large door opening and came

into a big courtyard round which ran a high clay wall white. Inside
the courtyard were two or three old tamarind trees and young syca-
mores under which there was refreshing shade against the burning
sun. In this court, near the wall, the camels and horses of my master
Nyebbu were tethered and there were many wandering-about black
ducks and red and blue fowls and a few sheep. On the other side of
the court, opposite to where we had entered, was a high wall which
screened the house beyond and another archway in the middle of the
wall, which was closed with a great wooden door. This my master
pushed open and led me after him into his diwan, a large cool room
with small windows high up and seats of clay running all round the
sides on which tanned goat skins and zebra skins and handsome
carpets and silk cushions were placed, all smelling of perfume.

My master instructed me as to my duties, which were to attend
on himself, to prepare his snuff or his pipe and to make his coffee or
his tea, which he bought from the wealthy Magarabi merchants from
the land of China, and to do his food purchasing and to run his
errands, and to keep his diwan clean. When he, Nyebbu, was laid
down to rest and had fallen to sleep in the burning heat of the day,
I stood up on the clay couches and looked through the small windows near the top of the walls and through these I could see into the
inner court of the house which belonged to the harem of my master,
where his wives and concubines and women slaves dwelt.

Now, the Fullani, although they are Muselmin, are not jealous
of their women as are the Arabs. Neither are the women allowed as
much freedom as they were in our country of Popo, so that whereas
my master was displeased if I entered the court and part of the house
set aside for his harem, still, he paid little heed if his wives or women
slaves conversed with me, Hadi Abbabba Guwah, when we should
meet outside in the greater court, or if I should encounter them in
the bazaar of the town. Indeed, he Nyebbu would sometimes send
me a-trading to the market souks in company with his Head-Wife
and some of her hand-women, in order that I might assist them in
carrying home the things they had bought and my inks and reed pens
they had bought for me.

And in this way I became acquainted with a comely woman
slave of the name Erega, belonging to the Marghi tribe over to the
East. And there sprang up a love in her for me and hence after my
words we sought many opportunities of meeting in secret, and this
the Head-Wife found out about and told my master, who became

exceedingly wrath to find out that I was an upstart slave and vowed that he would punish me. He, Nyebbu, had me tied to the whip stake and had me flogged until I fainted. And to another stake my Marghi girl who had love for me was also tied, and would have been flogged, but that she swore by All Holy Allah and all the earth that no harm had passed between us, and that the Head-Wife had only accused her out of jealousy, and as she was a young comely girl and now I learnt, Wo-ye, a favorite of the toothless old Fullani, he was inclined to believe her and so she was released. But he said that, on the morrow, he would sell me to the Turks. Puh!

And all that night I remained tied strong by my wrists and always standing to the post where I had been flogged. But just before dawn when everyone was sleeping soundly, my young, comely, Marghi girl, who had succeeded in escaping from the harem, came to my still bleeding side with a small knife and cut my bonds and then bade me run away and hide until my silly master's wrath had spent itself. This I needed no second bidding to do, and sore and weakly as I was with my beating I stood up and eased cautiously to the gateway of the courtyard and, putting aside the beam and opening the wooden door noiselessly, I fled into the town.

Before it was yet light, I had hidden in sanctuary in one of the big mosques and waited until daylight. Then I boldly approached one of the gates of the town thinking to pass out into the country and hide in the bush for a while, but four Hausa soldiers who stood at the north gate would not let me pass, seeing me again naked and my back all bloody and suspecting me to be a runaway slave.

When I told them with rapid words what had happened to me, disguising such of my tale as would make them think I had been altogether and justly punished, all four of them came about me and took pity on me and the leader of their number said he would take me to the Great Sultan of the town—the Amir of Yakuba. As I limped alongside of this soldier leader, who was now up on horseback, my heart quaked within me, for I said to myself:

"Surely but the Amir is a great man and will know the truth and not my lies and will return me to my master, Nyebbu."

But I dared not run away from this soldier, lest worse should befall me. And when the soldier dismounted before an arch and a high white wall and led me into the Sultan's palace, I could not feel my feet touch the ground such was the fear and awe that possessed me. After a while life came back to me and when my companion poked his finger into my side sharply I lifted up my gaze from the ground and looked up at this Sultan, who was called by the name Mohammed Nadiku. He was a tall Fullani with a yellow face marked with smallpox and with a thick black beard. Below his eyes was a thin blue veil covering his nose, mouth and chin and falling over his breast so that when he spoke his voice sounded far away and muffled.

The soldier told him my tale and he the Sultan listened attentively and then addressed me with somewhat of a kindness, saying that he would inquire further into the matter when he had leisure. He told the soldier leader to take me away and to wash the blood off my body and to salve my wounds and clothe me in a long taub and a turban and to give me food and bring me back towards eventide, when the Sultan should have returned from his prayers at the great mosque.

At eventide then the Sultan saw me again, and this time my heart was strengthened, for I was clothed in a fine new long blue taub and a clean white turban, and my belly was full with sheep meat in sauce and hot corn seed porridge and I thought myself a tall fine good fellow and a regular Muslim and the Sultan Mohammed Nadiku made me tell him all my history, from the time when I was first captured by the Fullani-Hausa and then especially he asked me questions about my master old Nyebbu inquiring about his wealth, and how much ivory and other trade goods he had, and how many slaves and long guns he had, and asking me to tell him everything else I knew about Nyebbu. And when I had answered as near as I could all these questions, and seeing from his manner that the Sultan seemed much jealous of Nyebbu, an evil spirit put it into my good heart to tell more lies that should hurt my master, and I told the Sultan that I had heard Nyebbu say many, many times that he, Nyebbu, was the greatest man in Yakuba, and then when a propitious day arrived he would depose the Sultan Mohammed Nadiku and make himself, Nyebbu, Sultan in his stead, and that he had sent a great present to the Amir al-Mumenin at Sokoto to gain his favor so that he might secure his help and aid.

And these latter words were not altogether a lie by me, for I had seen truly my master dispatch this present to the district of Wurno where the Amir resided, but for what purpose I do not know. And after I had finished talking, I could see that the Sultan was in a mighty rage against my master, for his eyes blazed and by pulling at his veil away with his hands he tore it. When I had done my work talking, he said nothing, but dismissed me and told me to return to all the soldiers in the courtyard, who would feed me and comfort me and treat me well all round. But on no account, he cautioned, was I to leave his palace, or he would have me killed.

The next day a messenger came to fetch me to the palace of the Sultan of Yakuba, and when I arrived there and wended my way round the many Fullani standing there, I was near the throne, so down I went and then arose from touching the ground with my forehead. I saw standing in the corner of this huge and much decorated chamber my Fullani master Nyebbu, who had two guards on either side of him with drawn swords. His hands were tied together behind his back and he looked in a sorry plight, with his clothes torn and his face very bloody, where some soldier had struck him repeatedly in arresting him.

When his eyes had seen me, they lit up with wrath but in all the time he said nothing, and I, knowing myself to be in favor with the Sultan, met his gaze proudly, and further, arranged my beautiful new turban and smoothed down the folds of my beautiful new long taub, so that he might see I was now in good circumstances. The Sultan was sitting on his mighty throne of carved stone and on his carpet from Persia smoking a water pipe. His executioner, a tall Kanuri man with a black fez, and naked to the waist but having a great red cloth round his fat loins, stood on the carpet by the Sultan's side with a drawn sword. When I had remained there waiting for some few moments, the Sultan removed the mouthpiece of his pipe from his lips and said:

"Repeat now the charges you did bring yesterday against thy master Nyebbu and if you should have lied to me and I find it out, I have already in my mind how I will deal with you."

Then my heart waxed faint within me lest the Sultan should of his wisdom discover the lies I had told. But I plucked up courage thinking that it was only my words against my master's and that the latter was jealously regarded by the Sultan, and so I resolved to tell the same tale as I had related the day before.

When I had finished, the Sultan turned to my master and said:

"You have heard the words of this your slave, O Nyebbu. What have you to say to defend yourself?"

And my master replied:

"It is a cunning mixture of truth and lies which my slave has told, O Sultan. This and this is true, but that and that is false. It is true that I have sent my ivory and gold pieces to your liege lord, the Amir al-Mumenin, as a compliment. But it is less and much less than the present I gave to you. It is false that the thought ever entered my heart or the words ever passed my lips that I wished to conspire against your power or make myself Sultan in your stead. It is true that I gave this hyena a flogging and I blame myself only that my heart was soft for this man I once liked so much, and that for the offense of trespass he committed against one of my women slaves, I did not have him killed outright. Now I take Allah to witness that I have sinned in nothing against my allegiance to you and your rule and I pray you, as a just man and one fearing All Knowing Allah, to release me from my bonds and hand over to me for punishment this lying dog of a slave. You have the power to do me to death I know, but assuredly, Allah and the Amir, al-Mumenin, your Lord, will not tolerate my blood at your hands."

When he had ceased speaking, the Sultan rose in wrath and called out to those of his guards and courtiers who were round him:

"Is not this man self-condemned? Do you not hear the proud fashion in which he talks? What care I for the Amir of Sokoto? Is he Lord over me, I, Mohammed Nadiku, the Sultan of Yakuba, of Bantshi, of Muri, of Soso? It is enough; the slave has spoken truth. Strike off the head of Nyebbu and we will see whether his friend, the Amir of Sokoto, can help him, and cut out the tongue of this dog and son of a dog, in that he has dared to evoke the name of Allah to support his false statements."

When my master heard these words he pushed forward then and shook himself free of his guards and throwing himself flat on his stomach and elbows, he managed, as best he could with his tied hands, to wriggle and roll over and over and to the Sultan's feet crying:

"Aman! Aman! O my Lord, be merciful—spare my life and let me live and I will be your slave. I will be content to light your pipe and boil the pot of water for your tea. Take, take all that is mine— my ivory and slaves and gold and guns and women—whatever you see that is your wish, but let me yet live a little while. I will start on the Haj to Mekka. I will pray for you there at the Holy places."

And thus he wept and groaned and called aloud and even turned his face towards me saying:

"Speak you in my favor, O Big Head! I have ever treated you kindly and favored you much with my liking since the day I did buy you at Yola."

And I spurned his face with my foot kicking up the dust and said:

"Who am I that I should dare to speak when the Sultan has just spoken?"

And I saw the Sultan Mohammed Nadiku call out in an angry voice:

"I am weary of this noise. Are you all then, as this dog, that you look to the Amir of Sokoto and not to me—that I speak and you obey not?"

And the guards seized with strong, sure hands my master without more ado, and dragged him spitting and choking to the steps of the outer court. Here while this Fullani merchant, my once master, was still screaming out at this injustice, the executioner's men pushed him down and thrust hard a large wooden gag into his mouth, breaking off his remaining few top and bottom teeth and forcefully they pushed it in slowly until it prised his lower jaw almost from his skull. And when this was done, the executioner with the black fez took from his red waistband round his fat loins a pair of blue iron pincers, and, seizing my once-upon-a-time master's tongue, tore it out by the roots. Then the executioner's men took him, with him spreading round the courtyard the blood from his mouth, and began tying him against a wooden block in the very center of the latticed courtyard. With this done the executioner raised high his sword and sliced off Nyebbu's head with one blow. And his head was dispatched to be stuck on a post outside the Sultan's gateway, and then the body of him I dragged about the town by the legs and all the while I shouting out that they should everyone bear witness; thus should all people of this town and all lands be treated so that despised the authority of the Great Sultan of Yakuba. And the body I afterwards flung outside the town for the hyenas to eat. And after old Nyebbu had been thus disposed of, the Sultan sent men to seize all this merchant's property, slaves, and all other goods and then he attached me to his own household and gave me the Marghi girl to wife, the same that belonged to my late master, and I, Hadi Abbabba Guwah, became a great favorite with Nadiku, the Sultan of Yakuba, and was much feared in the town for it was said by all and everyone:

"Whomsoever Big Head condemns, he the Sultan executes."

And so my affairs prospered for the space of a year or more. But meanwhile, some Fullani merchants in the town who liked not Nadiku, the Sultan of Yakuba, had sent secret messages to Wurno to tell the Amir al-Mumenin the things which my Mohammed, only a Sultan of Yakuba, had done, and the way in which he, Nadiku, had in wrath repudiated all his allegiance to his liege lord of Sokoto. After some fourteen months had passed, the rumor reached us that a great army on foot and on horseback was on its way from the town of Kano to punish our liege lord Nadiku, as well to set up another Sultan in his stead who should govern Yakuba and only for the wishes of the Amir of Sokoto, al-Mumenin.

And these things caused great terror to my new master, the Sultan, who sent messengers in all directions to all parts of his dominions to collect his fighting men of foot and horseback to defend his capital. And the walls of the town were repaired and made good. Much store of provisions were collected therein and there was constant drilling of all troops all day and serving out to them of gunpowder and lead to cast into bullets. And at length we could see from up upon the great mountain behind our town the smoke of burning villages and other signs of the devastating army. Soon their great host was encompassing the town on all sides save the mountain side. And seeing the great forces brought to subdue Yakuba, the Fullani notables of the town held council among themselves in some secret conclave and they whispered in desperation to each other:

"Wherefore should we join issue with this man who has been Sultan of Yakuba? His quarrel is not our quarrel. Why should we fight to save him only from the rule of the Great Amir of Sokoto? We are Fulbe and the Sultan of Sokoto is a Fulo and a Prince of the True Believers. Surely it would be a sin in Allah's eyes to fight against him. Let us send our messengers from this town to the commander of the host, and ask him for protection and a guaranty of our property if we negotiate with him and hand over to his keeping the man who has been the Sultan here."

And news was brought to me of what the Fullani elders had planned by one Zada, whom I had made my friend with planned and special favors, and who was—Aya!—in this council. And I went in to my master, the Sultan Mohammed Nadiku, and told him secretly what was in the words of Zada. And he trembled much, and turned ashy pale, and said then to me:

"I see clearly that these merchants of this town have no grati-

tude in their hearts for what I have done for them and will not be
faithful and true to me. When I call upon them to fight, the dogs will
join with the enemy, even if they the enemy do not first surround my
palace and capture me and give me over to whoever will be my
enemies of the moment. There remains naught to do but to escape
to the mountains while there is yet time. I command you, Hadi
Abbabba Guwah, to therefore make ready for me food that I may
take away with me, and at nightfall I will disguise myself and bear
an order sealed with my own seal, that shall let me pass out at the
mountain gate, and so I will hide among the hill people till I can find
means to escape East to the Kingdom of Adamawa, where I have
many friends and you, Big Head, you shall go with me and follow
my fortunes. And if you are true to me, when Allah shall again give
me property, I swear by Holy Allah the Merciful I will reward you.
I will make you a rich man, and I will by my God make you free.
See," he said, "you have nothing to gain by turning against me your
Sultan as those traitors have done, and you, Hadi Abbabba, are more
hated in this town than even I am, and they all would be sure to kill
you, but before this to slowly pull out your tongue, and all after I
am gone."

And this reflection by Nadiku was a true one, for reflecting and
then within an hour seeing that I had—Puh!—nothing to gain at all
by betraying this Lord to the Fullani merchant notables of the town,
I resolved to escape from this place with him and follow him, Aoi-yo,
wheresoever he should go.

So we hastily and secretly set to work to make preparations for
this journey of escape. The Sultan I watched fill a bag with silver
pieces which he then hung round his neck. He moved round and hid
about his person such small things as he could hastily lay his hands
on. He told me I must do the same. Then he had in his hand what
was to my knowledge a M'bum blow tube, but which had been sealed
at both ends. He took off one end and he filled the tube with fire
stones and putting together the end of the tube, then he did place this
tube up into his body. The Sultan said to me that this was something
a Francswari had shown could be, and that Allah would have to
forgive him for executing the terrible and the unclean. Then preparing some balls of cooked yam and maize cakes, we put over all these
things several rich long taubs and scarves and hid our faces with
lithams, or face veils such as the Fullani of the north are given to
wear. He wrote out with his own reed pen on a square of sheepskin

an order to let himself and myself pass out of the mountain gate. Only he called us by the names of two of his servants. And arming ourselves secretly with daggers and loaded pistols—the Sultan carried a pistol with six barrels, such as you English call riwolwa, which had been sent to him as a present by the Christian traders on the river Kwara—we left the palace.

Stealthily walking through the streets of the town where the shadows were deepest, we arrived at the mountain gate, and the Sultan speaking in a muffled voice showed his written pass to a much adorned Captain of the Guard and told him to let us quickly pass on the business of the Sultan. And this Captain of the Guard, suspecting nothing, touched the permit with his forehead in token of respect, and gave orders to his six men that they should cautiously unbar the gates and let us through. So we passed out of the town and climbed up into the mountain, where we hid ourselves amongst the great stones and bushes.

When the dawn came we could look out over the town and see the activity of the siege, and fearing to leave our place of hiding in daylight while so many riding scouts of the Sokoto army were scouring the plains back and forth, we resolved to lie quiet all that day until darkness should again set in, and we could venture to cross the open country of the plains at night. And soon after the moon was up we could see that there was a great commotion inside the town and outside, for the merchant leaders had it would seem discovered our departure and had sent to sit and treaty with the commander of the Kano army. When the dawn was over and the sun higher, the gates of the town were opened and after much yelling and firing of guns the besieging force marched in.

What happened afterwards Nadiku and I did not know, and as no one was sent searching for us, we crept down the other side of the mountain, where there were no inhabitants, stepping cautiously all the while among the huge stones and bushes and keeping ever a good lookout that no one spied us. When the sun was setting, we were at the base of the mountain, and there being a crescent moon that night, we made the best of our way on foot across the plain until we came to some hills, where we hid for a while. And the next day we waded across the shallow part of a river and bought a little food at a small village of Bantshi people who wondered greatly to see us Mohammedans on foot, but we explained to them that our caravan had been broken up by the invading army from Kano and our camels taken from us. And here with three of the silver riyalat, we managed to buy two small asses, which we mounted and then rode on as quickly as might be in a southerly direction, crossing a great plain between two ranges of mountains, and when we had been traveling thus for some three days, we arrived at a quiet valley between some small hills where there were no people dwelling.

The punishment of Allah fell upon my master the Sultan here. We had made ourselves a small camp for the night by cutting down dried and gray thornbushes and strewing them in a circle. Inside these we tethered our asses and the Sultan then lit a fire with his flint and steel and tinder. When we had eaten yams and maize and washed our hands with sand and prayed, the Sultan laid down to sleep and bade me watch all about us until it was the middle of the night, when then I should sleep and he would take his turn watching.

But after a while it was fated that my eyelids should grow heavy, and an unworthy slumber fell upon me so that I ceased to watch. When I had slept for a little while, I was awakened by the firing of a riwolwa, and then I heard the growling of a lion and the voice of my master Nadiku calling for urgent help. And it would seem, Aoi-yo, that while I slept foolishly, the fire had gone out and a hungry lion had leapt the barrier of gray thorn spikes and fastened onto one of the asses, who in terror broke loose from the stake to which it was tethered and struck my master about the legs with its hoofs as he slept, and he, starting up in a fright and seeing by the light of the waning moon that a lion was attacking the ass, pulled out his riwolwa and fired it at the body of the lion at the same time calling to me to help him, and the lion being wounded in the back and greatly enraged, left the ass which he was tearing up and fell on my master, whose arm and leg he tore at with his thick teeth and terrible claws, but my master, Nadiku, thinking to keep his life, fired off all the other barrels of the riwolwa into the lion's big head with the other hand, which was all free, and the lion left off biting him and then fell dead.

Then I, who had scarce known whether I was alive or dead with the fright I had had, arose, and seeing the lion was dead, I dragged his body from off my master, whom I also took for dead, but then I saw he had only swooned from loss of blood.

I got the flint and steel from his waistcloth and struck a light, and having made a blaze of dried twigs, I tore off long strips of cloth from my master's clothes and bound up the great wounds in his thighs and arms where the lion had torn him.

And when it was morning, I saw my master had opened his eyes and was looking around. But a fever had got hold of him and he could only wobble his head and talk nonsense. He knew not where he was and not what had happened to him. I tended to his wants as well as I could, and then bethinking myself that he was too ill to continue his journey then, and that the ass which the lion had attacked was also in a sorry condition, I thought it best to remain where we were till my master should have recovered. So I took our two gourds and went out to seek water that I might have wherewith to quench our thirst and wash my master's wounds.

And when I had ascended a little hillock where there was rain-water lying in the clefts of rocks, I spied in the distance riding slowly across the plain some Fullani soldier horsemen. Guessing that they were searching for my master, I hurried back to our encampment which was on the other side of the hillock, and by the fortune of Allah, shielded from their sight. Then I stamped out the fire so that its smoke should not betray the whereabouts of the camp to the soldiers and sat down to reflect on what I should do now. Seeing that my master still lay sick and out of his senses, and that one of the asses continued to be disabled, I resolved within myself that it was foolish to remain with my master any longer, for it would be long ere he could travel and then only slowly, and assuredly the Fullani would discover us and slay us. So, having considered all this, I went to my master, who was talking nonsense and heeded me not, and took from his neck the bag of riyalat and silver fingers which he carried, and taking a dagger, dug out from his body the tube filled with fire stones, and then I took the riwolwa and whatever other things of value that were easy to stow away. And then leaving him a gourd of water, a little food, and the disabled ass, I mounted the other and rode away towards the high range of hills in the west, knowing the hillocks where I had been to get the water would for some time screen me from the gaze of the Fullani horsemen, who were scouting us out. At nightfall I reached a village at the base of the mountains.

Here I gave myself out to be a Hausa trader, for all the people were foolish timid pagans who, seeing me dressed like a Hausa, believed me to be such.

I had not any clear plan in my mind as to what course I should pursue, but I, in all my ignorance of the many purposes of Allah, thought I was now far enough away from pursuit and would hence give myself out as a Free Man and would trade with the riyalat I had taken from my master Nadiku. So I then told all of the villagers that had gathered round me that I was riding in front as a scout for a large caravan of slaves from the Adamawa countries, and that I wished to know where in that direction I should find a great market at which we all of the caravan could profitably dispose of all our slaves. And the Head-Man in his foolishness said:

"At Yakuba there is a market, Hadi Abbabba Guwah. There is no better place to sell slaves than in Yakuba."

But I spurned him on this advice and told him that I had heard there was a glut of slaves in that market and asked if he or others knew of no great town to the westward? On that by and by several counseled me to proceed to Keffi, which should be a town nearly as big as Yakuba, lying to the westward. And they directed me to proceed along a certain little river called the Doma to a place where it joined a bigger stream called the Maja and after crossing at the ford, and skirting a great mountain and crossing another river the Tumdah, I should then see Keffi before me. And believing in the tale that I told them they asked me before leaving to give them some guaranty that the soldiers and captains of my big caravan, following me should not harass them as it passed through their town. Wishing to satisfy them, and also to get free, I pulled out the pass which the Sultan of Yakuba had written and gave it into their hands. They, of course, not being able to read what was thereon written.

And then by the earliest time of the morning I rode off in the direction of Keffi. And after several days' journey, which would be wearisome to recount to you, I found myself at the huge gates of this great town. I had to sleep outside all the night because I arrived after sundown, and the gates were shut, and I was much harassed all the night by the attacks of hyenas who would run in on me and snap at my own limbs or the legs and hindquarters of my ass.

When I entered this Keffi the next morning I and my big head was a fool believing that the town people of that place would as readily believe my lies as the simple villagers easterly in the wilderness. So in the marketplace I told all who stopped me, and questioned me, that I was a Hausa merchant come to trade there and to buy slaves with riyalat, and I said how the rest of my large caravan had been broken up and dispersed by the attacks of forest robbers and

I only, Hadi Abbabba Guwah, had escaped. And hearing this story four traders pushed away people and came forward and spoke to me not in the Juku trade language or in the M'bum but in the Hausa language. I stammered and I stuttered; I could not speak that tongue, so I replied to them in the Fullani speech and all four of a second laughed aloud at me and finally:

"What are these lies you tell us? You a Hausa merchant and you cannot speak the Hausa tongue? And the fulful-de you talk is the fulful-de of a slave. Perchance you are some runaway that has robbed his master and put on all his clothes. Come along with us to the governor of the town and give us a true statement of your case."

And though I had to back the ass away and protested and swore and entreated them and several times wrenched my garments from their grasp, but finally they altogether dragged me off of the ass into the dust and stood me up and pushed me toward the Hausa governor of that town, which, although in the empire of the Amir of Sokoto, is ruled, I found, by Hausas. Aoi-ye. When I was carried before the governor, so great was my fear now that my wit deserted me and I could not frame any lies that should satisfy them but was reduced to confessing the whole truth of what had befallen me in all the days of Nyebbu and Nadiku, and then all before I came to Keffi. I was long in the telling of the tale, and then encouraged by him to proceed slowly, and I cheered up in the telling by the laughter of the governor, who made merry over the things I, Hadi Abbabba Guwah, had done. When I had finished speaking he bade the four to strip me of my clothes and riyalat and indeed everything I possessed, so that I was once again stark naked, and feeling like a pagan once more.

"Now," he said, restraining his mirth, "you deserve death for the things you have done. But it is not in my heart to kill you, for you have made my sides ache with laughter. You shall live therefore but now become my slave, Hadi Abbabba Guwah. But you beware lest you play any pranks with me. I have more wisdom than both Nyebbu and Nadiku and no tolerance at all, so it will be easy for me to behead you."

Then he clapped his large hands and when they came he bade his servants give me a smelly old piece of cloth to hide my nakedness and ordered that I should be put to hard work in his plantations.

This was a bitter lot for me who had thought myself almost a Mohammedan gentleman and often I would stop to weep at the misfortunes that had befallen me. And thus when I failed to do good work with me dwelling on my misfortune, I got many a flogging from the Overseer of the governor's plantations. I could count over one hundred scars from the whip on my body, and then one day it was said to me that as I was a worthless and downcast slave, I should be sold in the market. O-ye.

So together with some others who were again wild bushmen from the Akpoto country that had been captured in a Hausa raid across the Benue, we were taken on a great fair day to the town of Keffi, and stationed there in the marketplace for sale. And a Hausa merchant of Kano looked at me, examined me, and asked many questions about me, and finally after much talking and waving of arms with the governor's Overseer, bought me for only three riyalat. I was of the opinion I was worth at least twenty riyalat. Two days afterwards my new master departed for the town of Kano with a big caravan that had many baggage camels and their small, thin off-spring and horses and asses and slaves and such. My tired neck was set in a great square wooden collar, the one side of which was fastened to the huge neck of one of the wild Akpoto slaves and thus again with pain and the familiar weariness, we had to walk on day after day after day in the middle of the caravan. Although I spread my hands wide and salaamed low and pleaded with gestures many times to be set free to walk by myself and swore before Allah and with many oaths that I would not run away, the leader of the caravan up on his horse had no pity on me, and said he had heard in Keffi that I was a cunning rascal and he did not intend to give me any chance of escape. Puh!

I do not know how I lived through this journey, so great was my suffering and so little had I to eat and no clothes had I to cover my scars. The great wooden collar that I wore round my neck was never removed, and its ceaseless chafing caused two great sores to come onto my shoulders, the scars of which are the largest I have to this day. The Hausa man who was the Maidoki, or leader of the caravan, was called Din Shekara. He was a cruel man with one arm and a hard heart and paid no heed to my whining nor yet to my compliments. For at first I thought to win his favor by extolling his greatness and the beauty of his countenance and the splendor of his horse trappings as he rode past me. But he would only aim a foul blow at my head with the butt end of the tufted lance that he carried,

66

and rebuke me for a saucy slave in so daring to comment on a person of his greatness. This repeatedly from this simpleton Din Shekara.

I, Hadi Abbabba Guwah, who had been a favorite of his mighty, lovely Excellency, the Sultan of Yakuba, considered myself as much a Muslim True Believer as any Arab or Fulful-de follower of the Prophet. Here, I was now forced to walk daily in step with an ignoble pagan Akpoto slave from the Ibo country, joined to him during the march by a Christian iron chain which united our two heavy wooden collars. Sometimes I would try much to show the camel guards of the caravan that I was a Muslim like themselves, and in a loud voice and palms out and fingers spread, I would recite the fatha, the prayer from the Book of Books, which I had learned from the Fullani Muselmin, or I would attempt to pray the Two-Bow Prayer. But so often as I did this in the hearing of the guards they would strike me across the mouth with their long Bassa knife whips and jeer at me, saying that Allah could not understand such jargon and mocking me for the nonsense that I spoke in the Arabic that I had taken all the time to learn by rote.

We sojourned for a while at a place called Saria, and here the slave to whom I was fastened fell sick of a town fever, and of a sudden he pulled me down with him into the dust and after rolling about and yelling, did proceed to attack me with his mouth and made to bite away large pieces of my body with his teeth. Then a guard was upon us and he pushed his spear point into the neck of this raving fellow and wrenched him off of me. And thus this slave did die. And a number of other slaves of the caravan also perished of this fever, so much so that the leader Din Shekara feared to lose all his profits. So he consulted with some of his merchant men and it was agreed that such of us as had survived the sickness should be somewhat better treated so that we might reach Kano in a fair condition. Moreover, the wooden collar was now taken from my neck and the sores dressed with oil. But a large rope was soon tied round my throat instead and this new collar in turn again fastened to another slave. I was given a little more food than before, just a little, and our progress became slower between Saria and Kano, so that the slaves might not become too exhausted.

At length one day the soldiers in front of the caravan began firing their long guns and shouting and rearing up their horses and the word passed all along the caravan that Kano was in sight.

This was a finer city than any I had yet seen, and although I was sick and weak and an ill-treated Popo black slave, even I felt glad and walked in a more upright manner as I passed through the great adorned gate and entered the wide streets of the town. I and the Akpoto bush slaves were all to the slave market to be sold the next day, but this did not make me sad in any way, for I felt that whatever my lot might be, it could not be worse than the previous sufferings, and I was even merry as I sat over a huge dish of cold corn porridge that night.

The next morning there was a great press of people in the market, and where each lot of many different slaves with their sellers were stood in a row for purchasers to inspect. There were yellow-faced Arabs, brown Kanuri people from Bornu, blue-skinned Tuaregs from the Great Desert, and Fulbe from Sokoto and the Kwara river, all wishing to purchase slaves. A Hausa man of Kano whose name was Gungi and who was a "Mairini," or dyer, examined me very closely and asked many questions about me. Of course, Din Shekara, the caravan leader who bought me in Keffi, spoke highly of my qualities and said there was never such a strong and willing worker as I, but the dyer looked doubtfully at me and poked me doubtfully because of my great leanness and the sores on my body. However, at last after much dispute, he bought me for thirty thousand Kauri shells and took me away with him to his house, which was in the quarter of the town called Sherbale.

When we arrived there, he spoke to me in fulful-de, which I then knew better than Hausa, and he told me that if I was a good slave, I should find in him a kind master, but that if I shirked my work or stole from him or ran away, I should find no pity in his heart. I spoke many sweet things to him and knelt to him and kissed his hand trying to win his favor, all the while thinking would I of a day kill him in such a way as I did with Nyebbu? Getting up from the dust and standing very upright, I found he was looking kindly on me. Wallah! Then he clapped his strange colored hands and when some women slaves came, he bade them lead me to a small tank of well water where I could wash myself and to afterwards give me food. He also sent a small boy to me while I was washing and on his arm was a common blue taub of cotton and in his fingers an old red fez, and the boy told me to wear these instead of the dirty rags I wore about my body. Having washed and put on my new clothes, I looked quite a better kind of man, but not as good as when I was with Nadiku. However, my new master—Baba Gungi as he was called—took great credit to himself for having made me such a cheap bargain in the market. Ayamaaa. . . .

In the afternoon of that day Baba Gungi took me with him to his Marina at the back of his yard. This was a steamy looking and hot feeling open terrace, or platform, of clay with a number of very big clay dyeing pots, and here eleven men slaves were stirring up the smelly indigo juice that was in the pots and mixing it every now and then with large spoon loads of some pounded red wood of a kind brought from Adamawa.

My master spoke to those other slaves and told them to instruct me in the work and make me useful.

When he had left us, his slaves, who were rather simple folk and mostly people from Bornu, asked me to tell them of my history—who I was and whence I came. To them I related much of my past adventures as I have told them to you, and in this way we sat long talking until they heard the sound of our master's sandals pattering slip-slip on the ground of the courtyard outside and started up in a panic to go back to their work.

Then I was shown by one of them, Brahimu, how I must fetch a white cotton taub from among a bundle that lay on a clay bench that ran along one side of the Marina, and soak it in a cistern of clean water, and when this was done, wring it out hard and nearly dry and then plunge it into one of the many dye pots where another man went from one to the other and stirred them round and round with a long pole. And then again I was to take other shirts from the other dye pots, the dyeing of which was finished, and having wrung them out to plunge them for a minute into another cistern of dirty water, and then again wringing them out, to hang them on the branch of a small and crooked-looking ponciana tree which grew through a hole of the terrace wall in the middle of the dyeing place. When this was done, and while these shirts were set to dry, I was given others that were already dried, and these I had to spread out on mats on the ground of the Marina and beat first one side and then the other with a long very pliant stick. This was a kind of business hard to learn, for the taubs must be beaten in a certain fashion so that the roughness of the dye leaves the cotton and a shiny appearance like silk takes its place. All through the day we would hear this sound of beating of taubs going on, for always day after day one slave or another was at this work, and as they beat they would sing this song in keeping with the sound of the blows:

> We are dyers, We are dyers
> Dyers are we
> First we dye it
> Then we beat it
> And then we sell it
> To a goodly and godly man!

For the first few weeks that I lived in Kano in the house of Baba Gungi, I sought only to gain the favor of my master and I was so industrious in this dyeing work that the other slaves reported well of me to Baba Gungi. But after a time I wearied of this dyer's life, although I had plenty to eat and it was good food and I had a master who did not ill treat me. Then also I began in time to assume a mastery over all the other slaves of the Marina and became a kind of chief among them—so much that I made them do all the work and passed my time mostly joking and laughing with my master's women. And one of these women named Dubra did for me a favor, and that was to purchase in the town, with her own Kauri shells, reed pens and another calabash of ink so that I could continue writing numbers and the words of the Arabic. I also got from her a knee table made from cypress wood.

And occasionally I would manage to have a little dyeing done privately for such friends as I had worked hard to make in the town, and for this, these work-friends would give me small presents, which I turned round to sell so that I could gradually store up money with which to buy fine clothes. And my master at first approved of my smart appearance, and told me I did credit to his household. But gradually he grew distrustful, and suspected that I had not dealt quite honestly with him. Moreover, he grew angry at my behavior with the women and at the saucy tone I took when he rebuked me, and I heard him say one day to another of the slaves that he would soon find means to reduce my pride.

One morning he found great fault with the dyeing of some taubs and ordered me to repeat the dyeing of the cloth. I called another of the slaves and bid him dip the taubs again into the dyeing pots, but my master angrily interrupted and said:

"My order was for you, you, you dog to dye the cloth and not Brahimu. It is time you should be punished for your insolence."

And he stepped into the house and unknown to me fetched then a great whip made of hippopotamus hide.

I was standing with my back to him mocking his anger to all the other slaves when he in a wrathful state suddenly began to lash me with this hippopotamus whip, and even through the cotton shirt which covered my shoulders he cut my flesh with the whip and drew much blood. I could not at all contain myself at this treatment, so I turned on him and with all my strength—for I am a strong man after feeding well, which is why the Arabs called Hadi-il-guwah—and lowering my head, I charged at him like a water horse butting him full and hard in the chest. Such was the force of my head blow that the whip fell from his hand and sank to the ground, then he clawed at the clay of the Marina which brought forth blood from his fingers and from his throat came the sounds of a dying man.

When the other slaves saw that I had seemingly killed their master, they raised a terrible noise and all the women came into the Marina shrieking and tearing at their garments and calling for help. Remembering what had happened to me at Yakuba with Nyebbu, and before any could detain me, I broke from them all and ran full pelt through the many streets round to the palace of the Ghaladima, or governor of the town, and heeding not the clamor and the hubbub of the guards, I rushed on blindly into the diwan where the governor was lying on a big and fat woman. Seizing the upper skirt of his long robe in one hand and pinching his bare buttock with the other, I cried:

"Aman! Aman! I place myself under your protection."

And he backed off and stood up from the woman and facing me proudly removed his garment from my hand, and let it fall down to cover his body and his little particle that made babies, then called his guards to seize me and then he angrily demanded to know from them why I had been allowed to enter his presence. And they bowing their foreheads to the dust mumbled and protested humbly that I must be a madman, a possessed one, that there was no holding me, that I had passed through them in a fury like one of the Genii of the Great Desert. And then the Sultan demanded of me to tell him my tale, and I related to him so much of my history as might bear on my own case, laying great stress on the fact that I was a Muslim, and had been a big chief in my own country having over a hundred slaves and that every one of the twenty or more concubines in my harem in Popo had her own goat, and that to be struck by a man

such as a dyer put madness into my heart. And the Sultan said
to me:

"Know you how to fight, how to aim with a gun, how to ride
a horse in battle?"

And I replied that I had been a great warrior in my own land,
and I had slain many people, too many of them for me at all to
remember the number.

Then he asked me if I were willing to become one of his soldiers,
and I said to him:

"Ayo Wallah, if you grant me protection from Baba Gungi!"

Then he handed me over to the "Sarki-n-Yaki," the Captain of
the Guard, that he should drill me as a soldier. This captain, who
I saw had his wits about him, and thus I knew he would listen
attentively to me, and so I expressed a wish not to be a foot soldier,
but one on horseback, and he said this would be done for me since
I was in the favor of the governor.

Once more my heart felt proud at the change in my fortunes.
The other soldiers among whom I now lived treated me with a
certain amount of respect as being a Popo slave who had murdered
his master and yet had got off scatheless. It took me some time and
considerable labor to learn to ride a war horse and the fighting
Tegama camel in the same fearless fashion as the other troopers rode.
But I had lost my great fear of both these animals, and also the horses
of Hausaland are smaller and more docile than those of the Arabs
in Tarabulus. I was given and told I must learn the use of the hemp
lariats and sharp hooks with which I was to pull the enemy from
their saddles, and the horrible Yataghan throwing irons to be used
after I had dispatched my arrows. I was also armed with the long
Masari straight sword which was hung on my left side, and in the
right hand, I had to carry and use a short heavy wooden spear with
an iron point. The officers of the troop wore great wide turbans and
leopard skin skirts bound close to the body, and long silver daggers
fastened in a belt round their left arm. A few of the horse soldiers
had muskets which they carried in place of the spear. I told the
Sarki-n-Yaki I wanted a musket, and thus I, Hadi Abbabba Guwah,
had a musket, which I had to daily practice with by firing at a target.

We wore red turbans on our heads and we dressed in large blue
shirts from the shoulders to the breast and down to the hips. These
were bound close to the body by means of a red shawl which we
wound tightly about us. Some of the officers had their black shawls

tied over the lower part of their faces after the fashion of the Tuaregs. We wore no sandals on our feet because they interfered with our grasp of the stirrups. This cavalry, which was in the service of the Sultan of Kano, was quartered in spacious and wonderfully appointed barracks at the back of the palace, and these barracks enclosed a square, or maidan, where we could practice with all of our many weapons and drill or exercise with the horses or the camels.

About what happened further when I went to war for the Sultan of Kano, I will tell you when I see you tomorrow. I am weary now. Insh'Allah!

When I had served in the army of the Sultan of Kano for perhaps six months, we were ordered to get ready to go on a warlike expedition. This Sarki—as the Hausa people called their Sultan—the Sarki of Kano had arranged a very clever plan. Some little while before, the Sultan of Gujeba, a town in the Bornu territories, had sent an invitation to the Sarki to join in a raid on the pagan infidels of Kalam. But my Kano Sultan excused himself by saying that he had other concerns in which he wished to employ his time and his army. Nevertheless, he urged the Sultan of Gujeba to proceed to exterminate in Kalam all such as should not have embraced the True Faith. As soon as the Sarki of Kano satisfied himself that the Sultan of Gujeba had set out on his expedition with all his war forces and that the frontier lands of Bornu were denuded of soldiers, he gave orders to the Commander of his Army, the Sheik-Abd-er-Rahman, a Moor from Timbuktu who had risen to a high position in the service of the Sultan of Kano, to get ready eight thousand cavalry and about four thousand foot soldiers, and with their bows and spears and muskets, invade the country of Katagum and the border lands of Bornu. Before our army left Kano, many of us wished for charms against death and several old m'alams came with their calabash inkstands and reed pens and knee stands and wrote out verses from the Koran on sheepskin.

When we left Kano we rode for about the space of half a day and then stopped to encamp for the night, and the villagers of the district opened a market in our camp and sold eating provisions. At nightfall the leader of the camp, the Sheik-Abd-er-Rahman, the Moor, sent for such of us as he esteemed for our ability and exalted temper and gave us many cups of black tea to drink and two or three

Kola nuts to eat, after which we all salaamed in deep respect. We started again at midnight, when the waning moon was risen, and then made a long journey up and down and round and even to the next evening. The day after that we arrived in the vicinity of a town called Gubu, which our commander, the Sheik Rahman, then proposed to attack, as it was, as he said, well populated and much bounty lay therein. Many of the inhabitants round this town had at our approach flocked into Gubu, intent on defending themselves behind its walls, and many others also concealed themselves in the palm groves, and the stubble bushes of durrha corn in its environs. They shot poisoned arrows and hurled darts at us, but we soon dislodged them from round the town by setting fire to the stubble and such of the dry trees as would burn, and the raging of this fire swept the ground nearly clean and drove all the people into the town. The next day we delivered the last assault with the whole force and easily climbed their walls and killed their army.

But the leader of our force, Abd-er-Rahman, the Moor, was angry at the resistance the town people of Gubu had made, and which took away in death about four hundred of our soldiers, and he ordered the cutting off of the heads of eight hundred of the defenders. And having selected about two thousand of the best of these inhabitants that we had made slaves, he dispatched them with a small escort back to our town of Kano while we others proceeded further towards Katagum, leaving the town of Gubu not quite empty of people, for as our wise commander said:

"We must allow some to remain behind to breed more people so that we may make slaves of another day."

The country of Katagum and the vicinity round we utterly wasted, destroying all of the dwellings with gunpowder, and laying bare all the plantations with fire. We carried off a rich spoil of slaves, guns, camels and cattle, cloth, saddles and skin-bags of rice, maize, oat, and pepper, and Kanopik jars of palm oil and diamond stones. After riding in a thunder and raiding as far as Fititi, we reassembled all our foot soldiers and cavalry and returned to Kano.

I had agreed with some of my comrades that we should mutually assist each other in capturing slaves and other bounty and share the profits between us. The custom in that country, which overall is called Sokoto, is that when a private soldier shall have caught, say, five slaves, he shall give two of them to the Sarki of Kano and retain the other three for himself. Three of every six camels we captured we would have to give up to the Governor, these beasts being more valuable than slaves. We—that is to say my five comrades and myself—managed altogether to capture forty slaves, and thirty-five camels. The slaves we bound one to the other with heavy wooden collars and iron chains like once I did have to endure, and the camels were tethered together with hemp, and both slaves and camels we drove back before us using our spear points from up on horseback during that time we were returning to Kano with the rest of the force. Of these forty Gubu slaves, some were old women, some were young girls and boys, and only three or four were able-bodied men. We gave up sixteen of the slaves to the Sultan, taking care to choose the oldest and least valuable among them, and of the twenty-four that remained we each got four. Of the camels we each got three. Altogether the whole amount of slaves collected with this raid numbered several thousand, and brought much wealth to the Sultan. At that time there was not a good market for slaves in Kano—there was no demand for them now by the merchants from the Kwara, so the Sultan of Kano resolved to send a strong slave caravan to Zinder, a town about eight days' journey north of Kano. He chose me as one of the armed escort, at which I greatly rejoiced, for I counted on selling at a good price my own four slaves and my three camels. At the same time we had to convey presents and a letter to the Sarki of Zinder, who had recently allied himself to Kano against the Bornu people.

The commander of this expedition to Zinder—the Sarki-n-bai, or the Maidaria, as we used to call him—was a very jolly good-tempered man named Ubanmasifa. He was fond of jesting and would often make us laugh loudly at his tales of the caravans he had commanded and all the raids he had in his time been on. I had seen he had taken a liking to me when we had been on the slave raid to Katagum, and on this long journey to Zinder he made me his Zaka-fada, or Aide-de-Camp. Wallah!

And as is the custom, my person was dignified with a bag of money and diamond stones and bags of rice and dried sheep meat and then I was allowed to wear the silk black tabu over which descended the bright silver chain of my office, and round my head was wound by the soldiers the white turban and ear cloth that comes down and must be wrapped accordingly under the chin and then came my long white ankle cape, two arms wide. Ayamaaa, I was exceedingly pleased. But did I not deserve it?

Several wealthy Moorish merchants from the great Fezzan

would accompany us from Kano to Zinder, and with one of these—
a man named Al-Haj-Ayub—I took care to become very friendly,
because he appeared to be the richest of them all, and now he talked
much to me over the camp fires of night in my new uniform of office,
of the many fine things which were to be seen all round in his
country, and in the land of the Turks at Tarabulus and advised me
to secretly leave the service of the Sarki of Kano, and accompany him
with his caravan on his return to Murzuk, where he was going with
his spoils of Fititi slaves and the Tegama fighting camels. He told me
camels were so cheap in Zinder that many people came across the
Great Desert to buy them and take them back to Fezzan to sell again.

In our caravan besides slaves, we carried a great store of sweet
potatoes and dried fish, which are things that may be very profitably
sold in Zinder where the people are far off from any big water that
holds fish and for some reason or other cannot grow sweet potatoes
in their plantations. The road from Kano to Zinder is unsafe traveling for small caravans because of the robber chiefs and their bands
that lurk in the distant rocks. Some of these are Daura people who
are pagans, and very fierce, and are constantly at war with the people
of both Zinder and Kano. They would lie in wait to attack even us,
and would endeavor to surround and kill any stragglers of the caravan and at them shooting poisoned arrows. Also the force of their
bows is so great that it is said their arrows will pierce three planks
of wood placed together, and the poison of them, which is obtained
from a certain plant they had not the knowledge of, causes you to
quickly swell up huge and die, even if your skin is only just pricked
with the point of the arrow. We lost in this way fifteen or twenty
soldiers who had lagged behind.

And another danger in this country between Kano and Zinder
was the many lions and hyenas; hyenas of a large kind and spotted
and not striped such as those you see in Tarabulus. We had to make
big fires at nighttime to keep off these beasts, and even then we were
not safe, for one night a lion and his female jumped into our camp
over the hedge of thorns in a place where the fire had sunk low, and
attracted some of our horses, endeavored to have a mouthful or two
of the flesh of them, but we drove them off with burning brands. The
noisy hyenas however, as we neared Zinder, got so bold that they
would surround the camp at night in their large numbers; perhaps
forty or fifty, and any man who should venture outside alone would
be attacked and pulled down, and they had a cunning method of

leaping at the throats of such as they found alone and unprotected, and by seizing the necks of these people suddenly in their jaws, they would prevent their crying out, and holding a man such, the other hyenas would eat the man's belly out.

After being about ten days on this route, we came within sight of Zinder, which we first discovered by the numbers of vultures that were circling round it in the air, for this spreading town lies a little low and is concealed by a lot of reddish rocks and low green hills. As soon as our horses and camels entered in through the gates of the town, we military men of the escort who were taking the letter and the present from the Sarki of Kano to the Sarki of Zinder sought and in a time arrived at the house of the Ghaladima, the Vizeer of the Sultan, and he bidding us wait in his outer court, hurried off to acquaint the Sarki of our coming and to arrange for an audience. The houses of Zinder we had recently passed seemed to us poor and of bad workmanship after those of Kano. The walls are simply of clay bricks baked in the sun and piled one on top of the other and which had not ever been even whitewashed, nor was there any attempt at decoration after the fashion of the Arabs. There was scarcely any furniture in this house of the Vizeer we were in, and no mats or carpets to sit on. Indeed, this Ghaladima himself had been sitting in the dust when we had entered.

After we had waited a short space of time, the Vizeer returned and said the Sultan was ready to receive us, and he, acting himself as a guide, he led us through the airless streets of the town to this Sultan's palace, which was a kind of mud fort. Herein we entered, and after passing many starving-looking Hausa cats surrounded by flies and passing through several courts where there were a lot of soldiers lounging about, all unarmed and bare headed, clad in very food stained taubs, we were ushered into a dark chamber where the Sultan was sitting on a mud bench. Instructed by the Vizeer, we all threw ourselves down and taking up the dust of the floor in our hands we threw it over our heads saying in Hausa:

"Baba-n-Sarki, Baba-n-Sarki, Sarki-n-dunia," which means, "O great King, great King, King of the World."

Then the Sultan having commanded us to deliver our message, we rose up and told him the occasion of our visit, and delivered to him the letter and the present which the Sarki of Kano had sent to him.

The Sultan then ordered his weakly looking people who must

be his servants to fetch an old Figi-an Arab from Wadia, who acted
as his scribe, for this goat of a Sultan could not even read. When this
man arrived, a cripple with no legs below the knees and swaying and
moving forward and back and forth on tiny crutches, he handed him
the letter. Its contents pleased the Sultan, and he said that in the
future he should trust to Allah and the Sarki of Kano for the mainte-
nance of his power and not any longer to the Sheik of Bornu, who
had no business in his country, for in Zinder did they not speak
Hausa and not Kanuri? And then he bade the Vizeer to give us each
a present of Kauri shells from the Treasury, and to supply us with
food during our stay. He told us that he would consider what reply
he should send to the Sarki of Kano, and would give us a letter and
a present to our Sultan when we should be ready to return to Kano.

After this we went out into this miserable town and visited such
people as were persons of importance, paying them, as is the custom,
many false compliments and receiving small and worthless presents
in return. And this duty completed, I was urged to buy me a wide
and sharp sword of shining steel tempered in the fire, and cut all of
this down like an old dead tree, dirty old town.

The next day we went to look at the slave market to hear what
prices were being given for our bounty. But we found to our disap-
pointment that they were of no more value here than at Kano, for
this Sarki of Zinder called Sadi-Radi-Hisham had made many slave
raids of late into the Daura country, and this town was full of slaves
for sale. As I did not see any chance of getting a good price at present
for my four slaves and three camels which I had brought with me,
I resolved not to be in a hurry to sell them, although the price was
going up because I had to feed them all the time.

The Sarki of Zinder was a cruel man and much feared by all his
subjects, and by even the blue Tuareg of the Great Desert who came
to Zinder to trade. For the least offense, he would sentence people
to death. When a criminal was to be killed, he was taken by the
executioner to an open place underneath a lofty tree with thick shiny
leaves of a kind called "Alleluba" in the Hausa tongue. Of this sort
of tree there are three or four only in Zinder, and each one is called
"Itatshe-n-mutua," which means the Tree of Death, for these trees
mark the places of execution upon the outskirts of the town.

A few days after we had come to Zinder, we heard that a

number of men who had been caught stealing in the Sultan's plantations were to be killed, and the Ghaladima sent a small boy to guide us to the place of execution, so that we men of Kano might see how such things were carried on in Zinder; this dirty old town.

We came then to one of these trees standing in the open space, which was bounded by great rocks wherein the hyenas had their dens and could eat the bodies of the people executed. The place under the shade of the tree was so clean swept and smooth that I went there to set myself out of the sun, but the boy who had come with us hastily snatched my garments and pulled me back away and made a noise thus:

"Do you wish to die Kano man? For," he said, and I saw he had few teeth, "all such as go under the boughs of that tree save the executioner must die. And it is fortunate the executioner is not already here or certainly you, Kano man, would have been hung up by the heels."

"So," I said to this drooling boy, "such is this, your grand town of Zinder."

But I thought it wise when I heard this Zinder boy's words to take the care to get a safe distance from this Tree of Death, and I then observed that its upper branches were covered with innumerable vultures, who seemed to know from the crowd of people standing round the place that an execution had been ordered.

Presently the men doomed to death by the Sultan arrived, and fear was struck into all our hearts when we saw the manner of punishment ordered, and my companions and I wondered not that the Sarki of Zinder had made himself greatly feared by his people.

There were six men this time to be killed. Their arms were bound to their sides and their ankles hobbled. Three of them the executioner tied round the neck and the ankles to the trunk of the tree, and then taking his long and straight sword he to each in turn drove it into their bowels and ripped them right up to the breastbone, after which each time he plunged in his hand and tore out their hearts, which he then cast out onto the ground and to the vultures who were now thronging round him waiting for the offering.

As to the other three, he first tied a rope round their ankles, then seizing them as a man would seize a man in wrestling, turned them up on their heads, and while his assistants held them in this position, he threw the end of the rope over the lower branches of the tree, and then hung the man up by his heels. After hanging thus for a long while, the blood gushed from their mouths and nostrils and in much agony they died.

But the last of these men when the executioner was wrestling with him had bit him several times in the arms so that this man took out pieces of flesh with his teeth and then spit them to the ground at the feet of the executioner. This so enraged the executioner that he changed the mode of the punishment.

With the help of his three attendants he drew the rope round the man's armpits and then pulled him up to the tree so that his feet were a few inches from the ground. And when he was thus hung up perpendicularly and swinging to and fro and turning round, the executioner took his sharp bush knife and slowly cut the man to bits in little pieces, first lopping off the toes and then the fingers and the nose and then slices from his arms and thighs and every now and then he turned and made a jest to the Zinder people who roared with laughter and clapped their hands in applause, after the Zinder fashion, and all the while the man who was being killed was screaming until my ears were deafened and the vultures were nearly tripping up the executioner in their eagerness to snatch at the morsels that he had hacked from the man.

At last the man had bled to death and the executioner had cut off everything below his middle and left the upper half of him still hanging to the tree. The Zinder people at the last shrieked and applauded and said there was never such an executioner in any town like theirs. But for my part, I thought this a bad people and surely such pastimes must be displeasing to Allah.

We had been in the heat of Zinder some three weeks, and still this Sultan had not got ready his letter and his gift for Kano, and also there seemed no chance of selling my bounty of slaves and camels profitably. And I liked not this place more and more, and ever felt fearsome and uneasy, for its people were now insolent and some who had seen me walk under the Tree of Death would tease me and tell me that by rights I should be slung up and executed.

This being so, I listened not unwillingly to my Fezzani friend Al-Haj-Ayub, who proposed that I should join his caravan and go north and cross the Great Desert with him, assuring me that I should sell my slaves and camels at great advantage at Murzuk, where the price is nearly ten times that of Zinder. Moreover, I, Hadi Abbabba Guwah, might afterwards journey to the Turks' country on the seacoast where I should see the wonders of the Nasrani towns and the great blue water and the Nasrani wind ships and other things, the like of which I would like to see.

The Fezzani, Al-Haj-Ayub, was a wise man who had traveled many times far, and had been in Holy Mekka and even in and round India, and he insisted to me privately that my land of the blacks was "batal"—worthless—and not at all to be named beside the lands of the Arabs and the Hindis where the great Engrizi ruled. So he harshly advised me to secretly make all ready for my departure without arousing the suspicion of the leader of our expedition, the Sarki-n-bai, Ubanmasifa, and then when he cautiously sent me word to join him, to slip away from Zinder at night and travel with the Airi caravan that he himself would accompany as far as the country of Azben. To render this easier, he suggested that I should make a feint of selling to him the four slaves and three camels that I possessed and should also make over to him the six camels I was about to buy with the riyalat and Kauris I had hoarded in Kano and brought with me to Zinder and also the bag of money and diamond stones which was my token of Aide-de-Camp, thus my friend could join my possessions to all his own and take them out of Zinder in the caravan without arousing any suspicion, and after I was well out of danger and on the new road to Azben, he could return to me all my own. This seemed to me a good plan, and I did as he directed, pretending to my Sarki-n-bai Ubanmasifa that I was tired of keeping and feeding these slaves and my camels and had got only yesterday a good price for them all from Al-Haj-Ayub.

When the long Airi caravan was ready to start—it was principally composed of Fezzani merchants and Ghadamsi traders returning across the desert with their slaves and dry goods and was escorted by Tuaregs who were paid to guard it safely from robbers as far as Agades—I received a secret message from Al-Haj-Ayub, telling me to leave Zinder at nightfall without arousing suspicion and ride out to a small village under the hills to the north of the town, where I could join the caravan which would halt there for the night. Accordingly, I saddled my war horse in the afternoon and, asking permission of the Sarki-n-bai to ride to the other end of the town and pay a visit to one of our friends, at whose plantations I said I would pass the night, I started. When once outside the town, I thumped my heels into the horse and rode rapidly to the village where I had appointed to meet Al-Haj-Ayub.

He arrived with the long caravan soon after me and paid me many compliments on my dexterity, telling me while looking at me in my uniform that I might rise up to be a great man some day and in the land of the Turks. I proposed that he should now restore to me my bag of riyalat and diamond stones and my bags of rice and my camels and my four slaves, one of whom was a comely girl captured by the Gubu from the town of Katagum, to which I had become much attached and resolved not to sell her. But Al-Haj-Ayub advised me in my own interest not to press such a request, for he said:

"I have told the Tuareg soldier leader of the caravan that these slaves and these camels are mine, and that you are my friend who will accompany me as far north as Azben on important business for the Sarki of Kano. So it will be better not to alter this arrangement till we arrive at Azben, otherwise knowing that you were once a slave belonging to Kano, they might send you back to the Sarki-n-bai at Zinder."

This advice seemed reasonable, so I held my peace though I was rather vexed that my woman slave from Katagum was placed with the women that accompanied Al-Haj-Ayub. But my Fezzani friend so talked to me over and over that I resolved not to make any fuss until we were well away and beyond the limits of the Zinder territory. In this manner, appearing as the friend and companion of Al-Haj-Ayub, I traveled without incident of note as far as the country of Damergu. And here my friend advised me to sell my Kano war horse, telling me that it would surely die in the Great Desert beyond, and directed me to exchange it for a riding camel, which I did. For the space of two weeks we traveled through the Little Desert beyond Damergu and the like of such country I never saw before. It filled my heart with terror.

Except at the wells and drinking places, which were of great distances apart, there was not a sign of a tree or a bush—nothing but sand and hills made of sand. Although the land we crossed was so dry and parched and windy and sandy along the line of the caravan, yet ever and anon where the sky met the earth, I could see large lakes of water in the far, far distance and also beautiful groves of trees. But whenever I pointed these out to my companions and asked why, when we were suffering from thirst, we should turn away from these lakes, they would laugh and jeer at me, Hadi Abbabba Guwah, and say to me while in my uniform that my uniform showed me false and that in truth I was a know-nothing pagan, and tell me I ought to know that these lakes were shams, and the evil work of all the Genii who inhabit both the Little and the Great Desert and that if anyone went in that direction of the lakes and the groves he would simply lose himself in the sand and die. I felt ashamed. Sometimes I know I know nothing and must learn. O Foyo.

And the farther we traveled through the sand the less I liked the Fezzani Al-Haj-Ayub. He became rude and insolent to me, for each time I hinted at his handing over my slaves and my other trade goods or paying me for the use of my camels on this journey, he threatened to betray me to the Tuareg leader of the caravan and have me sent back to Zinder and perhaps to the Tree of Death.

At length we arrived at the town of Agades and here with my hands and my mouth I loudly demanded my bag of money and bags of rice and my slaves and my camels from Al-Haj-Ayub and he replied:

"Assuredly Hadi Abbabba, on the morrow when we have rested I will restore to you what is your own. But speak not of this in the hearing of the Tuareg soldiers that came with us, lest they find out your secret and inform on you to the Sultan of Azben."

Accordingly, I waited with much impatience for the morrow. But on the morrow the Fezzani sent me word that he was very sick with the desert fever and he could not transact business, and moreover, it would be better to wait till the Tuareg guard was dispersed, but—Wallah!—he asked me to meet him on the next day in the marketplace, and he would make over to me all my property. So on the morrow I met him amid the throng of the market and he said:

"For safety, I have stored your slaves and your camels and all else in another part of town. Do come with me and I will show you where they are."

Then he led me through many streets to the house of a Ghadamsi merchant and when we entered he spoke to this man in the language of Ghadames, which I did not then understand at all, and the Ghadamsi looked very hard at me and said to me in the Hausa tongue:

"As you desire, I will show you where your slaves and camels are put and you would be wise to and it would also please me if you would dwell with me till the starting of the caravan for Ghadames."

Then my Fezzani friend said to me:

"I have a matter of business to attend to. I will leave you here."
And he departed.

And when he had gone, the Ghadamsi directed me to follow him and led me into a dark chamber and said:

"Look within that inner apartment and you shall see your four slaves."

And when I turned from him to look something struck me violently on the head and I swooned.

I know not how long I remained in that condition but when I awoke I felt very ill and found the top of my head and my lower features covered with blood, and my wrists before me tied, and my ankles tied. I was stripped naked of my uniform of Aide-de-Camp to Ubanmasifa, and also my sword and my dagger had been taken from me.

I began then to understand the trick that had been played upon me, and as I looked I found myself in the same dark wet chamber where the Ghadamsi had told me to look for my slaves. I staggered to my feet and wiped the blood from my eyes and tried to find the door with my hands. But it was shut and bolted and I struck it and its terrible thickness with my hands and called loudly many times, and then all the exertion made me swoon again.

When I once more came to myself I found the door open and the Ghadamsi standing over me, and when I looked at him, he spoke to me slowly and very distinctly in Hausa saying:

"It is time for you now to know the truth. Your friend that Fezzani has played you a trick. Here are no slaves of yours nor yet camels and other goods and I doubt much whether you have ever possessed any of these, for the Fezzani said you were a mad fellow that pestered him with your tales and he paid me silver riyalat to detain you here until such time as he should have started well on his return to Murzuk. Now, listen carefully to what I say. Whether or no you had slaves and camels is a matter of no interest to me. You are now my slave. If you are disposed to work for me without noise or clamor, it is well. I will give you food and clothing and treat you well. But if you are going to make a rumpus and bother me with your talk of slaves and camels, it were better that I put an end to you at once before your strength comes back."

And here and then he held above me my own dagger, and made a feint, as it were, to plunge it into my breast, but I, feebly staying him with my hand, begged for mercy and told him that since I could not recover my property and had nowhere to go for protection, I would remain with him and serve him faithfully as his slave.

At these words he put my dagger back into its sheath then lifted me up and unbound my hands and feet and led me into an outer court, where he bade me wash my wounded head in a tank of water, and during this procedure, I knew of a sudden I would look out to kill this man. Afterward, this my new Ghadamsi master gave me a filthy mess of porridge and an old long shirt vent with several holes.

And in this sorry condition I abode with the Ghadamsi for a space of some three months. And then he concluded his business in Agades, and having gathered together a large number of slaves, perhaps sixty, he made ready to return to his native town. So we set out with the next Ghadames caravan.

While we journeyed through the country of Azben my life was bearable, for although I had to walk on foot, the marches were short and there was plenty of water at each place we stopped at, but when we entered the Great Desert beyond, our sufferings were terrible, for all we slaves had to stay on foot through the hot sand and it became so far to go from well to well that many slaves died by the way. Then some would be able just to reach the drinking place and then would sink down and die before the water reached their lips. And if any slave could not have the strength to stand when the caravan was ready, he was either shot if once he was a good slave, or left to die of hunger if he had once been a bad slave, in punishment.

And in this way I nearly perished too, for when we had been journeying some thirty days a sickness of the bowels overtook me so that I could hardly drag myself along with the rest of the slaves, and I felt it was better to die quietly in the desert than to endure this agony day after day. So when we had reached a certain well where there was a broad wadi and many rocks, I managed to conceal myself among the boulders, and the rest of the caravan, hearing an alarm of the approach of some Tuareg robbers, hurried off and no one searched for me.

In the shade of these rocks I fell asleep and I must have slept a long time, perhaps a whole day and part of a night, for it was a morning when I lay down, and then the moon was high when I awoke, and instead of dying as I had expected, I felt somewhat recovered, though my body was wet and cold with the heavy dew.

I cooled my parched tongue by licking the drops of moisture from my arms, and in spite of my weakness, I managed to totter to the well which had been dug in the wadi and fetch up some water in a broken cooking pot that lay near. I also found some dates and a piece of maize bread which someone in the caravan had left behind in the hurry of departure.

While I sat eating, I had a great fright for there was all at once a clamor among the rocks and I thought it must either be the Tuareg coming back or the caravan returning. Then it seemed to me that it was not men that I saw leaping over the stones but Genii or Ghuls of the Desert, and I was so scared with fright that the sweat poured out over me and down.

And when these creatures came nearer—I being too dazed to think of flight—I saw they were only baboons of a kind not unlike those which were found in my own country. And they too were scared when they beheld me, and hesitated to come to the well to drink. But finding I heeded them not and seeing that I was unarmed, they gradually took courage and satisfied their thirst. And when they had left, I again fell asleep and did not awake till it was morning. Then I rubbed my eyes and wondered whether I was under any more delusions, for I now saw some thirty men standing and squatting about at a short distance away and also a number of camels tethered further away and these men had all of them blue skin and blue face veils and I knew they were robber Tuareg, and when they saw me move and bend up and look on them, some of them started up and yelled and then all surrounded me and one said to me in the Hausa language:

"We thought of you as one of the dead. How come you here?"

Then I told them so much of my history as would serve my purpose, and after consulting some time among themselves one of them that had a pack camel that carried a little baggage mounted me thereon and we rode away. After several days traveling, during which the Tuareg treated me kindly and gave me a sufficiency of food, we entered a broad wadi where there were many date palms growing and this I was told was on the outskirts of Ghad.

The robber Tuareg camped outside the town for a few days and then took me into Ghad and sold me in the slave market to a Ghadamsi merchant named Sidi-Bu-Khamsa. And here in Ghad I first saw the Turks. The governor of the town and a lot of the soldiers who live in a fort are Turks, but the Tuareg are masters of the place.

I do not think—although you are expert at traveling—that you would ever be able to reach Ghad, for the Tuareg will let no Christian come into the place, and indeed, men that I met there would many times boast and loudly and in my hearing of the number of Christians they had killed and how slowly they had dispatched them. All these Christians they said were Francswari who had come down to Ghad from the North where the Francswari ruled, and the Tuareg would tell how they had killed some with their spears and had made others drink of poisoned wells, and for this the Turks never punished them, for they had not the power.

I must say I led a quiet life in Ghad, which is on a plateau close to the clouds and such has good weather and hence I grew first fat and then strong, for up there was plenty of food. My new master, Sidi-bu-Khamsa, was a mild man and treated me kindly seeing that I again became a hard worker. He principally employed me in his gardens, which were in the largest wadi I had ever seen and among beautiful palm groves some distance from the town. Here I worked a waterwheel, which a camel turned round and round and round to bring up the water. I tended all the herbs and spices and vegetables in the gardens, most of which I ate all day long and which the Ghadamsi would sell in the souks of the markets in Ghad. I was happy there in the palm groves tending the waterwheel and began to forget the yesterdays and myself and all my troubles, for then my master taking me into great favor for the willingness with which I worked gave me one of his female slaves to take as my own woman, and who was a native of Bornu. I lived in the beautiful plantations and so little troubled me that I should have been content to have remained there all the rest of my days. But after about five years my good master Sidi-bu-Khamsa died, and all his property was divided among his heirs. I and the woman he had given to me and most all of the other slaves were to be sold in the market because there was some dispute among the young men who claimed the property; therefore a day was appointed when the sale should take place.

Now some merchants had come east from Murzuk for the purpose of trading, and when the auctioneer was leading us through the bazaars to show us to people who might wish to buy slaves, some of these Murzuk traders came forward to inspect us, and when one of them began to ask questions, I recognized the voice as a voice I had heard before, and looking into the face of the man who had spoken, I saw it was the Fezzani who had so well tricked me out of my bag of money and my slaves and my camels in the country of Azben, and also had nearly brought about my death. It was Al-Haj-Ayub, and he brought back that part of me that I reckoned I had lost. But I gave no sign of having recognized him, thinking if he purchased me, I would cautiously bide my time and take my revenge very surely. And he, looking into my face, knew me not, for I had grown a complete beard and was fat and was otherwise much changed during the time which had passed since we had last met. Moreover, this Fezzani Al-Haj-Ayub was suffering from the eye sickness which was common in Fezzan, and could not see clearly so that when I was offered to him for sale he was obliged to touch my body with his fingers and hands to ascertain that I was fat but also strong and well made.

And the auctioneer, who was a kindly hearted Ghadamsi man who had traded much with my former master, wished that I should not be separated from my woman from Sidi-bu-Khamsa, so he asked of the Fezzani a lower price if he should buy the two of us. And after much haggling on the part of Al-Haj-Ayub, he consented and I was handed over to him, together with my woman, for a sum of one hundred riyalat. Then he took us away with him to the house in which he lodged, and told me that he should return in a few days to Murzuk, and that if I proved myself an honest and capable man, he would give me more women and an ass for myself and he should put me in charge as overseer of one of his plantations there. And to all this that he said, I replied with sweet-sounding words and salaamed all the time, and though he then asked me many questions and told me he had a fancy we had met before, I said nothing but concealed my thoughts from him, naturally. But to my woman I told everything and we together arranged that we would wait for a good opportunity to revenge ourselves on this dog.

When he, Al-Haj-Ayub, at last had got together all his merchandise and his slaves and when he had overloaded his underfed camels, we set out for the town of Murzuk. Now at about this time the Fezzani had taken a fancy to my woman, and he had resolved to make her his concubine, and she conferring on this with me I advised her what she should do. In the gardens that we passed through outside Ghad that once belonged to Sidi-bu-Khamsa, I did pluck the berries from a thorn apple tree. At the first halting place, I gave these to my woman, telling her to bruise them and put their juice into this Fezzani's drink so that he might become stupefied.

This she was not able to do until several days were passed, for the Fezzani Al-Haj-Ayub sent not for her to come to him until we had arrived at a great wadi between two high cliffs, where there was much vegetation and an abundance of fresh water, for it had been raining in the mountains. Here Al-Haj-Ayub, who said he was ailing and felt weakly, resolved to rest for a while, as in this place there were a few abandoned huts where some black Moors had at one time lived and in which he could store his slaves. In the middle of the first night after we had arrived here, my good woman came to where I was sleeping and said:

"It is done. This Fezzani is now a dead man, or, likely to die. I mixed up these berries with the coffee that he bade me prepare for him, and now he is lying in his tent like a corpse."

The other slaves were all sleeping. Awake only were his Fezzani servants and these seemed to take little note of what was going on near their master's tent. So I crept into the tent with my woman and found to my consternation that Al-Haj-Ayub was still living. He had vomited much of the coffee my woman had given to him and during the moment I was crawling into the tent he was making some effort to raise his head.

Fearing lest he should recover, I seized a big sharp-edged stone that kept down one side of the tent and with that took the time to aim well then smashed in the Fezzani's skull before he had time to cry out. And after this, afraid of a second for what I had done, I hastily took such small things as I could easily carry in my hands and on my person—pistols and such like—and beckoning to my woman to follow me, we crawled out of the tent together and made our way very quietly back to the place where I had been sleeping. And being accustomed to this moving about of slaves at nighttime within the camp, all twelve Fezzani sentinels paid no heed to our movements. So I passed round among the other slaves such of them as were men and had belonged to Sidi-bu-Khamsa and told them how and why I had killed this leader of the caravan. And they consulted with me in whispers as to what I was about to do. I then asked them why we should always remain slaves to these Fezzani and Ghadamsi people. Now that our master in Ghad was dead, why should we not become free men? And they all agreed that these words were just.

Then I proposed that we should take the twelve Fezzani sentinels by surprise and kill them and then divide amongst ourselves all the plunder and afterwards go our own ways. This being agreed to before the morning light had come, such of us as were large and strong men armed ourselves, and stealing up to the Fezzani sentinels round and about through the rocks, we suddenly threw ourselves upon them before they were yet fully awake and wrenched their guns away from them. Then we stabbed them many times with knives and smashed in their heads with rocks and they, these dogs, were soon put an end to. And when the daylight came, we divided all the goods of the caravan, not without some wrangling and dispute among ourselves, and I being the leader of the men, took Al-Haj-Ayub's riding camel while the camels of the twelve Fezzani guards fell to the lot of other slaves.

When all these matters were settled, I, still the leader of the men, hardly knew what to do. Wo-ye. Some of the other slaves advised that we all should return to Ghad and tell a tale which should explain our case, and others counseled that we should continue on the road to Murzuk and enter the town separately. But as none knew the road and we feared to lose ourselves in the desert, I as one resolved to stop for the present where we were, inasmuch as the rains had left us a great pool of water in the wadi and we had certain provisions of our master to feed on. Finding me of that opinion many of the slaves agreed to stay.

For the first few weeks all was well. We made good repairs on the abandoned huts with branches from the athal and talha trees of the wadi, and took up our abode in them, dividing the women slaves among such as were the stronger men. We killed with stones and caught in snares the ducks and desert fowls that came to the pool of water to drink, and we laid in wait for the great gazelle, the big animal with the mane something of the lion kind which you may find in some places in the desert.

These gazelles would come down in the nighttime from the great cliffs that surrounded the wadi to browse on the sweet pasture which had sprung up round the pool. Our houses were away from the pool some little distance halfway up the cliff, and therefore the animals were not disturbed by our presence.

So in the darkness we would creep down and lie among the rocks near the water and if the wind was in the right direction and the gazelle did not scent us, we would sometimes manage to kill them with our guns. But after a while, whether it was that these were scared away by our having killed some of their flock, or whether the camels were consuming the herbage, I do not know. But they ceased to come and the ducks and the other fowl too began to leave the wadi now that the drought was commencing and the pool drying up. And in this way we began to be short of food, and were forced to kill the camels one after the other in order to eat their flesh. And when the scarcity of food was felt and before we had killed all of the camels, some of the other slaves were urgent that we should leave this wadi quick and proceed towards Murzuk. But it was now seen by me that Al-Haj-Ayub had chosen an unfrequented route in order to avoid the bands of Ajhar Tuareg which are always ready to prey on small caravans in these countries and that only he and his Fezzani companions knew in what direction the way should be taken towards Murzuk, for although we searched about in all directions, we could find no issue from the wadi which seemed like a track, and when we scaled the cliffs and looked round the horizon, we could see nothing but sandhills and desert—no palm trees or any sign of water, and I for one felt my heart fail me at the prospect of risking ourselves in the desert with only five of the remaining camels between us. So I was persistent in my resolve to stop here even though we should have to perhaps eat three camels one after the other, for firstly, we had found a bag of seed corn among the Fezzani's goods, and this we had planted in the moist ground near the pool, and secondly, there was always the chance that another caravan of travelers might pass by to whom we could tell some plausible tale, and whom we might follow out of the wadi.

There were also date palms growing near our house, but these being all females and no one having fertilized them with the pollen of the male at blossoming time, they were without fruit and all we could do with them was to cut them down and eat their hearts and young leaves. But as three or four months had now passed, we began to be in sore straights—less from the want of food, though, than from lack of water—for the great pool which had been formed in the middle of the wadi from the rains on the mountains began rapidly to dry up under the hot sun and soon there was no more water left in it, and then for a while we began digging holes in the sand to reach the water which sank ever lower and lower. And as the water became harder to reach and more and more precious, so too bitter quarrels arose among us for its possession, and we fought for each water hole.

Although I tried to keep order among the people, we were all mad with thirst and longing to drink, and in these fights one after the other was slain in various ways and all the females except my woman died from want of water, for the men had become greedy of what little water they brought up from the water holes and would give none to their women. I—thinking always to keep in the favor of my woman for some unexpected later time—always shared what little I could get with her. At last matters got to such a strait that I said to those men that would listen to me:

"Rather than wait here till every drop of water is gone, let us start this day as soon as the sun is down and it is cool to walk over the desert as fast as we can towards the west, so that we may perchance alight upon a spot where we may find water or meet travelers. Better were it even that the Tuareg should catch us and hold us as slaves than that we should die of thirst or kill one another."

Most of them agreed that there was sense in these words, so we hastily threshed some of the small corn which was ripe, and carrying this store of food and our guns and such things as we could readily carry about our persons, I and those who had agreed with me set out and walked as fast as we could with the thirst that tormented us, but whether it was that in the darkness we could not find the traces of any route, or whether the winds of the desert had covered them over with sand, I do not know. But in the morning we could not tell what place we were in or recognize any of our surroundings, and there was no trace of water anywhere. Our mouths were so parched that we could hardly speak.

When I dragged myself to the summit of one of the sandhills, I could only recognize one feature in the country round me, and that was the great cliffs of the wadi which we had left the evening before. And now we were in a sorry case. I knew not what to do. The heat of the day was so great that the sand seemed to burn my skin and make my thirst ten times more dreadful. Some of the men were struck down by the way with thirst and with the heat of the sun. When we saw they were likely to die then, we who still had strength to move threw ourselves on them and cut their throats and then sucked greedily such blood as flowed from their necks.

In such a manner, very few of us kept ourselves alive and were able to walk a short distance, lying down every now and then to rest in the shade of such rocks as could protect us from the sun, and by nightfall we had arrived at the base of a small hill where there were growing a few talha trees. The dew that night was heavy and in some places where the rocks were smooth and free from sand it lay almost as if rain had fallen, and here we obtained some relief by passing our tongues over the wet rock. Having moistened our mouths we procured a little corn and swallowed it. When it was morning we saw some date palms far away growing in a little hollow it seemed. Our hearts were gladdened by this sight, because we knew it to be a sign that water should be there and so we set out in that direction.

Now every day since we had left the wadi where we had lived several months, when the day was at its hottest, we would oftimes see in the distance before us those great lakes of water with palm trees on their shores. It was only by slapping my face and thumping myself on the head that kept me from running there. This I had to do to myself every few hours. For I knew it was some trick that the Genii of the desert play on such men as are lost in these regions, for I knew and cried to myself that it is only a deception, as I believe I have already told you. Yet I do not understand why the further and further one walks after these lakes, the more they do recede, until when the sun sinks they vanish altogether. And yet the sight of it is all so true.

The falseness of these seeming lakes and groves caused me to never let the men divert their steps to walk after and so to reach them. But on this morning when we set out to arrive at the date palms, my woman was distraught in her head, and as the day grew hot and the Genii's water began to show on the horizon, she would have it that a great lake did truly lie before us, and then again thinking she was back in her own country of Bornu, she pointed to it and called it the Tshad, imagining it to be the great sea of Bagirmi. In vain I reasoned with her as well as my dry tongue would permit. She would pay no heed to what I said, and although I was convinced that we should find water at the date palms, she would hear nothing of this, but set off full pelt in the opposite direction, crying out that she could see her mother and the house she used to once live in. My strength was too little to enable me to follow her and bring her back by force, and she too, after running for some distance, threw up her hands and fell down in a heap. And then the others, my companions, crying out that her death hour was at hand, ran away from me to her and threw themselves on her and cut her throat and greedily sucked the blood. And I, in spite of my thirst, had not the heart to join them, for although I was sorely tempted even in that time of madness, I remember that I thought it would not be fitting in the sight of Allah to drink the blood of my own woman and one who had been to me as a wife. And yet after a while a great stupor came over me while I watched them cut pieces off her to eat, then I swooned and I must have slept.

When I awoke, it was night and the moon was low on the horizon and yet very bright and thus I could see none of my companions round me. For some time I could not remember what had happened, but slowly when I gathered my thoughts together, I got up onto my feet and made my way, with what speed as I might, to the place where the date palms were growing. Here I found my companions lying fearful on the ground sheltered by a small mound of sand and watching men in clothes unfamiliar to me crawl across the sand like the crabs of Kroo Lagoon toward the grove, in which we saw the flames of the fires and rows of giant camels without their baggage sitting and chewing while all of the cameleers stood round their braziers eating. Then these crawling men raised up their muskets and the gunfiring commenced, and the guards of the caravan dropped onto the ground dead and some of the eating men threw up their bowls then slumped backward to death while many others that were unharmed by the guns ran from the light of the fires to the safety of the inner groves. But these were not to be exempted from being shot, for more explosions I did hear which told me there was yet another ambush throughout all that was dark among the palms. Then all was confusion and noise, for the camels had risen, and roaring they were running north, east, south, west, and several of the robbers were now scurrying and trying to catch them up. I resolved this was the moment for me and my companions to fetch us a camel or two for our use and on which we would again have an opportunity for an escape. My companions, because of their fear, said I was a madman and that my plan would produce another dead slave. Nevertheless, I left the mound and skulked in the direction of some camels who had departed the palms and presently stood confused near some rocks close by. I had made camel noises to these beasts as I approached them and hoped these sounds would keep them in place. So clever am I, Hadi Abbabba Guwah. Allah thought so, for the camels remained in their place. I had my hand grabbing the hair of one of the three camels when my movements were arrested by a shout of a man behind me. I saw he was one of the crawling men and dressed in the strange white taub with black turban and ear and chin cloth and black cape, and very surprising to me too was the fact that he was a black man. His words to me I did not understand at all, and the more I did not understand and showed him my palms, the higher his voice became, which then did cause a great moment of good fortune, for a cameleer who I quickly espied was near death, had come from his hiding place in the rocks, and was pointing his long gun at the robber in an attempt to dispatch this thief to the devil. His interest was only on this robber, so I pointed my finger up toward the cameleer, which I quickly thought was foolish, for a successful escape for me was in the hands of the dying caravan cameleer.

Now the robber in great haste pointed his weapon at him up in the rocks, and it was just as quick for me to see and hear that the robber's gun did not go off as he had intended it to, and by all that is Allah, I do not know why I took the pistol of a sudden from the cloth of my waistband and with my hand pointing it not at the robber but at the caravan man, I did shoot this fellow to death. Big Head having launched his only ball, I had a scant chance of escape. Indeed, the robber could now do with me as was his will. Wo-ye.

Having heard a commotion, a much armed party of this robber's other fellows had come up to us and then surrounding me, who was now working at looking greatly afraid and about to sob, then one of them drew his sword and came up to me and grabbed me by an ear and forced me down to my knees. Allah, I was beheaded. Ayammaaa Mammaaaa, such a fool. Stupidity deserves to be killed and not let it roam. So I was dead. And what will in seven days be left of me? Just a little heap of teeth in the dust.

Then a harsh command was issued and there came a quick silence and I heard nothing but the camel flies who had been disturbed by all the hubbub. On no account should I move and thus I remained until I was poked and pulled by my arms indicating to me that I was to stand up, which I did. The robber who did catch me stealing the camel pointed to the palm trees and his hand motions bade me to move in that direction, so I proceeded to the caravan fires all the while taking care to shake my body so I would appear possessed by a great fear. In this manner of being so scared I was brought to the biggest fire and behind it was a man whose visage so overwhelmed me I was thinking I would fall to the sand again. He spoke in his own language and my palms were up showing him I did not understand. I spoke to this man using Hausa words, then in the words of the Fullani and then in Arabic. Shortly another robber was at his side who was versed in the Hausa language. But before I could begin my tale and tell the interpreter all such lies that would impress him, the robber chief, or sheik, bade me be silent and then said things to the man who understood Hausa who then turned to face me and said:

"You have prevented the death of the first son of the Zahir ben Yazid. This action must be repaid, therefore he will not kill you."

Wallah, Hadi Abbabba Guwah succeeds once more! Now I would tell him my lies. But before I could begin I was silenced again and I thought cruelly so by this the Zahir ben Yazid and pointing his musket to my head put to me, "How do you make your way in this world?" A trader did I reply. On a command of this robber chief two men came to me and took the clothes off that I had and pushed me before the fire.

"Your body tells us that you have been all your life mostly a slave, and your large bones tell us you are from the south of Timbuktu and hence from the mountains of water. And it is shown on your body that you also have been a soldier, and now tell the Zahir ben Yazid in what army?"

"Not one army, your excellency, but six, first for the Sultan of Kano, then for the Sultans of Yakuba and Sokoto and Yola and—." And I was not permitted to finish but again I was gestured to silence by this sheik.

More words were said to the interpreter who then told me that I was of this moment his slave and he was now my master and further that I should be well treated if I behaved myself and in a befitting manner to himself and to his robbers and that if I was truly good he and his men would reward me. O Foyo.

And then this interpreter asked of me what did I consider rewards, that the Zahir preferred to know now what were my weaknesses so that he could pander to them.

"O Mighty Excellency," then I placed my palms quickly together and turned my head to the side and made my face as supplicant as I could and then into his face so disfigured by battle scars I said:

"A goat and all the corn I can eat and an ass to ride upon."

This would be granted to me puffed this desert lord, as soon as he saw that I obeyed his own laws and also complied with the laws of his band.

A goat, an ass, and maize indeed! Puh!

And so they finished robbing the dead and, placing all their goods up on their camels, rode away into the night and thus began my days with these men who I came to learn were called the Tebu Bedouins from Gandoga. But before knowing this I ran afoul of the Tebu every day of the day because of their Tebu habits and the strange fashion in which they did everything, which sometimes I did consider lunatic, and an example of which is this: even if I was in the good graces of all I was not permitted to speak. Thinking of this daily found me regarding it as witless. How could I heed so unreasonable a rule? I really could not. So I spoke. The interpreter then came to me and told me in a wrathful way and with the blows of his stick in plenty on top of my head and about my face and shoulders that it was not that his tribe were ignorant not to write or speak Arabic as did I, but that the Tebu abhorred that language and its noise and indeed all Arabs who were nothing but invaders in the land that belonged to the Tebu and the Goran and the Bidiat and who were all once too poor to retaliate and to resist the Arab exploiters but this situation was being remedied, he said. And that if I had a mind to learn to speak the language that is called Temejegh, or what you roumis call Great Berber, it would go well with me, but in that I was only a slave, I had to live within their law and hence in a condition of silence, like their brothers the Tchetadai Tuareg. O Foyo! And he said to me that I could not just be a useless mouth about the camp that just consumed their precious water and so I being the latest slave of the Tebu and since their last raid had yielded up, among other things, fifty-six Francswari chamber pots, I would now use all of my time day and night in the ignoble task of removing and emptying these pots then washing these same from Zahir ben Yazid's wide black tent. In this tent dwelled four of his wives and three that were concubines, each with her own pot. At least he was a sheik, and I tried to make this thought more or less soothing to my low spirits.

And so I began this duty of the pots and the details of which I will not go into, but only to say it was time consuming and always considering that I had more valuable work to do. I began to give respite to the other nearby slaves also engaged in this pot labor and thus I contrived in sign language for them to return my favors and so eventually I again obtained a reed pen and a small gourd of ink and an oil lamp and late into the night in the slave tent I did apply myself to making the scrit of the language Temejegh. And in between trips to the pots I did the Berber writing, and in doing these words I discovered a taub became the sound "jellabah" and which was always sleeved and hooded and then that a cape was now called a burnoose and which also had a hood. And instead of the turban I used to wind about my head, they wore a cloth called a Kafiyeh, and which was laid upon the head with its material falling down to the shoulders. This garment was kept in place by two strands of braided rope of fine camel hair called an agal.

And then I advised myself amid the language writing practice and the learning about the ways of these Berber people, which was done to make me look grander in their eyes, to begin to record in a book the booty which was brought back by outriders to the camp every two or three days and thus perhaps by this endeavor be promoted to better circumstances by being keeper of the Booty Book, which these Tebu could not keep, for none of these simple folk could read or write nor did they have a scribe. They could only put tally marks. But just looking at my numbers and scrit I realized would make them pleased and satisfied about their employment. Good fortune would come to me and as it should by all the decrees of my Lord the Prophet Allah. I on many nights and alone sitting high on a dune in the desert looking at the round moon did feel I might be the Madhi, the Chosen One, to whom all worthwhile things will come. O Goy-o!

I pause here to tell you things that I have forgotten and that were of some importance in my life at that time, me, Hadi Abbabba Guwah, for that is my name, Hadi Abbabba Guwah.

These robbers of the Tebu Bedouins most of the time every day mounted their camels before the dawn to ride out in search of caravans which they at first harass then fall upon and plunder. Although these robbermen I could see numbered about a hundred, I soon found it was false of me to believe that this was a true number involved in the constant raiding. If a large caravan of five hundred animals and a thousand cameleers and guards were sighted these Tebu of Gandoga stopped and couriers were immediately up on the swiftest of horses and dispatched to other camps of robber bands who had become allies in order to better lead the bandit life. When any of these men could not plunder because of some tribal alliance established against them, they would hide away, for they ranted a lot that they would never forego robbing and that if they built towns and changed their nomad life and their ancient habits they would not prosper, and that mosques and houses of the town breed mildness of character and it is only the fierce and warlike who dominate. And they decreed this in the songs they did sing in their tents when they were before their fires in the camp and one was:

> We are the Tebu of the Black Tents
> of Gandoga
> With fight in our blood and with
> our fathers behind our rifles
> Al-lah! Al-lah! Al-lah!
> Freedom is dearer to us
> than our money bags!

But it was not all the time they would go out every day, for as I have said, English, when the season came for the large caravans to commence their journeys all the fighting men young and old would mount their beasts and would be gone for a long space of time leaving the camp abandoned to only the women and the children and us slaves. And for me the first of these long raids I do remember especially, for it had been whispered to me a little while before that the Zahir was a wise and dignified leader who of a sudden would hugely reward merit in a man be he bandit or slave. Accordingly, I forgot all thoughts of killing him one day and thought in place of this that I would show him of what great value I, Hadi Abbabba Guwah, could be. And of course truly there was scant opportunity for a smart kill, seeing that if I did so how could I hope to escape with my life and a few camels from the Tebumen when I still did not know any trails or how to navigate the desert?

But after all the men had departed on this murder raid, I was warned that although he was a commander of more than a hundred and would dress himself in lion skins before an attack upon a mighty caravan, he became a sheep that nearly made the noise baaa-baa once in the confines of his own tent and in the company of his own women and because of his silliness his women were wont to treat all of the band inside and outside the tent as if they were all Zahir ben Yazids. Tish! I would make a lesson for my master to heed as well as the men of the band. And that he did not rise above this condition was seen on his return from this long raid and did make everyone sorrier for

him than before, I did believe. I resolved I would do work for the
Zahir and for the other tents and thus receive a gift from this one
and then a gift from that one since slaves were not in plenty. Then
also I was laboring over the Berber scrit which had to be done with
as much haste as possible and really I could not be tending to his
wives' and women's pitty-pitty pots all the day. Also to truly further
myself in his eyes, I on my account alone took up unclean work
duties in the cooking pot tent. But after the Zahir came back, however, there was no reasoning with him. And I admit to you, English,
that I rarely emptied his women's pitty-pitty pots although I always
intended to do so.

According to my mind his great mistake was in not leaving the
pots in charge of the day iklan, this word in the language of Temejegh
means "slave." No doubt I had faithfully promised to attend to his
wants but the Zahir deceived me by speaking as if all day emptying
pots was the easiest of pastimes. He said that since the time he had
captured them all his pot iklans got into the way of emptying these
things regularly, just as anyone said his evening prayers. That certainly is not the case. I always said my evening prayers and I cannot
say how many times I forgot to empty the chamber pots. Of course,
if I had been living in his huge black wool tent and sleeping with a
good goatskin bag of water beneath my head and these pots always
before my eyes, I might have done so. The Head-Wife said of me that
I never wanted to empty any of them, which is not only not true but
unkind. I told her my plan was to run to her tent from the cook tent
immediately after butchering and ripping out the entrails of the
sheep for the evening meal and give her pot a thorough emptying.
But one thing or another however, came in the way. I often remembered about all of the pots while I was in the slave tent putting down
the scrit of the language Temejegh. But even the Zahir could hardly
have expected me to cease my arduous efforts merely to get up and
run over to empty pots. When I had finished my writing my hand
was full of pain and my head was so tired and thus I was much
disposed to lay down and rest my body and not at all in a proper
condition for emptying pots. Then Fava Pavi would step into my
tent. I put it to you, English, could I, Hadi Abbabba Guwah, have
been expected to give up my friend Fava Pavi for the sake of a pot?
Again, it was my custom of an evening to visit the other tents to
inquire therein if I could do any work for which a few riyalat in
return would be welcome. Often when I was in the middle of one of

these labors Zahir ben Yazid's pots appeared before my eyes crying out to be emptied. His wives and concubines did not believe this, but it is the solemn truth. At those moments I would actually hesitate over my work and think should I stop what I am doing or should I not? Where I lost myself was in not stopping and hurrying to his tent at once. I said to myself during these times that I would go when I had finished whatever the others of the tents had put me to doing. But by that time his beloved pots had escaped my memory. This may have been weakness. I now understand I should have saved myself much annoyance if I had risen from my duties at hand and gone then and there to my master's tent and those of his wives and concubines. To show how honestly anxious I was to fulfill my promise to be a good iklan to the Zahir, I need only add that I was several times awakened in the middle of the night by a haunting Genii of the desert who said to me that I had forgotten to empty some pots, but lo, in the morning I could not remember whose pots they were. At these times I tried to do things that would make me remember again in the morning. I did reach out from my mat and took my knee desk and turned it upside down so that the sight of it when I rose might remind me that I had something to do. But I always thought of something else to do other than to empty his or his women's pots.

I come now to the day before the Zahir's return. I was cutting scrub for the cook tent when I remembered about his pots. It was my last opportunity. If I emptied them once I should be in a position to state that whatever condition the tent might be in, I had certainly been emptying the pots. I jumped onto my ass and minutes later one arm did I have on his felt door while the other arm held the largest number of pot cleaning cloths in the camp. Throwing the door aside I rushed in. The cloths nearly fell from my arm. There were no pots!

I found the day iklan and said:

"Where are the pots?"

What do you think the day servant said? He coolly told me that all of the pots being so full that they had been flung out many days ago and that the wives and the concubines had gone back to using the desert. I went to the cook pot tent to keep myself from thinking of my punishment. But with the servants flinging out the chamber pots faster than I could empty them what more could I have done?

When he summoned me I related to him all that I have just told you. Zahir ben Yazid maintained that instead of playing fool's tricks like these (fool's tricks!) I should have got up and gone at once to his tent. What? And disturb our neighbors? Besides, many of these nights had been overly chilly, and could I reasonably be expected to risk catching my death of cold for the sake of a few wretched pots?

On hearing these words my master pounded himself on top of his hooded head and his face all the while appearing very confused. He held me fast and shook my body and shook my bones all round the tent and called me a savage and said I was not trustworthy. I tried to soften his heart by yelling many times, "All Hail the Grand Master of the Tebu" which he heeded not and so I asked him to take pity on me and understand that emptying chamber pots was not a good way for me to spend my time. Then he pushed me down to the carpet of his tent and said his intention was not to beat me for he said he knew I was immune to the blows of any whip. And that he would punish me now in a way in which my life would become unbearable and that soon I would ever be a sorry sight. O Foyo Foy-o. No, he would not sell me to the Tuareg, so I thought it wise to plead before him not to send me to work in the cooking pot tent, that he should by all that was Allah beat me, or command me to any task but on no account not that of a cook. It was not to be, for he did not want to set his eyes upon me which he would do if I was in the cooking tent. He said the punishment I deserved was to aid Dun Abess, the camel Alim, a word such as you call a "doctor." As the guards began to pull me from his tent, I told the Zahir that I had mastered his language as he had ordered and that now I should be given the proper clothes with which to decorate my person, who was speaking Temejegh, which he had not noticed. I reminded him. And that I was certainly not a savage as he said, but a learned one and who would next study Mohammedan law and therefore worthy of a jellabah and a burnoose and the white Kafiyeh headress. He jeered at me and ordered his guards to drag me completely from his tent and in this like manner all the way round the rocks, O Foyo, and across the sands, Puh, to one of the many corrals of piled boulders that was the place of business for Dun Abess, the Alim. The guards shouted to the Alim that I now belonged to him and was to be instructed by him and thus become one of his four helpers. This was because during a raid the camels did fall to the ground and injure themselves. The women of the camp looked to the riders but only after the robbers had returned to camp and then as soon as they had removed the fighting trappings all beasts that had been hurt or were in a sorry condition from saddle sores because of the fast pace of long-distance riding were led to us for repair and solace.

Some of the corrals were small to contain one camel and some large to give shelter for many. Above these repair pits all the day long hours, and day following day, hovered fogs of black flies and always their continuous buzzz and buzzz-buzz. What made it unpleasant indeed was that we could wear no clothes save a rag of a turban on our heads and much of the same material round our loins. We had to remove these many times a day and wash them in steaming water to drain them of camel blood but mostly as the Alim said it was to keep the many diseases traveling in the air and on all of the flies from nesting in our loin cloths and thus jumping onto these beasts to go ahead and make them suffer horribly and then eventually die mad. These flies the Alim called Botcha settled on our bodies and faces and crawled into our noses all during the long day and mostly round our eyes to get the moisture and hence blinding us so that it was difficult for us to do the work. At night we lacked the strength due to weariness to sweep them away and because of this we each had our own number of sores which sent the flies into even a greater frenzy about our bodies. It was a loud rejoice indeed when the Alim discovered a way to keep the flies from us during both night and day. He found that if we all caught twenty or thirty scorpions each, and placed them live in large bowls of hot palm oil they dissolved. After we stirred the bowl round with a stick many times this lotion we did rub onto our bodies and thus the flies avoided us.

The Alim was a sorry old thin man hurrying about and always commanding in a loud voice. At eventide and after prayers I would watch him punish himself with a bound bundle of thorns and also he did not speak Temejegh so that I could understand him. The helpers were Kabyle Berbers from the north. Also not speaking Temejegh in any way, and captured by the Tebu during a revenge feud with the Kabyle five years before. From a pathetic man named Ramah who was versed in Arabic I did learn that the Alim was not a Bedouin either but a Dergaoua, and Ramah explained to me this was a cult tribe from the East that believed to whip their bodies with thorns brought them an ecstasy and this made them feel closer to Allah and such was why Dun Abess and his ears easily endured all the day the noises of pain coming from the camels because it reminded him of Allah also. The Alim, therefore, did feel his best after a large raid and when our compounds were crowded with wild and shrieking animals and he was pulling swords from out of their bodies and cutting slashes across their punctures so that he could thrust in his hand to find the musket ball.

The Alim taught me the many things that I had to know in this business and thus not be lax in any responsibility, and of course, to avoid the angry blows from his bundle of thorns which he said were truly wasted on me because I was not a Dergaoua pain-lover. Often also I got a harsh beating from the whips of the Tebu who would puff that I had neglected their animals which was not only unjust but silly.

Camels have very short lives and this is because they are too dumb and do dangerous things to hurt themselves. All of these bad-tempered and bad-breathed beasts will go ahead and eat anything and this includes also other animals and if you are not cautious a mouthful out of you and if the man is dead he will eat all of him. See, English, I withdraw my Kafiyeh to show you I have no ear. This which is not here did end up in the stomach of a Tegama fighting camel I was trying to cure of bad water sickness. If they eat the poisonous plant Aphasomzid these sad creatures come in from the trail with blood-in-the-head disease which was proven to me by the eyes being full of thick moisture and the head shaking quickly side to side till you would think he would send it flying off. If I did not make all the haste I could then, the beast would fall to the ground and after rolling round on it, along with his body giving him contortions, the camels would die of a stroke. Before this could happen, I ran to the jars and got the tabac then back to the beast to rub the tabac into its eyes. This would draw the blood now gathered at the top of his brain down to the lower part of his head and next I had to hurry and with a sickle knife cut the throat pipe below its left ear. Three hand cup hollows I would make next in the sand. The blood from his throat pipe was black for perhaps ten clicks of my tongue then slowly it became less black and when it was red for ten clicks of my tongue the hemorrhage is stopped. Then back to the top of its head to cut some hair which next had to be pushed into the cut I had made. After this I put sand in my mouth and once all soggy spit it into my hands and pushed the sand into the cut in back of the hair. Round this I spilled the Alim's scorpion lotion then went to the next camel to treat till I could stop at evening prayers.

With the morn and before the sun did rise the Alim made the

fires that had to last all the day and on these he put pots of water for the camel sores and pots of water for the tea for the Kabyle and for me. We Allah'd our prayers to the One God above All Gods as the sun came up and as the flies arose to hover again above the corrals. After putting on our turbans and loin cloths we were made to start the day. We had to see if there was any infection in the camels we had treated the day prior and caused by ticks or fleas or flies round the wounds and sometimes ants attacked the sores to cause terrible bleeding and the ants were immune to the scorpion lotion but not to the red paste the Alim had made and I would apply on these occasions. After a report to Dun Abess on the strength and condition of every camel in the compounds I gathered sticks for the fires to keep the water steaming. The feeding of the camels was of the next importance and barley and dates was the best food the sick camels could munch down.

Many times a camel in my charge became worse because of my treatment and the Alim would go into a wrath then ask me one tedious question after another about how did I proceed with this camel on this day and on that day and at length he would calm himself and be satisfied that I had acted in accordance with his instructions. He would often say that Allah had willed the camel to be worse. If the camel's wound had become infected he would make me withdraw the hair and the sand from the wound. Then with my hands I had to pull the flesh apart to see the cause of this new development which would most times be that black beetles had bored through the sand and hair to get to the flesh and these beetles would be followed by flies which entered so that they could lay their white worms. One time this happened to a fine Mehari war camel that belonged to Saadi, the son of the Zahir I had saved so long ago. And then again, I said to the Alim the stomach of this Mehari was inflamed. He said, as he would always say, that he had seen this. For this Mehari the Alim was bound to be the best he could as a doctor in order to save this expensive beast. And he made the beast swallow handfuls of mint leaves and dried orange skins which the camel would soon disgorge, thus ridding his stomach of poisons. The wound he treated by filling it with grasshopper waste. The day after the Alim did again look at the beast then say to me the Mehari would die and because he estimated many of the beetles had entered the stomach and in this position inside could not be disgorged in any way. So he would not waste any more of his barley nor his dates to keep alive a camel that was doomed. I led the Mehari from its corral with the flies coming also and slowly out into the desert followed by the corsair birds walking across the sand who thought of the camel as a meal as did the vultures that were beginning to gather in a circle high up in the sky. But these creatures would get little of the Mehari for the Alim had sent Ramah for the Saluki dogs, who were used by the Tebu in their attacks on the caravans, and who only ate camel meat and so after the Alim shot the Mehari these vicious dogs ate the camel leaving only the eyes and the tail as a meal for the corsair birds and the vultures.

The birds fared better with the beasts with the Tara disease because there was no cure at all for this frequent camel malady, which was a bone disease of the legs of the Giant Gheti and Tibesti baggage camels captured during the raids. It was at first instance a wasting of flesh of the legs whereby it shriveled then peeled off and second the drying up of the bones so that while the camel stood on his feet the leg bones would begin to splinter up and down till the weight of the camel at last snapped them and it would fall to the sand to die of apoplexy. But before all this was endured by this dumb beast in my charge I would lead him into the desert and because the Alim thought it a waste of a ball to shoot a camel thus diseased I had to use a long knife, which I was made to drive up into his brain then twist the blade to make certain of a sudden death. Then at a distance away I would watch the vultures and the corsair birds leap upon the camel and eagerly tear the flesh up and swallow it and all the while I would laugh for I was told by the Kabyle these birds would acquire the Tara disease and in some twenty days hence all would perish in the same manner the camel would have, as I have previously explained to you. Also to perish, if we were on the trail and near the great rocks, were the baboons who would come after the birds departed to gnaw on the bones.

And thinking of the baboons, it was the year the Tebu of Gandoga were again moving their camp north of Tuat in order to have better raids that the Alim, Dun Abess, died, and in my opinion of exhaustion, because of this sort of work. The Zahir sent his guards to fetch me and in his tent once again decreed to me with a grand gesture of his hand, puh, that I was at this moment worthy of the title of camel Alim and so be it I was so. I said to him I have been for the space of many months a camel doctor and that I did not like to be so a camel doctor and that it was puh and that he was correct and my life was unbearable and it certainly was not to be this again and therefore that I wanted to die and immediately.

He did look at me in a solemn way and said:

"Do you know why I want you to be the Alim?"

"My life is unbearable," I said loudly, now using my hand in a gesture, "and as you have wanted it to be. You have succeeded O Master of the Tebu and further I feel a savage and if it pleases you a dog."

"You are not a savage and I withdraw this word and will pay you a reward as a token of my respect for you. However, it is reported to me as said by Ramah the Kabyle that you are a fine camel doctor indeed and the gain is yours and also for my men who tell me you have made them take greater care of their beasts which Dun Abess never took the interest to do. So you have become one of much value to me."

"Do your men tell you O Zahir that they do not like to be so close to me, Hadi Abbabba Guwah, once a chief of two thousand men, because I smell like a sick camel?"

"I say to you once again you are only valuable as an Alim. You have truly mastered Temejegh and therefore speak to my men of the details of mending their camels. You will act as the Alim or I will have you put to death."

"My life is unbearable and I am exhausted with the want of sleep and further I cannot endure being camel smelly any longer and hence death is the only profit I can see to a wretched life."

He clapped his hands and his guards appeared and he said:

"Take this vassal away and tie him to a rock and introduce to him the death of a thousand cuts."

O Foy-o! This Zahir did again take advantage of my good nature and so without further display of a dispute or a rumpus I was back again in the compound among the sad Kabyle and I did think my misfortunes were all to continue till I died and in the sunrise and then again with another I would ever and anon walk wearily on the blood that covered the sand of the corrals and treat the hideous diseases of these accursed beasts and day after day push cobwebs into their many wounds to staunch the flow of blood then use thorns to bring together the flesh so that it may mend. Surely in Allah's sight, me, the wonderful Hadi Abbabba Guwah and a one who can be of the best value to all that do meet me should lead such an unprofitable life. O Pity on me, Allah, or else sell me to the Turks if it is so fated.

On that day with me so distraught in the head I recall I had risen from my sundown devotions to Allah when someone called my name. It was Saadi. Puh! He was back from a raid. This Tebu I once did save wanted me to attend to his camel before I did any of the others. He boasted that they had brought back a host of Arabs as prisoners. On the morrow he would present all these to the women so that they could torture them to death as an entertainment and also as a release for their vapors. And so?

With the night close to the morning and me bethinking that my life now was all extremely silly, I was off my sleeping mat and then standing, I took from its place in the basket a long knife and I was away and it was in my head that Arabs had only contempt for the Berber Tuareg and Bedouin. All Berbers were to them as dumb camels. A black man was not even worthy of a jeer.

And so I told the sentry of the prisoners to pick a strong Arab. I had a nasty duty for him in the compound. The sentry laughed and discovered such and then prodded the prisoner to his feet and ordered him to go with me. Well away, I cut the rope that bound this Arab. I said to him that I was a slave. After morning devotions the women were going to roast him alive then eat him like a goat. I was the camel Alim. If he did some mischief for me I afterwards would take him to a camel that was healthy and swift. He would escape. I led the Arab to the tent of Saadi. He used my knife to send the sentry pacing before it to the devil and without noise. Then he took up his sword and quickly entered the door. As the Arab was to kill Saadi, which was what I meant by mischief, I slashed my knife into the brain of the Arab and thought in a frenzy would all this succeed? Al-lah! Al-lah! Allah Yahmahrik! God be with you!

Saadi was in one click of the tongue on his feet from the sleep and in his hand was a sabre. Three of his concubines were now shrieking. I told Saadi a story of how all this came to be and ending it with:

"O Great Saadi, O Lord and Master and son of the Master of two hundred tents, this fiend out of hell was going to spill your precious blood and I, Hadi Abbabba Guwah, a humble slave, will pray to give thanks to Allah that I could again and at this time be of such service to my Lord of the Desert Saadi ben Yazid of the Tebu."

The Zahir entered the tent and put his gaze down on the fallen Arab and then lifting his head his narrow eyes looked long at me and during this time his camel dumb son gave the explanation of what had happened and how his life was again in debt to Hadi Abbabba the Alim of the Great Tebu. I held the gaze of the Zahir with eyes that said my heart quaked within me.

"So Alim," he said with what I thought was a sort of a smile, "as is our custom, a second payment on a life that you have already saved must be a greater one. What is your desire?"

"Freedom."

"No."

"I do not want to work as the Alim."

"I agree that you will not be put to this work again. So that is your payment, Hadi Abbabba?"

"No. It is not enough for the life of your son. I want next to work in the cooking pot tent."

"No."

"Then to be your Mullah and teach you how to read and write."

"Niwalla: no."

Allah was not with me at this moment, and to gain a mastery over this situation it was only wise to fill my face with glee and shout all the while flaying my arms:

"In the camp of the Great Tebu of Gandoga the best employment is to ride on the raids! O Lord Zahir, I have served well in the armies of—"

"—Yola-Fola-Kano-Baba Gungi and surely countless others. Yes-Yes-Yes," he said to harass me. Then breathing in much air into his stomach, he turned and spoke to his son, "Saadi, is it your wish to spend your time training this rascal?"

This baboon said, "Father, it is the Tebu way to reward service and deeds."

And the Zahir of a second fluttered his hand like the wing of a bird and his brows came together then lowered to nearly cover his eyes. And I heard my head say to me, "Oh, you Zahir ben Yazid, you can see Hadi Abbabba too well now. I must watch all the while not to anger you, you old lion, for on the next instant surely you will rear up your sword arm as the scorpion does its tail and you will strike me down with a smile then relish the act later that night sitting on one of your chamber pots. And I will anger you, O Wo-ye, that I do know. And so, I must kill you." Ayammaa-Mammaa, at times what Allah makes us do through his will can be wearisome. And it did not please me, English, to know that I must kill him and also

spend the time and make the effort to think of the circumstance in
which to do so.

On the morrow another mischief descended on me by the order
of the Zahir. Another rebuke meted out. Another laugh for the Tebu
in their tents over their bubble-bubble pipes. I was presented with,
and for the purpose of raiding, an ignoble soft-faced Filali camel with
one eye. I was not afraid, however, so I made a rumpus and said to
the master of camels many times: "What was the use of a war camel
with only one eye?" By and by he answered that it was because the
Zahir had said that the Filali had belonged to a terrible Arab and
thus understood only commands in this language, which the Zahir
had told the master of camels I spoke in perfection. To make me feel
I had not altogether been taken advantage of, it was said to me that
this camel's one gone eye on the right side was nothing beside the
fact that he could trot more than thirty days without water where
all others could only trot fifteen days. This reasoning I had to endure.
To my mind I knew that if I pointed this camel north this dumb beast
would surely be veering ever easterly until we ended up in the great
water that borders those lands. Puh!

Then passed the days that Saadi the baboon explained to me the
beliefs and rituals of the marauding Tebu. They believed that a thief
must feel better than the man he would soon kill defending his
caravan, and indeed better also if it is possible than the men he rides
alongside during the attack. In accordance with this custom my
Filali was dressed for me in very elaborate clothes. The head ropes
were made of many twisted goat leather strands each different in
color than the other. And onto these many large red and white tassels
were woven. Colored wool pouches were hung from its neck for any
amulets and trinkets of good fortune I might wish to put into them.
Then more small tassels and more bright ribbons were woven into
the bottom. Then using thongs and straps my beast was belted with
Perasi carpet blankets, and a decorated saddle with traveling bags for
food and water and sticks for fires and all of different soft leathers
on which were woven more patterns. All indeed very fine. And all
of it for this cripple.

For my property now that I was in raiding service, I received
only a sword and a buckler, a cloth without a pattern for the fighting
turban, and an ill-looking jallaba and a worn sash to prevent stomach

pains and belly strains from long distance camel riding. At my expression over this Saadi said to me: "Other clothes you must provide for yourself from a caravan." I was exhausted with the want of kindness. It wasted me. Better to be a one-eyed camel. But, as it was my survival to be a good marauder I took care to endure. I would try to learn quickly and then become rich so that no one would again laugh and jeer at me for a know-nothing pagan slave, and, no one else ever say to Hadi he would sell him to the Turks.

At first I belonged to no band of horsemen and this I was told was for my benefit in order to learn this difficult business. So after the sun had risen and all were mounted and on the trail, I would ride with the rear guard and sing to my camel as Saadi had instructed, for on the march the camel goes best when the driver sings to it and about the beast itself. Then with the sun directly above I had to ride to join the flank watchers to see if we were being tracked by soldiers of a caravan who were to spy out if we were migrators or a jewel caravan or if we were indeed robbers. If we saw the pigeon message birds let loose we knew these creatures would fly to the caravan and give warning that we were robbers. On this instance the Zahir would order a change of direction and hope to find another caravan to plunder.

And at night near the fires Saadi drew on the sand with his stick and instructed me on the routes of the caravan trails, and also on the sand he marked for me the names of the stars and how to use them for navigation if ever I got detached from the fighting columns. And how to use my shadow in the day for a compass and become very experienced. He promised I would become that, and I would never miss my direction and that I would be able soon to navigate my way to any of the big towns on the middle sea. I promised this baboon I would master this navigation. Now at hand I knew I would at last understand how one day I could escape these miserable Tebu of Gandoga. Then I joined in and said to some of the men that we would all be safer and the danger would be far less if we shot the beasts of the mounted men in a caravan then hack the head off the rider as he started to fall to earth—to my mind the quickest and safest thing to do for a thief, if he is to last to an older age. This was not so in their eyes and I was railed at loudly then all shook their heads at my foolishness. They said shooting the beast was unprofitable and that I must learn to understand to always shoot the rider who they said was absolutely worthless to them. Instead capture the camel whose value at that time in Murzuk was over fifteen riyalat. So this to them was the only profit. Their law I obeyed because it was only wise for me to do so. And yet after twelve times raiding and obeying the rule I had still received no money of reward for this and for the fervor I showed with my lariat and hook work, which only I could do, and, as well had dragged from the saddle and dispatched at least one hundred and eighty cameleers. Instead I was commanded by Saadi to take my camel and my property and go join the band of a hundred whose leader was Ali Gameel. What do you think? He did not like me. The display he made with his eyes and his brows and the manner in which he used his hands and his posture foretold he would abuse me, and issue this abuse in his high-toned voice that sounded like a one-penny whistle. And even at that time he was ignoring my lariat and hook work, showing I was greatly skilled in killing and mayhem. But now I had an enemy who dismissed all of what I have just said to you and who would sit at night on his chamber pot and dwell on me being beaten till I was a blood-covered feeble person with swollen closed eyes and scattered teeth and covered about my head with horrid cuts and bruises. I had even put out of my mind the killing of the Zahir. And for this Allah, as was his will, had handed me a life of punishment again. I did not deserve that Ali Gameel decided not to speak to the men of his band about me using my true name: Hadi Abbabba Guwah. To all he called me Seni-ah-anta. This word in Temejegh means "one pubic hair." My life was unbearable. But if I gave too much heed to this and other delusions Ali Gameel had, the mastery I had over my mind would fail. Lest I do this, I understood I had to remember that the only way to increase myself was in acquiring booty and promotions, of which right now I had none. Sadun, captain of my band of twenty-five, was the only marauder of Ali Gameel who did not disgrace himself in my eyes by calling me "one pubic hair." For this gentleness I told the captain that I was spending all my time now lamenting my plight and then of an instant to make myself feel better I told him I would work harder than ever before in order to gain the rewards that I, Hadi Abbabba Guwah, truly merited. And what do you think he told me, and told me only because I was now in full standing as a robber of the Tebu brotherhood of Gandoga, and that as such, I could not become rich through booty or money. I had not been told by Saadi that all thefts were the common property of the tribe and that no man could ever be other than slightly unequal to his fellow raider and that only in clothes.

To ease my new confusion and torment and also to perceive what to do, I went to my tent and sat at my knee desk and picked up my reed pen and, putting it into the calabash, I scribed in Arabic and not in Temejegh, over and over, that Allah was All Merciful and All Just and would punish all those who caused trouble to Hadi Abbabba Guwah. I scribed thoughts in different ways that I was in pain, and that all I had stolen should become common property and that I knew now I Hadi Abbabba Guwah could not become rich through slaves or ivory. Also I had to scribe the truth as I perceived it at this moment, that the Tebu would never be truly pleased with me. Knowing this, I must be cautious much beyond my reckoning and also make the effort and create a pretense to replace that which was once true enthusiasm. That is to say, when others were tired I would yell and fire my musket and thus bring attention to myself. Thus I was still entrusted with this fruitless raiding on the day following and the day following that. And as the tribe grew rich I had to exist with a one-eyed camel forever wanting to trot eastward. It would be just as likely I had a fat baggage camel or yelling and waving a sword ride into battle on a goat. Then I fell to scribing the longing I had for the air and the feel of my motherland and the sight of the palms above the grass and the look of the blue water of Kroo Lagoon. Of course, I wept at these thoughts for a long time.

Now when I rode the valleys all rocky and without trees I took to watching the birds that were very high up go north, or note that the ground in the morn sparkled because of the dew which covered hundreds of the webs which the tiny spiders had spun between the clumps of dirt, or let my gaze follow the wind patterns all along in the sand until I became nearly dizzy in the head. And day upon day upon day I listened to the soft slow pad-plot of the camels' feet on the sand. What would become of me? Aoi-yo. I was just a rover of the desert. The scars on my body have multiplied because of battle but not enough where I would be entitled the Tebu honor of being called "A man of a thousand cuts" and thus be able to retire from plundering. Sadun the captain of my band had ridden forth on four hundred and seventy-five assaults and the outcome was he had achieved only two hundred and eighty scars. Puh! Will I for the rest of my time live in a tent and ride after caravans for no profit? All of this silly business was due to the Berber Tebu considering stealing and slaughter more of a sport than a worthwhile employment and discussed as such round the campfires at night puffing on their long bubble-bubble pipes. Then I found also it was a sport of a kind with recognized rules; all of which did not impress me, further, it made my heart melancholy. I discovered about the rules only after I tried to make myself bigger in their eyes by suggesting a new strategy for them and I was again rebuked for it. I said with a strong voice why do we not poison the wells before a small caravan of a hundred reaches them then tell their leader that all of their goods we happily would trade for just some of our water and then simply they could continue on their journey. And later, when their stomachs were taunt from the poisoned water we had supplied them, we could swoop down on them and gather in all their camels. Wallah! Success! But tut! These heads of straw believe in all their Tebu hearts in the rules of recklessness and that ritual robbery and murder kept the men virile and youthful and that the greatest possession is not to have clothes or money or camels or ivory but to have a small skin of water and one skin half full of dates and a musket and twenty pieces of ball. Silly.

Also the only talk that I could have that did not give me up to yawning was with one of the Ouled-Nael dancing girls from the land of Moroc and who was in very good circumstances and which the Tebu had bought for the period of one year some months before. She now worked in our south tents because she had stabbed in the throat one of the Tebu in the north tents due to he had misused her. The Ouled-Nael are much tattooed on the forehead and cheeks like the women of my tribe in my south motherland. But other than this adornment all the day and eventide they are encumbered with many and heavy silver bangles and silver bells round their necks and wrists and ankles and in the braids of their hair and round their waists, so that their bodies made these bells and bangles go cling-tinkle-ding-bing whenever they moved. Perhaps seventy or eighty riyalat worth of noise. Even the three silver daggers she wore in her sash had bells at each end of their shafts, in my opinion, their value being at least five riyalat apiece.

Her name was Samonama. She was comely beyond all of the dancing girls I had seen in any of the courts of the South. And she impressed me with her talk of all her incidents in the many encampments she had lived under in the North and of the different caliphdoms she had trafficked to and of the many gifts that had been bestowed upon her. Because of my delight in her I saved myself much annoyance and left off the habit of going to the common tent to sit for companionship only to have to listen to the tedious Tebu burbul-burbul over their games of checkers. It was better to hear Samonama talk to me and relate to me of her adventures with her people the Atala Riff and then also every night to listen to her Pedireed pipes and her Moroc wailing and watch her thumping the tambours and pluck the one-string Bedouin violin that made the twang noise and to hear her dance song and gaze at her hips going up left and down right and down left and up right as she tinged the tiny silver cymbals fastened to her finger tips. And the more she danced the more her fragrant odor entered my nose holes and the more the musicians sang with heads thrown back and bobbing and with all their teeth showing and the elder leader clapping his old hands till I thought they would break.

But in a short space of time all my reveling ceased, for she commenced with many noisy wailings and then the pulling of her hair and also word lamentations that she had become possessed with a longing to be up in her Atala homeland with her mother and father and brothers because she had heard the Francswari had taken possession of her beautiful village and that the Francswari soldiers were conquering and pillaging all of the caliphdoms and sultanates in the land.

To myself I understood, "I will miss her talk," and then so that she could hear me I said to bribe her:

"It is better that you remain here. You would surely receive some injury if you travel then arrive at your place of turmoil. Moreover I will teach you how to write."

"I do not wish to learn how to write! I wish to be with the army that is being formed in the mountains by our great and mighty one named El Kabir. It is my place to also rebel with him and all the tribesmen and thus rid our villages of these accursed Francswari. I cannot remain here merely to dance for these Gandoga ruffians called the Tebu. Ach!"

With this she forced me to say: "You have given an oath that you would remain a year. The Zahir will not accept this new wish of yours. Perhaps it is better you dwell on the gold pieces that you will receive from him in good time."

"I do not also want that gold! I want to be with my warrior brothers and at this moment! Ohh, Yuhhh! Do you understand!"

Then on the morrow she confined herself to the Ouled-Nael tents saying she had the malade and it is prohibited to enter this area

so I could not go and see her day following day and more. During
this period I kept saying "Samonama" which by every eventide I
found the repetition of this difficult word had swollen my tongue. To
destroy this ailment I said instead "Silver Bell," for to keep her
presence before me made my life durable because all the rest was just
ambushing and looting and it varied little. I rode the desert and
watched ever the bumping up and down of the water sacks on the
crupper of my high saddle and felt the musket strap settle deeper into
my shoulders hour upon hour and my neck constantly chaffed by the
itch of the cord that was fastened to the long curved dagger with
holes drilled into the blade so that it would cause a deadlier wound.
And always the foul smell of the coating of grease that protected my
face from the bite of the sand and eating in the saddle by tearing at
strips of smoke-cured mutton or swallowing small dried curds.

Much in front of the columns was Yoluba the scout of the
strong eyes up on his swift Mehari who always rode standing in his
stirrups in order to gaze better over the desert. Then of a sudden he
would whirl about and signal with his long camel stick that he had
spied a caravan. Without noise I would tap my Filali on the head and
send him along into the fighting position. Then it was the attack and
shrieking out of "Allah-Allah-Allah" and the pounding of hooves off
the sand of the undulating ground and wishing that my beast would
not trip on the skeletons and dried-up corpses of camels and men
from the raids of days past or the raids before that. Then the dispers-
ing action with my musket and then the scrape of metal on metal and
the clang of sword upon sword and the yelling and the noise and the
whirling, separating, and more musket firing and the fierce thrusts
and then—tut!—off with his head and the body of him descending
from the camel to flop then to jerk about on the sand like a fish on
a riverbank. The Tebu dead did not warrant a second glance and the
wounded are a burden adding useless mouths to a band traversing
a waterless desert and dying men will soon be dead. I spied the rider
coming to me slanted over to one side in his saddle and his hand
flourishing his short sword behind him and because I was thinking
of nothing but Silver Bell in six clicks of the tongue he was upon me
and quickly he had dropped his sword arm and bringing it up and
with a whop-wup-o-foyo-o off with my arm which tumbled down to
the sand and me looking at that which was once my hand still
gripping a sword. He raised his weapon for a fatal blow. Was this
the end of my life? Only a one-armed man sitting on a one-eyed

camel? And as I was thinking Puh! the ball of a musket took away half of his face and the top of his head thus saving me, Hadi Abbabba Guwah, for greater things.

In the camp the stump that was left of my arm with all the flies and moths following it was at last attended to by Silver Bell and as she picked off the beetles that clung to it, I had to listen to all her hubbub of remonstration along with all her bingle-bangle-bangle-tingle-ding noises whenever she moved during this doctoring. To keep my thoughts away from the pain I said her name over and over, "Samonama, Samonama, Samonama," giving much exercise to my tongue and all the while thinking soon it will swell and I would feel good about that.

After days of a wet and discomfortable fever I was ordered by Saadi to appear before the Zahir, as was the custom, who I knew would tell me I was retired from marauding. Ali Gameel had been feasting with appetite and joy and saying to his guests that he was now rid of his "seni-ah-anta." On my mind was how would I now be employed? I can no longer be a scribe. Aoi-yo. "Tawakkul-al-Allah" rely on God. In this latest of my misfortunes I said these words over and over: "Tawakkul-al-Allah." Would I be returned to the smelly camel pens to help another Alim? Puh! How was I to gain from that.

Then I was escorted by a guard to the Zahir who sat on his thick cushions and in the finest of his clothes which my raiding had provided for him. Was this to remind me of my downfall? However, he did not look unkindly on me nor did he look well upon me who he once called a savage and a vassal.

"Hadi Abbabba Guwah, you are now in a plight that is much more troublesome to me than you and your camel with only one eye. Better to have lost one or the other of yours. Because of your foolishness of losing an arm you will have to work in the cooking tent and your task will be to kill and clean captured sheep and fat horses for our pots. That is your employment for all your remaining years with us."

"O Zahir, in your mind you still think of Hadi as a slave, but that is not the work for a man who now bears the scar of grace and who was once the raider and took your sacred oaths and served you well and, Aya, without profit."

"Ehwalla yes! It will be yes for you and yes for Hadi Abbabba

Guwah the very Big Head who can no longer serve me at all save
to serve in my cooking tent all day with a knife preparing my meat
with the one worthless arm left to you. That is my command, you
rascal."

And then, alas and again, my mouth ran before my head.

"Puh on to you O Zahir. You vex me. You cannot read but I
can do so, and because of this I have written down in a book all of
the ancient laws of all the Tebu in the North, East, South, and West
and that I will freely give to your Gandogas hoping one day all of
you will learn to read. It is written in these laws that I can demand
to serve on the raids as the Tebu custom allows. This you cannot
deny me as I am now one of the brotherhood. I will tell you I will
not be in the cooking tent cutting up your silly meat. I will tell you
I will become the fa-fasah. And your fashion says yes I can be this
and your own laws say it will be, O Zahir, which you could read of
if you were able."

The eyes of him became only black lines stretched above his thin
nose and bearded mouth. He fought to restrain a bout of apoplexy
for as he rocked back and forth on his cushions and gripped his
trembling hands he knew he could say nought at what I had just said.
With mock respect at his want of dignity I salaamed low and then
solemnly, and then left his tent so that he could have his apoplexy
in his own privacy. You see, English, by temper I am not an unkind
man. It is simply some men as the Zahir lack goodness.

A fa-fasah? Oh, as you call it in your tongue, he is a signaleer.
This was a plunderer who had been mauled in some part of his body
and who now rode by the side of the Zahir and by his orders directed
the attack on a caravan by using a long stick at the end of which was
attached long strips of cotton cloths tied up in knots with thongs
every hand-spread to form a whip. When taken from its water bag
and thrown out and snapped it made a whack sound and not a crack
sound like that of a gun. Thus with this method and various signals
the Zahir told all of the columns what to do during every part of a
raid. For this employment I was given a splendid trotting camel and
with two eyes. And thus I continued this weary life of migrating over
the sand and through valleys and over hills and bumping up and
down in the saddle in the hot sun and me singing to my new beast
of his merits and he in turn kindly repaying me with his constant
reply of burbul-burbul-burbul.

And it was at this time that Silver Bell had to remind me that the season of the great raids was here. It was a time the temperature had become its coolest and a time the clouds showed they might drop rain. These conditions brought forth the great caravans from Chat in the South and laden with sugar, cotton, tea, sandalwood, feathers, coffee, and ivory and all hoping to get to the cities bordering the middle sea like Tanger, Alger, Tripoli. The count was always over one hundred of them and each caravan could have over two thousand camels strung out over five or six miles with two thousand warriors to guard them and all and every one of these being Arabs and thus much hated and hence agitation in camp among the Tebu and other Berber tribesmen was awesome.

Because of the size of these caravans never would two or three hundred of the Tebu dare to attack them and—Wallah!—the Zahir had to open his money bags and pay other marauding tribes to join him in order to be successful in this venture this season.

So the fearful and terrible Igdalen Tuaregs of the lagoon blue eyes were the first to join the Tebu because the Igdalens had nothing to do since their blood feud with the Ibek Tuaregs was over having slaughtered every one including the old and the women and the children. Then in the camp and under the Zahir's tent at twilight and evenglow he served up to them a splendid feast. Late in the night Saadi came to my tent to inform me that the Igdalen captains had said that as a gesture of good feeling the Tebu had to offer them and without payment forty-five to sixty camels and perhaps later if the raids were not successful ten or twenty slaves. The Zahir had agreed to this but that, as a gesture of a very kind feeling toward his brothers the Igdalen, he would give them one slave now and that I, Hadi Abbabba, should be taken by them at first light. This they refused to do for the slaves would be used as dung collectors for their tea and cooking fires but since they lived now in the Tebu camp they would use sticks as the Tebu did and thus not waste their food on a slave who lacked work to do. Of a sudden I was so sad I sobbed. Then I kept shouting without any sense and jumping up and down until I was wasted and did feel weakly and all with the thinking of the Zahir's harsh intentions toward me. I took hold of Saadi whose eyes and mouth said he was in much of a fright and then wept to him:

"When will I be treated well? Is it fated that all will take advantage of my good efforts?"

I dropped to my knees and said to him: "Surely I have tried to be worthy. And is the way I am to be disposed of?"

I struggled onto my feet and pushed hard this baboon who then fell to the carpet while I rapidly raised my one arm remaining in supplication and entreated:

"O Lord Allah, Master of Thrones, O Mighty Excellency, O Magnificent Sultan, spare Hadi the Clean and the Godly!"

Yet again my heart of a sudden so did quake within me that I felt overwhelmed and near to a swoon with the fear that had possession of me and I had to tap my mouth and slap my stomach and drag up Saadi to pound my back lest in my grief I became sorrier than I was now. And in this dazed condition Saadi left and Silver Bell entered my tent and she came to me and she held me fast and said shouting at me like some harridan that this display and this commotion was quite hideous to her. Ah wo-ye. Wo-ye. And Silver Bell talked me into losing my trembling fear by soothing me quickly with her strong hands and also in a long embrace and at last saying in a rapid fervor that the Igdalens would not want Hadi because they needed a two-armed man to pick up all their dung and not an old man with one ear and one arm now useless. As I began to tremble all again and shout and wave my arm knocking her to the carpet she began yelling at me that although the fierce Igdalens hold slaves they never bought or sold them now since all theirs were the sons and daughters of slaves and knew and wanted no other life and that she truly believed the Igdalen intention was to sell me to the Turks who would put me in an Army house full of men who just served all their daylight hours to give pleasure to many men or to any soldier who wanted it.

"AYAMMAAA MAMMAAAA-MAMMAAA! Fo-yo! Fo-yo! Puh-Puh-Puh-Puh!" And so she jumped up upon my back and to take my mind off this employment she pulled at my hair with much strength and bit my shoulder and said over and over and over that I should think only and only of leaving the Tebu and venture north with her to her land of legend which is a place for all those who believe in Allah and that everything is possible and for all men, even me.

It was after many hours of sitting in exhaustion and seeing nothing with my eyes that I lay down and it was on this night that I bathed myself in my own water and had screamed out at my enemy

Ali Gameel in my half-sleep that I was not "seni-ah-anta"—one pubic hair. On the sun rising my own dancing girl told me she had been to the Igdalen camp and had spoken to their chief Ramah Rajala and told him of El Kabir and his war against the lowly infidel Francswari and their terrible practices against all the faithful. This information Silver Bell said had captured the attention of this chief, Ramah Rajala, as she reckoned it would, because these Igdalens practice the Moslem faith more scrupulously than most, praying five times a day which seemed to make them better warriors, although when the Zahir attempted it in past times it failed to be a success for him. And I remember Samonama took advantage also of the old feelings the Igdalen had for the Arabs who had taken their ancient land and persecuted these Berber people so that they had to migrate to these bitter deserts which they live in to this day. And since the Arabs were now allied with the Francswari she told the Ramah Rajala if he returned to their lands now and fought by the side of El Kabir he could mete out punishment to the hated infidels and also obtain retribution from the smelly Arabs. And she warned him that the Tebu would never stop being other than simple-minded thieves and all tallied up to be not of much worth to Allah or even to themselves, if he didn't mind her saying so. The chief said to Silver Bell that her beginning words had convinced him that he should break their alliance with the Tebu and on the event of the next raid escape to the northerly land and join the Holy War—or as they say it: the Jihad—that El Kabir had mounted for Islam.

And then she said to me that she had said to Ramah Rajala that I would be a worthless work slave to the proud Igdalens and as well to the Turks who she said to him would never pay what she Samonama of the Atala Riff was willing to pay if I, Hadi Abbabba Guwah, was permitted to go with her in order for me to be at her side in her endeavors to purge the lowly and the ungodly from all that is the paradise of their ancient homeland of Moroc and Alger. She would give Ramah Rajala the sum of sixty riyalat for me to go northerly with them and away from the terrible Tebu who persecuted me so. This she would pay for me; me with my weary sword all full of pocks and nicks in the blade and a buckler full of worm holes and beetle bites and a limp cloth for a turban and without any patterns on it and a patched-up jallaba with blood on it and of course taken from a killed Arab. O English, please pause here to consider that in Murzuk a camel was worth as much as fifteen riyalat. So you must understand that to Samonama the comely, I of the one arm and the one ear and in all old clothes was worth all of four camels! I looked up to her for I was still prone with exhaustion and tears came easily into my eyes. Sixty riyalat! Four camels! I now saw Allah had reached and touched her and all of her money bags and I regarded her smiling and glowing in her face as if she had it pushed into a fire all sights became a blur with my weeping and then tears destroyed seeing her any longer at all during those moments.

Now, hear me, you can recall that in times past I was once worth two pieces of ivory and at yet another time three goats . . . but never in Hadi's span of years has he been worth all of four camels. And English, the beasts I speak of were of course Mehari camels, which you do surely know are the best in all these lands as far as you can see from the top of a mountain north-east-south-west. With the weeping completed I fell to sleeping and my sleep became nicer when I stopped dreaming of Ali Gameel and in his place the dreaming of the kindness of Samonama with her riyalat, or, as her name is easier said when you use your tongue and not think of it: Silver Bell.

Then this fierce Igdalen Tuareg desert lord Ramah Rajala gave me a terrible fright when he opened the door flap of my tent and brought himself in enwrapped in his long blue and black cloak that stopped at his ankles and which was all decorated in patches and then the many times round the nose and mouth and chin veil and with his hair not covered with a turban but all in many tens of small greased braids which also had long black and blue ribbons tied to the end of each one and all of this hung first to his shoulders and then down and beyond. His smell was much of perfumed oils. He carried three short swords and a riwalowa and at me he looked with his lagoon blue eyes and I quaked and then stepping to my side lay a hand on me and said:

"Samonama of the Atala Riff has told me of your plight. She has told me of your enduring faith and that you touch your forehead to the dust toward Mekka to give devotions to Allah so many more times a day than we the Igdalen do, that I feel a shame and also humble in your presence. Your devotion makes you in our eyes far more of a complete man than you will ever understand Hadi Ab-babba Guwah. And for this virtue I come to tell you that parting with these Tebu who torment you unjustly will be successful and that I give my word that you will be able to die in a better place than in this land of the Tebu. I will start this day to prepare for our departure and our journey across the desert by having my men acquire the best of the war camels and by using stealth and trickery also day by day steal and hide the food that will be necessary for our traveling. The one God and the only God is with you, Hadi Abbabba."

I salaamed low and in my head I said, "Ehwalla yes, you shiny spider, and all because your purse contains sixty riyalat that once belonged to my Samonama."

And by and by I was alerted to an attack on a caravan and because of the Igdalen custom which the Zahir said he would obey we had to rise in the dark for the attack which would be at dawn. And because it was the first raid of the season the Zahir announced he would direct the fight and not Saadi as we all believed it would be. Besides, during the sun's rise, this baboon liked it better to lie long and roll about upon one or the other of his women trying much to make little baboons. Then too, my foe Ali Gameel insisted he would lead this first assault to plunder and no amount of angry protest out of the mouth of greasy shiny spider would sway the steadfast Zahir in his choice that Ali Gameel should do so.

Then it came the time to be on a small plateau above the mouth of a gorge and beside the Zahir as the signaleer. I remember I spied the caravan to be one which carried only salt and which, if you do not know it, is considered precious and is used to cure meat and fish in the cities that border the middle sea and these meats and fish in turn are sent back south to be sold for very dear prices. The caravan consisted of innumerable strings of camels one tied to the other and spread out in a parade one behind the other in precise line of order for perhaps two or more miles. Perhaps twenty feet away and abreast with them there was another string and there were perhaps fifteen to twenty strings as far as I could see in the morning's mist and one hundred or more camels to a string. Besides the Arab navigators and soldiers and guards there were the thin and poorly dressed Yakaba Tuaregs who were the cameleers and in line every twenty-five feet and pulling two or three camels by their rope leads and all the leads were tied to the upper arms of the Yakuba men.

The Zahir with an ugly noise from his mouth and a motion of his hand instructed me to take the length of cloth from the water bucket then to use my pole and snap the whip the number of times it required to signal the marauders below that the raiding should commence, which I did, and so did they all five hundred of them. And with their shouts and yells and the goading and the whipping of their camels they rushed forward in the damp ground from their hiding place in the gorge to build up their charge. And this was the raid shiny greasy spider said would be the escape raid of which I would in fifty clicks of my tongue be a part of, for sixty riyalat. And as I watched these riders who I would now see no more and had spent so much time with, I felt deep in my heart and of a sudden and without considering any of it at all, how would I, as you would say in your tongue; how would I sitting here feel "goodbye" to the Zahir? He who once long ago had saved Hadi's life at the date palms. I do not forget this, no. Then I turned my gaze to him to find an answer to my question and I saw this old lion had stood up in his stirrups for the better to see and his excitement caused his knees to bounce him up-down-up-down-up-down in the saddle like a very small boy before the pot of the evening meal and then he began with choke-choke sounds to laugh at the watching of this grand sight of all of his thieves riding forth into a fray amid much clamor and hubbub and who were soon to fall upon all of the Yakuba and their camels and all of the Arabs and their salt. The Zahir laughing as if he were a man taken with madness, and further, English, laughing as he had laughed over Ali Gameel naming me "one pubic hair." And all the while I endured the abuse of him ignoring me as though I were not there beside him and after all the work I had done for him and then me forgetting it was me who had made myself signaleer while he insisted that I should be only a butcher. Also it was he who had tormented me and had harassed me and had made my life unbearable and also made me work at emptying all those chamber pots. Puh!

Now remembering that I was still weak in my body of exhaustion and yet also much distraught in my head and remembering this I do not truly know how I received the thought to say "goodbye" to the Zahir in the way that I did nor further how I had the strength to do so. But of a sudden that was so quick that I scarcely believe it all once did happen, my hand did find my scimitar and from its buckler I did pull it and up it went and descending s-s-ssssh the scimitar it cut the Zahir from the very top of his Kafiyeh to all the way down to the shoulder bones where began his pretty patterned jallaba. My goodbye I knew of a sudden was the will of Allah. Such is the will of Allah. To finish my goodbye was a broadside swipe through his neck and this ceased my mighty bodily efforts, and I saw the end of my labors were two pieces of the old lion's head down on the rocks. This was at first, English. But then one half slid off the

rocks and fell down to the gorge below and this English I truly did
not know would be my goodbye feeling to the Zahir. Sitting here with
you now English, I know it is true that toward Hadi he was not a
good man. And not to be good to Hadi is foolish.

Then I started to sing mightily to my camel to make him go
hua-hua-hua-hup-hup-hup down the rocks clippity-de-clop-bop and
on the gorge ground hastened to join the raiders riding mightily to
the plundering and I did try to keep singing with all the remaining
strength of my breath and with all the fervor of my heart about how
I adored my Mehari camel but of course only to make him run faster
and faster.

Samonama had said to accomplish this escape she would ride
in disguise with the Igdalen. And that they would all the while and
with every action pretend to attack the caravan but instead ride
through it without killing anyone then continue to keep riding on
and on all the way beyond leaving all the hubbub behind. The Tebu
would not pursue us because they would only think of their ancient
rituals and this was to complete the attack and then to gather in the
booty and then kill off all of the wounded of the Yakuba and then
afterwards—Wallah! Success! For it was their custom to take much
time—perhaps one upon one day—torturing the Arab prisoners to
death.

As I rode into the damp sand globs raised by the Tebu and the
Igdalens, the air round became now filled with the many cries of
ADAR-YA-YANE! ADAR-YA-YANE and all from the Yakuba
cameleers and which was the command that brought all the baggage
beasts down to their knees and also by order of the Yakuba the
camels knelt in line each behind each other while the Arabs were
dismounting and running to these salt camels to point their muskets
to begin to shoot their ball at me and the Tebu and the Igdalens. I
applied hard strokes of my whip onto the flank of my Mehari then
let it dangle so that my only hand could apply pressure on the left
nose rein so that I could bring my beast up behind my comely Silver
Bell who without reason was riding her animal vigorously and seemingly in order to gain on Ali Gameel. With much effort she had
managed to become very close to him. Then this strange action she
solved for me by raising her arm high into the air and quickly it
snapped down in front of her and there was a tinkle-tinkle-tinkle of
a bell on the handle of her dagger and this piece of silver worth five
riyalat went all the way end over end and into, thud, the back of Ali

Gameel. But I did not have any moments to dwell on this unseemly behavior for all of my exertions in dispatching the Zahir and the riding down to the gorge and all this loud singing to my beast and this up and down galloping across the plain to the attack had undone me and due to it all my arm stump was bleeding all over me and I felt dazed and that I would soon swoon and then fall off my animal and down to knock my head on the stones, which I did.

But not yet the end of Hadi. Samonama had my body kindly thrown across the neck of a stray camel and two times I can open and close my fingers of my one hand to give you an account of the days I was slung and had no sight or mind at all except for the hurt in my stump of an arm and the pain in my head. I quite now felt I had a big head. And now I bring up fingers to let you see the days I sat squeezed into a trotting camel basket yet ever attended to by Samonama while under the sun of the day travel and then under the moon and the stars during the night travel and always day after day she trying to keep the top of my head cool with warm water and she wrapping and unwrapping the cloths from my stump to wring out my blood and she telling me with every click of the tongue that I must live and then feeding me and if at a night stop being next on the ground to me and rubbing my arm and shoulders and telling me she would henceforth only dance for me, but for all of my part, I wanted her to tell me again and again of the things she had said of her land and how every day they ate plenty of different kinds of fishes in sauces that were made of shellfishes and which I did think I would favor much and how they wore great robes and jallabas of patterned cotton and also silk and I did sleep much better dwelling on eating the fishes and the wearing of many robes in this land of legend where all pleasures are possible to a good and godly man.

I remember little of the next event because in my weakness I could not give it a proper attention and also I could not see because without a moon on that black night it was not possible to do so. The event was that our column entered the walls of a town. The town was large for it took some while to ride round through the thoroughfares. Then I was carried by three men up the many dark stairs of a house. This is all that I can recall of this.

But next—wallah—I of a second opened my eyes to see the rising light of the sun on the palm beams of a ceiling and also feel that I was enwrapped in a strange gown and then with my hand groping, feel that I was on a mound of cushions that were piled on top of a sleeping platform. I saw that I was in a spacious chamber and there was a table beside my bed and there were carpets of many confusing designs spread on top of a large shiny wooden floor and then more tables and also many stools and all different in shape and size and then wall hangings on which were written one-two-three wisdoms from the Koran and then curly latticework of sandalwood covering the windows.

The air in this chamber was cool and all sweet smelling as if I was in a garden. Then I took up a great fright which caused me to fall from the cushions and the platform to a carpet below for my thought was: "Is Hadi dead and in Allah's paradise?"

Puh! Niwalla no, for I heard tinkle-clinkle-ding and then Silver Bell parted the curtains and came into the chamber and also following were two girls dressed in slave clothes and who carried trays on which were great dishes of meat and dates and rice and oranges and limes and then too, tea.

She told me in a tremble of a voice to get off the carpet quickly and to get back and lie on the cushions on the platform. Then with those eyes that pierce as one of her five-riyalat daggers pierce she looked at me and: "You will now become healthy and quickly so that we can fight for El Kabir."

I said: "You are foolish. I can no longer go on the raids for camels or hope to kill for booty with one arm. I can now only be useless as a bandit."

"No, Hadi Abbabba Guwah. This Chosen One is not a bandit. He does not steal. The Great One fights for his people and for freedom from the invading infidel Francswari and the smelly Arabs. He wants no camels and no booty but only freedom!"

My head of a sudden said to me and while I was picking up the meat with my fingers and eating, "This thought of freedom that I once did have as a young man is as dead as the Zahir. Puh! Now I truly know there is no freedom, only employment." But I asked her out loud what was it to her this freedom that she, Samonama, spoke of.

"It is to be rid of the unbelievers and their stealing of our land and to be free of the Francswari law of taxes."

I said to her, "Taxes? What are taxes?"

And she then at me answered, "Taxes are like the Romans had taxes, and which means they took riyalat from my ancestor fathers to build they said roads for our trade and then schools for our children but to teach them their laws and customs and about their gods and then houses of healing they said so that we could not die of oldness or illness in our own homes as is our custom."

I halted the chewing on a piece of tasty sauced goat meat. "Aya. Taxes! In my opinion money to build roads for trade and schools in which to—"

"—Yes," she said, looking away from me in anger, "but not by the hand of the Francswari and the smelly Arabs. We of the Berber Riff and all the Berber Morocs should do so for ourselves alone."

My mouth was again full. But I had to say: "Then why have all your Berber people not done so before this is what I now ask?"

"We are too poor, but now we will, I say. And because of El Kabir the Chosen One." And again her mouth became all a tremble.

During some sipping of tea I said, "Does El Kabir have much riyalat?"

"No, Hadi. He is poor." This was said in a solemn way.

Then I said, releasing some belly wind, "How does this Chosen One think to live of a day and obtain the food and the goods to give to his men which they must have in order to fight infidels and the smelly Arabs?"

"My people and all other people will provide food and goods for him and all of his men and without payment because they know he loves them after he loves Allah. And this mighty love will also make every village and town and woman fight for him. This love makes the Jihad. And this love says that you with your one arm will be accepted to fight because you fight for Love and Allah and not plunder."

She talked more and said other things in this manner while I gave my attention and my hand to the food the slave girls had brought to me.

"Your face is the face of protest Hadi Abbabba Guwah. I have paid much riyalat to the Igdalen for you. And I have never before ever paid for a man in all of my life. And now I am making you yet again well. I want you to eat and you must eat much but you will do so because that is my desire and so that in days you and I will ride as one to El Kabir, and offer to him for the fighting, and without payment, the Igdalens that I have persuaded to come here and then ourselves. I have killed six men and now I want to kill Francswari and Arabs and I have come to know you are an enduring and wise and noble old soldier of more than two hundred scars and musket holes and who as you did tell me in the Tebu tents has led four times a troop of five thousand men of cavalry and foot soldiers when in war service with the Sultan of Yakuba and then the Sultan of Kano and the Sultan of Zinder and then for the mighty Sultan of Agades and with all this riding and sword swinging and pillaging of towns I will tell the Chosen One you should therefore of course lead all of the Igdalen Tuaregs into all of El Kabir's battles and also by his side. As you say, 'Eh Wallah! WALLAH!' "

"Ayammaaa Mammaaa" the inside of my head shouted.

When she had left the chamber I did quickly drop my face into my hand and weep and then moan at this the latest of my misfortunes. I had now after all my trouble with the Tebu to kill for love. I lay back on my cushions and did dwell on what my Samonama had said to me. She had said this love she believed in was a feeling like for Allah. Does El Kabir think he is God? My confused head that was in turmoil could only say this love should only be for Allah who is the one god while Mohammed is Prophet and near his equal. Then she told me and strongly so that El Kabir the Chosen One truly loves all people and for what reasons she could not explain to me properly. But further, these words said to me that this leader would then also love that goat of a Sultan of Zinder Sadi-Radi-Hisham and that treacherous one Al-Haj-Ayub of Ghad. Then if El Kabir loves me, I Hadi Abbabba Guwah would be the like of the goat and the deceiver. I am not the dung that these men were once. So, I charge that his love was all unreasonableness. From this I could only be disposed to think that this El Kabir was false and ignoble and a bit witless. All this rumpus for love. How long will this love of his endure? Puh! And freedom. Puh! In this life I know there will always be masters or a master. Surely this mighty El Kabir the Chosen One will not now try to be my latest master; that would indeed be foolish. Stupidity deserves to be killed not saved. But what I did feel that was more terrible was that I foresaw no profit to me in this oncoming fighting. Ayamaaa Mamaaa! O perhaps it was fated I thought.

When I was not eating or resting or Silver Bell was not laying or sitting on me on top of the cushions on the platform and all the while moaning and gasping that she loved me—Puh—I did practice writing in a book with my only remaining hand. And again at other times Samonama would put on her clothes and gather up her money bags and go down the stairs and into the town which was called Talsinit and walk to the market. And on the first of these occasions brought back to me in the chamber as gifts a bubble-bubble pipe and four Persian pistols and a sack for each of packing and powder and ball. These she said were to help me regain my strength and my good nature.

Of another day she brought to the chamber a tent which she said would be used by us in the coming days of the fighting. Ayamma Mamma. Next into this chamber and to me came precious jewels that I would wear against misfortune and also a horse and a saddle and both as black as me and the horse was of good blood and quick on all feet and had a fire sparkle in his eyes as there was in hers, she said.

Then too, in this period and at this place Talsinit, I heard from her that she spoke some of the Francswari language of which she said she had had to learn when a child and when the Francswari were nice and gentle and they were only traders then and not as now with soldiers pillaging all over. I asked her then to speak this language to me and I heard it was spoken using most times a nose noise with little clicks of the tongue as in the Xhosa language. It is a very softly spoken language and was pleasant to my remaining ear and also over all the languages which I have heard or learned. So we sat together at the chamber window with it open and looked down on what she called the jardin publique de la cité and which had a fountain with flowers in the water and I asked her to speak to me more of the sounds and then tell me of the meanings of this Francswari which she said should be les Français and then I did write these into my book but also badly.

In the night also I would work on her on the cushions on the platform and at times on the carpets after which she would make ready for me to smoke my bubble-bubble pipe and then I would tell her to talk to me and inform me of more things that would be well for me to know of in this land of legend where all things are possible and to all men. Then she did quickly leave the carpets and run to a chest and from which she brought forth a sack. And to the window she did make me come. And from the sack she took sand and bones and strange small squares of wood with designs on them which I did not understand and she scattered them upon the carpets. Then she said that soon I would ride beside her to the plain of Ajagubub and she would take me to her brother who was a holy man and who in turn would take me to his high priest and the great mind that is Sidi-Abd-Al-Hadj-Ghirha. He was the powerful sheik El Senussi and who is a mighty holy man and leader of the Senusiya Brotherhood and a political kaid under the Turks at Murzuk. This was the first time I did hear this name and it was wise of me to have her tell me that it was only with the spiritual assistance of the Senussi sect that all of the tribes were organized against the Christian dogs and that this mighty King of Kings will have his followers preach the Jihad in Tunisia and Egypt and that in Moroc and Alger all the great chieftains and Emirs and Sheiks and Caliphs and Sharifs and leaders of the tribal confederations were sending words to Sidi-Abd-Al-Hadj-Ghirha that they were prepared for the great day of the Islam state in Afrique and the overthrow from bondage and the extermination of all unbelieving roumis and all of the unfaithful from the Nile water to the Tanger water. To this the greatest Islamic powers round the Middle Sea were pledged.

In a mud house strengthened with stones that is one of the houses that is the University of Senussi I would sit before a knee tea tray. There would be a heavy brass teapot and two small brass cups. Sidi-Abd-Al-Hadj-Ghirha would pour you tea. At my left I would see a white rock which is a loaf of sugar. I would drink a bit of tea and then with a hammer break off a chip from the sugar rock and suck on it. Tea-hammer-chip-suck. This is the ritual. And to him Sidi-Abd-Al-Hadj-Ghirha I would say:

"I breath Allah and in me Allah is breathing."

Drink tea–use hammer–chip a bit–suck the sugar.

"And Allah the Compassionate and the All Merciful will smite the infidels and the unfaithful smelly Arabs!"

And then I would further say:

"I, Hadi Abbabba Guwah, am a true son of Islam and an eternal father to all of the oppressed and to all of the poor and I Hadi promise to purge Islam of the pagan Christians!"

Whereupon Sidi-Abd-Al-Hadj-Ghirha would produce a silver box wherein is reposed a hair of the beard of the Prophet bought in Mekka for an enormous sum and which he would permit my forehead to bend and touch. Then he would produce the extremely holy and potent charm which was the knucklebone of one of the holiest marabouts who had ever adorned this land of legend. After touching this he would say that he would pray for me and in order to have my soul and spirit enter into the Jihad. His pose would be to form his hands into a cup shape and place them on his breast. Then his breath would stop and his head and hands would bow and pray for a long moment. After which he would raise his head and expell his breath in a long slow hiss as relief from the prayer. Then he would make the gesture of drawing his fingers downward across my face which was the gesture that said I would absorb all of the blessings that would flow from his prayer. Wallah! Shields for Hadi against misfortune.

Then I had to say with him the five pillars of the Koran: that there is no god but Allah and Mohammed is the Prophet of Allah and then that the prayers should be done thus so: onto our knees and then that our bodies must bend ever forward toward Mekka until our outstretched palms and foreheads touch the dust of the ground, and next Zaka—almsgiving—must be practiced every part of a day. Puh! Then also that the fast of Ramadan must be exercised and there must be no food at all of any kind—Ayammaaa Mammaaa—or drink or carnal pleasures with Samonama and for one month. Tish! And then lastly the promise of Hadj—the pilgrimage to Mekka.

"I will do this—I will do this!" I said strongly to this holy man leader Sidi-Abd-Al-Hadj-Ghirha.

He said to me, "In the name of the Prophet I pronounce you blessed. May Allah increase you in spirit. May Allah have mercy upon you for all of the time you have left here in our land of legend."

And as he said this he did insist that we leave the tea drinking and that I walk out of the house beside him to the plain of Ajagubub in order for us to watch the sun go down. All of the university houses round me in this waning light turned as pale as all of the gold that you have ever seen in all of your life and at one time. And in this light, I was blessed to look upon the high peaks and which were clothed in snow of the magic and beautiful Atlas mountains over in the northerly sky. And slowly their snows became as red as a thousand campfires and all round me of a sudden, standing there, it all seemed hushed and as if I was waiting for an unexpected event. But then that did quickly come. For then just as the sun was half behind the faraway sands it did happen. A white flag did flutter up to the summit of the minaret of the great mosque of the University and on the balcony a muezzin did appear, and then face westwardly, he did wail forth the evening chant. And from all of the hundreds of other minarets of the University five thousand six hundred voices clothed in body in the white garb of Holy White did take up the words: "Al-lah! Al-lah! Al-lah!" And Sidi-Abd-Al-Hadj-Ghirha, the Great Mind, did raise his arms to the disappearing sun and said to me:

"Twelve hours before and half our world away this mighty call to our prayers had started. In far Philippiniya when this sunset that is here was there. At a thousand leagues an hour over the earth and the water it had run before the coming night to Yava and to Singapore and then onto India and our words were chanted from the minarets of the great Muslem city of Delhi. 'Al-lah!' Through India and its deep passes and over its mountains it will sweep on and on and into Isfanhan and soon Kurdistan and then across all of the sands of Arabia and then to Holy Mekka itself. 'Al-lah! Al-lah!' Then on to Cairo. 'Al-lah!' The cry will be heard all over Tripoliana and on to Tunisia and then, Hadi Abbabba Guwah, down to us once again in our place in the great sand sea of the Sahara.''

In my fervor over his words and this moment, I fell to my knees weeping and screaming "Al-lah-il-Allah! Al-lah-il-Allah" one upon the other. Then after the prayers Sidi-Abd-Al-Hadj-Ghirha of a sudden ordered and caused two sheep to be brought before me as a sacrifice. In the Holy manner an Iman recited the invocations of Islam to me and then grabbed first one sheep by the horn and then the other and with a large knife he quickly cut their throats. And all of the blood of each was poured up and over onto my head and shoulders and it did drip down my body until the Iman started to wipe it away with Holy Water and to the accompaniment of suitable prayers and the recitation of the principles of Islam and the Koran. And as he finished his wiping off of the blood the Iman said to me: "And now and henceforth you will be called by all men by the true name of 'Mohammed,' Hadi Abbabba Guwah!"

And the holy men who had gathered round this ritual all shouted:

"Mohammed Hadi Abbabba—Mohammed Hadi Abbabba!"

To which I shouted back to them:

"Wallah! Wallah! Wallah!"

And Sidi-Abd-Al-Hadj-Ghirha said, "And all men will recognize you as a genuine Muselmin created so by the blessed action of me and thus you are now able to wear the hood over your eyes and to enter any mosque or Juba and display to all your orthodoxy and also your new self as the most pious of men."

And English, all this that Samonama did say to me in this chamber because of her sand and bones throwing did come to pass. She was my great fortune this Silver Bell of the Atala Riff. And back then and because of her words and saying that I would become a true Mohammed I could not in my excitement do other than lie on her and she on me and also sitting and hour upon hour all the night through we did this baby work, and me laughing and laughing, and all she could do was moan and moan. Ayaa.

On the plain of Ajagubub and with my new name I could only say to myself, but softly and repeatedly, that now I was again in good circumstances. Then aoi-yo. Saying this appeared to me of a day and of a sudden as if I was attempting to lie to myself and to soothe he that was Hadi. I at last resolved that it was all false. That I was not now truly in good circumstances. As I looked upon the days before me and the many.many days to come even with the mighty name of Mohammed, I saw no true profit to myself in occupying my time in killing for love. But did I, Hadi, dare to dwell on this while sitting in our tent and all the time looking upon the chest where Samonama kept her money bags? Ehwalla yes! Aya! What would become of me in these days of Samonama and her leader riding about killing les Français and how long a period of time would they be at killing these les Français? Puh!

I asked myself should I go to the tents of the Igdalens and suggest to them that we steal away to once again become bandits? Niwalla no. It was worthless as a plan. There was now to my mind no profit in being a plunderer even with the fierce Igdalens before whom all tremble. I said that to steal away alone on my horse at night after taking her money bags and her horse was also foolish. I knew not this land or the ways of the people. And how would I employ myself after all of her money bags were empty and the riyalat gone and I had sold my horse and her horse and all of the jewelry she had given me against misfortune?

Then I resolved it sadly and said that all I could do was only sit in the tent and put my face down into my one remaining hand and weep over all that had happened to me and was happening to me and was about to—Ayammaaa Mammaaa—happen to me. Wo-ye.

Then presently day upon day riders came onto the plain and all in different clothes in their mode and in their colors and all were much armed and noisy with their shouting and musket shooting into the air and some were harsh-looking men with perhaps five or six crisscrossed leather bandoleers about their shoulders and waists. And it came to be that as I did look round me day upon day north-east-south-west there grew perhaps forty or fifty thousand tents all about on the plain. How could this El Kabir love all these noisy people? Or even be pleased with all of them? Samonama said he was. Tuh! And still she could not make me understand love.

As we walked round the plain Samonama would use her arm and fingers to point out information to me like that the tribe in the blue and white clothes were the Zaquig Bedouins and that those there in black were Bedouins of the Zowaia and the Chamba and on she did talk until I could no longer retain all of the different names nor did I much want to retain all of the different names and their strange customs. This may have been wrong in me and I said this to myself back then at that time. The days ahead made me understand that I should have listened to her.

Then Samonama said of a day that El Kabir had pronounced that there would be five days of his hospitality and by the generosity of his heart and that to all who entered onto the plain of Ajagubub what little he had was theirs and without payment. Was that the voice of love? Yet bazaars were set up and in time hundreds of dirty-looking men squatted on their mats round all the tents and sold to the horsemen by shouting at them, sweet rice and oranges and fried maize sticks and teas and at a cost that was much more than I had ever seen in any town, in all my life. But the horsemen paid out the riyalat and I saw the money bags of the sellers were heavy. O this was much better than love in this land of legend.

Then Samonama's tribe rode in and in long brown silk robes and white gondourahs which is a long flowing garment that is attached to the head and also they had brightly colored scarves at their throats and on their feet long yellow curly toed slippers and with five riyalat silver bells at their tips. And Samonama with some excitement said:

"I must go and visit with my people and I will be with them perhaps days." And tinkle-jingle-dingle of a second she had tied up her clothes and money bags and was off to the corral to get her stallion and mount it and ride away. Aoi-yo. I was vexed at such a departure. Then that night and with my bubble-bubble pipe I remember I sat outside our tent and did dwell much on "how long would she be gone?"

The day after she had departed great feasting was decreed by the Senussi leaders and which I did welcome strongly for it had wasted me not knowing the answer to my question and also fear and awe possessed me because there were so many different family tribes

round me and I was all alone. So scared and tormented was I that
I was sure I did appear weakly and I understood this was not wise
to do. And at this time and into my head came an old song of long
ago and that I did once sing:

> Ayamma Mamma I am a stranger
> I am a stranger
> I do not know where I come from
> And I do not know where I am going to
> Ayamma.

Then many strange sounding voices in my head would answer
me:

> We see you are a stranger
> We see you are a stranger
> Tell us where you come from
> And where you are going to, Ayamma!

I could not resolve and answer my song. Then I only wandered
round and watched the tribesmen in their tents raise the sides so to
admit the air and let loose the cooking fire smoke, for I was told that
the law of the plain was that before the killing and for three days it
was that if any warrior would be drawn to the cooking smells of
whatever tent he could freely enter and eat his full and then so depart
and without obligation. I did recall that once it was said to me that
the eating of too much food could come and aid a saddened spirit
which was indeed mine of the moment, and also would make me
leave off of the thinking of my question. So I was quickly lured by
my nose and because of the smells to a tent filled with twenty-five
or more laughing Ahaggars sitting round in their white robes drinking and eating and of a sudden singing. I was welcomed noisily and
with their hand gestures they pleaded to me to remain. Then their
words insisted that I sit and accept their hospitality. I salaamed
"Ehwalla yes" and then I sat and I was offered all of one of the many
newborn roasted lambs just freshly killed and just out of the fire. The
dark and oily roasted animal was being in my hands and at my
mouth then my teeth found in tearing at him that between the skin
and the meat of this lamb they had stuffed thousands of raisins and
almonds and pistachio nuts. The whole of this lamb and nuts I did
eat and also the many bowls of the fried and sugared rice and the
trays of hot baked breads covered with liquid butter and also I drank

different teas and coffees. And after the washing of my hands I did walk away and without obligation. Wallah. I had in some measure succeeded in ridding myself of my sad spirit.

My stomach made big burbul-burbul noises but I walked on and on and round and round with my head back and my nose at the proper angle best to catch any new scents. Smells like those of Samonama drew me to a bell-shaped Azben tent and to four gracious desert Lords in green who salaamed me while sitting then bade me by Allah to enter and sit upon their cushions and to watch and wait while one of their women poured small cups of butter over ten chicken bodies above a large fire of camel dung. When they were brown here and golden there and shiny and reflected the firelight as water does the sun she slid them off the spit into a large tray of powdered cinnamon. Then each chicken body she rubbed all over with the cinnamon and completing this she then dumped the chicken bodies into a tray of powdered sugar and then the rubbing of the sugar into their bodies commenced all again as with the cinnamon. The chicken bodies went again onto the spit and again over the flames of the fire until the first drops of melted cinnamon and sugar began to drip into the fire. At this moment she slid the chicken bodies from the spit and two by two they went onto smaller trays spread wide and deep with green grapes. A tray was served to me and along with a large brass bowl of black olives that had bathed long in strong herbed oils.

The more I did eat the more I did rid myself of my sad spirit. And so I wandered and wandered and at one Tamahag tent I ate goat stuffed with dates and then to an Iklan tent and I ate horsemeat slabs and then to a Kel-air tent and feasted on twenty roasted pigeons stuffed with sugared breads mixed with raisins.

In the passing of time and eating and eating I could no longer remember all of the different tents in which I received hospitality. But I remember that up from large piled trays and bowls and into all of my big mouth went pilafs of rice and butter and ginger and dried goat cheese together with earth nuts and palm fruits and chicken bodies stuffed with oranges and melons and cooked grape leaves and washed with a whisk in mint sauce and then fish bodies with the salt beaten out and then oiled and baked whole on top of the dung of the fire and then eaten with different hard breads that were fried in oil or in butter and also soft breads stuffed inside with wet green olives.

Then it came to be that between all of this filling up of my big upturned mouth with food, which did go down to my now much bloated stomach which did look like that of camels five days dead, I could only again eat after drinking three and then shortly thereafter, four and then soon five large bowls of lemon juice, which I was assured by all of my many hosts would aid my appetite so that I, Hadi Abbabba Guwah, could carry on with it all. Then after each of the evenglows and after prayers, I did wander my body alone to my tent. Then all of the night I did lie askew on my many carpets that Samonama did buy for me, but even then I did flop about like a fish on a riverbank. I would wake of a sudden and sit up to speak to myself and say: "I cannot think of my answer for I can no longer think of the question." All because of the hubbub and burbul-burbul of my terrible stomach, which did cause me to roll round in order to make my belly feel better.

And in this state of sprawling about in different positions, Samonama with her chains, bracelets, charms, and bangles entered the tent. And kneeling noisily close to my body, she did take into her hands my sick head. I remember I thought she did smell like that of chickens rubbed in cinnamon and then sugar and all of which had been served to me on a spread of piled rice in turn sprinkled with the juice of green grapes.

She said to me in a way of anger, "Get up from this wasteful laying about after stuffing your stomach." She did twist and squeeze my shoulders and shake all of my body violently and kept shouting to me: "Come, you fattened goat—sit up on your messy sleeping mats—wake! Wake! You have lost your stomach three times, you fat goat! Wake! Sit up in your stomach mess!"

She took hold of my one remaining ear in her fingers and pulled me to a sitting position, then shouted again and this time up my nose, "All commanders of the fight are now to appear before our wonderful, brilliant leader who hates these Christian roumis—El Kabir!"

"Puhhhhh . . .," I moaned. And the rest of the food that remained in my belly made burbul-burbul noises as if in answer to the noise of what she had just said to me. And, as you say, English, in your language, I "passed wind" and then more "wind." She slapped my face as is the traditional custom of the Berber people. I was supposed to be humiliated. But I was not, because I am not of the Berber people and, furthermore, I, Hadi Abbabba Guwah, like to "pass wind" whenever I want to. But before I could feel good about this, she began to hold my nose and shake my head from side to side and continued with:

"I have spoken to my brother. He swears by saying that all is our Lord Allah, that he will arrange for you to receive very much payment for this battle. But only, only, if I tell him that you will fight fiercely. Very fiercely . . ."

"I will fight fiercely," I did say.

And on my asking about all of this payment, she did relate to me what would be the circumstances of my rewards for fighting in this silly battle. In a high amount of excitement she did say that her brother promised that all of the Christian prisoners that I did capture would be mine to torture as only I wished.

"Torture Christian prisoners? What profit was there in torturing Christian prisoners? Puh! You make prisoners slaves or you kill prisoners. You are a stupid woman."

"You do not understand because you are not of my people!"

"Next you will say 'in this land of legend.' Phew. I do not like your legends."

"Will it satisfy your greed to know that also for each pagan infidel prisoner my brother will give you twenty camels?"

"Twenty camels a prisoner? Ehwalla yes! Twenty camels a prisoner . . . O Goy-yo."

Then, because I was a bit pleased with my Samonama, and these feeble endeavors on my behalf, I grabbed her with my arm and pulled her down to my sleeping mat, even though it was smelly, with the intention of laying on her in that terrible excitement I had for her; and doing this, I had to say, as she did say, that she was the best woman I ever did lay on.

"No!" she did scream out to me. "You are too smelly. Also, even when you are clean, you cannot do this."

Then quickly, with a difficulty of breath, and softly, laying there on her back, she did say to me, "You must not do this now and also for a long time. For since you are the best man that has laid on me —but now smells like a dead horse!—it is nevertheless that Allah has begun in me a little Hadi Abbabba Guwah. If you lay on me at this moment I will have another Little Hadi in me, and tomorrow another and another and another. I want now one Hadi. Not four or five or six. So, you must stay from me until much after the birth of one Little Hadi."

"Aoi-ye . . ." over and over I did say looking down onto my beautiful Samonama and her beautiful body. I did then roll over into my smell and did keeping saying aloud "Aoi-ye—Aoi-ye . . ." over and over. These words to her did not at all say truly what I did feel in my heart. And yet as I could so easily frame lies and had done so all through many years, I could not now frame words that I did feel for her because they were true words of feeling and not lies. I did feel love for my Samonama. But I was fearful to tell her that. So too I could not lie to my Samonama. Puh! What have I become that I cannot frame a lie? Am I getting old? I did feel weak. Have I lost my reason? As she did look at me, my then speech to her was:

"Now we will not ride into battle since you have confessed to me that there is a little Hadi . . . I want to attend to you . . ."

"No. We will go into battle!"

"No! We will *not!*"

"Yes we will!"

"No no-no we will not, you whore of a thousand tents!"

"What?"

"No, we will not, you whore of a thousand tents . . ."

It was so fast that I did not truly see it. She had made a fist and three times: bam-bam-bam! She hit me on the jaw. I did drop to my mess on the carpets, shaking my head as I was stunned so. She did stand up and turned to leave the tent. I left the carpets and did grab her leg and with a mighty pull, fell her down and she screaming and yelling rebukes at me and kicking at me all the while. As I crawled up between her spread legs, she did pound me on my head with more of her fists. When I did at last reach her belly and began kissing her belly and yelling "Little Hadi" she did stop pounding me about my head and shoulders and I began to weep to her as I kept kissing her belly: "You must not fight—you must not fight!" Her strength was such, she having two arms, that she did push me down and I found myself between her legs; whence I did weep and say up into her, over and over, "Little Hadi—she must not fight—she must not fight . . ."

She was suddenly still, and no longer rained blows about my head and shoulders.

"No" I did hear her say. "This you do and say does not change my mind. My mind will not be changed. Nothing can change the mind of Samonama once she has made up her mind. I say to you that I will fight nevertheless of Little Hadi."

I did say: "I have made you a Little Hadi . . . I say to you that I will not fight in the battle because of this . . ."

"And I say to you again, no-no-no. And you will not speak to me and say to me that I will do this or that I will do that. I am not your slave. It is instead that you are my slave. You must remember that I could pay much riyalat for you because I was 'a whore of a thousand tents.' Because I was that I could pay much riyalat for your horse; and the saddle that you do admire so much, and all of your clothes, and all of the good food I did provide for you to eat. All because of this 'whore of a thousand tents.' Look and see what you are now, Hadi Abbabba! You are *my* possession. I am not yours. Then also, as I have just seen, because of your feelings for me and your weakness for me, you are a slave most of all in your heart. Now I want payment. For the money I have given to you, for the things I have given you, and for the time I made you well from the sickness. And for all the times this 'whore of a thousand tents' danced long for you so that you could get up a heat to lie on me. So you will, for me, I know, fight in the battle for *my* people and for no profit, and fight for their freedom and for not profit, and kill for their fashion of living. And I do now know, lying on my back and looking into your eyes, that you will fight because I, who you feel for, ask you to fight. Fight for what I, Samonama, do feel and think. Say this to me: 'I am your slave.' "

I did say: "I am your slave . . ."

"No! Say it this way: 'I am *your* slave!' "

"I am *your* slave."

"Good. Now say to me, 'I, Hadi Abbabba Guwah, will be a slave to the whore of a thousand tents forever.' "

I did command myself to decree this to her: "I Hadi Abbabba Guwah . . . will be a slave to the whore of a thousand tents forever." Then I said, pulling myself into a more upright manner, "In my opinion, you are sick in the head as the camels that I did once doctor. Do you not see you might die in this battle: you 'whore of a thousand tents'?" Then with this and with more of my burbul-burbul, I did note I was overwhelming her: specks of foam were coming to the corner of her mouth and she began rocking back and forth on her knees. I quickly tried to gain a mastery over this situation by contorting my face and opening wide my eyes as I was wont to do with all of my other slave masters, so that she would have pity on me, plus perhaps it would make her stop this witless fuss.

Instead of this deception being a complete success, she did rebuke me and shriek out of her own contorted mouth: "fool's tricks!" Then did hit me across my face with the open palm of her hand. I was exhausted with this want of kindness. In more anger and shaking her fists at me and amid the noise of her silver bells and bangles and necklaces and bracelets, she shrieked: "It is true! You are One Pubic Hair!"

"One Pubic Hair!"

Then her making hissing noises; wiping the foam from her mouth with her sleeve, she stood herself up from all of my many carpets and pulling up her belly clothes, departed the tent her silver bells, brass bells, bangles, beads, necklaces, and anklets clanging, clinging, and jangling.

Wo-ye. All of this silly rumpus and her drooling at the mouth did not make me feel well at all. I felt no gain: I had made no gain. Indeed English, I felt pain. This, the latest of my misfortunes, in this land of legend, a place where everything is possible and for all men, even me.

It came into my head that I should quickly now go to the bazaar and soften my terrible pain. I did not want to bow my head to the dust to pray. I felt not to pray. I would instead, indeed, spend her money. Spend the riyalat of this blasted whore of a thousand tents who now wanted only a witless battle and not my little Hadi. Pouf! I would adorn myself instead. I would force myself to feel better. Yes, I said to me: "Force yourself to feel better. Do something!"

I took up several of her money bags and to the bazaar I did go. Very quickly I did pour out her riyalat onto a carpet and purchase a blue and green and white striped jallaba of Chinese silk. Then I did add to it a wide red sash of twenty yards and over this a black waistcoat with fine red embroidery. Then unto myself and falling off all of these new clothes, a white cape. Then my purchases were new strips of white ear and chin and neck cloths. All over these went necklaces. Onto my arms went charms blessed by Holy men. Onto my wrists went bracelets. And to spend her money more, I did buy and adorn my head with a black and white striped Kafiyeh headdress with three thick bands of agal ropes of camel hair to hold the Kafiyeh firmly onto my head.

But I did not, I do know, feel better in spirit after adorning myself in this way. No, English, I truly did not feel better. Instead of walking about in my new fine clothes for all who passed me to admire, I did go and just sit on my many carpets in my tent quietly and then begin to think wearisomely of my Samonama. I did sit and sit and, in great lethargy, await the summons to El Kabir. But so badly put out was I in thinking only of my Samonama that I did feign sickness of my stomach, which the Berber people understand because they eat too much, and do not like a poor stomach to make a mess on their carpets. And so I said weakly to the young messenger-boy who had no teeth that Samonama would lead the Igdalen Tuaregs into battle.

I did not rest all the night. Then with the morning sun, and as if it were not another new day to me at all, but still only in my head the sleep pictures of the night . . . of my Samonama . . . talking to me. My Samonama and her thousand silver bells, brass bells, beads, bangles, bracelets, necklaces, anklets jingling, tinkling, jangling, clinking, dingling, bing-binging everytime she took a deep breath. I confess, English, I was confused and in turmoil. I did stumble as I tried to walk.

And in this state of mind, English, and by and by, I did find myself strangely sitting on some dumb beast of a camel and beside my Samonama and with all of the hundreds of the Igdalen Tuaregs behind. In this moment she did shriek out: "Where did you get those clothes? You are dressed like a fool! A madman! You will embarrass me up to my teeth to all! All this, with my money! You idiot!" But I remained composed. I did just point to the Igdalens. On the necks of the new Igdalen horses, which were Barbary black horses, long-tailed, pedigreed, with fine bones, arched necks, and fiery of spirit, now hung the silly sacred verses from the Koran which commented on War, and which had been burned into very long red leather strips and then tied with sheepskin strings to the tufted strands of the horses' manes, which in all made them look like lizards. All of these horses had made the tedious pilgrimage to Mekka and hence were referred to as the Noble Ones. Some had magnificent leopard skin trimmings on their saddles, which were of carved teakwood covered in velvet. And for what was to come—what gain? Puh.

Wearily I remember I did pass by on my camel next to Samonama what I did believe were the rich guest tents set up for the chieftains of this rebel baboon El Kabir. I rode slowly beside her nearly slumped over in my saddle because of my strangely saddened heart and if I would have fallen off my camel in my apathy as to this occasion I would have babbled:

Ayaam-maaa, Mammaaaa
I am a stranger, I am a stranger . . .
Where am I going toooo . . . I don't know.

Ayaaaa-Mammaaaaa . . .
Just as a stranger; Just as a stranger,
Do you know what you are doinggg . . . ?
No.

Soon our troop came to an area containing the largest and most colorful of the tents in all of that long row, tents that were the finest that I ever did see in all my life. None of the low black and patched Bedouin kind that are all spreading and squat and smelly. But rather of the tall pavilion type that go high into the air and with a sort of bulb on top and having many colored stripes and designs on them. These tents at night contained the tribal chiefs that would take part in the coming battle. Before each tent were flags flying from tall spears stuck into the ground. These were the fighting banners and family history of the chiefs of each pavilion tent. All these believed in this fool they called and referred to as: "Oh Magnificent excellency My Emir El Hamel El Kabir." Their further adorations were, "Leader of the Faithful." Also, "Shadow of the Prophet." "Commander of one hundred thousand in the army of his Lord Allah." These tents led to the Grand Circle where El Kabir would give us his blessings.

As I did ride slowly beside Samonama up to this circle I did take a long look as this commander of one hundred thousand. All I did think at that moment was that I wanted a beard like his and I also wanted his clothes. They were better than the ones I had on, which I confess, English, did not truly have dignity, only variety and color, as Samonama had indicated.

A chorus of perhaps fifty or sixty Holy men that stood behind him chanted over and over as we did pass, "As the merchant trusts in his stuffs for profit, the rebel puts his only hope of freedom in his bravery." Then we in turn mumbled: "Allah–Al-lah–Allah." Puh. As I looked at El Kabir my head said, "This silly bug was just another desert lord who had burbul-burbuled himself into good circumstances." All of this rumpus of these simpletons about me made me bitter and feel more strongly that it was witless to fight these invading Francswari soldiers who had no caravans to plunder. They dealt not with trade goods. They only wanted to conquer a worthless desert and make the inhabitants pay taxes. I should have stayed with the Tebu of Gandoga. Or even in Kano. Or even with Baba Gungi. This was ridiculous.

On a small sign from his majesty the Sultan or His Magnificence, the Prophet who had an army of one hundred thousand men, Samonama reined her horse to a halt and then turned the beast to face this lord of the wastes. And so I had to do this also. He raised his old bony hand to signal silence to the chanting of the Holy men and I did see he had many riyalats' worth of rings on it and, wiping his lips with his tongue, I knew he would issue a decree and with much emotion. The only noise now being all the silk battle banners on spears stuck into the ground and flapping in the breeze about him, he said:

"I remand to you O Samonama, leader of all Igdalen Tuareg in this battle, and she who seeks revenge, that we of the Great Sahara Berbers have fought mightily against the Vandal Kings and their terrible soldiers. Then again also the wily Phoenicians when they did come. Then again the bronze soldiers of Carthage. Then yet again all of the thousands of marching Romans under their cruel Emperors Caligula, Caracallus, Scripio, and Octavian. Then beloved Samonama, O patriot of our land, came the hordes of the Byzantine Caliphs. Then alas, the smelly Arabs. Allah has not been merciful. All of our noble ancestors believed in our land and in our traditions, and in our freedom. Freedom. This is what we fought for. These values are worth fighting for. Now, now, my patriot child O Samonama, come these Franks. And again as in our past, every league they penetrate is a threat to our peace and our way of life and our tribal structure. Now there has been a call to arms—to arms— to fight to rid the newest of invaders from our beloved land. And again, and again if need be, we shall harass our new enemy and we shall ambush and we shall do battle this day with these Christian pagan infidels. And we—we the Great Berbers—will win. As we have always won! Kill-Kill-Kill-O Samonama-Kill!"

This drivel did not impress me. In fact, this drivel wasted me. But it did impress Samonama. She repeated this mad old pretender's words of "Kill-Kill-Kill!" And as is the custom at these rituals raised up her arms up down up down above her head as if they would leave their sockets and with clenched fits and with all of her emotion shouted "Kill-Kill-Kill!" And so did the Igdalens all along beside us decree this witlessness and also too the Holy men. It was all so sad, English, so sad.

Then as you at times think that you are dreaming in your sleep and you do not know what will come to you next, I did follow her motions of raising her horse's head and turning and I followed her down and passed neat rows of the yellow goatskin tents that were the shelters of this moron El Kabir's bodyguards. Perhaps five hundred of them.

Soon we all reached the gathering place. And when we numbered perhaps thirty thousand of only the front rank, we wheeled in very stately movements and all of us now by fours progressed round and toward the vast field of the charge, and as I remember, in squadrons of one thousand. Slowly, as was the fashion, the fours became eight abreast as we began to move into position on this plain called Bal-al-Din. Hoofs shuffled through the sand and over the stones and I reached down and tightened the saddle strap, thinking this was not a good way to spend my time. But beside me was Samonama. And all about were the jingles of thousands of bits of accoutrements and the sight was thousands upon thousands of swaying tassels of all colors. I do recall that on the south of our Igdalen Tuaregs were the white-robed Ahaggar Berbers and on down the front rank were the Azben Berbers, who were still forming into eights. Beyond them another tribe of blue-clad Tuareg of which I did not know. Samonama kept following her signal cloths tied to spears stuck into the ground which would lead us to our charge start. Looking north there were the thousands of the camels and riders of the Oulied Sidi Chelkh Berbers and past them many thousands more of the Hamacha Bedouins. Beyond these on the plain of Bal-al-Din I could not see.

Then we reached our signal spear that decreed stop and form twelves in a line and behind and all the Igdalens did so. I kneeled my grunting dumb beast to its knees by shrieking "Adar-ya-yam! Adar-ya-yam!" to wait on this soon to be terrible plain of Bal-al-Din for the charge signal to be ordered. All round was simple scrub and some bare rock. No flowers. A few knife-edged plants called Bru grass. Thousands of wind patterns were in the sand that had been blown onto Bal-al-Din from westerly. We did wait.

Huge swarms of the black string flies had followed the camels and many of the horses. Now many of the swarm dropped to attack the small red ants living beneath a dead pistachio tree in front of me and my camel while on the ant heap was a lone sand skunk with his nose in the ant hole licking up the little red things with his long pink tongue. The rest of the flies settled on my beast. Soon he burbuled and snorted and tossed his head. I did look only westerly and not at my Samonama, who sat on her horse also waiting.

In the charge to come I did resolve to watch all of her movements and to try to protect this foolish woman with all of the cunning I could muster.

In the distance ahead and through all of the heat waves that shimmered and watered your sight, it seemed there was no enemy, just the orange and purple hills on the far horizon. But we were not to be deceived, for time and again scouts on swift, small horses brought words that the Christians were there and also what they were doing.

The heat of the sun now drew the moisture from my skin to wet my new clothes as I sat quietly and from time to time tried to calm my restless camel with the least effort. Every one hundred clicks of the tongue a hot wind came from the East and it did seem to contain little knives but in truth it was the tiny weightless thorns of long-dead Ayatashi bushes that blew about your face and hands and made you claw at the skin continually.

We did wait.

It appeared that El Kabir, master of wastes, in order to keep us excited about the coming battle, had instructed his guardsmen to ride before the long line of the first charge and in packs of twenty or more men. In a festive and fervid and wild mood they galloped their horses along with their trumpeteers and drummers before us for a short space. Suddenly they did rein up short at different intervals and at the last moment of this time, fired their rifles into the air and shrieked prayers. Time and time over these guardsmen galloped to the signal of the trumpets and the drums. There would be sand dust, a rush of waves of horsemen with flying capes and turban neckcloths; swords waving at the air from one hand, shooting rifles in the other, guiding their horses with their knees and the din of them shouting for Allah to send down blessings upon this idiot endeavor. After they had stopped short, the smell of powder was carried by the wind and drifted among us on this plain of Bal-al-Din.

Soon the guardsmen before us doing this tedious entertainment were quite beyond reason. Now each of these considerably witless soldiers of El Baboons did want to outdo the simpleton next to him in a wilder performance. At the brutal spurred rein-ins, their horses' blood all covering their bellies, each dirty rider made his stallion rear up angrily in pain and made his forelegs paw the air. Then these beasts neighed in exasperation and then down to the rocks and sand of the ground to, in their fury, show their impatience to all this nonsense by twisting and turning in the dust communicating to us they were feeling: "Let us get into the battle and let it all be over with." To control the horses the guardsmen drove their spurs deep, drawing more blood. But the beasts swirled in faster circles, kicked up rocks and sand, and tried to attack the legs and feet of the riders with their teeth. To gain a mastery over these maddened animals, the soldiers beat them hard with rifles and the flat of their sabers and tried to make them leap forward and to again make them turn and ride back down the line for another display. They were now shouting war cries, maddened themselves, and standing up off their saddles and in their stirrups, and turbans became unfastened and quickly streamed in the wind that the horses created in their twirling, bucking, and leaping, and the guardsmen continued to brandish their rifles in the air space above their heads. Having the horses now in some control, these riders, having reloaded their rifles, did shoot ear-deafening fusillades to the sky. And then for greater display, threw their weapons in the air only to catch them up a second later. All was endless sand dust, noise, and ferocity.

Amid this hubbub a young child scout rode up and before us and reining in his swift little horse abruptly, started to shout to Samonama that the Francswari Christians and their bloody Arab allies were advancing across the plain. Also, information that there were two regiments of them that were light foot infantry, each consisting of five thousand men. Also from this bewildered child scout, that there were six battalions of their cavalry following the infantry; and behind these horsemen, three battalions of silly Cannon du Colonialiste, which were what we used to call, when I was a savage years ago in Kroo Lagoon, "tubes on wheels." But to you now, English, they were what in your tongue were called, "screw guns," or, as you at times called them, "donkey guns," that were in pieces and carried on what were called "Missouri mules." Large and powerful beasts that could move about at a very steady pace and even on high mountain trails and at an even steadier and more rapid pace cross mountain passes only five hands wide. The caravan leader of these "Missouri mules" could stop their running pace of a second and the crews of these "screw guns" would take off the parts of the guns and put them into one piece on the ground in a time that would take me ten clicks of my tongue.

Also the scout did report that the Francswari had for this battle what they then called "Krupp guns." Larger "tubes on wheels" and pulled along behind by four to six horses and then behind the guns wagons for their bullets. These "cannons" were used, as we were told, for "long-range work."

However, understanding all of this sad situation before me, I resolved not to take offense nor take flight but to remain at the side of my Samonama and to look after her and the Little Hadi that was in her belly. My head did keep asking, "Am I a fool?" My head replied easily: "Ehwalla yes." Then, "Would I succeed in protecting her?" Sadly, I did not think so. These thinkings in my head were stopped when behind me and in the distance came the beating of drums—the huge war drums of shiny copper the size of tribal cooking pots which were carried two by two on each side of Mehari racing camels and the drums beaten by their riders with two long thin clubs made from the frangipani tree and they went "Boo-umm-Booo-umm," which was just really the alert signal. Then these "Boom-booms" were followed by the blaring sound of the long brass trumpets that give the signal to camel drivers to beat their chewing, grunting beasts from their kneeling positions by shoutings and shriekings of "Ahh-ya-da, Ahh-ya-da!" And he did roar as I beat him to his dusty feet and all the while preparing the beast and myself for the forward movement; which meant adjusting my five new twenty-riyalat pistols that Samonama had sent to my tent and their cartridge belts that crossed each other over the shoulders and chest of my new but too loud clothes. I tossed my cape over my shoulders and raised my black veil to just below my eyes. All this amid hysterical shoutings of "Al-lah–Al-lah–Al-lah!" And soon Samonama's horse and behind me the Igdalen horses and, indeed, all horses along the lines were neighing and coughing and pawing at the sand and creating dust with their hooves. To all the "Allah-Allah's" I kept saying in my head, "Puh-Puh-Puh." But out loud to all round me and so that I would not bring a rebuke down upon me, I also "Allah'd" loudly, and raised one of my pistols into the air and shot her bullet hoping Samonama would look at me and be pleased. She didn't.

The long trumpets again made their signal noise known to us above shrieking "Al-lah!–Al-lah-al-lahs" which instructed us that we all should forward across the plateau in as orderly a line as was possible. This is difficult, English, for twenty thousand men in one line. My beloved Samonama with Little Hadi in her belly straightaway went slightly into the lead. Suddenly all was silence now but for the soft, slow pad of my camel amid the dock-dock of Samonama's horse and the noise of the Igdalen horses behind. We struck our beasts into what was called, as is the custom, the "walk," which was truly just more of a forming maneuver. Some one hundred or more smaller drums signaled back those that were too rash to keep in line of the charge while the remaining bigger copper drums kept pounding out the steady beat of "go ahead" which was this "walk" rhythm. My war camel and the fighting stallions behind now knew the Christian enemy were ahead, and that there would be a battle, for during this "walk" period they haughtily threw their heads back and chortled and grunted and whinnied and from side to side tossed their heads back and forth; all to each other, to each other all across the entire plain.

I kept my looking on Samonama. I could only have a gaze for my Samonama. Why would she do this to Hadi? And perhaps to herself? Why would my beloved be so foolish? Are women such as she always so foolish? Are all women inclined to die in a mess of witlessness? I concluded in this "walk" across the plain: "Women have the brains of a camel." Yet in my heart, even though I did say this, I knew truly I was tormented. Do women really have the brains of a camel? Yes, women have the brains of a camel. Then why was I tormented? Why was I confused? What herbs could I use to doctor this woman's mind, as I did with the camels when I was with the Tebu of Gandoga? As with all camels, I again then concluded, women are creatures of folly; creatures without reason. I, Hadi Abbabba, accept with a wave of my hand that all men are witless fools. Deserved more to be killed than to stay alive. And indeed, soon most of the charge would be. Well, better to be with Allah than to be alive, so these simpletons believed. Such I think, English, is the history of mankind.

But for a woman to be without reason makes me sad. Indeed, English, it makes me weep.

My confusion was halted by the big copper drums. They had changed their "walk" rhythm beat to the next signal in the movement forward. This was called "the pace." So we of the squadron tapped the tops of the heads of our beasts into "the pace." This continued and again the smaller copper drums signaled us to keep our animals in a perfect line, which was becoming more difficult as the drumbeats entered their blood. In this "pace" period many of the Igdalens began to eat from their skin bags tied to their saddles. This was due to what your language calls fear. The Igdalens behind began shoving long strips of dried mutton into their mouths then tearing off with their teeth huge mouthfuls; all as they rode and bobbed up and down in this time of "pace." Others stuffed their mouths with figs. Their rifles were still slung over their backs and all their sabers jungle-jangled as well as the many daggers that were slung round their necks.

Slowly the big drummers increased their pounding as they felt the camels and the horses were feeling more and more of the "warfire" within them, and that they were even now more impatient than during the walk. This was what war drummers were for. And the animals understand all too well these rhythms. So you see, English, it is not easy to hold them in a perfect line.

After the proper period of time the drums and their beat again changed, and the rhythm told us that we should move into the "swift march," or what you English call "the canter." And all of us, of course, should stay in a perfect line. Puh! However, all of us that were on camels tediously again raised our long sticks which dangled from our wrists and tapped their necks in ritual signal even though the camels understood perfectly well what all this new noise meant. During this movement it was much more difficult to keep my beast close at the side of my Samonama, now who I called "my torment." Or was this idiot, "my disease"?

The order of the line, as I remember, was good. I, Hadi Abbabba Guwah, was impressed. Dust from this maneuver now made invisible all of those behind Samonama and me. We were getting to the silly charging speed. And the drummers saw this, and as is the ritual, their beat changed in a faster way and signaled "fast trot"—Boom-boom-boom . . .

Now I needed, in the dust swirling about me, to stop tapping the camel's head with the long stick and start beating the dumb camel's flank; beating him terribly and not ceasing this during this "fast trot" movement and its rhythm. All these beasts did like this strain on themselves: they did like war, as my Samonama liked war.

My idiot torment. Ahh-ye, I must rid myself of this nuisance: my Samonama: the latest of my misfortunes, in this life of punishment. How was I to gain a mastery over this situation of charging toward the Franks on a camel? Here, in this land of legend, a place where everything is possible and for all men, even me. Yet as I bounced up and down going across this plain at the "fast trot," I could think of nothing as a solution at this moment of my life.

As if the beasts were not straining enough to the drums, men now started to shriek even more encouragement to their animals by yelling at the top of their voices: "Ya-ya-ya!" Thousands and thousands of "ya-ya-ya's!" sounded over the plateau. Then came the "Hua-hua-hua!" These cryings-out blended with the rhythm of the yet new terribly fast copper drumbeat. And again these poor animals lurched forward and strained all the more for speed. It was agony for the small drummers to keep them in line, and they frantically did signal for all of us to do so, but to no avail above now the "ya-ya-ya!" and the "Hua-hua-hua!"

All, all with my one arm, English, I controlled my beast. Believe me, it is not as if you were resting on Persian carpets.

Faster and faster across the plain of Bal-al-Din did all of us go.

All was noise. My horrible Samonama was still taking the lead on her sand-colored horse; and now to me there was nothing but the incessant pounding on the sand of twenty thousand hooves. Rushing forward little birds flew up in a frightened, swirling swarm and fled before us toward the Christians.

Yet I only had time for twenty hits of my stick and then the drums said, before they would no longer be heard above the din of Bal-al-Din and the "Hua-hua-huas" and the "ya-ya-ya's," that we of the front line could "break," and each rush forward as he willed and thus completing the full charge ritual, and all the others behind to follow. All men with two arms dropped reins and unslung their rifles and drew swords from their scabbards. Now their noise to their chargers became sounds like that of a corral full of different animals, and above the pounding I frequently heard the Berber yell of "Isk-na! Isk-na–Iskna–Iskna!" which was even more encouragement to the animals to go faster.

Now it was a terrible effort for me to stay close to my Samonama and only with one arm, mind you. But I have never known a camel, English, to run so fast; so fast that it was only wise to tear the Kafiyeh from my head and let it fall to the storm of the dust behind. All our capes now bellowed out beyond the tails of our charging beasts, and the clothes we wore caught the wind and made us feel we would be dragged from our saddles. So now off came my cape, and I tossed it to the wind—which fouled the legs of the horse behind me and he did tumble onto the plateau, throwing his shrieking rider before him. Who was promptly ridden over by about five hundred other Igdalen Tuareg. Wallah! This, the latest of his misfortunes.

Thus disposed of, I rode on, staying at the side of my Samonama. It did not please me to do so. I truly did not want to make a rumpus with these Christian pagan infidels, or these "roumis" as the Berbers called them. I wanted to lay on Samonama and give her more Hadis. I wanted to . . . what, English? The charge? Oh, yes. That. Well, I am tired now, English. My mouth is dry. The sun is going down. It is time for refreshment. And if you are still interested, I will come to you tomorrow again.

Good morning, English. I come to see you before the sun is up and a cool breeze is still blowing. But the promise is of a day of heat. So I walked here to you at this hour to freshen me. That is, before the day grew old. Yes, I will have some tea. I see on your table that you are still writing in your book. Is it still about my life? I—continue the charge, English? What charge? Oh, the charge on the plain of Bal-al-Din. But first, may I have some more tea? Yes, that is good . . .

Oh yes . . . well, we were rushing, rushing across the plain of Bal-al-Din, as I did tell you. When we were in this state of like birds flying across the plateau in a frenzy and rifles were unslung and sabres all out, the flag bearers who were also in the front line of the charge had to untie from their saddles at this wild full gallop very long poles. Then against the wind that pulled at these long poles, raise these staffs to the vertical and then put them into foot stirrups. Then they did begin to twist these long poles round and round. Then came amid the shrieks of the men and the pounding of the hooves of the animals, the slow unfurling of the huge flags attached to the staffs, all of which they did continue to do at a full mad gallop. As they slowly twisted the poles they did moment by moment unfurl the long dark green silk fighting banners of Islam, on which were the writings of the great prophet Mohammed in white. Thousands of flags were being unfurled along with their red and blue and brown

Jihad streamers on which were inscribed promises of loyalty to the cause of El Baboon. The flags were bigger than most of the men themselves; and the great long flags and streamers now fluttered and flapped and snapped in the wind created by the speed of their charging animals and to the sound of thousands of "Isk-na–Isk-na–Isk-na's!"

Samonama, now in a more sillier mood, signaled that I and the Igdalens must yet encourage ever further our frothing, maddened, charging beasts to a greater and to a more thundering speed. Amid this incessant and horrible pounding noise that the exhausted beasts made on the hard plain, the Igdalens responded to Samonama and the hundreds of them did begin to yell all above the noise "Mutee–Mutee–Mutee–Isk-la-na! Isk-laaaa-na–Muteeeee–Muteeeee . . ." Amid our green fluttering flags and with their sand-filled throats now began the shrieking out one to the other of the battle yell of "Hal-lo–Achba! Hal-lo–Achba!"

I could at last see the roumis on a rise in the distance and which was the horizon. The green silly flags of Islam and their streamers slowly dipped forward due to this new excitement of seeing the pagan Christian infidels before them. All about me this nonsense started, in this land of legend which I believed once of a day would place me in better circumstances. I ask anyone now—were these good circumstances?

Samonama was well in the lead of our troop. And I was yelling out "Samonama-Samonama-Samonama" and working my beast closer to her when came the new noise of "Ssshhhhish-boom-ssshhhish-boom!" And then a "crack-whooommm!" The ground shuddered as the Christian bombardment came through the air and fell amid us. The ground and the sand and the rocks went up into the air as with a water spout. As in columns and we were all enwrapped in dust, sand, pebbles, but especially me, all of this puh hitting me about my naked head and face and capeless shoulders . . . ripping through my new clothes that I did have left . . . I had to endure the sudden gusts of earth whipping at me and my camel and to give a great patience to the whistling noises that came before the Frank missiles landed. Every second of a second the whistling, the "whooshing" of air; the explosion and the little snap currents of it whipping at my face and again swirling my new clothes almost up over my head so that I could not see where my camel was going. One explosion and smoke became mixed with another explosion and smoke and this continued and continued as we rode forward through it all and my remaining ear was drowned in constant roaring sounds. Now beasts and men and flags and streamers and "ya-ya-ya's" were constantly falling to the sand about me. And in all the noise and smoke and shell I could no longer see Samonama ahead of me. And what was even more of a nuisance was the pieces of torn and shredded war horses that began to dirty me; and also pieces of the Igdalens and their clothes who rode them splattered me about my face and body and all I could do is keep riding and riding hoping to find my Samonama. I kept thinking, "How long will this nonsense continue?"

Then I was overwhelmed. Of a second, these things did happen to me and almost all together: Down headlong my war camel went with a long bleating cough and a bellow. Up and off of him and forward and all through the smoke and air I went; the blast burning my one remaining hand and all of my face and then most of all my new clothes remaining were whooshed from me; of the cannon blown away. This the latest of my misfortunes. With the next explosion that instantly came, half of the war camel's head I could see was terribly ripped away and sent bobbledy-bobbledy along the sand until its final stop at some distance. But, then, I, Hadi Abbabba Guwah, who was down and to the sand ground and then rolling over and over almost naked. All about me was still smoke rolling, like, English, the color of once my inks, but, mind you, with more blue in it.

Then, I had to spend my time getting out of the way of the riders that were still rushing forward past me and very swiftly and shouting this nonsense of "Allah-il-Allah! Allah-il-Allah!" Ahhh, Puh!

About and around me north, east, south, west, were also the screams and shriekings of many other men who had been torn and blown from their beasts and who now were unable to get off the ground but were bleeding and trying to summon this last strength to say their farewell prayers to this magic ground of legend on which they did now lie torn and gasping and sprawled and on top of their coughing, bellowing, dying camels and horses. Then, because of the hurt in my head and all of the blood that covered my face, I did swoon.

When my eyes were again first opened, I saw the sky. It was a much lighter blue than my inks. I did slowly roll over as is the custom, and with much effort; O Wo-ye yes, I with great effort did stand up. Then I turned all round. The smoke had all gone away.

Wheresoever I turned, north, east, south, west, there was destruction. All for Allah-il-Allah. I was not impressed. Bodies were lying about smoking like lambs on a spit over a fire. None made their noise of "Allah-Allah" now, either in their dying prayers or their shriekings out in pain. Soon there would be no living man at all round as I took this time to survey about me. I, Hadi Abbabba Guwah, "One Pubic Hair," was all alone, and, you must understand, English, hurt badly, on this vast plain of Bal-al-Din. My mind did not have to work so hard for it to tell me I was not in good circumstances. Next it came into my head, where was my Tinkle Bell with all her bracelets, anklets, beads, bangles, necklaces that went dingding-ding-ah-ling? I would now think of only to take the time to walk crookedly about this wretched battlefield and round all of the dead to look for my Samonama.

I fell down sometimes . . . in this task, and it was not an easy thing to again get into the erect position. I looked at the mangled bodies of each and every one and then quite some distance away on this terrible plateau, I did come upon a piece of what was a part of her. I found her shoulder in some clothes of her and with an arm to it that had been separated from the rest of her by the Krupp cannons. On the wrist of the arm I saw her bracelets of silver bells enwrapped round. I did not wish then to search out more of her or find any other pieces of her. As I held up her shoulder and arm with its silver bells about the wrist, I did recall then of a second that she used to say much to me that she "loved me." Ehwalla no, all to her own self was "Allah-il-Allah-Allah-il-Allah." This shoulder piece I held, with its arm broken and falling limp and bleeding onto the sand, was all that remained of this "love." Where was Little Hadi? Where was Little Hadi? Where? But I did not want to explore for her belly or her head on this plain of Bal-al-Din in this land of legend where all good things were possible to all good men, even me. All now I shouted was "Allah-il-Allah" and over and over I did shout it. "Allah-il-Allah" —are all men like baboons hanging from trees and scratching their bodies than like men? Then I fell down onto the earth of this plateau because of the pains of my body due to the battle and in my stomach due to my Samonama.

I lay on my side feeling sick just as if I were one of the camels in my compound on the edge of the camp of the Tebu of Gandoga. And just as if I had eaten too much, I did lose onto the sand the contents of my belly. Then reaching out and pulling and tearing and ripping the remaining rags from the dead, I wiped my mouth clean. Then I rolled onto my back and looked to the sky.

I saw way up high, so high they looked as small as flies on a camel, the huge black-blue vultures and also what they give the name to: the marabou storks. . . . These were of a white color and with long legs and with long red beaks . . . the number was many hundreds or more. I did watch them. I knew they could smell the bodies that were all covered in blood and also see that mostly they no longer moved. Slowly as I did watch up at the sky and watch the vultures and the marabous, I began to breathe in a deep fright. The vultures and the storks came down slowly dropping and then again slowly dropping in circles. Hundreds, all circling above and riding on the winds with their big wings motionless, and being cautious as is their nature to be. In the proper time they would come down and land on the smelly dead and begin to eat them. In the distance and flying low and fast over the dead and dying were also hundreds of what are called the small "corsair birds," who also I knew wanted to eat off what was left of the torn soldiers of El Baboon.

In a mind crazed with pain and poor circumstances, I stretched out my one remaining arm and shrieked into my one remaining ear: "Where is the rest of my Samonama?" She of the oh lovely restless eyes, that spoke to me in a language despite her stupidity. In those eyes there was beauty, and feeling for Hadi. In them dwelt delight during our good times. Always before the sun was up and a cooler breeze had blown across our bodies, in promise of a day of heat. And I would sniff in her garden to freshen me, before the day grew old . . . and from that came Little Hadi. Where is the rest of my Samonama? She who has given me Little Hadi? And the plateau of Bal-al-Din is laughing at Hadi, who is not a rascal. Nor is he "one pubic hair"! But, now the vultures are winging in the air and the plateau of Bal-al-Din is smiling at Hadi whose death is now appearing. Was this the end of my life? At the mercy of Allah-damned birds? The cruel sun shines on those now dead who went to war. And me, Hadi Abbabba Guwah, who by nature is tender and kind of spirit and also in exile from his homeland of Popo, see the ground is dead again and yet again spattered with blood.

I tell you, English, if you are not dead but hurt badly as I was back then, and all alone without a live comrade on the ground, you must expect the vultures and the marabous and the corsair birds soon enough. The big birds in the sky will soon come down low, to suddenly fly in on you in a whush-whush of halting wings to deal with you. I did know that when this event happened, I had to quickly roll over onto my face and stomach if I did not have a weapon, which I did not have, or I could not keep moving which I could not possibly do really. How could I gain a mastery over this situation? If I had stayed in a swoon or swooned again, nothing would have helped me in this circumstance. The vultures and the marabous together, when they land, will walk in on you and then crowd round you with their wings raised to frighten you and make a lot of their "aik-aik-aik" noises. First they will try to rush in one by one and attack your eyes to pluck them out and then when they do so, they know that you will be helpless. If you are faint from your wounds, perhaps the pain will make you wake. But still you have only one eye left as I, Hadi Abbabba Guwah, had only one arm left, and aoi-yo, one ear. On the side where you have lost your eye they will keep attacking you and climbing on you covering you all over and if they are very hungry, they will be tearing at you angrily and "aik-aik-aik" and then more and more will surround you and climb onto you with the smelly feathers of their bodies smothering your nose as you lie helpless on the earth trying to fight. If you do have some strength, you might have time to save half of your face and your eyes. Then others, of course, will peck at your new clothes, if you still have your new clothes on you, and tear them away to get at your kidneys, which they seem to favor as that part of your body which they want to eat first. All of which I did not like. With the vultures and the marabous coming down lower and lower and now with the excited corsair birds already attacking the dead, and with my head so painful and smelly with my blood, I had to admit yet again that I was not in good circumstances. Ayaaa. It was then that I did spy many horsemen coming from the West and from the direction of the Frank cannon and at the fastest gallop that they could possibly come, stirring up in their pace much dust. I more or less remained on the ground to await the passing of these Franks, and I lay as if in a swoon so as to deceive them that, I, Hadi, was alive. What other trick could I play? Ah-ya. I wiped the blood from my face and admitted that I was considerably exhausted with the want of any other trick. Then of a few moments, with my eyes watching them come closer, I did see that they were not Franks, but our own soldiers riding from the battle with the Christians. I did, with great pain to my body, stand up and then begin to wave to my comrades in arms. My intention being for them to halt and aid me in this, my latest desperate situation. The birds began to fly up and away before these horsemen could trample them to death. The air round and above became filled with fleeing vultures and marabous, while the corsair birds headed easterly in low flight over the ground. The rider leading them all, his cape flying and flapping in his own wind, did see me. But he did not rein in his horse to help Hadi; he passed by me and rode on. Then other horses came and all started leaping over all the bodies of men and horses on the ground one by one and some of the galloping horses even catching up their legs with the dead horses and the jallabas and falling headlong with the rider being thrown through the air forward into the torn and bloodied bodies of beasts and men that they were riding over. This happened many silly times, with my comrades screaming and the frightened horses whinnying. But the fallen tribesmen would wipe off the blood they had gathered in their headlong plunge, and quickly with no more ado rush to their now standing horses, then mount again, and—off they went while I still waved and shouted at them to aid me. The ones that did not fall headlong over bodies just kept riding by me, and, all round me; rushing by in dust and sand; not giving me, Hadi Abbabba Guwah, heed. I now picking up a more colorful rag, continued to wave to make them stop and save me. I did try to shout above the pounding of the hooves to them all speeding by me and covering my blood with sand dust and little pebbles. I did yell at them:

"I am Hadi Abbabba Guwah! It is me: Hadi! Hear me—I can speak all of your languages . . . I am not a "senti-ah-anta," in Temejegh: one pubic hair! Stop for Hadi! Stop for Haaadiii . . ."

But in the noise of the thundering hooves and in their own turmoil, they did not hear me, or they did not want to hear me. Where was my reward in this life? After all of my good efforts? All I know was that I was exhausted with this want of kindness. I, Hadi, was forsaken. It would be the death of Hadi. I lowered my rag. I wept. I looked round to find a good place to lay down and put my teeth in the dust. Then, one of the last of the horsemen who were rushing by, a blue-veiled Thitsh Tuareg, himself covered in blood, reined up his horse to my sad and panting breathless figure. His horse's body was covered in sweat like that of foam at the seashore, and more foam dripped from his horse's mouth, but this bloody trooper looked down at me with a face happy and satisfied with the day's work.

I implored: "Be merciful unto me, my comrade. Let me come onto your horse as Allah would wish it . . . so that I can ride and fight another day." Which was, of course, one of my lies. I did not want to "fight another day."

He said down at me, trying to spur his horse to a calmer state: "*You* my comrade? Your days of fighting are over, old warrior. I cannot strain my horse more with a man with one arm, one ear, and about to lose one leg. It would be well for all of us in this desert if you just lie down and be quiet and then die and then let the birds peck away at you."

With this sad decree to me, he slashed his horse with his whip and starting up continued on his way, leaving me, Hadi Abbabba Guwah, there alone on the plateau of Bal-al-Din with nothing but dead people and dead beasts.

So it was then that I did fall to the ground in my grief. Then I did have come into my head: Would the mastery I had over my mind fail? And what do you think my mind said to me? It said: "A further risk was to remain here." For it was a waste for Hadi to die. For I had not yet been in good circumstances. I did think it would be wise for me to go westerly; to go away from the birds that would come back. So, as I had fallen to the earth in my grief and confusion, so now I had to stand up. It took me about twenty clicks of my tongue to stand up. Then I fell down again. O foy-yo. How to stand up again with my wounded leg?

I put my forehead onto the plateau sand, and with my good leg pushed up and up and up until my good leg was rigid but trembling, and my backside up into the air pointed at the circling birds. But with only one arm to support me, I fell over sideways. Again, lying on my back in the sand, I could only think, did I have the prowess to make it westerly?

How to stand up? I could not crawl westerly . . . sand would enter my wounds . . .

So I, Hadi Abbabba Guwah, sat up there on the plain of Bal-al-Din and thought of Samonama's promises for me in this, the land of legend. What legend? Where was my Samonama? Where was my Little Hadi? Then I forced myself to stop thinking this; for I saw the marabous and the vultures were descending again to do their mischief.

I had to stand up if I was to live. To do this, you must understand, I had to use two legs, not just one of them. So I did stand up;

blood now flowing all the more because of my total effort on my wounded leg, to aid me in standing up. And then, with still the pain in my head, the hurt, I began to slowly limp my way onwards westerly. And I had to take much additional time to limp round and round and round the bodies in my efforts to flee away from the greedy birds. I did see that most all of the only partly living had no strength to get up off the earth in order to limp with me. Soon enough they would be food for the marabous and the vultures and the corsair birds. And most of these half-dead looked up and spied out and then listened to the birds in their again descent and the marabous excitedly made their "aik-aik-aik" noise as they got closer down to their meal and the half-dead knew their end and those that could scream screamed, and those that could not, wept. And those that could do neither prayed.

One of these unfortunates, a tribesman of the Chlur Berbers that I was at the time limping round, did grab at my ankles, then did put his hands together, showing me that he could not speak at all because of his wounds and so used gestures to beg me to stay over him a moment and with his hands he pointed to his Heft sword with its two sharp cutting edges and its long sharp point, and then, he pointed to his heart. With gestures, he showed me that I should plunge his sword into his heart and thus kill him instead of the storks and the vultures eating him alive piece by piece. It would be, he gestured, Allah's mercy unto him if I did this. I thought of a second of the birds ripping and tearing away at his body and so I did pick up his sword and then stand over him in Allah's mercy, and considered, if it was I, I should beg the same . . .

And I put the sword point onto his heart and he watched me and before wearily pushing it down he blessed me elaborately with his sign language. He imparted that I was a good Hadi, and that he and his family would remember me and pray for me all of their days.

I pushed the sword down quickly with a jerk deep into his heart. Blood burst up and all over me. Puh! Then I bent down and took up his dried goat-meat bag and also his dagger and also his large water bag and slung all slowly, in pain, mind you, over my shoulder. Then pulling out the sword—ugh! I did wipe it clean on the clothes that he did have remaining about his body, and put the sword over my shoulder also. Thus ended this fool's witless dreams of "Allah-il-Allah."

I could see up in the yellow sky that more birds had arrived and that many had now landed because the riders had passed, and they were already tearing off the clothes again and ripping at the flesh of the dead, and also of the half-dead and I think I remember I could hear hundreds of screams float across the plateau of Bal-al-Din.

I continued to limp as fastly as possible considering the pain in my knee and the hurt in my head and I limped round and round of those that lay on the sand and the half-dead called out to me and raised weakly their arms and if they could make a voice, begged me to give them Allah's mercy with the point of my sword into their hearts because they did not want the agony that would come from the beaks and jabbings and the claws of the marabous and the vultures, all of which were at them already.

As I passed them in my condition, I did the best that I could to kill those who begged me to kill them, yet, you must understand, only those in my path westerly. I could not, mind you, manage to go any way north or anywhere easterly to just kill people. This task would take days. Just westerly. And on and on over the plain and past the feeding birds I did endure my painful walk and dragging my bloody sword behind me. Yes, I did heed the summons of them that were near, and then without undue pain to myself, but yet with my head hurting, lift the Heft sword to the summons, then plunge the point down deep into their foolish hearts. My weariness was great. Then because of this, I had to cease this task of mercy killing. All I could best do is now wobble crookedly westerly tiredly, weakly, leaving those still shrieking out for mercy and intoning Allah-Allah; and begging for mercy . . . but again, English, I had to be and was merciful to only a few more of these wretched yet foolish people . . . so, I, Hadi Abbabba Guwah, did use my last strength Oi-yo to just put the point of the sword to their hearts and plunge. I remember, what did aid me in this was shrieking out "Samonamaaaa." And then I would shout: "Women have the brains of a camel!" And then I would plunge the swords into their hearts.

"Women have the brains of a camel!" Over and over as I pushed down the sword. But I knew, English, in my anger, I had to conserve my body so that I could get away . . . for the vultures and the marabous wanted Hadi's eyes and Hadi's kidneys. To change my anger I kept dwelling on "Could there be any improvement now?" Aoi-yo, Puh!

Then I did dwell on: "Who would be merciful to me, Hadi?" A poor weakly, tired Hadi who has nothing but good intentions? Of a sudden I shouted: "I can read!" Yet my leg limped me . . . I was all over blood, smelly, with sand over all over everything . . . my head hurt . . . then my heart asked again: "Where is my Samonama?"

Over and over westerly my heart betrayed me with this on this walk on Bal-al-Din.

Then my heart asked: "Where is Little Hadi? In the belly of a vulture? Yes. So are her brains . . . in a belly of some dumb bird . . ."

I tell you, English, I did weep these things . . . and I did look at with my tired eyes all those of the payment of "Allah-il-Allah" . . . yet after this the profit is vultures and marabous. Allah then the vultures. Are all lords of wastes? All El Baboons? "Where is my Samonama?" my heart did keep saying to me limping and dragging the sword behind me, going westerly, across the plain, of a second killing some tribesmen, but mostly, even when I was killing for mercy, thinking of my Samonama . . . then not to think of Samonama, I tried to think of other things: Could there be any improvement now? A man can only try all the time not to be witless. But if he talks too much with other men of a day it is likely he will become witless. That is, if he is not witless to begin with. It takes great, great care not to be witless.

And having these thoughts of life going through my head as I did ever limp on ever westerly, I did spy five-six-seven-eight young marabous glide in, flap their wings to halt their flying, then plop down on the earth behind me. Marabous of a white winged color, and on long legs with long redlike beaks and with their heads always bobbing back and forth. Then came and landed on this earth, stirring up the sand dust with their purple blue flapping wings, the young vultures, but clumsy vultures as vultures are clumsy, with necks that looked as if they had been broken then mended improperly. Sand was beginning to move across the plateau with the wind that came from the southerly-easterly . . .

You see, English, these young dumb birds did come for me now because most all of the other bodies of the concept of Allah-il-Allah on the plain of Bal-al-Din were now covered with the old and the strong vultures and storks who would not give the young a chance to eat or to interfere and thus partake of destroying a body.

Twenty or more of them now followed Hadi who was hastily limping alone across the plain and they remaining behind me at a distance and all the while flapping their wings to keep up with me and making their "aik-aik-aik" noises, then snapping loudly and clacking loudly their long beaks: "clack-clack-clack," which of course, all saying to me: "We want your eyes. And then after, your eyes, we want your kidneys!"

I did take my sword that I was dragging off the ground and put it on my shoulder and to turn and look and see and await their attack as I limped wobbily and on . . . this attack would be as planned as that of a troop of cavalry. Soon and all together these young dumb birds would rush at Hadi . . . perhaps three or four of the young marabous would flap their wide arms and take to the wing and then get to as high as my shoulder all the while coming directly to attack my eyes. The remaining birds on the ground that were following as I did look over my shoulder would then of a sudden race along the ground waving their wings wildly to gain ground speed; their necks out, their sharp beaks thrusting before them and all the time aiming for my kidneys.

It was wise, of course, that I now stop my limping, and turn to look at them in order to await this attack, as was best to do in this situation. Then these birds stopped also, yet began to flap their wings more quickly than before and this was to get themselves more excited and moreover they began their "chuck-chuck-chuck" to each other, which now meant they would charge.

Two instead of three or four ran along the ground then took to wing and gained the height of about my shoulder all the while coming for my eyes. Others started to flap and run across the sand coming for my kidneys.

I swung the sword at the proper moment and Hadi did well; for —puff and Wallah—of a sudden two headless dying storks lay flapping about sprouting blood on the sand. Actually, English, as I remember, one headless dumb bird and one dumb bird with only half a body left to him.

But do you know what, English? They heeded not this display by Hadi. No. These incessantly wicked dumb birds then all rushed at me at once. Then I did go into a frenzy during which I did spend some time killing these birds.

I remember feathers were all floating and twirling in the air and bodies laying about were shooting their blood over my own blood and I was becoming all completely red over my own black body. However, two of these dumb birds did arrive at my body and one dumb bird lunging plunged his beak into my side at where my hip was and forcing his beak into me as far as he could, which, mind you, was only to my bone, while the other's beak plunged into my kidneys. I did manage to slice the head off the one attacking my kidney, but in my terror and the growing madness of the other who had left off at my hip and now was attacking my kidney, I released my sword to the ground and used my hand to grab for his beak that was attacking my body. When I had his beak out of me I did grab for his throat. He was a strong and greedy and young and hungry vulture, English. And his strength and fight and flapping of wings did force me to fall to the earth and all with now his fast wiggling neck in my hands and his sharp knife beak trying all the while to hurt Hadi everywhere. With my bloodied feet I held his body distant, pulled to me his neck, and then with all of its soft, flabby, smelly, wriggling skin in my hands rushed it into my mouth and tightened my jaws and my teeth onto that greedy, dumb neck with all of the strength that I did have remaining in me. In his own fear of his own life his legs and nails attacked at my body and skin and his claws made more wounds. I did keep gnawing at his fighting neck to try to eat this tube into two separate pieces, which was difficult to do, but which I finally did succeed, at last, in doing. Wallah! Then in anger over this rumpus I did throw his head to the north and then push his terrible body to the south and away from me.

I was weary. But I knew that I had to stand up and continue westerly, for I did know the young marabous and the young vultures would come again, so I did accept the pain it took to get myself onto my legs, and discovered, although I had hitherto been limping, I now had to contend with leaning sideways and to the south because of the wound the marabou stork had done to my kidney.

So, English, to get away from this situation, and with hurt still in my head, my kidney almost food for the birds, I limped on and on, on my blood red legs westerly. . . . I remember I tried to talk to Allah; mind you, not "Allah-il-Allah," but Allah. Yes. I asked him to give me mercy. I repeated many times limping, leaning over sideways, "My Lord Allah, you cannot let Hadi die because of birds . . ." And then I remember saying over and over that Hadi was not senti-ah-anta, one pubic hair, but only full of good intentions . . . that Hadi just wanted to go westerly . . . trying to get away from birds . . . also, I could read.

And thus, reassuring myself with these remarks, and trying to smile up at the sky easterly and saying my remarks again and again,

I did have new strength to continue my weary way westerly, weakly, leaning to the south and limping.

But I say to you on this present day, English, and I swear it to you in the name of any God you can name to me, that I thought I would fall down to the sands and die altogether. . . . In my misery walking, I *even* agreed, that yes; Hadi is senti-ah-anta. And that, at last, that Hadi would die. No more Hadi. The sand would cover me with another wind . . . I stopped limping and fell onto the sand and lay with my knees up to my chin and holding onto that side of me where my kidney was attacked, and I wept. Hadi: eaten by birds . . . salt from my eyes did roll down my face and onto the earth and with a sobbing breath I did ball my one remaining fist and shake it at Allah to the east. I shouted with salt tears in my eyes and all of the voice I could command: "NEVER HAVE I HADI ABBABBA GUWAH BEEN IN GOOD CIRCUMSTANCES IN ALL OF MY LIFE! AND NOW THIS! EATEN BY BIRDS! THIS IS NOT A GOOD THING THAT YOU DO TO HADI; YOU MUST UN-DERSTAND!"

With my shrieking out, then Allah took note of me; there laying on the sand, or perhaps it was, English, your Christian God, or, his prophet: Jesus Christ. Some God heard me! Somewhere! Who? For I can tell you, English, I did feel better in my heart after uttering my pleas . . . and I felt a strength in my body that I did not have before . . . and I was of a sudden, untired.

Slowly, I did roll across the sand and pebbles, and then, with this, I did commence to stand onto my feet with new blood dripping, but thinking to myself, I wonder how long all this would take? But I had the strength. . . . Nevertheless, with this strength, I put my Heft sword onto my shoulder, cutting my neck in my clumsiness, and leaning south, thus tried to continue limping my way westerly, weakly.

By and by I heard more "clack-clack-clack" of the marabous and the "aik-aik-aik" of the vultures and I raised up my head and with my eyes I did spy a sky full of them; mostly in the air winging and yet some on the ground eating . . . those in the air slowly circling and then of a sudden sliding sideways down; and down, circling again . . . then sideways down . . . I was coming onto the battleground of the Christian Franks; whereon hundreds of them lay amid the soldiers of our own charge who, yes, had reached them and then did their slaughter only to die themselves. There was enough on the ground for the birds, so I did not think it was a risk to go through them. However, to be cautious, I made the fastest pace I could endure round and past the birds. Then I spied a thing truly most remarkable: I saw that on this earth, as I limped by, all of these dead Christian soldiers wore all of the same clothes. Every one of these pagans wore the same coat the color of blue. Each and every one. All wore sashes of the same blue color. All wore the same white pants and all had tied on the same gray leg wrappings round the lower portion of their legs. All of them seemed to have worn little round white hats with long white neckcloths attached at the end that fell down to their shoulders. . . . How silly that all and everyone should dress the same . . . I did think these Christian Franks deserved to be dead—all dressing the same. Puh! These infidels were indeed simpletons.

I passed round these Frank soldiers covered over with birds ripping and tearing away one by one. But even in my haste, I did spy a Frank laying on the ground in truly splendid red pants and only two birds on top of him. He also had a blue hat and he wore very shiny leather tall shoes; as I did call them, then, of course in my ignorance. I know now that they are called "boots." But more importantly, I did spy a rewolawa in his outstretched hand, or, what I now know to call, a revolver, as it is in your language. This revolver, and his red pants, I did think would be useful in this my latest journey through the dead. So I took my sword off my shoulder and limped to this Frank Red Pants, and killed the birds. In making this energy, I almost swooned. But in pulling hard the revolver from his hand, I did hear a flutter of large wings behind me, and, as I had dropped the sword to take up the revolver, I had to think only of the revolver and to use this that I was now pulling at with one remaining hand.

As I did tell you, English, I did learn to use this weapon while in the service of the Sultan of Kano, now far away in the south. Do you recall, English? So, I spied over my shoulder that more greedy dumb birds were behind me, and would now probably come onto me again. But what do you think? The hand would not let go of the revolver. Then to a great fright, Red Pants opened his eyes and looked at me. Aya-mammaaa—and I shrieked and shrieked again. Some birds flew away while the remaining backed away deciding not to charge me in their fright and all the time I was pulling at the revolver and shouting out "The birds! The birds!" and pulling at the revolver. I only had one arm—how could I point at the birds and pull at the revolver both at the same time—I ask you? So I had to let go of the revolver, and so as this dumb pagan Christian Frank stared up at me, I flapped my one arm to pretend I was a hungry bird and I said to him over and over: "Birds—birds—birds, you Christian simpleton!"

This idiot at last had understood my meaning, and he relaxed his hand grip on the revolver. I quickly stood up, turned, took the aim, and pulling back the little spur that is as you call the "hammer," squeezed the trigger. And the revolver exploded and—Wallah!—blew one bird's head off. Wallah! This made me feel jolly good. Truly jolly good. And so I took up my aim again at another dumb bird and pulled the little spur and—boom!—the bird exploded! Jolly good. What a revolver! Then boom at another and then at others: "Boom-boom-boom!" Then with feathers and heads lying all over the ground they started to take to wing. But I put more pellet bullets into the revolver and "boom-boom-boom!" Three more bodies together, and along with their hundreds of exploded fluttering feathers. They, these birds, fell to earth and made, each one by one, a sad plop, plop, plop noise onto the ground, except for the feathers, of course, English, which made no noise at all: just fell onto and covered the bodies of these roumis with white feathers.

And so, now I did begin taking the beautiful red pants off of this half-dead infidel, then I, Hadi, would get my legs into them, and thus I, Hadi, would continue westerly in these beautiful pants, the purpose of which was to hide some of the scars of my life.

As I did work to fight off the difficulty of undoing what you call his fly buttons, at which time I did start thinking of my Samonama, and which I did finally achieve; I thus began to pull this ridiculous garment from his body: down, down, down. But then, his pants would not come away free because of his tall black boots, which as I remember, I did want also. So, English, I began tugging with a panting breath, and trying to pull off one of his boots, all with one arm and leaning westerly, when I did hear the sound of, in the far distance, barking dogs. So I stopped myself at what I was laboring to do at this special moment, and did straighten up as best I could and then I did espy about twenty dogs coming toward me and all the while generally jumping up and over the Christian troopers scattered all over this desert plain of Bal-al-Din.

The dogs too also scared the remaining birds round me and they raised their wings in fright and pecking out the eyes of these foreign dead and all of them in a flurry took to flight and then almost covered over the light from the sun in their retreat easterly. These barking dogs, as I did now shade my eyes to see them, appeared still to be coming directly at me. O puh! O wallah, wallah, wallah! Wild dogs! Rushing to me, Hadi, who in all of my life had nothing but good intentions and thought of nothing but improvement. O Allah-Allah, where is your mercy? Would I with all of my excellent efforts ever live without fear of birds, blood, battles, and the beads and bangles of a Samonama?

Then I did espy behind the dogs, and following and running through the heat waves exactly in their path, perhaps seven or eight or nine of these infidel soldiers. Then I became confused. But I will always remember that they were all dressed in the same silly blue coats and all had white pants and all wore little white round hats as looked like cakes and with the neckcloths fluttering down and behind as they did run following the dogs and always coming toward me. They had in their hands these dreaded Christian long rifles, which had those sword knives attached at the end where the muzzle is, and carried them up close to their chests in what your English Army calls "the ready position." And so I let go of the boot of Red Pants and wiped all of the moisture from my face with my one hand.

Aoi-yo, would I be dead now? And join Samonama? Or would I swoon first and then be dead with their sword knives? Could I get out of this situation? I, Hadi, could not shoot all of the dogs with the revolver and then all of the roumis and still hope to live for greater things. So I thought to use Red Pants' revolver would be foolish. . . . I yet again knew I had to act and to pretend and to fake and to tell my lies. But with Red Pants' pants down round his knees and with one boot gone. . . . O Foy-yo.

Then in my panic, I resolved to pick up the revolver and shoot all of its pellets at these dogs. Then, of a sudden, I decided, Ah-ya, niwalla, no! There were too many dogs for the pellets in the revolver. Then I fretted: O my Samonama Silver Bell, perceive what you have done. O my mad woman. Look Samonama, look! At one particular moment, birds. Now dogs. Oh, it is enough to damn Allah. I breathed heavily. I wearied. I accepted. Now I would be eaten by dogs. Ah, puh!

As I did dwell on my plight, on this new fate, looking up at the yellow sky, thinking on my coming death due to hungry infidel dogs, they had all now, with much noise, arrived all round me; in a circle, all barking, some jumping up and down in place and also too some coming at me and snapping click-click their jaws at me, and when I did shriek, retreating away from me, and I all the while terribly afraid to discharge the revolver because naturally of the soldiers following at a run behind them. So I took to only waving my one arm at the dogs as the only action I could do, however, keeping safely the revolver in my hand in the event that at any moment they would attack to eat me.

These dogs I did see, while I did flay my arm at them, and shrieked out at them, were of all sizes and of all different colors and of all assorted kinds of fur, and of all various breeds. None of which I had ever seen before. Some had tails and some did not. One had only three legs; and then another, only one ear like Hadi. All had body scars of many battles. Yet all together, even with the scars of their lives, they continued to come for me, bump up and down and circle round me, bark and snap their jaws at me, who had more scars than they did. Then too making their terrible throatlike growls at Hadi.

The leader dog, a big dog, who was black and had no tail, would rush at me and jump at me for an attack at my throat. I did strike him with Red Pants' revolver and knock him down. But then, the other dogs small and large would come to attack, especially the brown little dog with only three legs. Then, as one dog bit deep into my leg and another at the stub of my arm, I did shout out: "By Allah, this life is not worth living!"

The dogs continued to charge and attack me and bite at all parts of my body and I did nearly weep yet I did fight in a fury. They tried to drag me down. I knew that when they would succeed in doing this deed, these dogs would kill me by tearing my throat out. During this fight with these beasts, English, I cursed my mother Teeta for her selfish womanly want in that she would give birth to a child that would forever live in a dreadful and horrible and idiotic and foolish world. A life of pain and strife and of every second of a day. And in which the only feeling in your mind and one does think of constantly is to endure, endure, endure. Then I screamed at the dogs attacking me: "For what reason? I have done nothing!" Then they had me down on the sand.

And I did shriek out to sand and the sky and to the dogs: "You stupid selfish mother woman, Teeta. You also had *only* the brains of a camel! And now, because you gave birth to me: dogs are going to eat me!"

I was striking out at the dogs with the revolver, kicking out my feets and trying to roll about incessantly, during which time I also shouted at the dogs: "Samonama had the brains of a camel! And all women have nothing but the brains of wearisome camels!"

And yet as I did fight the dogs, I understood that I was selfish. That I did want to bring little naked Hadi out of the belly of Samonama and into this selfish, horrible world. So I also was guilty of being as foolish as my mother Teeta, and then again as foolish as my Silver Bell, Samonama.

Then as one of the dogs did seize me by the neck, I remember thinking as I slammed over and over his head with the revolver, "Ah, it is stupid to live at all. Where is the profit?"

I then did hear yells, and all of the dogs suddenly left off attacking all of my body. I saw that the running roumis soldiers had arrived and as they continued to shout at the dogs to calm their tempers, so too did this party circle about me just as the dogs had done, but this time slowly, their rifle muzzles with those knives at the end pointing at Hadi. I released Red Pants' revolver to the sand. Now, in my new terror, I sat upright and did attempt to bid and gesture to them as much welcome as I could under these new circumstances. I smiled and waved my one arm at them and flapped at them the stump that was left of the other, imparting to them that I had nothing but good intentions. Then, not wishing to die in the sitting position, and trembling all over, I did get into a standing state. It was natural for me to lean westerly and breathe in great draughts of air and hold in my kidneys. But also too, I thought it wise to force myself to fill my face with glee and pant at them the words, "Ehwalla yes," and smile and then I thought perhaps it would be better that I should be sad and sob. I did not know. I was too confused. Would these pagans kill me? Or would they sell me to the Turks? O Wo-ye. So it was then that I decided not to be sad and sob but to rather fill my face full of innocent supplication, ehwalla yes, and further, to lean my head to the side, open my mouth, and look humble and stupid, all with my knees bent and leaning westerly. I did pretend to be dead already. I knew that I would not swoon. Perhaps Hadi would just die. But not because of birds and not because of dogs. I would have good fortune and die with a bullet pellet or perhaps by quick thrusts of those long knives at the end of their roumis rifles. I did lean sideways and did think of this; yet even in my panic, I could not but help to observe these invaders. I was unimpressed. Their silly same blue-back coats were torn and dirty. And some had much blood on them. Also too, blood on their torn white pants. Several of these Christians had little white sticks hanging out from the corners of their mouths, and these little white sticks were on fire and smoking.

There was a terrible aspect to the bodies of these pagan soldiers. They were tall but yet also very wide across in the chest and on top at their shoulders. They had short thick legs. And each one had the biggest feet I had ever seen on men before. They had wide and square faces that looked only of muscle and jutting bones, and, as some had a reddish color to their white skins, others had faces the color of copper. Their eyes were the cool color of the waters of Kroo Lagoon. But also eyes like those of falcons, piercing and mean. Their hair was straight and the color of sand.

Now, I did observe, their leader, a Christian soldier with a bent and crooked nose and no eyebrows and with that little white smoking stick hanging down at the corner of his mouth, began to walk toward me while the other soldiers continued to circle about me. I shouted out to them to allay any fears that they might have that I would hurt them, or harm them in any way, "I am Hadi Abbabba Guwah; the gentle, the kind, and of course, sirs, the ambitious."

They were not impressed. Closer and closer this leader soldier came to me. In all of my fright all I did then was to watch what he would do with his rifle pointing at me with that the knife at the end of the muzzle.

Then he stopped and looking down at me said, his speech harsh,

"Mein Liebling, lebst du noch? Eh? Hein? Lebst du noch?" And pushed his rifle muzzle toward me.

I made my noise: "Welcome to the plain of Bal-al-Din, O Mightly Excellency. Welcome!"

His noise was: "Eh?"

"Welcome to—"

"Lebst du noch?" he interrupted.

Wo-ye. What is "Lebst du noch?"

Then he grabbed my hair and pulled me up to a standing position. Then he slammed his rifle against my chest forcing me back and back and then further back all the while kicking me and then he shrieked at me, with the dogs again barking:

"Das is keine gute einstellung." And he said this silly thing over and over with his little white stick going up and down between his thin, stupid lips.

I did not understand. He should perceive that I did not understand. I did grab at his rifle and did breathe heavily and sob out in Arabic and with my head leaning westerly, that I was Hadi Abbabba Guwah, and that I had only good intentions. Then I did commence to speak to him in each of the trade languages, in Fulde, in Marghi, Juku, Popo, Batta, Hausa, Temejegh, Fullani, M'bum, and even in Mandingo, that please do not be unkind to me. That I am not a rogue; just a slave, a poor slave—a water carrier recruited for the battle of Bal-al-Din!

But this dirty simpleton did keep saying to me: "Lebst du noch?"

In this confusion and fear, the latest, I could only think: "How could I frame any lies if this barbarian foreigner could not understand me? Any prowess I could have used was valueless!"

Again and again he did kick me and the dogs did keep barking and this beast did continually thrust his rifle into my chest and then he started to make the decree, or whatever, "Noch immer nich tot?"

What, English, to me, was, "Noch immer nicht tot?" I ask you?

This madman pushed me until I fell over backwards due to a dead body of one of these blue-backs that was on the ground. Then he was in anger shrieking out to me as he looked down at me: "Ja, noch immer nich tot, hein, ihr scheiber? Eh-eh-eh?"

O Lord Allah. Mercy. Spare Hadi. I do now recall praying. Then I did think perhaps I will just get a punishment. . . . Then he pointed his sword that was attached to the end of his rifle at me, and his speech did become at that moment, a bellow to me:

"Liebst du mich, du schwein?"

What were these commands? Why punish Hadi? What did I do? I began, because of my terror, and because it was wise, to begin to weep and wail all over again, but even louder, and I said to him in Arabic, with all of my false tears dropping down my face: "I would like to see in you something more like dignity, you bug, you monkey, you unbelieving white infidel; you stupid Christian first-class one pubic hair!" At this, the dogs began to howl out and then go berserk.

Of a sudden this ignorant pagan blue-back reversed his rifle quickly to the butt end and raised it above his head, a gesture that bespoke that he was going to knock out my brains. This was finally the end of my life, here on the plain of Bal-al-Din. And what do you think English? I thought of my Samonama. I thought of the days that before the sun was up, her body was the coolest breeze, even though the morning wind was blowing and promising nothing but a day of heat and that I was walking with her side by side in some formal garden, which was freshening to the both of us before the day grew old. O lovely restless eyes of my Samonama that spoke in her own language despite that stupid tongue.

And so, English, with me thinking this was the end of my life, what do you think really happened? The red pants on the ground with his red pants half off and one boot gone was now sitting up and while in a jerking manner he was now pulling up his pants and he was saying to the "du schwein" trooper in a voice that was weakly and choking:

"Allez vous! Allez vous, s'il vous plait . . . garde-a-vous . . . garde-a-vous, mon enfant. Regardez: n'importe mon enfant, eh bien? Ah bien."

This invader in this haste with his rifle raised up high to knock away my head, of a sudden turned to look at Red Pants. Then slowly, still looking at Red Pants, he saw a sign made by this Red Pants with his hand to this "du schwein" soldier, that he, "du schwein," should lower his rifle and not knock out my brains, which he did do, thus saving me, Hadi, for greater things. Of course, English, if Allah, the All Merciful, would will it.

Then this rascal conqueror "du schwein" soldier looked down at me, took his rifle in one hand, and with the other took his little white smoking stick from his silly thin mouth and threw it away onto the sand. Then he bent over me, and cursing at me, which entailed his spraying a kind of brown spittle all over my naked body and which seemed that this was all his mouth contained, this Christian shouted:

"Du; achtung—achtung! Auf-auf-auf, du schwein—auf!"

He grabbed my only one arm and pulled me easily onto my feet as if I were weightless. Then with more shouting from this soldier leader, four of the other invaders, one by one, quickly picked up Red Pants by his shoulders and then also by his legs, and began to carry him westerly, while "du schwein" at this time did grab me by my neck and pulling me close to his messed-up face said: "Marche! Eh —marche!"

It was then that, when he was close up to me and breathing up

174

my nose, I discovered that he had the breath of a camel. Then he further abused me by again pushing me with his rifle indicating that I should follow the soldiers carrying Red Pants and all the while shrieking out: "Marche-marche-marche!" This soldier was a moron.

I thought at this time that it was their fashion to behave in this manner. More importantly however, during this silly "Marche-marche!" while all of the time I was making the sound of Xhosa, which is by the way of a clicking of the tongue at the bottom of the mouth, I dwelled on: Would I get out of this circumstance scatheless?

Then too, I must tell you, that when he was very close up to me while pushing me before him with his rifle, I could not and I did not dwell all that much on: "Would I get off scatheless?" Because, English, besides "du schwein" having thick, bad breath, he was also very smelly. It was not as of an Arab smelly. I did think that, at this first time, that perhaps it was a roumis smelly. Or that perhaps it was a Christian smelly? It was not a camel smelly. Nor, was it like that of a goat. It was just a new smelly smelly, and the like of which, I Hadi, had never before smelled in my life. Then I thought, maybe it was just a "lebst du noch, hein" smelly. Or a "du scheiber" smelly?

I was wrong about all that I had dwelled on of this moment. Do you know what this smelly was, English?

It was caused by a liquid these Christian soldiers did spill about their necks and down all over their blue coats as they did drink it. Underneath their blue coats, the white collar button tunics that they did wear would be stained with this liquid all down the front. So, too, that part of their naked body called the chest, when, of course, I did see them naked.

This liquid was called "Madame La Pinard." It was dark red in color, as with blood, and thickly and stickly, like that almost of the honey that comes from the bee, but which most of the time these soldiers did mix with water, but not always.

"Madame La Pinard" I did discover was made only for the soldiers of this army, and was made from small berries but are "grapes," and which I did discover only grew in the lands across the Middle Sea. And where the "Madame La Pinard grape" was let to ripen on the tree to where it was almost rotting and then collected along with their bees and bugs and put into large old tubs whole with the seeds still in the berries and the bees and the bugs still alive. The grapes were then mashed by feets and then dumped into another tub and then onto this mess was poured in a liquid called "cognac." Then it was carried away and buried in wet earth by the farmers who made it and who also always kept the ground wet.

Soon enough, these tubs were sent across the Middle Sea to these infidel Christian soldiers, who did then put this "honey" into smaller wooden casks and then did pack them into wagons so as to carry these casks of "honey" about with them wherever they went. When the Christians did drink this "Madame La Pinard" mixed with water as I did say, some would become wobbly and fall to the ground and just sit giggling. Then some would become sleepy and just lay out on the sand. Then some too would simply become happy and smile and desire to dance about the sand with their other roumis. If it was taken without water, most became harridans and shrieked out their fears and also too their nightmares, while others became and acted as completely afflicted as madmen.

And so, with this smelly "pinard" Christian behind me, I did limp and lean sideways as I was pushed along over the hot sand of this dirty battlefield and all of the while stepping over their sightless dead amid the barking and wounded dogs round me and who were constantly about my feets and legs trying to trip me up. And at every click of the tongue, I held my kidneys in to prevent them from oozing out.

Then it came that time that I could see that I, Hadi Abbabba Guwah, was coming on to a column of these white dumb beasts who were forever saying "Lebst du noch," and who were, I did now see, at a halt and sitting tiredly about with all of their belongings lying on the ground and with their white sticks in their mouths and most all drinking "Madame La Pinard" from their little tin bottles.

There were perhaps two hundred filthy-looking soldiers. And, of course, every one in exactly the same silly, smelly clothes of blue and white. Very dull, English, very dull.

"Noch immer nicht tot" again pushed and pushed me but at this moment did force me along the length of this column, till I was of a sudden grabbed by the throat by him and pulled to a stop before another roumis in red pants and black boots.

"Noch immer" did shriek out, striking me with his rifle and in much anger: "Achtung! Achtung! Du Schweine!"

Then this warrior in red and black did say again these words: "Regardez vous, monsieur, s'il vous plaît." And then he said something to me which was a question, but which of course, you must understand, English, which I, Hadi Abbabba Guwah, did not at all understand. I am not a moron, as you know. But I simply did not understand this yet again language of "Regardez vous, monsieur, s'il vous plait." What was this rubbish?

And instead of trying to kiss his hand in an attempt to win his favor, I did try to make him feel as a moron as he did make me feel a moron. So I did say something to him in Arabic and then in anger and with my arm thrown out and with the stump of my other arm flaying but in no wind, I did say to him words in every language of the trade tribes. Yet again I did speak to him in Marghi, Fulde, Juku, Popo, Batta, Hausa, Temejegh, Fullani, M'bum, and Mandingo.

And what do you think, English? This Christian baboon did not understand any of the languages I did speak and only did reply to me with: "Mon Dieu, Mon Dieu . . ."

However, I did think his Frank sounds as he did continue to speak to me were now becoming pleasing to my one ear. Not as with the sounds of the language of "Noch immer nicht" which came out of a bad and afflicted throat. But Red Pants' language was more of a speech as if it was coming out through his nose. Nose language. But nevertheless, how was I to understand his drivel? And all the while leaning sideways and holding on to my kidneys from oozing out?

This blue-back in red pants said to me, "Excusez-moi, monsieur," then shrieked out something toward his soldiers along down the column and finished all his words with "Vite-Vite-Vite!" and all through his nose, and his words were repeated—Ayammaa—by each man all down this ragged dirty-looking column. Then eventually I saw riding toward me on a Mehari camel, not a yellow-faced Arab and not a light brown Berber, but a black man; who almost looked purple; who had a beard, and who wore a flowing loose white robe as what we call a "jibber," which was a kind of loose taub sewn all round and up with black patches and reaches down to the ankles, all of which flapped in the wind as he rode. On and wrapped about his head he wore the longest white turban I ever did see. A Frank rifle was slung across his back and bobbled up and down as he rode toward me through the heat. He had but only two desert daggers pushed into a long, wide blue sash that was wrapped round his waist and jibber, and in it as well was thrust a scimitar also. Two leather pouches that contained his Frank rifle pellets were worn crisscross over each of his shoulders. To this sight coming toward us, Red Pants bespoke: "Voilà—voilà!"

This purple-looking black man reined up, then expertly brought his camel to the kneel with his stick. Then the Red Pants said something to him through his nose in this nice-sounding nose language. To this the purple-black man touched his hand to his forehead and said:

"Oui. Eh bien, Monsieur Le Major."

Fo-yo. He spoke their language . . . Le Major? So, these red pants are officers.

This blue-black man then took the rifle off his back and approached me. He was very tall and also young and of a stern face. When he had stopped before me he put his hand on one of his daggers. However, he did not look a moron nor did he look unjust. So I did try in Arabic: "My name is Hadi Abbabba Guwah. I am from Kroo Lagoon in a country called Popo, which is a land far to the South, which I know you have never seen, so I do not expect—"

He interrupted me in Arabic and quickly: "My name is Dres Ali Mohammed. I am from the Sudan; a land far to the East. From a small village that is on the river Nile. I am employed by this Frank army as a scout and as a guide. They pay me in many good Frank louis. Hence my loyalty is to them. So I say to you, 'Bonjour!' Do you understand, mon cher?"

"No," I replied. Then I thought: This answer was folly, and I quickly realized it. So then I said, "Yes, bonjour mon cher."

Although he had a strange accent to his speech, it was nevertheless Arabic. So I did think: "Ahh, now I could speak Arabic to him and frame all of my lies so that they would soften his heart toward me, and then that he would perhaps be gentle with me and then also even be kind to me. So I shouted out:

"Oh, the Sudan! Aya! All have heard of this great land of the Sudan! Aya! On the Nile, O yes. O master; that majestic river. O to be born on the Nile, to—"

He whacked me on my head with the blade of his dagger: "I am not your master," he said quietly.

My words were: "It is the ritual address for a slave. I am only a poor slave sold to the army of El Kabir and to be only a spear carrier on the plain of Bal-al-Din."

He squatted before me pulling up his jibber and put his rifle across his knees. But in his hand he held his dagger, and pointed it to me. "Oh yes, Hadi Abbabba, I can see by the scars on your body and the fetter marks round your ankles and those also round your neck and then too the whip cuts about your back and arm that you have been a slave. I also, Hadi Abbabba, have been a slave, once. But I also can see that you have been a soldier, and if I am not mistaken, probably a mercenary soldier and also probably a bandit and caravan robber, and for a long time also. Your body all over is a history year by year of battles, caravan raids, ambushes, and general mayhem. Undoubtedly you have killed many men or you could never have survived."

Then he tapped me quickly on the head again with his dagger blade: "You are also undoubtedly a sneak thief of the night, a liar, and a complete rascal."

I thought in my head, "Ahhh Puh! Puh! Puh!" However, my speech to this young vulture was: "Ahhh no, Dres Ali Mohammed of the Sudan on the Nile, I was also just a poor water carrier in this battle that was on the plateau of Bal-al-Din. I did not kill any blue-back. I just rode beside my Samonama, only to watch her die . . . I—"

He raised the dagger that was in his hand to silence me, and I thought it wise to stop and look at him.

He said, "Do not give me your self-pity, you goat."

"Goat?"

"I said goat," said this Dres Ali Mohammed. "And further you are a thief, a liar, a rascal, and, nevertheless, a goat."

I replied calmly and in a very quiet voice to this vulture, all the while slowly pushing away his dagger: "It is not wise nor has it ever been, to be unkind to Hadi. No, niwallah no. Indeed Dres Ali Mohammed, it is quite foolish. Others have had to learn this truth, sadly. And of course, my fine peacock of a friend, they are now all unfortunately dead, so that they cannot tell you of what I say."

He did look at me quietly for many clicks of the tongue. Then he said calmly, "Yes, old man, I believe you."

"Old man!" I shrieked out.

"All right. Then an old snake."

Then he lost his humor and slapped me hard on my head with the blade of his dagger and shouted at me, leaning toward me: "You have been spared death, you one-eared, one-armed old goat, and only because you shot the vermin birds from away from Le Capitaine so they think, these roumis. Thus they spared your miserable life. Because now Le Major is grateful to you and Le Capitaine is grateful to you. And so, now, I have been instructed to look after you. But

I tell you true, you are a burden to me. I do not look after anyone.
Do you understand? Make one mistake on me, who will be watching
you all of the time, and I will use the edge of this dagger and I will
cut your throat. Do you understand old man goat?" Then he quickly
turned and said something to an invader soldier in this language of
the nose, and of a sudden this roumis blue-back took me up by my
one arm. He proceeded to pull me along down the column and past
all the staring infidel warriors and to its very end, at which were five
covered-over wagons, drawn by four "Missouri" mules each.

I was pushed past these to the very last covered wagon. At the
rear end of this, and on the ground sitting and resting, were some
of the conqueror wounded. Most every one of these was hurt badly,
and mostly naked and with their wounds of the head and chest and
shoulders wrapped about with white linen and each man surrounded
by their dogs and by fogs of flies. All of these men rested near, and
at intervals, beside eight long ropes that were on the ground and all
of which were of different lengths, and each of which was attached
to the wagon at the axle. I was taken to one of these ropes, and
pushed to sit down beside it. From this position on the sand, I could
see inside this last covered wagon and through the clouds of thousands of flies, that also many other blue-back invaders were in there,
all wrapped in white linen and who I did now understand were shot
to pieces so badly on the plain of Bal-al-Din that they could not walk.
All these invaders were sitting and lying tightly together, some sleeping, some weakly drinking their "Madame La Pinard" out of long
green bottles; one soldier was also then singing loudly and sadly.

It was then that a heavy, healthy-looking soldier moron appeared walking from whatever out of the wagons . . . carrying linen
and two large leather bags. He was absolutely coming to Hadi. Then
he did stop over me, and look down at me, and then he also said
words to me which I again did not understand, like "Come sta?"
Then "Sta bene?" He gestured for me to stand up. In a fright of this
new roumis, I did so. He looked at my kidneys and at my leg, nodded
to himself, and bespoke: "Malto bene, ah si."

He did take from one bag one hand full of a paste looking like
that of maize before baking, which he kneaded into a ball. He did
drop this into the other leather bag and proceeded to shake and toss
it about in the bag and also to put his hand into the bag and seemingly squeeze the ball, and with much difficulty, as I did see by the
expression on his face. Then he brought forth the ball from the bag

and it was all covered with assorted tiny green leaves. This he kneaded and slapped between his hands shaping it into a round disk, then of a sudden said, " 'Scusi," and slapped it onto my kidneys and then of a second he was wrapping me round with the linen. In six clicks of the tongue I was shrieking out in pain while this blue-back was shouting " 'Scusi-'Scusi-'Scusi" and I was trying to wrest the linen from my kidneys. At this action he grabbed my shoulder with his strong arms and then did hit me in the face which was followed by this man pointing one finger up under my nose and shouting into my face, "No-no-no!" His eyes did tell me that he did have good intentions. And it came into my dumb head that this blue-back was like me, Hadi, who had once been the doctor to many frightened camels. This "doctor" invader repeated the same procedure with the same paste to my wounded leg.

Shortly, with tears dripping down from my eyes and sobbing from the pain at this linen and this paste which was now wrapped about my kidneys and about my leg, I leaning sideways all the more because of it, I did hear that a harsh command was being related all down the column, the words of which, of course, I did not understand. The dogs all barked and each of them began to tiredly get onto their legs. These resting wounded invader morons sitting about me slowly stood up also, all looking like eternal death. The column far ahead began to me to move. The blue-back "doctor" said "Ciao." Then: "Arrivederci," and added quickly, "mon enfant monsieur" and left me to return to one of the wagons.

Lastly of course, the wagons began to move. Then each of these wounded infidel white people, each and every one, did pick up and then proceed to tightly hold on to a part of his rope. I did the same thing to my piece of rope and thus the wagon did begin to pull us all along behind it, helping us to go northerly in the pain of our wounds.

And so, I continued this weary life. And to accept yet once again that I still did live with only fear of my life. I did try to force myself not to feel my pain as I was pulled along behind the last wagon, and only to dwell upon the thought, how could I make myself worthy to stay alive, now that I was with these barbarian roumis. My success would depend upon me every second of a second trying to walk in a more upright manner behind the wagon full of these wounded soldiers and their fogs of flies. And it was also the time I accepted that I had to learn, even in my day of a day pain, the terrible blue-back beetles' fashion of marching up and down and over the soft shifting dunes, a march step which is used only by them, and additionally, it is a most difficult way to move that I have ever experienced in my life. Their own peculiar gait, taught also to the "Missouri" wagon mules, is a slow, long stride; a slow one-two, one-two, one-two. It is agony. I asked in my head again and again, "Where are the camels? The horses? Even burros?" Did these simpleton blue-back invaders walk everywhere? O Allah, Allah, in your everlasting mercy, be kind to Hadi. At least deliver unto me a goat!

It was terrible for me to endure, English. I had to grasp and to hold on to a rope that was mostly oily and I had to continually all of the day to throw my good leg in a circle forward then use my wounded leg to keep me on in a standing, hopping walking position; all to keep up with this witless one-two, one-two pace of these people. But of a day I would bespeak to myself over and over to lift my spirits: "This is not yet the end of Hadi," and to keep my head up further, I would continually chant to myself again the old song of so long ago:

> Ayammaa, I am a stranger
> Stranger!
> I am a stranger!
> I do not know why I've come here
> And I don't know where
> I'm going tooo.
> Ayamma!

Every day of those first days thirst did swell my tongue because water was not plentiful. I would be short of breath, and then too, coughing all of the time between the singing and the talking to myself because of the sand dust caused by the mules as well as the moving wagons. But I could only hang on to the rope. Lean now to the west and limp along. Hadi at the end of his breath and strength, listening to the cursings and the lamentations of the wounded in the wagon filled with flies and also their moans and the whinings of the dogs, and also beside me the groans and the swearings of the many blue-back foreigner soldiers that were hanging on to the ropes as I, Hadi, was doing. And none of these cursings, lamentations, and complainings did I understand. It was vexing to me to spend my time in ignorance! So at the rest periods, where we fell to the sand and we tried to rid ourselves of our exhaustion, I nevertheless did try to begin to force these stupids to talk to me so that I would at least learn in a more leisurely manner the precise sounds of what they did say, which would further aid me in understanding these conquerors from across the Middle Sea. Mostly I discovered that these soldiers of the ropes were from a tribe by the name of the Germani. Then in numbers and language next were the Frank tribesmen. Then too came those of the Italani tribe.

Of course, English, I did not have my knee desk or my pens or a calabash of ink or my parchments, instead, as we were everytime sitting down resting, legs crossed, some of these stupids did write on the sand for me with their fingers and in their strange forms using what they and you call "Roman letters," which I did not know of. Yet I would have to know of these "Roman letters" in time. But as quickly as possible I did try to learn and to understand. I did not mind that they laughed and jeered at my own Arabic writing with my finger in the sand and which they did sneer at and all called "fish-worm writing."

Then too, English, it was also difficult for me in another manner. Mostly, these blue-back foot soldiers could not, as with the Sultan Sadi Radi Hisham of Zinder, not write for me in the sand at the many rest periods. They did not know either how to make the letters of this "Roman alphabet" or how to put them together to form words. They could not read. Again, sadly, these ignorants were mostly from the Germani tribe, as was I did discover the beast who pushed me from the plain of Bal-al-Din and who was forever repeating "Nicht ist tot" and was always clicking his boots together and shrieking out "Jawohl!" and always addressing me as "Mein Lieber," or was it if I can remember, "Mein Liebschen"? I do not recall. I have now so many languages in my head, you must understand, English.

Also too, many of the Frank tribesmen could not read. But not those who wore the red pants who were all of the Frank tribes, and who never used the language of "Nicht ist tot." But then, the red pants could only speak this Frank tongue; their own language and to my surprise never any other. All of the Italani tribesmen, however, did not only speak and write their own language, but also the tongue called Latino, and yet again, English, they could speak and write well the tongues of these Franks, and these the Germani, and those called the Spanaro. Some also "Slav."

By and by with the many changes of the paste and the linen

round my kidneys and of my hurting leg which I did endure in agony, I did find I could walk "one-two, one-two" across the soft sands in a more upright manner. Niwalla yes. Hadi succeeds. I was in better circumstances.

It was then that I, Hadi, was told by this always angry Italani doctor tribesman who had treated me with his paste and linen, day by day, that I was to employ myself by aiding him with all of the wounded in not only the one wagon but the other wagon and also those who grasped on the ropes. I took care to be jolly about this labor, lest I fall into bad favor with this "doctor" and be cast out.

So I too did learn day by day to carry about the two leather bags and the linen and to mix the paste which was mostly made of what you call sorghum and gelatin. Then make the ball, then squeeze into it the tiny green leaves which I discovered were a variety of herbs that had come back to this land from across the Middle Sea. These herbs were a mixture of mainly what we used to call "the grains of Paradise" when I was a young boy. It comes from the aframomum plant. You call it white pepper. Added to this white pepper, this Italani tribesman did try to show me how to mix in with the pepper the proper mixture of what you call cardamom, then too coriander, also sage, nutmeg, cloves, garlic, camphor, Arnica and cinnamon, the oil of which was used by this Italani for mouth diseases.

Then I of a day made, by flapping it between my hand, as he did show me, the so-named "pattie" of all these herbs and to whatever size according to the wound. I either climbed into one or the other of the two wounded wagons fighting away the fogs of flies, and took off the old linen, as he looked at the wound, then on his angry instructions put on the new paste and enwrapped the soldier with the new linen, or also, during these rest periods, I did have to go back to attend to and do the same to the wounded hanging on to the ropes of the last wagon.

Also a necessary task was to distribute "Madame La Pinard" to the wounded in both of the wagons, and which was done about three times a day which I did do by me using a funnel and filling their empty tin bottles with "Madame La Pinard" from the casks that were in the cook wagons. Then another duty, for Hadi, was to return to the wounded wagons, climb up into the fog of flies, and to give to these mangled and tortured invaders a narcotic called hashish, which had been wrapped in these little white paper tubes and which they did light up with so-you-call matches. This I was led to believe, besides drinking "Madame La Pinard," was to kill their pain of their wounds, and also the thoughts of still being alive in this wretched desert waste.

Again and again these roumis soldiers did offer me to puff on their paper tubes of hashish because they took pity on my one arm and my one ear. I did a puff once. It was like chewing betel nut along with chewing sand. Or should I say, swallowing sand. Who wants to do that? Phew.

Yet I did learn day by day and slowly some words of each of the languages of these wounded, knowing all the time that I must continually fill my head with more and more of these words. Besides, it vexed me now not to know of what they spoke of. What they did mean when they laughed and said to me: "Bonjour, mon enfant extraordinaire pour le mal."

Then too, I did learn during this period of my life, how better to mix the herbs and also how better to pack the paste with them so to help the wounded more efficiently. I was to learn that this was to add more clove powder, a little more coriander, nutmeg, and cinnamon and leave off with the cardamom, sage, garlic, and camphor. These changes did work, and as I, Hadi Abbabba Guwah, had been a success in the doctoring of my camels for the Tebu of Gandoga, I was becoming a success with these wounded invader morons.

Also, you must understand, English, that I did all of this labor while living with my painful genii of Samonama, who did haunt me all of the time. As you say, I had this problem, which was that I had been unable at this period of my life to make myself think of her less. And thinking of her made me suffer. Then often I would ask myself: "Why are you not tired and exhausted of thinking of her? Why do you not surrender your thoughts of her?" Then, at other times, mostly at evenglow, I would dwell in anger on the thought that constantly the demon of Samonama inhabited me, and to fight this demon of her, my head would think of what a moron she was. This all through the day. Yet always came the thought to intrude: "My greatest joy I owe to her and then also my greatest sorrows. The best mixed with most bitter."

But many duties and the pain remaining in my body from my wounds helped me not to think of my Samonama. Mostly it was my duty of burying in the desert the wounded that had died despite my treatment of cloves, coriander, nutmeg, and cinnamon. Then always washing the linen free of the blood which I had to take from the bodies of the blue-backs that had died.

Also that which helped me take my thoughts away from my Silver Bell Samonama was closely watching those blue-backs who were surely to die, if not this day, then on the morrow. From one of these invaders, who was of the Nederlandi tribe, who was of the name Hans David Bowerman, and came from the city of Utrecht which belonged in the land of Holland across the Middle Sea, and who was to positively die, I did learn the name of this doctor and this master of these five wagons. This barbarian's name was Monsieur Anatolini Bagolini, and that he was once a teacher of the language Latino in a religious school for young girls in the City of La Roma. But that he had laid on too many of them and for too long a time, which the mothers and fathers of these girls eventually did not like. So he had to flee. Now his occupation was to dwell here as an invader of these wastes. This doctor Anatolini Bagolini was also the cook. So, after burying a soldier who did die, I had to rush to and work the cook wagon. This did mean that at each rest period I had to fill the tin water bottles of the soldiers, that is, if there was water. And if there was truly water about, take the large leather water bags, fill these up, then return to the cook wagon and pour the water from the leather bags into the wood casks, or into the buckets that I did use to wash clean the bloody linen. Also to give water to the wagon's Missouri mules and then back to burying a dead invader or to aid Monsieur Anatolini Bagolini cut off a leg or an arm of a roumis with a big square knife and a saw, because the limb had with time swollen and smelled foul, looked putrid green, and was altogether diseased.

Mostly these soldiers wanted the severed limb given to their beloved dogs to eat. "Why waste meat?" they did say. Then it was near to the time that Hans David Bowerman, the Nederlandi tribesman from the town of Utrecht in the land of Holland across the Middle Sea, was coming close to death. This tribesman of blue eyes and the hair the color of sand did not want to be buried at all. His thought was that his entire body would be of more use to his dogs and for them to eat all of him.

He said, "I cannot give this remaining wretched body to science or to the Royal Medical College of Amsterdam, so that the young students can cut up my body in order to learn, which I once promised

I would do. This is because I myself was once a student at the Royal Medical College of Amsterdam. And mostly back then, we had no bodies to cut up and with which to learn from. Now, I cannot even give them mine. So why bury me in the sand, only to be scratched up and eaten by the foxes when the column marches on, which you Anatolini, or you Hadi, know the foxes will surely do as they always do. So use my body in the most practical way. Cut me up in pieces and feed my body to my dogs, who have served me so well."

Then he took into his hand the hand of Anatolini Bagolini, doctor and cook, and said in the language of the Germani tribe, "Mein Lieber, ach, da leben is so saumabig," which means in your language, English, "Ah, life—it is so rotten." Then he said he did not want to prolong his death. And he said, "Signore bellissima, per favore, per favore, s'il vous plait . . ." And then he took his dagger and did force it into the hand of Anatolini Bagolini and said, "You know the old proverb, my comrade: 'Leben ist lebensgefahrlich,' which in your tongue is 'Living is always dangerous for your life.'

"Please my friends," he said weeping, "kill me now and feed me to my dogs. Bitte-bitte-bitte . . ."

But Anatolini Bagolini was also now weeping, and of a sudden thrust the blade into my hand. Of a sudden I pressed the dagger deep into Hans David Bowerman's heart and twisted it and he did expire. At the evenglow rest period, we took his body from the last wounded wagon and placed it on the ground. Then with this big square knife, Anatolini Bagolini ordered me to chop away and sever the limbs; and with a long, thin knife from the cook wagon he instructed me to cut out his stomach, liver, kidneys, and heart. Then he did point, Anatolini Bagolini, that I should go a distance away, dragging Hans Bowerman's parts in a blanket. Then Anatolini Bagolini did put his fingers to his mouth and make a whistle noise. Then the dogs did come. And I did feed Hans David Bowerman to his dogs.

There were too those invaders that killed themselves by either their own hand or by that of a comrade. These men Anatolini Bagolini would cut up himself, never giving me the task of doing this work, and all of the time shouting over and over as he did his chopping and severing, "Tu se baats—tu se baats!" or else: "No capito—no capito!" Or, and, "Tu se baats no capito!"

Then I would feed the dogs.

And also I did learn what you Europeans call 3 A.M. in the morning, because this was the usual time for the blue-backs to begin their one-two, one-two march with their dogs running along the flanks, since an early start permitted the column to reach the day's destination by noon, including rest periods, and so to avoid much of the terrible heat. And always, we had to walk thirty miles to the day. However, there were periods these conquerors called the "Pas de Route," which was an order given to these non-horse soldiers whereby they could, for two thousand clicks of the tongue, go slower and break their step of one-two, one-two, then adjust the burdens upon their backs in any way they did like, and just, as you say, walk, walk, walk. Allah-il-Allah, how they could walk, if only three miles by the hour in the "Pas de Route." Extraordinaire! Ah, OUI, Monsieur Anglais. Le desert disappeared away behind easily, as they all in a jerky manner, un-smoothly marched; steadily, never stopping. This one-two, one-two pace was equivalent to your four English miles by the hour.

And so with me of a day doing my duties and thinking wearisomely of my true torment, my Samonama, with a quiet saddened heart, the march did continue northerly, one-two, one-two with the inevitable interruption of "Pas de Route." However, these bluebacks did poorly marching over the sand and all in the heat of the sun. Why they did bother to dwell and suffer in this terrible land just to collect taxes even, I, Hadi the Humble, could not understand. But only at this particular time, Anglais. Soon it would be explained to me in a sorrier fashion.

But to continue, these forces of the desert did eat poorly, as I did also, the slave Hadi Abbabba Guwah. Most of these barbarians and truly myself had only to eat continually a cupped hand of dried goat meat to sustain our efforts on this march, which I and Signore Anatolini Bagolini did chop up into tiny pieces on the sand if we had a rest period and fighting off the dogs all of this time of labor. Then we had to lick off the sand, clinging to this ration, spit it away, and then put the hard goat meat into smelly, fly-covered buckets. I did carry these buckets up and down the column. But they were too tired to eat at the rest period. It was on the march they did eat this carrion, chewing it slowly almost to the rhythm of their march, then swallowing and then followed by Madame La Pinard. And also true, slowly chewing one hand-cup of dried-up vegetables.

And further northerly, where the nights had no mists, it nevertheless became even colder in this desert where the days were horribly hot. So I did gather that this was the reason why these invaders were issued their heavy service overcoats. At night these ragged bluecoats were all tightly buttoned up to fight off the chill. But even then, these pathetic tax collectors did shiver most all of the night.

During these days I did continue to do my most important work, which was, at the rest periods, as "Le Monsieur Bidon Enfant," or, as you say it, "Water Carrier." Also at these welcome rest periods, the soldiers of this doomed tax collecting expedition took off mostly all of their clothes.

Off of their backs, and which should have been carried on camels or asses as reason dictates, these idiots portered, as they marched, leather bags as you call "knapsacks," that contained, as I have said to you, dried goat meat tied up in tubes of skin made from the stomach of a pig. Also maize. Then too little bags of black beans from which they made a liquid they called "Jus," which is what you call "coffee," also metal plates and cups to drink from, linen for their wounds, needles and threads, tins of leather polish, an extra tunic, bottles and corks for their issue of Madame La Pinard. On top of these "knapsacks" and enwrapped round and strapped they carried a section of a little tent, which could, when put together, cover two soldiers in sleep. Piled on top of these tents they carried a metal tool with which to dig in the earth with. And then, English, mind you, on top of this, these mules carried large but neat bundles of firewood tied up into tidiness with leather thongs, the sticks and branches of which, I, Hadi Abbabba Guwah, had mostly gathered up and brought to them.

Then each of these invaders did remove two one-liter bidons of water and Madame La Pinard which they wore slung crisscross about their shoulders. Next they did unbuckle from about their waists eight large leather boxes which were full of pellets for their rifles, which they called "Lebels," in honor of the person who invented this weapon. Then off came their large and heavy blue, bloodstained, ragged, ugly overcoats, and after that, these dreaded Fuhrers of the sand, these heathens unwrapped from about their waists eighteen of your English feet of broad "ceinture bleue," which was a sash a foot wide and woven of raw silk made in Cathay and dyed poorly in blue. And now, they took off their dirty white tunics that had a silly little tiny collar which by regulation had to be buttoned tightly at all times. Why these imbeciles did not just simply wear elegant taubs and ride camels I do not know.

Their naked chests and arms exposed what you, English, call

"tattoos." Mostly all were designs in black, blue, red, and green. These "tattoos" depicted women of large proportions, without clothes. Also sailing vessels and flags, and words like "Helga," "Janine," and "Mother."

And all of this period of my life I did struggle mightily in work for Anatolini Bagolini, who now did refer to me as "Eh, Stupido!" and for whom I tried to do, as only Hadi Abbabba could do, all of my duties. That which was for me at every break period and at night in the cold to scout out and to gather up woodbrush for the fires for these first-class barbarians. Then make their tea if they wanted tea and in the European way in which they wanted it, and also to take the time to dig and bury those who had died in the wounded wagons, and further to incessantly change the linen of those still alive; wash these rags free of blood and spugh, reapply them, then hobble to attend to the sorry state of the wounded being dragged along behind the wagons by the ropes. All to the chorus of "Eh Stupido," which all of these savages had picked up from Anatolini Bagolini. But after they did say "Eh Stupido," they all did laugh, even those who could not really afford to laugh due to the pain of their wounds. But they did laugh nevertheless. Then I, Hadi the humble, found that I laughed along with them. These idiots did not mean any malice toward me. It was their custom. Anyway, you do not expect too much out of baboons.

Additionally, this "Eh Stupido" did fill water bags and the casks if there was a well, mind you. Then too, hurry to mince herbs for the various wounds. Now when the treatment of herbs did not succeed, occasionally chop and saw off legs and arms that had become a purple-red in color and throw them out to the foxes, which did increase in number by the day as I did cut up more or cut off more or buried more that had died. As the foxes tracked the column on the flanks, so too did the corsair birds, who always made a big rumpus in fighting with foxes over the dead meat of these soldiers that I did throw out to them. The corsair birds always did win a fight. The foxes were afraid for their eyes, which these birds will attack in an instant and very swiftly also. Then you have a blind fox. Which the other foxes will turn on and rip apart and attempt to eat, which never succeeds because the corsair birds wait for the foxes to kill the blind fox and as the foxes try to eat the dead fox the corsair birds will attack and to pick out more eyes. Then this entire ritual begins again. Dead foxes and the corsair birds getting fatter and fatter. So fat that they cannot sometimes fly. Then the foxes chase them along over the sand until feathers and all ends up in the bellies of the foxes.

Also always the buzzards with their wings stretched out were gliding high up in the air over the foxes and the corsair birds and following the wagons due to the flies and the very foul smells of the wounded. But mostly the buzzards looked for the blue-backs that in their exhaustion would fall to the sand and be left behind while the column continued northerly. This was a regulation in this army. The fate of these turistas was to be eaten alive, but usually not by the buzzards. Because as the soldier lay on the sand, the buzzards would fly down for their meal. But by that time the foxes had already buried themselves in the sand and waited to attack the buzzards, who they preferred as a meal, using the soldier collapsed on the sand as bait. But it was continually stupid for these small foxes to try to jump from the burrow they had made to attack the buzzards, which the foxes did in pairs. Because the large and powerful buzzards would just fly away carrying the small foxes with them until they attained a great height then did drop the foxes to their death. Then the buzzards would come down and eat the foxes while the corsair birds tore the still-alive soldier to pieces and ate with much screeching and rumpus this enfant pour la Madam la République.

During these days of suffering I used to dwell, especially when I was with much fatigue during the terrible heat of the over the head sun, on my genii that was my Samonama, and in my mind-sight see her dancing before me and then too relish how I did feel when I did once lay on her beauty and then from between her legs came so much delight and from which also came Little Hadi. And I would try much, and of course, I Hadi Abbabba Guwah succeeded, to hear every night of a night the sounds of her little silver bells and riyalat bangles all tinkling about her wrists, ankles, and her headdresses and about her waist and attached to the bottom of her skirt and about her neck and then too the bells that did dangle and ting-ting-ting and that were attached to her headband. . . . At this period of my life my dreams and dwelling of her did soothe all of my dreariness of this march, which I could understand day by day was not over. Nor, English, were my tedious duties and then again those that were yet to come, as you will soon learn of. This march was heat, cold, struggle, anger, grief, and haggardness. But I had known as you do know, English, hardship before this period of my life. So as I did

stretch out and put my hands behind my head and did look to the
black sky with all of its shining blinking starry tinkles so much like
her bells, bangles, and beads, would my Samonama not go away from
me if I did want to will it? Now what can I have of my Samonama?
Who did give me many dwellings and bought me clothes and weapons and a horse. I did conclude that my Samonama could not be just
riyalat and a horse. Or clothes or weapons. But more. She made so
soft my heart within me, which, mind you English, is not always a
good thing according to your circumstances. And now she is in
pieces and scattered about the plain of Bal-al-Din. Now that plateau
is laughing at "Allah-il-Allah!" Just so. Also I could be angry that
she did make me feel like a child playing, and that this life could be
one of smiling, and one where new clothes always appearing. . . .
Then I would wake from my sleep and shriek out: "Why do women
have the brains of a camel?" Every night of a night I did call out to
the sky at her, of course, and call her a demon; the demon that was
once my great joy, but now a demon that is my great sorrow. Why
do women have the brains of a camel? Why cannot they be born with
the brains of a leopard? Or perhaps a lion? Can you tell me, English? I see by your expression that you cannot tell me. Perhaps some
day . . .

But English, you want the story of my life, so, to continue
. . . . I then labored at learning the languages of these savages; so
called "Europeans," from across the Middle Sea. I did learn much
of their strange-sounding tongues from listening to them sing their
songs. These blue-backs did sing much, and all together, in what you
call unison, and all of the time. Especially those in the wounded
wagons and those also being dragged along behind by the ropes. The
walk called the "Pas de Route" was when I did experience the best
of their singing. . . . Then too, Anatolini Bagolini did sing all of the
time, even when he also did take the time and work at chopping off
a leg or an arm with his big heavy square knife. Or at times, mind
you, he used one of his saws. Nevertheless, he did always sing and
in that language which was the Italani, and which, it seemed to me,
is a language natural for singing, as it is also when spoken. "Ehhha
. . . Stupido!" Now, English, does not that sound nice to the ear? Oui?
Ahh oui.

Back then: "Ehhhaa Stupido, Signore Hadi Abbabba Guwah:
tu se pazzo!"

192

To which I did learn to reply to and with dignity: "Grazie, grazie, grazie," or "Malto bene Signore Anatolini Bagolini" and to which I always did add, "Ciao."

To which he would shout back at me: "Basta—basta!" which means, in your language, more or less, "Bugger off."

However, to return to the subject, from these imbeciles which always Dres Ali called "the exploiters," I did learn much of their languages from their singing, mostly, as I have said, in the "Pas de Route" march. They did sing mostly songs in the tongue of the Germani tribe. At times, at night, round the encampment fires, I would weep at the sadness of these songs they did sing, because they would of an instant make me think of my Samonama. Then also too, Puh, my wretched life that was of that moment in the desert. And I would think of the old thoughts of: "Is this the end of my life?" Or during the walking: "What a way to spend my time." Then, as well, there were other songs that would make me feel happy. However, Anglais, the red pants soldiers would actually order all of this singing. Oh yes. They did sing by order, and by this army's law called "Au pas gymnastique," which to them means, "Do it and don't think." This is not a good translation. But then, most of how these troopers communicate cannot be literally translated. It is up to me to tell you what they mean as to what they say; mankind's greatest demon. Do you not agree, Anglais, mon enfant?

Nevertheless, most of these horseless soldiers did feel, to my mind, even if they could not think. The Germani tribe song that did make them feel the most was called "Ein Heller und ein Batzen." This was, as you Europeans call it, a "romantic" song. But which was also a song sung to struggle forward by, and truly it did absolutely make the march easier over grounds that at this period in this terrible land had become completely all sharp with knifelike rocks for long stretches. Then the ground would become gravel with stones to walk on that were about the size of chicken eggs. Then the earth would become the sand again. Then a few hundred meters further, and so, Ah puh, rocks and eggs again. But even over these sharp rocks there was the horrid incessant "one-two, one-two" march step. And of course, I, Hadi Abbabba, the Good, did toil endlessly with all of the bidons of Madame La Pinard on one shoulder and all of the bidons of water on the other shoulder, and keeping them from falling off by holding constantly the leather straps together across my chest. And the song which they sang mostly for the "one-two"

walking, for it was the rhythm of this march, was the sacred and
all-powerful sad happy song of all of these Les Français soldiery.
They did sing it in the Frank tribe tongue. No! they did *chant* it, as
you say. It was called "Voilà du Boudin." Do you know what this
song means to them? This "Voilà du Boudin"? No. You cannot
know. Again English, language becomes difficult because the meaning behind words and song is mostly unclear. Or, should I say that
the feeling and the associations are unclear. But I think what I say
is unclear also. However, English, do you know what it means this
"Voilà du Boudin"? In your language it means, more or less, "Great
the Sausage." And I might add that sausage is holy with these
monkeys. Yes. And the story of this, and why it is their sacred song
and why it means so much to them, I will tell you of later. But I will
tell you this about their sausage. These blue-back simpletons will
collect many of what you call "pigs" and put them in a huge and
square metal pot. Then with their knives they will cut these pigs all
over so that they will bleed themselves into the bottom of the pot.
When these pigs have all bled to death their bodies are removed and
placed into a bin. Then all of the blood is scooped up with ladles and
poured into smaller pots arranged all along a long waist size table.
Like the ones you sit at, with the tall legs, as you say. Into these pots
of blood is added an equal proportion of wheat and barley. This they
then knead together with their bare strong fingers for a long time.
I have seen them with blood covering their skin up to their elbows.
Twenty or thirty soldiers hunched over all doing this kneading together along the long table. Then they will add herbs as they knead
the blood and the wheat and the barley. Soon the pots are put onto
fires and once hot stirred constantly. Later they remove the contents
and pour this mixture which is a kind of sauce into many trays, all
of which go into ovens. But only for a short time. Then they remove
the oven-cooked trays and empty the contents into yet more clean
trays on the long table. They did spread the now lumpy contents out
as flatly as they could with their thick stubby white European fingers.
Into each tray was now poured a certain portion of oil from olives.
These men now also kneaded this lumpy mess and the oil together,
adding all of the time a herb called garlic and also too other herbs.
When this was done completely to their satisfaction, this globby mess
was shoved into casings of pig gut and very tightly rolled into tubes
the length of your arm and as round as the hole you can make with
your thumb and first finger, then tied off at the ends with very thin

194

leather thongs. All of these snake-looking tubes were next placed into
boxes of wood from the cedar tree and piled up one on top of the
other and yet again returned to the ovens, but with a low heat and
now they would remain a longer time.

The finished sausage is purple-black in color. The length of it
the size of your forearm. These blue-backs say it completely satisfies
your appetite. Puh. It's as if you eat mud mixed with sand.

And so did we march and sing, and always march. Yet I, Hadi
Abbabba Guwah, I must confess, was truly a bit more fortunate than
the rest, for I did much ride in the wounded wagon brushing away
the fog of flies, and singing along with these soldiers while cleaning
their wounds, and applying my newly washed linen onto their
cleansed wounds by the magic hands of Hadi Abbabba Guwah. Then
too, I had the opportunity in this land of swordlike rocks and gravel
to jump from the wagon with a sack in my hand during the day and
to run about to overturn the rocks and grab up scorpions by their
tails and drop them into the sack. Some I did catch, of course, while
they scurried in the open across the egg stones. I would of an hour
catch perhaps thirty to forty scorpions each.

And since Allah has seen fit to make them the most ferocious
of the fighting insects, the scorpions did all fight together in the
sack so that when I did catch up to the wagons eventually, half of
them were dead, having killed each other off thus making my task
easier.

Then I did collect the "soupe" bowls from the wounded during
a rest period, build a fire, put some cooking palm oil into each bowl,
and put the bowls onto the fire. When the palm oil was hot enough,
I did drop live and dead scorpions into the hot palm oil. Of course,
they dissolved. That is, the dead ones. The live ones first had to pop,
as you say. Then they dissolved. After I had stirred the bowls round
with a stick many times, my lotion was ready. I then insisted, I, Hadi
Abbabba Guwah, that all of the wounded rub my lotion onto their
faces and hands and indeed, onto all over their exposed bodies, and
especially onto the linen of their wounds. And Wallah! the flies
avoided us. And yet again I had yet another task of a day and for
those many days during those days, that is, when we were in the
lands of sharp rocks and gravel. Mostly though, I did sometimes
walk and sometimes ride on the "Missouri mules" that pulled both
the cook wagon and the wounded wagons, and help Anatolini

Bagolini in the preparation of food for these savages. It was then that I did hear the most beautiful song that I did ever hear, and perhaps in all of my life. It was called by the name of "La Montanara," and sung very slowly in the tongue of the Italani tribe by Signore Anatolini Bagolini, who was once in the Regiment of the Alpini, whose chant it was. In your English language, it is called "The Song of the Mountain." It is, as you would describe it, a song of amor. There is no word in any of the desert languages for amor, or indeed, the Frank word "Romantique." So too in my Southland. The only word we can use that you can translate into the English or the Frank tongue is the word "possession." However, this concept word of "amor" and its attitude toward women is very interesting an idea. That is, I think of it when I think of my Samonama. But then, how can you have "amor" or "amour" for a creature that was so utterly stupid as Samonama? Eh, English?

Nevertheless, I used to try to sing this song "La Montanara" along with Signore Bagolini of the Alpini. He did sing it over and over and over with all of the sadness that he could bring to this song of lament. But I, Hadi Abbabba Guwah, do not have a good voice. Yet, since I did try to sing he did not curse me. Also I did learn to sing other songs, all of which I did think were beautiful, and again, as if written by genii. One was a Germani tribe soldier song sung to supposedly all the girls like the Ouled-Naels, or what you call "prostitutes." It is very touching to the soul and was sung only by the Germani late at night round the encampment fires. No other tribe would sing it. I did ask the question "why" but I did not ever find an answer nor could they tell me who was this Lilli Marlene. But I will tell you that this song made other tribesmen of Madame la République angry.

After a night of singing, at the hour of not yet light, which is as you call it, 3 A.M., I would carry all of my bidons to all of my soldiers who would then have a full one-half liter of "vin" which they drank as if it were water from Holy Mekka. More could be bought from the supplies stored into the cook wagons. This they did do. It was done all of the time by these morons. Always "Madame La Pinard!" Their red, red "vin" not like water but very thick between the fingers in ordinary circumstances. But in the heat of the day it would become like the slime that one could find deep in mountain caverns. Dres Ali Mohammed did shrug his shoulders to me and say,

"Ah, old man, raison d'être por La Legion. Ca va? Comprende vous?"

"You say to me that this Pinard is of a day the Allah-il-Allah of the Legion?"

"Jawohl, mon tigre," answered Dres Ali. "They drink, drink, drink.

"All of these mercenaries were already sick with this dependence upon their roumis alcohol long before they were either in this rogue army and especially before they did arrive here in this desert. These rascals only continue to drink in La Legion and now the difference is only Legion vin. They mostly laugh with too much of this alcohol and push each other about the encampment as little children are inclined to do."

I did nod my head toward Dres Ali's knowledge. At these certain times there was no dignity to their manner or bearing. Yet even we as children in Kroo Lagoon were not as rough on our fellows as these full-grown blue-backs who many times did begin to, in the European fashion, strike each other with their big clenched fists about the body and about the head and the face, always causing blood to flow from broken mouths and smashed noses. Then they would laugh and fall onto the ground and of a sudden begin the vigorous polishing of their leather belts and pouches and straps and knapsacks and all of the time singing all together as I did distribute among them the wine along with the help of Anatolini Bagolini and as these soldiers did have their fill sitting on the ground laughing and singing between each other then I and Anatolini Bagolini would return to the cooking wagons and then return to the column with our buckets and a scoop and go among these heathens who had by now stopped their singing and polishing and so too the red pants and with our five or six food bags about and hanging from our necks and shoulders along with more six or seven green glass bottles of Pinard, we would distribute a certain scoop "soupe" portion to each consisting of dried dates and goat meat which was for this day's march.

But most importantly, for Hadi the Humble, but also Hadi the Vain, was I would be greeted by these idiots with a "Bonjour, Monsieur Hadi Abbabba, merci." Or a "Buongiorno Signore Hadi," or "Buenas días, Señor Guwah." Or "Gutentag, mein lieber," or mostly from these Germani tribesmen it was: "Tisk, lebst du noch? Tisk." This meaning was: "Are you still alive? Too bad."

But I did take the opportunity to profit myself on these occasions by pronouncing properly, "Ja danke" and repeat, "Ja, ja, ja, danke, danke, danke." Or one or two or three or more of the Germani, who drank more than anyone else, would laugh together at me while the Pinard did spill from their mouths; they did point at me and with a voice like that of a wild dog, and spittle out:

"Noch immer nicht tot?"

To which I would try to reply with: "Leben ist lebensgefahrlich." "Living is dangerous for your life." They would laugh and clap their hands as children and rock back and forth on the sand. I had learned that most all of these Germani tribesmen always did think this return was a very funny thing to say to them. So I thought it wise to say it much to these dumb beasts. And my reward was always that they did raise their arms and wave their heavy green glass Pinard bottles to me and laugh all the more plus break wind and then drink and then reply: "Ja! Ja! Ja! Das leben ist so saumabig." To which I had yet again learned to reply: "Grobartig," which means "marvelous." This caused them to start laughing anew.

Then when "soupe" and Pinard was finished and the little tents rolled up and put on top of their knapsacks, their leaders would shout, "Northeast!" Then the cry, "Marche ou creve, marche ou creve!" which for you English means, "March or die." Many did absolutely keep up in the heat this one-two pace of these soldiers or during the "Pas de Route" and but also many did collapse to "creve." And did fall to the sand and prepared themselves to die. Not one of these soldiers would look back over his shoulder to see the last sight of his comrade, who he did know was lying in the sand to die. For the medical wagons were full and so too the ropes dragging behind and those clasping onto them.

Because of my good help to the kitchen wagon driver, I persuaded him to let me ride his machine that had special wheels with which to conquer the terrible sand. Now I could ride and not idiotically walk across the ground.

What English? Oh, oui. Dres Ali taking me to this Major Red Pants whose clothes I did once try to steal and all the while he did think instead that I was trying to save his life. . . . Yes, well Anglais, I did stand briefly back then before this fool sitting cross-legged on the sand during a rest period, and then I, Hadi the Humble, was quickly down on my knees and then salaaming low and did say in the language of the Italani: "Oh, si, oh mighty excellency, come sta?" or "How are you?" And I did think he would say to me, "Sta bene, grazie, grazie, grazie," which is nice to the ear and which Anatolini Bagolini always did say to me. Then in the language of the Italani, I did say, "I am your servant, I am—"

Dres Ali did rap me on the knee and whacked me on my head with his camel stick and then looking down on me, scolded to me in military Arabic:

"You first-class beast, do not address him or this roumis in this manner. Try to say 's'il vous plait' and say, 'At your service, Monsieur mon major Gar Yar Sasha Prumm."

This was this tax collector's name. Gar Yar Sasha Prumm. Later I did learn he was of the tribe called the cossacks, and came from a land called Ukraine in some greater land named "Mother Russia."

I said back then to Dres Ali in Arabic, "Cannot I say, 'Come sta'? And then he can say to me, 'Sta bene, grazie, grazie, grazie. . . .' "

But Dres Ali, now on his feet again, and looking down on me, said to me in Arabic, again:

"You first-class beast, he is a Francswari speaker and of that tongue and not an Italani tribesman or of that tongue."

To annoy this haughty Dres Ali Mohammed, I said, "No capito." Then: "Tu se baats."

He raised his stick to strike Hadi. I shouted the nice-sounding "Basta, basta, basta, stupido!" which Signore Anatolini Bagolini of the Alpini taught me in the Italani and which means, "Enough, enough, enough, stupid." Then this Gar Yar Sasha Prumm Major still in his red pants now dirty and ragged, did shout and waved the both of us to a silence. He used more, to me, incomprehensible Francswari words on Dres Ali and I said, "No capito."

Then lo, Dres Ali brought his stick down upon Hadi the Humble and many times he did do this. However, at this particular moment, I did observe that this Le Major Gar Yar Sasha Prumm's wounds had not at all healed well. And from his face I did see that he was in much pain, which he did attempt to relieve with a medicine these officers called "bal," which is a liquid you English call cognac, and that he was at this rest period drinking it from a canteen.

Then dirty, ragged red pants Gar Yar Sasha Prumm Major, whose life I, Hadi, did save, did take this "bal" cognac medicine from his hand and put it on the sand. He did wipe his mouth with his sleeve and then yet again did gesture Dres Ali and I to silence, who at that time were still arguing. Dres Ali stopped hitting me over the head with his camel stick and did sit down beside me and with a motion made me get out of my salaamed position. We were all three sitting there on the sand. Dres Ali then said to me that this Gar Yar Sasha Prumm Major was not going to have me shot and this was because I saved his life and that I was a good aid to the wounded and cook wagons of Anatolini Bagolini. So I would not be shot. Then, with drinking more of this cognac, this Prumm Major asked through Dres Ali what was my life? Who was I?

I did say to Dres Ali in Arabic, "Tell this afflicted donkey that I was once a king who had thousands and thousands of subjects and had lands as far as the eye could see north, east, south, west. But you see before you now only a poor slave without the dignity of clothes. But it was not so once. Alas, alas, I was made a witless slave by the cruel yokes of the—"

Whereupon Dres Ali did again slap me with his stick and then cover his face with his hands and did shake his head back and forth and then he imparted: "Oh, Allah-il-Allah-il-Allah" over and over, which I did not immediately understand. But then I did. So, of a sudden, I did kick him on his shinbone and angrily said to him in Arabic, "Tell this red pants my lies, tell what I tell you to tell him, you malignant idiot from this Sudanland. And further, stupido, it is not wise to laugh at Hadi, ever. Others who did do not live today. Understand? And more so, again accept the fact that if you tap me with your stick again about my head and shoulders as have done, I, Hadi Abbabba Guwah, will take it away from you, then I will push it up your nose."

He did lean across to me in a wrath, and with his purple-black face close to me, I smiled. Young people are foolish. It is sad. But then, I was young once also, and foolish. What is life without being a fool? Are not all men and women, English? And especially women? Like my Samonama? And then I said to Dres Ali of a sudden, "Yes, as you say, I might be an old goat to you, but carefully consider, one day you will take my place as an 'old goat.' If you live long enough."

He said after a pause and clicks of the tongue, "I apologize to you, Hadi Abbabba Guwah. I perhaps have misjudged you and misunderstand you. Let us have some peace between us. Yes, I admit I will one day be an old goat also. I just thought that you were only a liar and a thief and a rascal. You do only present yourself as a rogue. Forgive me, please."

"No," I did say to him quietly. "You do not insult Hadi. I am all of what you want to say about me. A rogue, a liar, a thief, a rascal. And actually, anything else you wish to call me. Greedy, vain, full of deceit, and now as of late, corrupted by lust for a woman. I am also a murderer and will probably be forced to be one again. Do you think I enjoy this? Or, to put it to you more intelligently, do you think any of what I have just confessed to you can be actually enjoyed at all? Am I happier being all of what this life has taught me, or what you yourself, Monsieur Dres Ali Mohammed, would try to teach me about not being a liar, a thief, and a rascal? Now tell this pubic hair baboon what I tell you to tell him. Please."

Dres Ali did tell Red Pants precisely this: that I was once a great and powerful king in the southlands who was made by force a poor witless slave by terrible caravan Arabs who roam all of these lands just to secure victims to sell. That it was they who cut off my ear and also too my arm.

Then I said to Dres Ali in Arabic, "Tell him this. . . . that at one period of my life I had ten thousand, no, you say to him that I had twenty thousand subjects—no, that I had one hundred thousand, and that I have never been a soldier ever, nor that I have ever killed anyone. I was just once a simple king who had thirty wives. In addition, tell him that I was a teacher. Tell this animal that I can read and write Arabic, Temejegh, and Marghi and Fulde and Popo, Batta and Hausa. And that I can add numbers and that I am able in bookkeeping and that I can navigate by the stars and also during the day by my shadow, and that I can draw maps and that I have been a doctor of camels. Include also that I do know of all the tribes all in this wasteland of the south. I know of the caravan routes coming up northerly from the lands of the Niger of Benin and I do know of the wells and the water holes and where the oases are in the south where begins this Great Desert."

This Dres Ali did impart. Red Pants Gar Yar Sasha Prumm did regard me steadily and with an unsmiling eye and also too with an unsmiling expression.

I did look at Gar Yar Sasha Prumm and put on my face of worry and woe. But he quietly did nod to me that I should just continue.

Nevertheless, to ensure my safety, I did begin to shriek out as

if to save my life; that I am now once a slave, a poor slave of the Tebu
Bedouins of Gandoga! I have been a poor and a wretched slave
of recent times in my life of the Igdalen Tuaregs. I was forced to
ride onto the plain of Bal-al-Din and if I did refuse, the punishment would have been that of death. I was just again a slave—a
slave!

Gar Yar waved his bandaged hand at me for silence. He spoke
and Dres Ali translated to me in Arabic that this was what this
moron was saying:

"You say, mon enfant, that you have recently been a slave. You
say this with a sad expression and much self-pity. You say it also as
if I will give you privileges, or sympathy for it. As if you think slavery
or being once a slave is something that entitles you to a special
treatment here. You have not learned yet that all men are slaves.
From the day they are born. You will also have to learn that the word
'slave' has no meaning either to me or among my soldiers. Look at
these men about you. Do you possibly believe that they are free? Do
you believe that I feel that I am free? Absolutely not. The original
legions for North Africa were started in ancient Rome, and as you
name it, by a mere slave. So the French took the idea from an ex-slave
who knew quite well what slavery meant, not in bondage, but in the
heart and in the soul and spirit. A slave captured in Germany. He
was brought to Rome as a slave in chains. He was forced to be a
gladiator and fought in the arena two hundred and sixteen times.
They gave him the ancient Roman name of Serviv Tullius. This
so-called slave was honored with freedom. This man, this German
Serviv Tullius, this 'slave,' created a Roman army that in a short time
conquered the known inhabited world. He created all of the North
African legions. Every aspect of the French Foreign Legion today is
a result of the mind of Serviv Tullius. A slave. He conceived that only
foreigners should enroll in the legions that were destined for North
Africa. Then, as now, poor pay but the best of officers. Prestige was
important. Also the discipline that they all seem to need of grueling
back-breaking labor, of building roads and pounding rocks and putting up forts with their bare hands, which every Legionnaire does
need to do for the many reasons he wants to and enjoys doing it. A
kind of penance for their past lives? For their childhoods? Absolutely. But you can be sure a Legionnaire not only needs this life of
hardship and death but nearly begs for it. Perhaps his own interpre-
tation of some sort of salvation. However, we today are the true lineal

descendants and are just like them as they were 'slaves.' These 'slaves' were once the most powerful army in the world of that time, the marching legions of ancient Rome, who created miracles. But underneath we are all 'slaves.' And we shall be always to the day we die. It is only a question of what you are a so-called 'slave' to. And how each individual is going to survive what he thinks his own personal slavery is. Whether it's positive or negative. We so-called humans are all 'slaves' and for all of our lives to whatever. You yourself, Hadi Abbabba Guwah, are a slave other than an ex-slave and to something. You will expose it to me and all the other men in time. Chains of the mind and emotions. Chains that are scars. Or perhaps continual fears. Or dreads. Or again desires. Perhaps loss. Maybe pain. Regrets? Folly of the past? So do not please show me your body scars. That is nothing. I wait. We will all wait, to see and find out what is inside of you. What you are a slave to. The extreme of which all makes up Les Français La Legion Etrangere. And so, you are welcome to La Legion. La Brave Legion. All because we in the Legion accept with great humility that we are extreme true slaves to our souls and there is little salvation for us but death, that is to us, of the Legion. Are you, Hadi Abbabba Guwah, a slave to passion? Or is it to romance? Or is it the violence and excitement of battle itself? Perhaps you like to indulge in despair and relish this daily practice of abject self-pity? Or is it that you are a slave to La Adventure? Or, as most of us, a slave to your own unknown personal anger that can at times become a fury and a rage at what mostly you do not know of, but that can make you a berserker and then beyond that of a berserker, the long step to the boundary of madness? In spite of all of this, I believe, if I live, that my mission in this Legion is to soften my Legionnaires' pain of being alive at this point in time and then get them to live with, as best he can, his fellow Legionnaires. Each of these soldiers has learned quickly enough in his life to despise his life and all that about him. Then comes his enlistment in La Legion. Then to learn with expertise to kill his supposed fellow man for any rationale he can dream up. This too is slavery. Emotional slavery to a past he never asked for or wanted but had to live out as best he could. We are also still slaves to remaining dreams. That is, if killing can be a dream. Negative or positive, political, economic or physical or romantic, or psychological, we are slaves. A slave to the inability to communicate. Or the inability to love or to feel truly. There are those who are slaves to stupidity and fear and

inertia. These are the worst. Stupidity, fear, and inertia slaves. But
we in La Brave Legion adopt the attitude that the only single approach to our pain over being alive is to go further into it and actually
embrace and desire as an exorcism the suffering of extreme and abject
pain. And it works. It is not God that I or my Legionnaires want.
It is not amour that they want. For all have lost those senses long
ago. The result is that the Legionnaire has an appetite for grief in
which the results are a desire for pain. So, the officers and sous
officers of the Legion provide this. To these men lying round you,
pleasure and the sense of being a true human being has not been
strong enough to get them to rectify what is basically to them sub-
consciously their stupid, or neurotic and somehow wretchedly useless lives. So, these men, they have chosen another alternative, which
is to die. But most importantly, to die on their own terms. To die as
best they can. That is, usefully in service. Not just to jump into the
river Seine or Rhine. Or if their problems get them into trouble in
the bistros of Paris, then 'Les Flicks' come and drag you out with
hooks attached to the ends of their hemps. No Legionnaires are
usually like that Hans Bowerman, who accepted that life was all
finished for him long before you ever did stab him days ago after he
begged: 'Kill me. Then Hadi Abbabba Guwah, cut up my body and
feed all the parts of me to my innocent and faithful dogs.' It is a
whisper. But again I say to you, it is a Legion attitude that life is
rotten, which you will understand in time and as you march with us.
Now, Monsieur Hadi, a so-confessed 'slave' with that wide-eyed
innocent expression of yours, do tell me, s'il vous plait, what are you
a slave to?"

"Monsieur mon major, s'il vous plait, I do not understand your
question, s'il vous plait."

"I see. Let me put it to you in this fashion . . . I want you to
understand that I myself am a slave to Russian Nihilism, or in the
French sense, a student of all that is corrupt and negative in mankind. Or, if you will, I am a slave to hate. Hence I am in La Brave
Legion employed in killing off as many of our species as possible. For
the greatest preoccupation we supposed humans have, and all
through history, is either continually to commit multitudinous
crimes upon each other or to kill each other off. This is what I have
said and witnessed men and women spending their lifetimes doing,
each of them in their own particular way. This is called, in the new
science of psychology, or en academie, as 'being human,' or 'inevita-

ble human behavior.' Which generally means that we must by our human nature, and for every reason you can name, slaughter, steal, rob, cheat, maim, and, of course, to lie to ourselves before the mirror and to others face to face on a daily basis. All due to our accepted human so-called insecurities and anxieties which are labeled and tolerated as excuses for misconduct and general stupidity. I personally do not accept this. To my mind personally, all this thick merde is inexcusable. For we are supposed to have intelligences that animals are not blessed with. Even animals do not kill and eat their own kind. But humans do. So I rebel at mankind. I rebel over the constant practice of petty adolescent power humans practice on each other in no matter what field of employment. I rebel over all physical and emotional cannibalism humans practice easily; too easily on themselves and each other and especially to our supposed so-called 'loved ones.' The true eternal human daily preoccupation is to continually strive and drive oneself along with as many others about us that we can affect into a kind of madhouse. But we ourselves alone each go in our sleep every night, in our own lovely particular way, to our own peculiar madhouse. Hence, La Brave Legion, which is nothing less than one huge, noisy La Pinard walking madhouse, where each one feels as he sees it, and reaffirms it each day after his midnight dreams, that all over again to him life is rotten because people are rotten and there is nothing to gain, so each wait to die and truly want to. Every day for their own special reasons and most of it is subconscious. Life for these since they were about five years old had been little deaths. And so, La Brave Legion is nothing less than a temporary hotel for self-suicides. And so . . . I now ask you again, slave, what are you a slave to? As I am, as we all are?"

"No, monsieur mon major, s'il vous plait, I am a true slave to good circumstances. And I do not want to be sold to the Turks."

"I suppose next you will tell me you only want a 'loaf of bread and thou' . . .?"

"Oui pardon, monsieur mon major?"

"Pass it by, please. Now, Dres Ali tells me that you are learned in daylight and night navigation in this God-forsaken desert. That you can draw well maps and can read and write Arabic and also know most of all of the Berber languages of the desert?"

"Oui, oui, mon major, si. Jawohl, jawohl, achtung."

"Speak French, please, Hadi Abbabba. Eh bien. Comprenez-vous?"

"Oui, yes, Your Big Excellency."

"Merci. So, you have also said to Dres Ali that you know of all of the caravan of this South Sahara and their water wells and also all of the oases for respite at night?"

"Oui monsieur, mon major; Big Excellency."

"Bien. Then again, I will not have you shot. If you live through all of this, I think you will be valuable much later on. That is, if you do not lie to me . . ."

"No—no monsieur. I no lie. Been well told by slave masters never to lie or cheat or steal or kill anybody."

"Très bien," said this tax-collecting Major to me. And still sitting on the sand, he did grab up his leather mapcase and he did take from it a pen from a box, a little glass container of ink, and a fat book that he did open and begin to scribe in it, taking time to say to me while doing so, "You must absolutely learn better the French language, Monsieur Hadi."

I did shout to this idiot, my deception being a complete success, "Oui, oui," and I did salaam low. Then to him I said hotly, "And I will learn besides the Français tongue also this Germani Deutschen rubbish. It is a good way to spend my time to my profit, Monsieur Excellency Major. Also, oui sir, I am still strong and active and of course, good tempered."

What did this Cossack of Mother Russia think I was trying to do with my time? Wasting it trying to learn desert Temejegh? Or Fullani or Mandingo, or M'bum?

I calmed myself, English, with the thought that life can be altogether bearable if there is learning to be done for the rest of your life; or, as it were, all of the time every day of a day. Do you understand?

I did at that particular moment, far way back then and of a sudden due to principally my frustration, complain in much anger to Dres Ali about these smelly, dirty, unshaven, coarse foreign soldiers and also about their day-by-day abominable rude manners. And I did say to Dres Ali, "If stupidity should be killed and not saved," which you know, English, that I believe in, "then why are these imbeciles that are in such a sorry state still alive?"

And he did reply to me:

"Yes, I know of what you feel seeing these soldiers; what you must think upon hearing the Major's words and thoughts. I do know what you are attempting to say. I too felt the same once, in the beginning of my service with these invaders. I understand what you see or, better, what you think you see. In the towns that these soldiers occupy, that hopefully you will yet live to see, all of the Franks who are called civilians insult and name these Legionnaires 'La Lie Humaine,' which translated means to these civilian people, 'the dregs of humanity.' "

But I tell you, the true dregs from across the Middle Sea or in the East would not have the absolute courage to come along here into this service of La Legion. And even if they did, they would not be accepted after being interrogated in the depots of Paris or Marseille. If by chance a true dreg is accepted into this service, he would soon be dead with a bayonet through his blanket in his sleep."

Again we marched. Day on the day now through the vast sand lands of the Chlurs, those fierce, light-brown-faced Berber Bedouins who came at us like thunder over the dunes from the sides and rear, with their beautiful robes flowing out behind them in a wind they themselves were causing. We would come to in our march upon bodies of the sentinels who had been stolen away the night before and now laid out in our path so that we could not avoid seeing how the Chlurs had worked on them. These Legionnaires had been staked out without clothes and little fires made under their hands and feet then tortured with a tool I once did use when I was the camel doctor with the Tebu Bedouins of Gandoga, where nothing was possible for anybody and before I escaped to my Samonama's land of fogs of flies but where all things were possible to all men, including me, Hadi. These tools which I did once use were called by the Tebu "garas," which, English, were short and very sharp knives only so long as my biggest finger and curved like the crescent moon. This tool I used mostly for the delivery of camel babies if there was much difficulty with the female giving birth. But then again in the afternoon, I did also use it as a cooking tool to clean vegetables and skin goat meat. But always in times of Berber tribal war, this tool was used for torture.

The Legion clothes had been taken off these sentinels by the Chlurs to use as gifts to their families and relatives and for themselves also. Firstly, on the staked-out Legionnaires, these Chlurs did slice with messy methods, the belly with the Tebu garas as if it were filet de boeuf. Then, holding the tip of the knife by their thumb and first finger, these imps would muddle through and cut further inside, scratch and dig their hands into the cavity of this still-alive blue-back's stomach to feel out that which in a man makes babies. From the inside and using the gara again, cut off and rip out all the fibers and the muscles of that which makes babies. This the Chlurs thought the worst insult to an enemy.

However, this was exactly as I had to do at times with the old male camels when I was a doctor to them. All this was to make the old male camels calmer while milling and sniffing about the young female camels, who in turn were being violently courted by the younger and stronger and perpetually unpleasant and bad-tempered males. But the old camels retained their instincts even after I had worked on them with the garas. The old snorting ones were forever and always amorously trying to climb up upon the insensitive females to make them sit in order to lay upon them and make babies. All this incessant cutting I had to do was to try to prevent noisy and total chaotic fighting all the day between the old and the young who were of every second trying to give the females babies. So I never did succeed. However, camels are at best mean and thoughtless beasts, even in the best of times.

Fighting between them for to lay on a female meant the death of an old male camel who had spent perhaps thirty heated years slaving back and forth on the caravan trails. Then all you could do when one was killed was to use the garas again, cut him up, piece by piece, and throw his meat to the foxes and the jackals, and take his skin to the marketplace to be made into water bags. Puh! And so, to keep trying to prevent the death of these old ones, I did decide to use the garas late at night and when no Tebu was awake to stop me, on only the young males who were perceptively and continually nasty in character and out for the blood of the old.

I did, when I was with the Tebu, pound stakes into the sand and then to club a young one to somewhat of an oblivion. Roll this camel onto his back, spread and tie the legs out onto stakes. Then straddle his stomach and while still half awake and laughing at me, he would shoot urine on me as they always did do. As you English say, a pee bath. I would cut into the young peeing one with a gara and try to work and chop and pull out this instinct to kill in order to make babies.

I, with the Tebu, was eventually successful in my skillful, en-lightened work with the garas, especially on those of the arrogant and pesty Mehari breed—wallah and voilà!—no fighting between them. Besides, these testy camels brought a bigger price in the camel marketplace, which would not ordinarily be forthcoming with their baby-making material. Traders in the marketplace were very pleased. Hence many riyalat in Hadi's money bag, because only I, Hadi, knew which camel I had chopped up, so skillful was I with the garas the merchants could never tell.

But to finish with these unfortunate Legionnaires staked out on the sand. . . . Many indeed were yet alive and baking in the hot sun and tried to speak when the column came upon them. But their tongues had been cut out. And no action that I or the others could take would relieve their pain. They would just have to be left to die a slow death after cutting them free. Many requested to be shot to death, which was accorded to them. Then they were buried quickly in shallow sand because we had to begin again with the one-two, one-two.

Then, as I did say clicks of the tongue ago, the Chlurs became très angry. All because none, not one of the quaint tactics that these Chlurs could do ever did win out against the Legionnaires. So began the capture of the stragglers, and not sentinels, that were just trying, in desperation, to keep up but doing their one-two in a reeling fashion far behind the column. The young baby Chlurs would swiftly come over the dunes and race up from behind and, with leather ropes, lasso these dying struggling stragglers and drag them over the sands to their Chlur mothers and young girls to again be tortured to death.

The torture was an entertainment and a release from pain for these mothers of dead sons and young girls of dead brothers and not yet married to some Chlur fool, and to be enjoyed very slowly and to be applauded with hand clapping and to be laughed at. And very different from the method in which the sentinels were killed. The women and young girls did prove themselves to be more pitiless than any of the Chlur men in inventing horrors onto these blue-backs who should have had the intelligence enough to shoot themselves as soon as they saw the Chlurs come over the dunes. But Wallah, no. So the women and girls had their own la festa by taking these soldiers and tying them up and then beginning to do their work on these tax collectors. I say to you, English, the females took many days to mutilate the blue-backs, the ways of which I will not tell you about because they are too disgusting. But days before death, it was an apertif to these mothers and the not married and those younger and not ready to have breasts.

When finally the stragglers did absolutely show signs of expiring, then the women and girls would crudely slash open prisoners' stomachs by sawing back and forth with lances and then fill up the cavities with fruits de encampment, or hot stones. And it was soon bon nuit for the Christians. Then they cut up these soldiers into pieces and did throw them to the jackals who roam round the Chlur camps after eventide, and soon these animals would be laughing all night with full bellies and laughing at the Francswari medals of the Croix de Guerre or the Medaille Militaire, and at "Honneur et Fidelite" or "Valeur et Discipline."

Also did begin the practice of leaving in our path bodies not from the Legion, but those of soldier columns that were escaping and marching many kilometers ahead of us. Men who were once in bright red uniforms and in tall round hats. Dres Ali called these people "Alger Saphis." They were desert camel cavalry guides and explorers for the blue-back army in all of the north, east, and west. Also these men were unappreciated Berber village police and gathered taxes as well. The Chlur women after staking with ropes these Saphis down on the sand, would work on them with the garas. Slice their eyelids off so that the Chlurs could watch them when the sun did rise on the next morn. They did linger about to see the Saphis slowly go blind with the rising sun. Naturally, por favore, after that these stripped-naked men were also a little roasted. Actually they became rather black. By the time the Legion came upon them they were blessed with the sight of Saphis' skin peeling off as do lambs over a roaring fire.

These "messieurs Saphis Coloniste" soldier guides, tax collectors, and policemen never buried their dead captured in a fight with the Chlurs. But so it was with these fool Legionnaires that they halted every time and did the sad duty of collecting this sort of pot-au-feu which were roasted, blinded, bloated, falling to pieces, and mostly eaten bodies due to the foxes and the vultures—for one large together grave. It was not an easy task to dig in the sand in their very weakened condition. Nicht ist fantastisch.

At last then we came to the level gravel plains and our march was in yellow air and the heat causing the blue-backs to tuck their long white and dirty scarves between their collars for them to suck up the perspiration from their smelly, sweaty necks. All to endure this windless blunt heat. But as you say, English, we whipped the cat and soon we were approaching a police-fort: a large walled tomblike-looking building with four towers going north, east, south, west, and with a flag on a pole rising out of the north tower. A flag of red, white, and blue in broad vertical stripes hanging as limp as the bodies from the Death Tree of Sadi-Radi-Hisham.

This structure was called by the name of "Fortress Paradis," which I did learn from Dres Ali was a thousand kilometers south-westerly from our principal objective, which was a town in this new country still northerly and called Sidi-bel-Abbes, the central city or "home" for all these blue-backs in all this land they called by the name of Alger.

Sentinels stood immobile upon the walls which were covered with running red and orange lizards, which you call "skinks," and running about on all of the towers under a horrible sun. The fortress itself was a structure about one hundred "one-twos" long on all four sides. Each side, which was like all of the fortresses in Alger, was a smooth wall four bodies high. The tall sentinel and fighting towers at each of the four corners were about twenty bodies high. This entire maison mud mound was surrounded by piled-up dried desert thorn-bushes but interwoven with each other as with cloth. It had been constructed with blood and "la bayonet" as well as with mud obtained from wells and made into bricks reinforced with sand and stones. All of which had a tendency to melt if it rained, which happened every fifty years. With each of these fortresses it had once been all the same, the Legionnaires were given building tools in Sidi-bel-Abbes and then just sent into the desert to built fortresses. Soldiers had to become masons and learn to use a spade as skillfully as a rifle or a bayonet. The construction of each of these bastions had meant battles all during the building of it, and it was said that it usually cost the life of one Legionnaire for each one-meter length of the walls. When a soldier fell, he was taken by his live comrades and cemented up within the walls. That is only one of the reasons these posts are named "Houses of the Dead," or what you call them in English, "cemetaries."

Past the gates that were opened after our bugler gave his signal, the weary column was greeted by even more dogs that did belong to those in this wretched "Fortress Paradis." The reason for all these dogs is that once in careless moments these sentinels permitted Chlur warriors to come wiggling in through the thorns in the darkness and up onto the ramparts and even into the fortress. Sentinels would be found dead with their throats cut and their Lebel rifles and their bullet pellet pouches gone. Hence these ragged-looking dogs who warned the sentinels. Each Legionnaire did not have only one faithful dog who hated all Berbers, and mainly Chlurs, but perhaps three or four inherited by him because of dead comrades. Then too, female dogs were forever making babies so a Legionnaire could, and did, in time end up with six or seven dogs, all of which were barking all the time along with the monkeys forever climbing the walls doing their chitty-chitty-chitty noises and the parrots flying about doing awk-awk-awk sounds. It was not peaceful, English, I can tell you.

Inside, amid this chaos, was garrisoned a Red Pants in charge and all of his two sergeants, four corporals, and about fifty men. Bringing inside our dogs and flies, I could see all of the shelters had been built against the skink-covered walls, leaving only a large court in the middle. Hanging down about the ramparts I did see perhaps sixty or seventy large boxes suspended on ropes attached to pulleys so that they could be raised and lowered. In the boxes were growing desert flowers of many colors. The reason the boxes were hanging by ropes was so that the dogs could not lift their legs and pee on them, thus ruining them. This was because the blue-backs of this bastion ate these flowers, just as the skinks did eat at the fogs of flies attracted by the flowers, who in turn were eaten by the birds. One of my daily duties did become the raising and the lowering of these boxes so to water them and the fighting off of the many different dogs who wanted to lift their one leg, if they had one, and pee on them. Many of these dogs had only three legs, and others had only two. Several had no legs at all, and were carried about high up on the knapsacks of their masters when transferred from post to post. All dogs with only one eye and one ear and severed tails and large festering wounds about their bodies and with only three legs or two or none were the result of these animals fighting in constant combat with the horses of the Berber Chlurs who were attacking their masters.

Our column had reached this outpost encampment a day after a supply column with its own dogs and monkeys and birds and food wagons of tea and rice and flour and dates and Bedouin butter in liquid form, which are standbys in the desert, plus many Girbas, which are sheepskins of water lined with tar which keeps the water cold, had arrived, along with the Money Master and an amorous collection of about fifteen old smelly Arab dancing desert flower girls, or what you call popsies, or what the Franks called "poules," which you English give the real name to as "prostitutes" and who follow the Money sous officer about from bastion to bastion.

Then daily, after eventide "soupe" and Madame La Pinard flowing into the mouths of these blue-backs, some Legionnaire of a sudden would get wobbly off the sand of the courtyard and onto his feet and, reeling about, eventually did grab up a "poule" and begin, without music, to dance with her in circles round and round the courtyard. Then other hulking soldiers grabbed the Arab "poules" and in grotesque couplings these half-naked unshaven barbarians did shout in the Frank and Germani and did begin to link arm in arm and start to stumble round and round together in the moonlight. And faster and faster they did twirl, laughing, most still wearing the boots with the nails on the bottom, some barefoot; all with their great moustaches dripping Pinard, their very muscled backs wriggling and rippling their blue, black, red, green ink tattoo pictures of dragons and flags and women with no clothes on that had been etched into their skin long ago and all going up and down pointing to the Sahara north, east, south, west. Yet, also some did dance all alone round and round while slapping their hands against their metal "soupe" plates, as an old almost hairless poule sitting beside me drinking did begin to sing lowly and slowly and soon louder and better and better. Then most all that were dancing on their feet wobbly and full of Pinard did stop their dance and commence walking round in a circle and trying to sing along with her in the beautiful song that she was singing.

Her melodious singing became a finer thing that caused me to think of Samonama, and, as I did watch, more Pinard was sloshed out to these poor beasts so they could drink and sing along better with her. They again did start to dance, on the tips of their toes, going round and round and then twirling out of tune with her song, which was "Wacht am Rhein." The activity continued most of the night with all the Germanis at the exhausting end, sitting and drinking Pinard and singing over and over the slow, beautiful song, "Wacht am Rhein."

As the days went by, these blue-backs wandering around the courtyard did seem in better spirits mostly due to the Arab poules and the services they did give all of the day and night and even if there were attacks without warning by one hundred or two hundred Chlurs at a time wanting la festa, mostly at night, when there was nothing to shoot back at from the ramparts except the flash from a Chlur rifle. However, those who lived through these onslaughts knew that in the morn they would be dancing round the courtyard with the poules and the feeling as to knowing that they would be killed on the morrow was dispelled. All because of the poules who cost, in your money, sixpence to lay on, and, if on their knees between your legs, fourpence. Dres Ali said to me that soon the sixpences and the fourpences would be gone, and when that happened, the poules would depart, as is their fashion, and then the best that could occur was that the Chlurs would assail the fort day and night because it would take the Legionnaires' minds off the departure of the poules.

He also did say to me as I did sit doing my language lessons on the sand of the courtyard in the shade, "Yes it is good for you to learn well les Français and Germani and the Italani so that you do not remain an ignorant savage."

I did say to him, "Have you ever known anyone who was not, in this life, as you name it, an ignorant savage? I have not. I would like to meet one who is not an ignorant savage. I now just do quietly accept that no matter what tribe of people you present to me, or what a person he is, that they are all completely hopeless, in which all will eventually end in a kind of death of one sort or another. That is their fancy. A death of their liking or how they choose to do it. If they and their minds are not hopeless, then they are in a hopeless situation, no matter what that situation might be and willfully creating for themselves yet again some sort of untidy tiny mess. Better Allah gave us the brains of a goat. We humans are the misbegotten. That is why we have the rules of Allah and why these Christians have the rules of their God and their Prophet Jesus Christ. All three state that we are hopeless." I, of a sudden, salaamed to this young fool as an excuse to get away. Even at eventide when I would get up and step away from Dres Ali, the heat of the day still did cling to the hot court of this fortress. The blue-backs and so too the Arab flowers that had chosen to remain, not for sixpences or fourpences but out of a sudden amour for several of these idiots, had shed most of what they named clothes for coolness' sake and for to better enjoy eventide.

I did not want to continue to think of my lessons in Francswari, Germani, Italani, or Español. Instead I did climb a ladder that did lead up to the flat roof of one of the towers from which these Francswari could overlook this desert. I did climb to this place to have a moment to dwell sadly upon my Samonama. Then one of the Arab poules spied Hadi out, and she too seemed impelled to climb to the roof where I stood to dwell upon the remains of my Samonama scattered all over on the plains of Bal-al-Din. To be polite to her I did talk and did point out that in the distance there were mountains that did appear to have vast sweeps of snow and shadow and to rise high to the sky of the Jinns. It was very beautiful, English. A full moon was appearing more and more giving light to this terrible Alger desert in this land of the violent Chlurs, and all making white the walls of this fort, radiant with the strange soft light of the rising moon, all trying to help me dwell upon my Samonama. But instead, I was too aware of the presence of this haggard and weary and naked-to-the-waist Arab dancing girl reeking of Pinard. Then this poule looked down at the half-naked blue-backs yet again singing and she also began to sing to be a part of these Legionnaires and her comrade dancing girls below. But this poule also did possess a voice for singing as with the other, a powerful voice and as she started to sing in the language of the Francswari, it caught the attention of her blue-back who obtained his flute from the barrack and, staggering back, began to play it up to her, and never did I hear and see two people act and make noise together such as this. As with all of the songs of the blue-backs, it was a sad song. It was named "Mon Legionnaire" and I never did hear anything like this before, yet it did belong to the feelings I also felt in my heart. Sad. Of many clicks of the tongue she did sing and I did come to hold her up under her arm lest she fall off the rampart and into the thornbushes. But then she did collapse and did begin to be sick and empty her stomach of Pinard all over my feet. And all I wanted to do was dwell on my Genii that was my Samonama. Now I had Pinard all over my feet mixed in with her water, crawling with pests, and little evil-looking lumps of bad Legion food that the stomachs of these flowers of the desert do not normally digest on a day-to-the-day basis. How could I think that I cannot get myself, as I was trying to do, to care for this poule less and yet keep dwelling on my Love Goddess Samonama with all of this smelly stomach mess all over my feet and all over the tower? And to keep constant and consider that I, Hadi, was her Great Love God. My greatest joys I owe to her and also my greatest sorrows. The best and the most bitter. A demon had inhabited her . . . also, she had the brains of a camel.

There was talk again of leaving this Fortress de Paradis for a trek through the yellow airless desert in order to continue to Sidi. It was good. Yet the Chlurs would again be able to kill me. All these passionate and incessant Chlurs and riding in the cook wagon wasted me. O Foyo. Yet at the fortress my head had become swollen with

the words of the languages of the Frank tribe and those of the
Germani, Italani, and the Espagñolis. And I had taken much care
to be well employed and useful and in this manner, I achieved the
name of ce-bon Hadi, the steadfast. And these roumis soldiers did
offer me as presents their precious little tubes of white paper in which
were dried black leaves and were to be inhaled. Then all of this smoke
came out of their noses as smoke after a cannon has been fired. These
tubes were called "Caporals" or as you say in your English, cigarettes. I did try this indulgence of these Legionnaires out of respect
and courtesy, but it was as if I had one large mouth full of old
coconut husks mixed up with unripened and raw betel nuts that had
been soaked in fox dung and caravan trail sand.

But my life had been bearable in the Fortress Paradis even in
the filthy rags that I, the eleganti, was forced to wear. And I was in
good body circumstances, for I could stand in an upright manner
without pain. And now I could depend upon some of my lies being
absorbed because the blue-backs could understand my speech in
Frank, Germani, Italani, Español, which did mean I had gained
more mastery over my situation. But I again contemplated longingly,
could Hadi succeed in this new trek? Ewa-lah yes, Hadi would
endure. He will live. There is no profit at all in being a rotting,
tortured Chlur victim. Besides, I wanted to see the Middle Sea.

So began again of a day by day we crawled like scorpions across
the many leagues of the thick sands towards our final destination,
Sidi-bel-Abbes. And without incident, except for me watching the
flamingos always migrating, the Chlurs continued to track us but
they feared to attack a now much reinforced column divided into two
and also realized they would have to contend with the beautifully
dressed and mounted Saphis. And in this manner the two columns
and the Berber camel police, the Saphis, tempestuous, excitable folk,
were also riding into the town of Sidi-bel-Abbes, with their mouths
all afroth, as was their fashion.

From a great distance, I did spy that a huge and formidable mud
brick and plastered clay wall did surround this city of the blue-backs.
I could also see from a distance tall minarets and large white domes
and many towers and I did think this was a town of great populousness and splendor. From very far there were cranes flying above in
a circle fashion, plus you could hear clacking from those settled on
the rooftops along with the squawks of high-up migrating flamingos.

Urging my wagon closer to this bastion, I could see the tops of these walls and the bottoms were crawling about with swift, black-haired, long-fanged Machabar baboons from the nearby Ashue Mountains. Later I did understand why the town of Sidi had many packs of large Machabar baboons, with babies riding on their backs, who did later sleep and rest in the trees of the town. In the beginning of their residence, they were permitted to crawl all over the walls, then permitted by the elders of the town in through the gates to wander about because they attacked, killed, and consumed the large rats that littered the Street of the Souks of the merchants which any of the dogs would not do. The baboons were outside the walls and inside the walls and mostly in the market squares where they did eat up rotting garden produce bothered by swarms of hungry but fat flies and slow sluggish crawling beetles and fitful lizards which were mostly eaten up by the starving rats who in turn were eaten up by the waiting quick-witted baboons who inevitably ended up eating everything anyway; the large gray flies and the fat-bellied beetles and the quickie-quickie green-colored lizards, the yellow-spotted mosquitos, and the butchered cast-off goat tails and legs and ears and all other piled up produce which had gone bad and would never be purchased by anyone. This disgusting town refuse was thrown on one huge five-meter-high pile in the easterly section of the marketplaces so that the produce would not have to be donkeyed back by the merchants to their distant villages in the hills. And this mess is what the baboons lived on. And they were allowed to go anywhere. Even within the souks themselves, also into houses. Hence the baboons got into a way of thinking they were kings of this place and lords of all they surveyed. However, the result was that Sidi-bel-Abbes was the cleanest town in all of the land of Alger.

Inside the legion encampment baboons were also permitted and roamed freely amid the dogs. Baboons muchly enjoy eating dogs; actually their favorite food. But not these tough legion dogs who had fought valiantly in unbearable desert conditions for survival of themselves and of their masters. If one of these Machabars attempted to attack a legion dog or steal away to eat a baby dog—not one chance, English. The cry of pain and fright was given by some dog and fifty or one hundred desert dogs would be on him and that Machabar baboon would be ripped and shredded into little pieces in about two clicks of your tongue and spread all over the compound. Baboons began to know this. So absolutely they did not try to eat legion dogs. Bonne chance on other stray dogs, yes. But the problem was that the baboons had already attacked and eaten all of the stray dogs of the town. Voilà. So legion dogs and Machabars had to exist together, even though the baboons constantly gave a hungry eye to our dogs.

When we came to the gates, the columns and their weary dogs, already barking at the baboons, were in a loud way ordered by the Adjutant de Compagnie to change their marching condition so that the blue-backs should march one behind the other. Some of the mounted Saphis rode off easterly, and I rode in the wagon and through the south archway, called the Gate of the Wind. Following me were many excited, scrambling Machabar baboons.

It was of a sudden very dark due to all the morning streets were covered over with interwoven lattice woodwork whereon were about five hundred years of red grape vines, which made it cool underneath and put onto the walls and down on the streets thousands of snake-like patterns of shadows. There were bougainvillea with the smell of jasmine everywhere.

This I did discover was just one of the many dim arched streets in this crowded walled town and given again the name, Street of the Souks, souks actually being little conclaves in small mud houses under lattice over-your-head work and all noisy with the cries of babies and water peddlers with terra cotta jugs slung on ropes across their shoulders and the barks of dogs. Many jabbering people crowded and pushing through these lanes and all dressed up in much color representing many different tribes of the lower and upper desert. But I was soon to learn that wind and sand dust storms were frequent and when rain came in from the Middle Sea it turned the souks into collapsing mud as when you melt butter in a pan over a fire. Now aspidistras, plants of these northern lands, lurked by the walls in Allah's early morning merciful shadows. With further progress our procession weaved past barefooted gypsy women with their entire fortune in gold and silver coins hung about their necks blithering loudly away in their Romany tongue and sweetmeat sellers jostling shellfish vendors with their flat wicker trays slung from their necks. Then we were pushing and kicking our way through goats with empty udders from their morning walk through the town having delivered fresh milk to the souk merchants. Most all of these animals know their routes so well that the Berber goatherd is hardly necessary.

Then we came to a part where over my head were also buildings perhaps one hundred meters high with iron-barred Spanish balconies brilliant with geraniums and all these flowerpots carefully tied to the bars.

I did spy also that there were awnings in front of these souks as well to keep out even more heat coming in at high noon and made of thin bamboo poles from Egypt with their merchants all sitting before them, legs crossed on their little Persian carpets. From the "restaurant" souks came drifting smells of cinnamon couscous, sweet overripe grapes, wet rice semolina with slightly oiled fried green and sweet red peppers mixed throughout with large shiny peas and women in the back of the souk constantly making up pyramids of all this on great round platters of pounded silver from Moroc.

I was much impressed, English, by this new place, for here were many things that I had never before seen in my humble life: soothsayers, snake charmers, and magic potion sellers and story tellers, then, too, spice sellers, tea makers with the scissors cutting up the leaves into tiny strips and sweet goat meat makers, coffee makers, hammers pounding their beans into little pieces, then putting the bits into shiny copper pots ready for tiny brass cups and little-finger coffee spoons. Also too in this market square were moaning bandits and thieves suspended in cages hung high up on thick, straight palm poles who had been captured by the Sultan's men and who would soon to be transported out to the desert to hang on their poles in their cages until they slowly died of thirst and starvation.

The pink-walled Legion encampment was in the absolute center of this town, surrounded by what I would soon learn were named in the Francswari, bistros or cafes, about which were many squatting Arab poules waiting with their legs open for business.

The soil inside the compound was not sand, but mostly red chips brought from the nearby hills and raked clean every morn. Entering the compound the dogs of our column hobbled in and met the dogs amid the baboons of this encampment. And remembering the desert Fortress Paradis, the inevitable had occurred here at Sidi. Dogs of other columns had made friendships with the permanent dogs of the Sidi barracks and made dog babies. Fortress Abbes was over-populated with whining and yapping and excited dog puppies, or, as you say, English, the place was a veritable kennel along with the continually chirping Egyptian hunting cats and the squawking, quacking parrots. In your English history, a sort of Bedlam of Alger.

As these blue-backs greeted each other as friends, a round-shouldered follow came and took hold of the mule traces and began to lead the wagon away. Of a sudden I was thinking it would be profitable to remain with the blue-backs, but how could I now be of value to them? Just be a good Hadi and hope they don't try to sell me to the Turks? Again I would command myself to be wise and put on the face like that of a water carrier and a simpleton and all the while being humble in manner, as it were. Manners maketh man. Even feign being fuganta, one pubic hair. I would salute every sou officer. I did not want to be a pagan, nor ever become just a little heap of teeth in the dust.

My round-shouldered guide eventually led the wagon to the hospital where the soldiers with great gentleness began to unload wounded from the wagon.

So I did worry what would be my corvee or, in your language, work detail. A man with one arm. Work in the soup kitchen for Anatolini Bagolini and stir pots as I did in the desert in the cook wagon? There would be no dead Chlur horses to chop up with the big square knife then spice them. Would I make bread, then scrape the pans? Crack nuts with my teeth? I saw no wood I could gather.

It ached in my heart not to know how I would be employed.

The guide led me to where I was to dwell. Up many stairs to a small hot room filled with buzzing fish flies and with walls painted gray. There was an old red table with the wall end lined with candles and whose ill-cut legs did not let it properly rest in balance on the creaking, sloping gray floor. A red chair's legs were not better. In one corner was a pile of reeds with a canvas draped over it. The pillow was a roll bag stuffed with marsh grass. Out the window and not far to the east were fields growing large brown sugar beets, which later I did learn the Legion did mill and then sell to the people living in the mountains. Also easterly were perhaps hundreds of immense black olive orchards and these silver green trees were planted in long straight rows. When came time for picking every Legionnaire available and his dogs, with a few curious baboons, did collect his basket then did tiredly stumble out to pick these olives then to spread them out on woven trays to dry in the sun for two days. Hence then to the press house to make dark olive oil that is sold in jars in the town and also in goatskins to all the hill tribes southeasterly. Another window presented a good view of the parade ground northerly, where at sunrise drums rolled and trumpets did blare. Always was singing out of the mouths of the rascal sergeants, as I translate into your tongue: "Move your bloody asses!"

It seemed to me that the beast that you rode on was forever being associated in name to that of the white man. But I will say the lot of the men below was hard. Waking up they were in a sorry state after drinking their Pinard half of the night.

The first morning sunrise call was "Rassemblement pour rapport," or parade for daily orders by company. Then it was "Garde-a-vous!" If it is said, means you instantly spring to rigid attention. The sous officer saw their attitude was "We will take up waking up some time tomorrow." So it was au pas gymnastique; these rogues in company formation two by two running around in a wide circle as the blowhard sergeants shouted "Vite! Vite! Vite!" When sufficiently awake the order was "Rompez!" meaning fall out for eating, and a tin mug of black coffee.

Then came the collective field service punishment marching parade. On the parade ground the sergeants carried whips as the caravan masters did during the days when I was being sold in the south; sou officers with snapping whips in hand. The prisoner Legionnaires were released from their confinement cells to run to their barrack after their names were called. This spectacular melodrama named Parade Inspection ordered them to dress in their costume of white kepi, ankle boots, white gaiters, blue greatcoat with four centimeters of blue sash; round this a wide leather belt, leather pouches, scabbard for bayonet, four more extra ammunition pouches filled with sand and with their enormous red epaulettes fixed in position on their shoulder straps, full knapsacks containing all kit, water bag filled and slung at the belt, needle and cotton thread stuck into the lining of their kepis and in each of their pockets paper for the lavatory and the regulation five louis of money.

After inspection it was punishment drill around the parade ground yelled out by sergeants snapping whips in the now hot sun. "Attention! Right turn! Forward march! Double march! Left, right —left, right! Halt! On all fours down! Rifle across the elbows! Forward crawl! Double crawl! If I see a single rifle touch the ground the holder is to solitary for fifteen days on half a kilo of bread a day and one bowl of water. Don't arch your knees! Pull yourselves forward with your elbows! Halt! On your feet—up!"

For nearly an insufferable hour as I did try to sit at my table I did hear the commands issued by sous officers and the cracking of their whips, round and round the parade ground, marching and alternately crawling. "Halt! On your feet! Garde-a-vous! Right turn! Forward march! Now sing!"

Marching songs are nearly all German in origin. But for punishment drill the traditional "Boudin" is required: the march of the Legion:

"Tiens, Voilà du boudin, voilà du boudin."

One duty I had was to be pig führer. I did feed fifty pigs. Fifty bambini pigs that again came on ships along with turkeys. These were to be slaughtered regularly by me hanging them up squeeling by their hind legs. Then cutting their throats and letting the blood fall into other buckets placed below their throats. This blood would be made into sausages mixed in with large gherkins, along with vinegar.

I was ordered to feed the pigs carrots, oranges, barley, dried dates, cooked rice mixed with bread without leaven. This to the pigs three times a day. Then collect all of the lemons eaten and sucked along with the officers' roasted pork. I was not ordered to make use of the lemons by squeezing the remaining juice into barrels to mix with water which the Legion drank for the long desert marches to other outposts. I was a good Hadi to do this on my own.

My last duty besides putting out waste from the cookhouse was to go to the threshing house. Here were bundles of unthreshed grain. I laboriously beat the wheat with my one arm to separate it from its straw. The wheat went into baskets and I had to drag them to the fort mill where two donkeys walked round drawing a heavy stone in a well-formed circle about fifty meters in diameter. Then let rest two days before it was winnowed. I had to go over the grain repeatedly and sift it all into a large, round mound.

When at last I did return to my room exhausted, I spied Dres Ali Mohammed sitting on my bed. With his chin he indicated the table. On it was a pile of Chinese rice paper, four bottles of black ink, and a tin mug of quills.

"To feed the animals is but a part of your day and night. The caring of the animals must be finished well before the noon meal." He spoke to me in Arabic which did my heart good, for I had not heard it in some time.

"If you do want anything, do ask me. I am responsible for you. Now come with me," he said somberly.

I did follow him to the administration buildings and, entering,

222

followed him down corridors going left and right. At last he and I did come to a door with written on it, Colonel Mizrat Novotny.

Entering this room I did hope I would impress him. He sat behind a desk leaning back in his European chair, waving about his fly whisk and which only did scatter the smoke curls coming from the evil-smelling Gauloise cigarette between his stained brown fingers. He was picking his nose and was a fattish, heavy-faced blue-back with eyes like a falcon's, piercing and mean. Also sitting was a very thin man in white clothes and white shoes and whose name I would soon learn was Professor Hercule Lubinacque of the Sorbonne school. But mostly visible in this room were books on shelves, the amount of which I, Hadi Abbabba Guwah, had never before beheld. This meant Colonel Novotny could read. O-ye.

He gestured for me to sit on a chair. He indicated a book and that I should pick it up.

"Open it, monsieur, and tell me what it is." I did so, turning the pages rapidly to impress him with my prowess. I decreed giving the book back that it was a trade account book of purchases made and monies paid to some trader. I spoke in Arabic. Dres Ali translated my words into Francswari.

Then this Colonel Novotny informed me what Dres Ali had told Major Svos, Novotny's under officer, about me. That I truly did know the trade languages Mandingo, M'bum, and Juku and also Hausa-Fullani. Did I honestly know of the main caravan trails and tracks leading up from the south of my land of Popo? Did I know the lands of M'bum? Did I know truly how to navigate the desert using only the moon and stars and especially the pole star as the main guide for traversing the desert and did I know how to use my shadow to travel the desert in the day? And did I know how to draw maps?

I said, "Oui," I, Hadi Abbabba Guwah, knew and can and could do all of what I have just sworn to you, my monsieur.

"C'est bon," said Monsieur Professor Hercule Lubinacque.

Then the professor did ask me many more questions. Did I know of the wells and the oases in the Great Desert? How far easterly had I been? How far westerly? Did I know the names of the tribes that lived there? How many caravans had I been on? What kilometers in a day did they make? He inquired of me about vegetation, the weather. Was I familiar with the land looking at it with the eye?

"Dres Ali has translated my list into Arabic of the reports and maps that I require. I want you to start in these projects immediately."

I did put on display much enthusiasm to this Colonel Novotny, for I knew I must succeed in pleasing him.

I would be provided with another desk. I did get it: unpainted, full of many holes due to woodworm, stained with many years of Pinard.

And to my unattractive room I did return after my morning food and the feeding of the animals. In days I was important enough to be attended by another blue-back by the name of Doques, who was of a day to sweep the room clean, kill as many flies as possible, fire the stove for the cold of night. Always this motley derelict was unshaven, and a sad-looking fool deserter in a ragged uniform. Doques came from the punishment cells. I ordered him to also bring me new pens when I did break them in my haste and larger papers and bottles of inks of different colors.

So in the skin-itching months that did follow where at night the flies were gone only to be replaced by clouds of moths that did flutter about and kill themselves in my candles as I scribed with a hurting hand, my religion became that of paper and inks, writing out report upon report. I did never scribe sitting on a chair before leaning over a table. I did not like it. So I had Dres Ali make me a knee desk so that I could start sitting cross-legged on my bed with my maps and charts and essays spread out before me in order I could make additions onto one piece of paper or another as I would think of them over the long hours of day after feeding the animals and the long time at night. My modus operandi. My lot was hard but I was loath to quit until I was so tired that I, many times, fell to sleep over my work. It was also true that I found myself enjoying this labor.

I did draw "cartographic" maps of all that I knew of the south lands in different colored inks. I did draw the caravan trails in red, the names of the towns near them that I had visited in black; also, the distances between them. This was the first time I did not have to draw maps using a stick on the sand. Now I had large pieces of paper and pens of the European kind. It was difficult, however. Francswari paper was made with too much cloth and no chicken fat at all, which made the lines blur indistinctly. Pens were forever splaying due to their weakness. I had to redo many times the track maps going from what you Englanders now call Lagos to northeasterly Banyo and then northerly to Kashka, Yola, Yakuba, Kano. Then separate maps had to be drawn that went through Bornu to Zinder, near to Lake Chat. Then I, "Hadi, the cartographer," drew track maps on how we got to Agades, Air, Ghat, Murzuk.

With much labor and little sleep I scribed maps indicating routes through the mountains, maps of wells and oases so that the Legion could build more forts there and have much of a supply of water. I indicated the name of each sultan who owned these wells.

In the interim I would queue in front of the cook house twice a day for my soup. Many of the Legionnaires of the long ago wounded wagons were now able to leave the hospital without bandages and greeted me with: "Voilà! There is le ce-bon Hadi!" with that and other voices of good cheer like "Cher Hadi, the stubby-armed miracle of the trail." Words like this spread to others of the bastion. I was also given the title "Chapeau Hadi," which means a good and wonderful fellow. Me. Ehwalla yes.

Many of these mischievous fellows insisted that I let them take me to the boissiere, or as you call it, the outpost canteen. I protested that I must return to my work. They replied that I worked too hard and needed relaxation. Besides, it would be an insult to them to refuse what they thought of as a very kind invitation. Oi-yo. I did fear greatly to lose my standing with them. So after soup I followed them to the boissiere which was candle-lit, airless, and smelling of tabac and cognac and did sit at a damp table with four of these afflicted Legionnaires, who ordered a four-liter pitcher of Pinard while I asked for as an hors d'oeuvre a beer in a glass.

I did not want to make any faux pas with my companions and, after the pouring out of the rioja wine, we all shouted "Salut!" and drank. Mama mia! It was awful to the taste. Then after another glass of beer and another I felt a change come over me, but more so with my sorries who did drink three tin mugs to my one glass.

I did forego my hors d'oeuvre and chose now to drink Pinard. The taste was just as untasteful as beer. Then I fell to thinking of my Samonama and her brains being in the belly of some dumb vulture. I nearly collapsed to weeping over this reverie with the feeling I would drown in my black memory. I had more Pinard. I did understand I was weak inwardly over Samonama and the foulness of loss spreading and spreading until I could see one day it could devour me completely. I had finished the wine and Jacques poured me another, which I drank quickly. I felt then some peace and calm. Samonama broke that peace. Merde! And I, Hadi the Brave, wiped the tears from my eyes and mouthing more Pinard and like a wind it was that I felt, the blasts of rising wind but then the feeling in me grew until it was as a storm of vultures distant and terrible and all coming lower and lower while all wanting my brains in their bellies at the same time trampling all about me was the pounding rumpus of lightless armies galloping and retreating across the plain of Bal-al-Din. Then there was no more noise or memory visions because of the Pinard. I had swooned.

They did carry me back and up the stairs to my room, my head inside now going boom, boom, boom. I tried to draw on my maps. I spilled ink on one because my hand could not hold the pen and my head was too fuzzy.

I did awake to the shrilling blasts of the bugle and ta-boom of drums. Sitting on the desk I did note two middle-sized baboons who were doing nothing but staring at me. The door of my room was all the way open. But now it was rompez or call out for soup, bread, Camembert cheese, sausage, and a tin mug of black coffee, or jus. In the meantime, I did go to the window that did look out upon the parade ground. I did see a shipload of recruits for the blue-back army which did arrive every month. In line not far from the new blue-backs and being whipped as an example to the new ones, were two lines of bald-headed Legionnaires that were almost completely tattooed and called Fort-a-bras. These, who were all scheduled for the prison called Battaillion d'Afrique, were large and very tough men who liked to fight, but better to them than that, liked to lay on young soldiers. The Legion, although tolerant, did not tolerate this.

My ragged little servant Doques brought me my morning meal. I shouted the baboons off my desk so that I could eat. I was out of sorts this day and told Doques to go fetch Dres Ali Mohammed. I was vexed as I ate with hunger, that I did not have my knee desk and a calabash of ink as I was used to, and had lost. When Dres Ali appeared I told him what I wanted. "Yes, master, it will be done," he said with a leer. Puh!

I had to do my duties and feed the animals, of course. I was very responsible, besides being a slave to my somber, piteous room. I was a good Hadi Abbabba Guwah.

When I did return to my room with my baboon following me, a large female who day after day had chosen to be fond of me, and who I now called Saadia, I found Hercule Lubinacque looking over my maps. He said he was very pleased with my work and that I had a talent for it. Of course I have a talent for it, you idiot.

"It is a pity that you do not know French properly. Come tomorrow I will bring you a French handbook which I hope you will study." He wished me bonne chance and departed.

So my work continued and for more days and days in the hot room and the cold of night I did scribe the Niger River from northerly to southerly as it ends at the water called Benin and indicated the town named Cape Formosa, and how it is connected in the north to the Sokoto River, then also too its connection to the Darorro River, all finally feeding into the Great Benue.

I did not have a visit from the thin Lubinacque for the number of days I could count on my fingers and toes. Then he did come, bringing with him his personal collection of "cartographics."

Lubinacque said, "These drawings come from the keeper of the library at Alexandria, who was but a Greek who lived and studied in Egypt. That is because the Egyptian King Rameses the Second by his own hand drew maps of his lands along the Nile with little crocodiles on it and pictures of all the birds that lived near the river and all the animals that came to drink in this river. All this on papyri and see, these maps also show the location of gold mines in the Nubian desert, drawings of his ideas of irrigation ditches; maps of how to navigate what he called the Middle Sea and how it can connect with the Red Sea. Also this man, this Greek named Eratosthenes, using measurements of all the ancient Egyptian surveyors, calculated distances from Alexandria to Aden by using his crude gnomon, or as you use in the desert, a measuring stick. He created with this tool what is called a meridian. From that he attempted to estimate the distance around the known world of that time. Another idea was to use on his maps, see here, a network of lines to locate places we call latitude and longitude. You see here, Hadi, on this papyri, is a discussion of stars, and the mathematical problems of geography and cartology, and here, the length of days of each season. The sun's course and differences in time at different places. These maps show how traders traveled from Rome to Alexandria, then up the Nile to the Red Sea. Next they traveled down around to the Indies and charted the Indian Ocean in order to get silk from Cathay. Here, Hadi Abbabba, take these maps and study them. Take these scrolls and read them."

I looked carefully. They were maps from Arab scholars at Baghdad. You see, English, Islam was making maps and also globes when similar Christian work was still primitive.

I did read these scrolls from after morning soup till evenglow, and discovered how Arabs used a compass long before it did reach the lands of the roumis. That Arabs were trading for silk with Cathay early in the eighth century, that a busy Arab merchant colony was settled in Kanton. That Cathay junks were steered by a magnetized iron blade set in the bows of their ships . . . and that these Cathays made regular trips to the Sea of Persia to trade. Baghdad under the Abbasside Caliphate was profitable for hundreds of years due to these maps that showed routes of trade and tides and rough passages. As a result, Baghdad became the center of learning, along with the riches and splendor of its architecture and the design of this city.

During the time of the Caliph Al Mamum's reign he created his School of Science and ordered his scholars that all the works of Ptolemy and Aristotle be translated. This Caliph Al Mamum ordered a large library made in Baghdad, that all copies of book covers were to be beautifully carved in leather and richly put together with the best paper and stitching. And many volumes of these books that did show and explain the names of places in his empire and what was their latitude and longitude and also he did commission charts to be drawn of all his towns and cities.

And then, of course, English, as a relief from my work, I began alone to venture out of my room to the post's boissieres. The worst of my Samonama sadness did begin at evenglow when mostly the colors of the sky were dyed deep purple as with the taubs of Baba Gungi, and westerly the horizon going to blue and then to green with thin streaks of crimson.

Also, I did go to the boissieres to learn by listening to the European language better. So I, Abbabba Guwah, would force myself to sit at one of the boissiere's many zinc-topped tables and uncomfortably in a European chair.

I was naturally welcomed by all of these connoisseurs of wine as ce-bon Hadi the humble, the vain and the scholar. I would encore on the red wine and everybody would encore also. They drank as if they hadn't had wine for months. But here I did learn the words of the Legion are of many languages, mixed up together in every sentence. Everyone understands at least a part of what is being said. Also they speak in what you call slang or argot, or jargon, in German, Russian, Polish, Italian, Hungarian, Spanish, Arabic, and Annamite, the tongue of the Berbers. Then there are special sentences used only by the Legion, as if you say to a vile Legionnaire, "Ich habe suppe von Deinemkopf." Only the blue-backs know what it means. In your tongue, English, it is interpreted as "I'm fed up with the sight of your ugly face so bugger off."

Too much grape of the gods also brought out strange behavior and thinking. At my table was Wolfgang Wentzhoff. Last time in this canteen he said his name was Hans Ashenhausen. Suddenly he erupted and said his name was Hans Holn. We all agreed his name was Hans Holn. He informed us he came from Magdesburg. We all said, "Très bien," and "Oh la-la-la!" Then he commenced to talk to me about pigs knuckles and heaped with mustard and bowls of potatoes and sauerkraut. Out of no reason he did shout out, "Verdammit-schnapps! Schnapps!" And to calm him down I did shriek out, "Jawohl, Herr Leutnant—Jawohl!" and then yell, "Achtung-Achtung! Schnapps! Schnapps!" which pleased him awfully. At times I would reply to his outbursts with "Ja, mein Hauptman." Then he would drink his Pinard and talk to me of wiener schnitzels and different ways to make apple strudels and all his comrades would pound his back spilling out "Ja's."

I had taken ten mugs of wine, mon dieu. And I called back old misery and pain to help my mind recall what I cannot regain. Samonama. That feeling for her was like feeding your heart to the beak of the hawk. It was time I returned to my room. My determination snapped when she looked at me. She knew that her knives were edgeless and that in a click of my tongue my life would begin. Life that I did think would be forever.

I would return to my room unaided. However, I did stagger and was very wobbly in my knees. Outside the darkness was dangerous. I must get to my room staggering or no. Ayammaa. At one point in my journey I did fall to my behind. Pathetique Hadi. Much labor on my part got me to my feet but about as steady as a Popo palm branch in a fierce sea wind. But I was not senti-ah-anta, one pubic hair.

I could smell her hair. It smelt of new forest leaves and the wind. Then, too, feel the hardness of her clean flesh, smell a fragrance stronger than my wine breath. My terrible beauty. At last I did reach my building and with mighty effort I did climb the stairs making capital progress and crawled into my room. What was there? I saw my baboon had her face on the floor and her bumper raised while a wild-eyed male baboon was there pounding away giving my Saadia quick and violent dicky-dicky, as she grunted, groaned, and sighed. Obviously a halcyon situation for her. Oh, my Samonama. Delight in her made trouble in my mind.

Now it was time for Hadi to collapse in sleep. Trying to do so I kept thinking Lubinacque was sad at me that I scribed so badly the Francswari. That it was terrible, and that my caligraphy using the Roman letters was terrible. He could not make sense of what I did write down. I asked him please do not be cross with me. I will do better and the Legion will find satisfaction in Hadi Abbabba Guwah.

In the morning I worked on trade routes, indicating their frontiers, rivers, mountains and climates, what goods could be obtained from those native to the area, and then notations of markets in distant lands for these various trade goods. I did read about the use of Italani ships built with keels, a device it was said, taken from the Viking tribe, and caused new charts to be made by the Italani sailors called "Portolano maps," or in English, "easy maps." With these Portolano charts the Italani sailors of the Middle Sea no longer used the Greek "Periplus," which was the golden book of sailing directions which described the appearances of towns all round the coasts of the Middle Sea and its capes and promontories as seen from out at sea. But of course, ships, as in my motherland of Popo, were only sure of their position so long as they hugged and cuddled the coast.

The life of this scholar I did find written in these reports was that for this man everything was maps, books, trade, and learning and reading all the time. Then also much of this was destroyed in one raid by the Mongol demon Hulaku Khan. Throughout the land there was nothing but raids, the burning of libraries, and the destruction of books and maps by all of the horde of Mongol demons. To escape the raids, and the death of learning, the scholars took up their books and maps and fled to the land of the Italani and to an island called Sicily. There with their books and charts and Portolano maps, a new industry came to be. It was the building of the ships of Sicily. Ships were built which had the Viking keels. Many copies of the Portolano maps were made and sold to merchants who in turn sold them to visiting trade sea captains, who now did see they could sail their newly purchased and well-constructed Sicily ships out of sight of the land.

And these scholars developed the Portolano maps even further by using a network of lines from the cross staff of the ship and also an instrument they invented called an astrolabe, all aids to navigation, and thus better trade.

Lubinacque said enough of maps, that I was becoming too interested in maps, which I, a sly devil, was. That I had to again write up my reports and tell the name of each sultan who ruled whatever area; how many soldiers did each sultan have, how effective were their military operations. How much did they have in money, who did they trade with, and lists of vassal tribes who pay annual tribute to smaller nobles. Then too, it was my own idée fixe to include the names of the many clan families and how each wanted the spoils of the sultan's conquests or to be included in on a great raid and night thefts of passing caravans.

All this Professor Lubinacque would have translated into Francswari by Dres Ali. I was pathetique in writing Français, which made me very sad, and I began to become fearful they would have no use for me. This gave me bad sleeps and at times no sleeps at all. I became frantic and would get up and write my reports or look over my maps to see that all was neat and correct.

Of one day I did ask, "Why do you want all this information?" Lubinacque did answer me that La Brave Legion wanted to become and would become, in time, a wealthy corporate body because eventually they wanted to become the biggest landowners in Alger. And that they do already have a grand agricultural program that foresees one day retired Legionnaires will tend their flocks of sheep and other farm produce. Their farms will one day supply meat, vegetables, fruits to the Legion only. Also, all farms will employ and be managed by partially disabled Legionnaires, many of whom will marry and settle down to this agricultural life and perpetuate a family. "But all must be conquered, as the Roman centurians conquered North Africa hundreds of years ago. That is why we ask you write these reports and make your maps. These will aid us in our conquest enormously. You will have a lot of work to do. Work hard and long, Hadi."

I did, until my eyes seemed to be burning and inside my head was going boom, boom, boom. So it came to pass that every evenglow I had to venture alone down the steps and over to the boissiere to seek grateful relief from my duties; try to use wine to calm my head and eyes and perhaps purge my feelings for Samonama.

I even got to like wine.

Legion rule was that you could get as drunk as you liked without committing material damage, and as long as you were inside the
encampment. However, if you traveled into this Arab-ridden town
it was full dress and steady on the legs since you were inspected at
the gate and easily turned back by the sentinels if you were not
properly turned out.

All of us stepped out, I, Hadi, just following wherever they
went. Soon they turned into an alley so narrow that we all had to
walk single file. Eventually, we came to the Cafe de Bulbul and
walked into noise and a large candlelit room with hundreds of moths
of different sizes fluttering about the candles at the bar and those on
the tables and all making moving shadow patterns on the ceiling and
through all the layers of Gauloise and Caporal cigarette smoke.
Besides the acrid smell of the burning cigarettes there were the
overpowering smells and sounds of sizzling goat meat and frying fish
mixed up with the reek of raw cognac and floor soap. The room was
full of staggering and drunk soldiers and the sounds of drunken
singing of "the Legion is our homeland," and the shoutings out of
"Verdammit! More beer! More! More! More!" All the Germani when
drunk only thought about food and endlessly about drinking their
brown bottles of Germani beer in a biergarten. Every thousand clicks
of the tongue, the gendarmes de la police militaire walked into Cafe
de Bulbul to observe that all was neat and tidy. They disregarded any
diables spread out in a swoon on the beer- and wine-covered floor.

With now in me much red wine and my beer bubbling the wine
I could feel it spreading up into my head and all through my body,
and thus I could dwell with intensity upon my Samonama. Perhaps
with more vin, that lovely intensity would increase. I boldly asked
the soldier sitting next to me for a cigarette. He gave one to me and
said, "Mon enfant, your face is the color of Hollandaise sauce."

Samonama—Samonama, my black memory that creates a despair is drowning me. Send me mercy from your home in the vulture.
Oui. But you are not in a belly now. You are vulture dung; nothing
but droppings, little pellets of merde spread out all over the plateau
of Bal-al-Din. Sacre bleu. What's left of you would probably only fill
two cupped hands, wo-ye-aya. Aya-wo. I rested my throbbing, tired
head again on the table in the spilt wine, closed my eyes. There, there
is her ghost when the night is old. All night long like a moving stain
across the sky until darkness sat in my mind like her riderless horse,
never bridled or tamed. Then I saw she was on her horse, her

beauteous face with her honey lips veiled. Yet to my fancied sight, I still did see the foolishness in her person so clear . . . then I was awake and she did flee, and waking brought back my night.

I lifted my head dripping with wine and took my mug and did drink all of it down. Clicks of the tongue and slowly my chin came to rest on my chest. Oh, if she could only have been a melting woman safe from ideas and just be my dancing Samonama with hips going up and down and around and forward and back while her arms did weave in and out of the smoky air clinking with her noise of silver finger bells now accompanied by her humming here in the land of legend where all things are possible to all men, even me.

Instead of "You will not speak to me and say that I will do this or that or I will do whatever. It is otherwise. It is that you are my slave. I can see it in your eyes. Say this to me: 'I am your slave.' "

"I am your slave."

"No, say it this way: 'I am *your* slave.' "

"I am *your* slave."

"Good. Now say to me, 'I, Hadi, will be a slave to the whore of a thousand tents forever.' "

"I, Hadi Abbabba Guwah, the tormented, will be a slave to the whore of a thousand tents forever."

Then I heard in my head her silver bells ding-binging, her brass bells and bangles clinking-tinkling, as well as her necklaces and anklets. Noise, I did say to myself. All noise. Puh!

How can I rid myself of this nuisance? My horrible Samonama. My phantom.

I had four more mugs of wine. I wanted to see if it would turn my body into corruption, as they did say it did. Living is dangerous for your life.

Then I did hear loudly, Oh la-la-la! shoutings out, breaking my reverie. I saw across the cafe a giant of a Legionnaire who was going to be rash with his fists that hardly opened before they shut again. The two had had their tête-à-tête and now began to push and strike each other. Soon their blood would be hot. Of a sudden, the smaller man had grabbed a knife from the table and threatened the giant with it. O-yeee, ahh mammaa, because it was of that time the gendarmes should be arriving again. Then someone let out cries of "basta-basta-basta!" meaning that all and out the door we should flee. At once an animal rush to escape this frolic. We met the gendarmes rushing to the ruckus and about to come through the door; we charged into

them knocking both down and they screaming also, getting out
European profanities, the number of which you could not count on
your fingers and toes. Count what teeth you have and the hairs on
your head and add them to your fingers and toes. That's good bookkeeping. Better yet, count the number of hairs growing out of your
nose and ears. Voilà!

We surged out from the alley onto Rue General Fleu. Some of
my comrade worthies fled right and others decided left. I was for my
room. Slowly walking mostly sideways as if I were a snake curling
across the sands, I, Hadi the sinless, tra-la-la, eventually did reach
the painted pink main gate that led to my own little casbah.

"What happened?" said one of the sentinels.

"N'importe, mon enfant," I said in magnificently good, clear
French. Lubinacque should have heard it. Oui. Hadi, the good fellow, ce-bon Hadi, had now to navigate his way to his casbah, which
was more difficult than finding the pink gate because I did keep
falling down. Two Legionnaires viewing my condition were gracious
enough to take Hadi by his feet and by his shoulders and carry him
up the steps to his casbah. One of them lit my candles, then both
again carried me to my bed, and putting me down started laughing.
With effort, I did look. There was Saadia, one cheek again resting
on the floor while her bumper was raised high into the air. Another
lover was imparting dicky-dicky. Probably like her mother, Saadia
was a young, lusty, wanton female who by her nature always kept
her bumper raised high hoping some male would come along and
give her a lot of moaning and groaning and squiggling while she
snorted for faster action. However, Saadia did like me best after her
dicky-dicky and always came and gave me her hand, making her feel
more secure. Then jump onto my shoulder and search my hair for
ticks and lice. If not this, chase and eat all of my big cockroaches
roaming in my room seeking orange and melon skins that I had
untidily or in haste left scattered about on my table and floor.

For me in the morning it was back to writing about Berbers:
incessant bickering by blood feuds involving additional offensive and
defensive alliances and further tribute paid to help the offended tribe
with ambushes, kidnapping, ransoms, thefts of camels and slaves.

Reports I tiredly put aside to work at the Francswari grammar,
its adjectives, verbs, and nouns for this Lubinacque because he insisted I do so. And I must remain in favor with this roumis.

After hours of this, my eyes began to hurt. When the ache was at its worst at the back of my neck I would forsake my work and go to the canteen. No. It was too noisy there, I would remain here and drink from the bottle of cognac Colonel Novotny had given me days ago and think about how long would I be of use to these rascals making maps and reports. How could they next employ me? Not just feed the chickens and pigs and turkeys and chop up goat heads. Ewallah no. Too little to do. Work with Anatolini in the cook house? Perhaps. Best would be to volunteer my services as a scout and guide to the Middle Desert. Oui. I would speak to Novotny at the proper moment. Voilà. Hadi thinks he is saved once again. All I had to do was to learn to eat pigs' blood sausages.

Nevertheless, lovely me, in the town once, drinking and thinking out my employment woes at the Cafe des Artistes, of a sudden felt hands grab my throat from the back and pull me out of my chair and throw me to the floor. Wo-ye-aya!! Turning, I saw a man with a patch over one eye. Lo, it was Ubanmasifa.

Recall, English, Ubanmasifa was the caravan leader in the employ of Sidi Bu Khamsa, the farmer with the water wheel that I used to tread and who died on me, then Ubanmasifa went into the employ as caravan captain of Al-Haj-Ayub who, as you remember, I also did desert once on Ubanmasifa's advice. Only to be captured again and made a slave once more. If you remember, I eventually killed Al-Haj-Ayub with rocks.

Ubanmasifa was not satisfied and laid onto my back and shoulders many blows with his walking stick because I did desert him once, and he is right, for I had no reason to truly desert him. When he had exhausted himself in about twenty-two clicks of the tongue, he of a sudden did shout at me, why was I in this city?

I did say I was working for the Francswari. That, most importantly, I, Hadi Abbabba, the humble, the vain, and the scholar, was no longer a slave. To the Legionnaires I was now cher ce-bon Hadi, and beloved. I told Ubanmasifa I was mightily pleased with my new employment and that I didn't have to kill anyone anymore. With this, Ubanmasifa stroked his beard, then laid a hand on my shoulder and asked me to come with him to a cafe he liked; to have tea with him and to tell him exactly how I was employed by the Francswari, which I did do and explained everything of my life from the time that I did desert him. He was impressed with many of my experiences and yet not too impressed with others.

Then I inquired what was he doing in Sidi-bel-Abbes.

He informed me that he had given up managing the caravans because of bandits. All during the year there had really been no profit for him in this business. Now he was in another business: being in charge of sending cargo from the port of Alger to France.

He told me he shipped across plantains or, as some call them, long figs, what you English now call bananas.

His cargo was also coconut milk which Frank women liked to bathe in, huge roped bales of sugar cane from the Southlands, and oakum, pitch, tar, dyes, resin, copra in large bags of canvas, rattan in bundles, and palm oil in small barrels.

On the return journey, Ubanmasifa brought articles for barter for the Berber cameleers, who would carry these trade goods south, such as fishhooks, iron mongery, crystals, gunpowder, all sorts of guns.

He was an emissary to many war-harassed sultans of the Middle Desert and those in Moroc whose crying need was trained and experienced European drill soldiers and all would be paid handsomely if they would come into their employ and could train their armies.

We parted saying both together that we must meet again at this cafe. He was eager to do this. So was I. Voilà.

As always, sacre bleu, it was back to my room, and my work. On this particular occasion, English, during the time that I was working on my Francswari grammar and my adjectives and verbs and nouns, Lubinacque did come to me to say that I had been working too hard. He added that I had been drinking too much Pinard and brandy. "Be careful," he said, "or you will have no employment with us any longer. Here, keep yourself busy but relax your mind. I have brought you easy work. Here are some of the legion account books for the post." But at that moment I could not think of account books, only what Ubanmasifa had told me of, an island he did know of called Amboina, an island in the Banda Sea, and that on Amboina one man had the largest plantation in all of what everybody called the East Indies and he only grew "clous," or the Spanish "clavo," both meaning as you call "nails." These little "nails," or as you call "cloves," grow on small evergreen trees and under the sun these trees exude a powerful odor that could be smelled far offshore in his Egyptian dhow, and one dhow load brought back to Alger and placed before the Arab merchants could be sold for more than the entire cost of a three-year European expedition. This island Amboina also had other plantations that grew nutmeg, cinnamon, or cassia, and pepper. But cloves or "nails" are used by the Francswari and the Germani across the Middle Sea to preserve the insides of their dead people with so as to make them last longer in the grave. The Italani, he said, stuff their dead with white pepper berries, after they have removed the black outer hulls, and garlic mixed with camphor mixed up in a pot with a jus called "vinegar." Why not just make a hole for the dead one and throw them in without "nails"?

Ubanmasifa repeated angrily, because there was much profit from these East Indies places named Moluccas, Sarawak, Siam, and the Malabar coast of west India. He had said it was much better than being a caravan captain. All he had to do was sail to the Malabar coast, then to Ceylon, from Ceylon to the Moluccas.

That the profit from Sumatra of pepper for Salem, Massachusetts, was a profit of seven hundred percent and that Salem is called the "Pepper Port." That the Italani cities of Venetia and Genova were built due to spice, but still, he said, that there was not enough spice because of the Gallic reverence for good food and many spices are involved in their preparation of good food. And then that for the roumis sickness of what they call leprosy and sleeping sickness in which the little nails, or cloves, should be mixed with coriander and nutmeg and, yet again, cinnamon. Then again, the demand and profit was high for these spices, while pepper, coriander, nutmeg, and also too, sage, to make Germani and Swiss sausage, or wurst.

But always it was back to my candlelit room and the endless copying of Lubinacque's maps and the studying of his ancient scrolls and studying my Francswari grammar which again at this time I did practice on yet everybody I could talk to. I did read about this man, Vasco da Gama of the Italani tribe, who reached Ubanmasifa's India in his big fat boats by sailing round westerly along coastal Africa, veering and reeling out of every bay and river all down the coast until he reached what was called the Malabar coast of western India, as Ubanmasifa said. But I read old scrolls that were diaries of Arab traders who did veer and reel along the coast to Cairo hugging the shore so as to avoid the corsairs and then who traveled down an Egyptian waterway all the distance to the Moluccas to obtain spices. I also did study maps of routes by sea to these places spoken of by Ubanmasifa.

Now it came a time that the professor Lubinacque said that he

was becoming pleased with my progress in his language and thought
that my Francswari grammar and my adjectives and my verbs and
nouns and my reading of the old scrolls and the old books splendid
enough that he would take me into the town and to the library of
an Arab friend of the blue-backs and called by the name of Mograb
who, I did come to learn, did own most all of the fig packing houses
and the sugar mills in Sidi-bel-Abbes. Also he did own over five
thousand camels that carried in goods from Lake Chat. I had seen
in my wanderings that the houses of the rich Arabs who did cavort
with the Francswari were in the middle of this town and mostly
always surrounded by old narrow, twisting lanes and hole-in-the-
wall shops and cul-de-sacs which were, as Lubinacque used to say,
"like going nowhere."

The going-nowhere houses of these fat, rich, smelly Arabs hidden behind high blank walls were all the same. There were firstly the
houses of the hidden gardens, circular gardens, then next two levels
constructed around the gardens, or as you call it, English, "a court."
And around these courts most always many small arched colonnades
or, at times, the roof of dark red tiles was upheld by these columns.
Sometimes there were many of these courts, and the tops of the
arches were filled with lacelike patterns that you see on the veils of
the Arab women. But these lacelike patterns all painted in many
different colors. The air of every court and its corners and its center
was filled with all the perfumes of flowers. Also, sometimes in the
courtyard of these houses there were large, elaborately designed
pools in which you sit into in the heat of the day.

To these houses only deplorable, monied Arab merchants and
insufferable Francswari could come, always in the best of their
clothes. Then also, only those Arab dancing girls that merchants
believed to be the most attractive were permitted to come.

Everyone who was to be a guest at these houses, especially at
Mograb's, had to be in good spirits. No one who was solemn or
severe was admitted to Mograb's. To be admitted also called for
rituals of entering uttering gleefully, "Lab es dilla!" "May you be
spared from all trouble." Say that to any drunken Legionnaire and
he'll laugh you out of the courtyard, s'il vous plait, tout de suite.

Then there was the ritual of spreading the hands and the many
tedious salaams which is the custom of these Arabs.

Every eventide after prayers there were dancing girls and the
music of the Arabs with their bagpipes wailing and instruments

called by the name "tambours" thumping incessantly. Then also their one-string violins squeaking frantically. These musicians, as with the desert Berber tribesmen, sang as they played; sang with their heads thrown back, mouths open very wide, in shrill voices, or truly, in a kind of exasperating Arab wail that sounded much like that of the noises that came from baboons during their mating season of the full moon.

And this sort of shrieking hubbub vibrating all over the court gardens and pool gardens nevertheless made these large-looking, veiled Arab girls dance violently moment after moment after moment, stamping their big flat feet on the colored tiles of the court-yards while the fat of their hips and bellies and arms jiggled and flapped north, east, south, and west. Most all of these Arab dancing girls had patterns of olive leaves tattooed in blue ink across their foreheads and down their cheeks and around their lips. And all and everyone had these drilled in for beauty's sake and had had their two front teeth knocked out with a sugar hammer and replaced with gold front teeth. As was the desire of the Arab merchants, nails and wrists of the girls were stained with henna leaves, which sent forth a strange odor as they danced round and round.

The reason, as you know, that the professor brought me to this place was for me to look at the library of this Mograb, whom he called a "bibliophile" although this merchant of figs and sugar and camels could not read. The library was only prestige to himself and his family and to impress other merchant families of the town as to his culture and intelligence. Nevertheless, I would be permitted to use his library to see if there were any corrections I could make to my map that the professor did not have. In a word, steal every bit of new information I could place my hands on.

And so, every day of a day back then I had permission to go with my pens and inks and my papers and with Saadia to the library of the merchant Mograb, there to steal. His cartography library was excellent. There were sea charts of stops along the coast trade routes of west Africa and gravure pictures of the fat ships that ever veered and reeled southerly toward my motherland and then south again to Lip-land. As in Popo, these sea routes hugged the land and traveled by the day and rested at a stop at night and the entire voyage was sailing in and out of points, bays, and river outlets; hence, nosing along the shores was easy in this manner. All navigation points on the west coast and all down to Kroo Lagoon were clearly marked,

and where, at each point, what the crews of these ships could expect
to find to eat: rice, chickens, tapirs, sweet potatoes, pineapples, plantains, mackerel, and tuna, all of which could be easily obtained by
trading with the natives.

Here in the library also I did find books of notes written in the
language of Spain which were really lists with small maps drawn into
them. Mostly, these books were what you call diaries of commerce
and trade and geography, and tales of mutinies and mutineers who
were on these heavy, fat-looking European ships and of the blood
they eventually did shed on the land against the resident tribes.

Mostly it seemed that these were perilous journeys because of
how the mightily armed ships of the Portogee, Nederlander, and
those of Spain and England would attack and shoot at each other in
order to prevent anyone but themselves from trading in spice. In
these diaries were writings about sailing along coasts and the worst
was to be followed by a Nederlander or an English ship from
the British East India Company or the dreaded Portogees who
would try to board you to steal your spice. Such was the value of
these spices.

Also, there were old account books. In these were lists of purchases and how they did sell and for what profit and, as Ubanmasifa
said, more than seven times what they were purchased for. They
stated that from among the many isles of the spice came also nutmegs
from the islands of Amboina and Banda; cinchona bark or what was
called "cassia" but in English what you call "cinnamon" from Ceylon, and from the Malabar coast of western India; and words that
said this spice was used in cooking and also as incense in the lands
across the Middle Sea. And from the Malay islands came the spices
of caraway, coriander, cumin, poppy seed, ginger, laurel leaves; also
sage, thyme, and white pepper; and from the Molucca islands,
cayenne, paprika, dill, fennel, and mustard.

Then I did start adding up the figures in the account books that
did tell that all these spices were very expensive in the lands across
the Middle Sea. And further writings that I did read said that one
successful return voyage with a full cargo from these isles of spices
called Malay, the Muluccas, and the Malabar coast would make a
profit for the merchant that would last for twenty-five years!

In the beginning I did not know how the Europeans used spices,
just that Anatolini Bagolini did show me how to rub spices into meat
of Chlur horses. For what reason I did not know. But I did decide

to spend more time in the library of the merchant Mograb and to read and reread and to be wise and learn. Yet all this profit from these little seeds, buds, leaves, roots, berries, and bits of tree bark? And these writings did show that the lands across the Middle Sea were devoted to these spices, and that several cities became rich, as with a city named Venetzia, all because of seeds, buds, leaves, roots, berries, and bits of tree bark. And the books then did describe why Anatolini Bagolini did make me pound spice into Chlur horse flesh: it was because his spices helped preserve meat in the heat of the desert. Then I did read that Europeans used spices to make a newly dead person last longer so that his family and relatives can keep looking at the body long after that body was supposed to bubble up and fall to pieces and rot. And that spices make perfumes and ointments because Europeans, especially the Francswari, do not wash. And thus they cover up their smells with spices when in the company of other stinking Francswari.

In time, I did again and again examine carefully maps of the isles of the spices: maps of the Philippines, those of India, Ceylon, Sumatra, Goa, Java, Madura, Celebes. There were books in English with drawings of the phraus of India, docks of Columbo, how Celebes phraus manned by Malays cruise among outlying islands and coastal towns of the Malay Peninsula, then go northeasterly to the center of these isles of spice, which are the Muluccas, and to their capital, Malacca, from which the best of the spices nutmeg, mace, and turmeric come from.

Then I, Hadi Abbabba the undaunted, studied with resolution lists of names of the Bengal Sea shippers, and learned how it was four months to travel by sea to Mombasa, and that black pepper, or what was called "chine," came from only India and Malay, and cloves from Zanzibar, and that the best of red pepper for spice grows in Mombasa and Zanzibar from which paprika is made, and then little notes on that if a man feeds paprika to a yellow canary bird which the Francswari like to do to their canary birds, soon the bird's feathers will turn red. Also, that to force live fish to swallow Mombasa red pepper is to make them last longer in the shops when they are dead. Thus also a way to preserve fish, as Anatolini Bagolini did with his spices into the fresh horse meat.

And at that time, due to the inside of my head hurting, my eyes in pain and dropping water and tears profusely, I did take up drinking wine and smoking Caporal cigarettes in my room during the writing of my reports and making better my fantastique charts. This went on for days.

It was reported that twice I did not feed the animals, and Doques saw I had spilled wine on my charts and I had in a drunken moment fallen down the stairs; indeed, I had even rolled out of my bed onto some cockroaches who were going to have babies and who did swarm over me severely in their anger. Sacre bleu. Even biting me. Puh! Then it was the professor who came to my room tout de suite while Doques with his bad breath was sweeping out the door the dead cockroaches and Caporals, to say that my condition was disgusting.

"You are drunk now!"

"Pardon Professor. Excuse moi. Hand me my bottle, s'il vous plait . . . have one with me and the flies and my melange of moths. Let's become as silly as a hat full of worms, absolument."

"No! There is wine all over your work now! You have become a typical Legionnaire. A drunk!" He spoke in the sharp, clipped manner which had long been the Legion style.

"Samonama," I said. "My Samonama . . ."

"Samonama? Who is she? Some harlot you found lying in an alley of the Cafe Bulbul?"

"Actually, my dear, Tebu of Gandoga proudly and in a merry jest referred to her as the whore of a thousand tents . . . no more brains than God gave geese. Her mother mated with a scorpion . . . a river to her people . . . mind like a cul-de-sac. Now just a little heap of teeth in the sand. Aoi-yo. . . ."

Then the professor told Doques to put me to the pallet, that I had had too much wine and was about to swoon.

In the morn before I could not feed the animals because of more of the night wine, Lubinacque came to me up my stairs with a bag of louis money and dropped it on my chest and said to me when my eyes did open that I was to immediately depart. That my service to La Legion was over. That Hadi's work for Novotny was worse and worse Novotny said. That I was to go out, out, out. Immediately. That the Legion was the home for lost hearts but that I was not in the Legion and could not be put in a punishment cell with no Pinard and could not be sent to Bat's d'Af and couldn't even be whipped with twenty-five lashes because I was not in La Legion but just a one-armed employee with one ear who would be intellectually useless because of being a total slave to Pinard!

"A slave to Pinard! A slave!" I shouted out.

He said, "A slave to your harlot! A slave to a woman. You fool!"

I could not frame my lies. I stammered and did try. Sacre bleu. I was too much with Pinard.

With Saadia holding onto my trousers and my one hand carrying my sack of bottles of Pinard and my louis money and my maps and charts, I did depart.

Past the parade ground and the ragged simpleton deserters with tin buckets who walked about all the compounds looking for the slightest trace of leftover Gauloise or Caporal cigarette butts. One fellow was this morn forever dropping his bucket whereupon he got three lashes across his back almost tearing his shirt off while others not on bucket duties ignored the whipping scene and continued playing Petanque, a form of boules.

La Legion's pink gate. At least they did not try to sell me to the Turks. The professor said I needed an education. What is that? Education? I can read. Sultan Mograb cannot read. Look at his wealth!

Hadi never did his dictionary for the Legion with listings like a stony desert is called a hamada; rocky plateaus, tassilis. Hassi-ain named a well or a spring.

La commedia e finita. The latest of my considerable, extensive misfortunes. Enough to drive one mad. Allah was not with me anymore so that I might gain a mastery over this situation. There was calamity as Hadi propounded his silly drivel? It pleases me to do so. Yet I am not pleased with my overmuch Pinard. Puh!

At last, Hadi the sot did come to the Cafe des Artistes through the corn husks that littered the streets of the town with Saadia and entered and did shout in French, "Blessings and peace upon everyone in this bistro." Nobody answered. They all took me for a drunken sot.

I did wander, then did sit at a table and Hadi withdrew from his sack one bottle of rioja. And I did drink with vigor. Lit up a Gauloise cigarette and flicked my matchstick to the floor. And I heard my head say to me:

Another rebuke meted out. Another laugh against Hadi. Exhausted with the want of understanding. Samonama wasting me. This life of punishment; abuse, insult, offensiveness. I swallowed more wine. The mastery I had over my mind was failing. How to make my life bearable? Where is my reward for being a good Hadi? And all of my good efforts?

Love hovered as a vulture within my mind. Once I did lay tangled in her hair and fettered to her lacquered eyes. Dancing girl of the Ouled-Nael, her hair caught up with a fillet . . . very subtle in swaying those quivering flanks of hers in time to the castanets' rattle: half drunk in the smoky tent, she dances. Lascivious, wanton, clashing the rhythm. And what is Hadi's use if he's tired of being with the chamber pots out in the dust and the heat, when he might as well forget chamber pots and lie still and get drunk with rioja on his settle?

Here's bottles and tin cups and measures and roses and Gauloises and one-string fiddles and a trellis-arbor cool with its shade and somewhere somebody is fiddling as if it were not the desert but a grotto. My thin little wine just poured from the bottle into my mouth that is pitchy, dreaming of Samonama beside a brook streaming by with the noise and gurgle of running water.

It is very hot. There is a noise shrilling, ear splitting; the lizards of the Artistes are hiding for coolness under Hadi's hedge. If you have sense you'll stay still and drench yourself from your wine bottle.

Across the bistro some red-fezzed Zouaves, a battalion of such that were in Sidi, were in violent argument with some Saphis of the native cavalry of hot-tempered Moors and Berbers of good families because these lunatics were devils although they rode beautiful white horses. So a fight. Should have been a "scusi" before a Zouave punched a Saphis in the mouth, or a "por favor, gracias," and then punch him in the mouth, without as is the custom of this language, to utter "de nada." And in the midst of this boisterous dispute, I did swoon.

An ocean of water ever rolling and pitching up-down surrounded me, and I was in a vessel with maps and charts under my good arm and yet more under my arm stump. From the head stays of this vessel, looking back, I saw land that was truly islands made up of huge sacks of cloves, black pepper, caraway, coriander, cumin, poppy seed, and all of the other spices I had encountered in my reading of Mograb's library. I was on a perilous adventure building an empire for Hadi Abbabba Guwah. The seawater did hit me in the face roughly and soaked my maps and charts. I did weep over this. But the good French ink stood up to the brutal attack of the salt water on my excellent Legionnaire paper. Up and down this ship did go, yet I, Hadi, was going forward in my life of incredible misfortune. It was although with the rough sea, a beautiful day of good sun and strong sea winds coming from Russia. I moved about like an infant learning to walk. The front bow disappeared of a sudden in a white explosion of the seawater, attacked my ship, the foredeck and waist filled with raging water and a large wave did sweep along my runners, dark, severe, and immense, with so little noise too; with but a faint hissing of foam, as in a deliberate silence. My wet and slippery decks were bleak, windswept, the mirror of salt water on my wood surface constantly renewed, reflected, and flashed the wild lights in the sky as my ship rolled and pitched. My wood structure was full of voices of pain, but the weighty sea which drove against my charts and my shrouds and kept them strongly vibrating was all invisible.

The light released from the sudden storm in the sky streamed over my ship again as my side of her lifted in a rolling motion, the water of the ocean falling down her wood sides as far as the end of the ship.

The ship went under. A wave stopped my ship with the shock of climbing onto a beach. The concussion scattered my charts and maps from under my arms about the deck, water did drench me, into my mouth, up my nose, all over my body. . . .

I did wake to Ubanmasifa pouring water onto me from a tin bucket. He did help me from the floor and set me into a European chair. I did nervously light up a Gauloise and send the matchstick over my shoulder.

"Ubanmasifa, I have had a dream of what will become of my life now that I am useless to the Legion; of what we must do. . . ."

"We?" As he sat down slowly, and I checked for to see that my maps and charts were still there—all there, I said a prayer: "Almighty Allah. Thou seest my afflictions. Thou knowest my need. Grant that I may acquit myself like a man in the trials and dangers that lie before me. Watch over me. Strengthen my heart; and in thy divine mercy and compassion, bring me all in safety to the haven toward which I now direct my course. Amen."

I did grab my wine. "Cheers," I said.

"No," he said.

"Bah. That attitude is enough to provoke Allah to madness. Let me, Hadi, the seafarer, present you with my idea." I commanded myself not to be so excited, not to shake my bones. "You say they want no slaves in France, no oats. That they want ivory and ebony wood and ostrich feathers and the feathers of owls. What do they want more? L'épice—cloves, peppers, turmenc, and all the rest! Voilà! Then with Allah's blessings we should provide that. Eh? How? By going the easterly route along the Mediterranean instead of westerly. Yes?"

I did, drinking rioja, outline my plan. Showed him my maps and charts, showed him with my finger pointing; my reasoning way, the time in travel saved, the profits. As a vicious trader his eyes did light with a spark of fire. But he just looked at me. How could I impress my intentions and myself onto him? Aya maa-mommaa.

"We need ships," he said. "I will see about it now. Be here when I get back."

"Si-si," I did say. "Très bien. . . ."

Hadi the navigator was tired. No more rioja. I fumbled with my sack and grabbed Saadia and staggered dragging her to the bistro keeper and asked to use his back room. Oui. Good man. In there, the back room, dark and cool, I found and lay down on a pile of straw. Would I dream again? Was the storm a bad omen? Would it be a disaster for me to venture into such an undertaking? Will there ever be no more bad times for Hadi? And nothing but dream time for Samonama? It was wrong of me to dwell on success? The gain would be enormous. Yet would I have prowess as a trader? Are my efforts all lost? I resolved within myself to be of good cheer. Absolument, n'est-ce pas? Rid myself of this distraught, unvaluable life.

Then I began to scratch myself. Another bad omen, as with the storm at sea . . . I did drink. . . .

Ubanmasifa woke me from my stupor, I scratching myself with much of a fury.

"You are to bring your sack and come with me. Quickly."

I had slept in straw permeated with sand fleas, the latest of my misfortunes. Scratch. This is really too much for cher Hadi to live with. My piteous self scratching all the time. Unmitigatedly unamusing.

Past lambs I pushed to follow a hurrying Ubanmasifa until finally he did turn sharply into an alley almost covered over by roses. Down the alley we went until he did stop before a large wood door of two partitions. He raised the knocker and let it fall three loud and one soft.

One portion of the door was opened by a servant and he did enter, turning to motion me inward. Where was Saadia? The inner courtyard was flowers and trees of the type I had not seen before and were grouped round a large pool along with orange trees that were only four hands high and with fruit the size of your thumb round. The dwelling itself was enclosed and guarded by a beautiful hand-hammered iron fence and door. In such surroundings it was embarrassing to be all the time scratching my sand fleas.

Through this door and down a high-ceilinged corridor I followed Ubanmasifa who followed a hurrying servant until we turned and came to a courtyard filled with flowers of every color and size. The walls were most ornate, all curves and sculptured juttings. All painted in green and red. Flowers everywhere and the smell overpowering me. This was good.

Ubanmasifa indicated I should sit on a silk-covered divan of red, and he placed himself on one of blue. Refreshments were served to us immediately by two very young Bedouin girls with tattoo marks across their foreheads and chins. The liquid was tea. Puh! Also small cakes.

"This man," said Ubanmasifa in a low voice, "is Fong Fun Fu Wong, a money lender. Chinese. Very rich and powerful. Owns half the quays in Arzeu, a seaside town not far from here. He—"

He stopped speaking. Fong Fun Fu Wong had entered by an archway to the left of me. He was a short, fattish old man waddling and dressed in a silken gown neck to feet of red, green, and blue with designs of lizards on it in white. He wore a small red bowl-type cap on top of a long train of hair tied in a pigtail and wound round with a blue ribbon. He crossed waddle-waddle to the center of the room and let one of the girls ease him down on some huge pillows, one piled upon the other, and, drawing his legs up, crossed them beneath him in Hadi fashion.

"Good afternoon, Mister Hadi Abbabba Guwah. My name is Fong Fu Fun Wong. Ubanmasifa is always incorrect in pronouncing my name. Sometimes he introduces me as Fong Wong Fu Fun, or Fong Wong Fun Fu. But mostly Fong Fun Fu Wong, which is assuredly wrong. Is this all clear, Mister Abbabba Hadi Guwah?"

"Oui, Monsieur Fu Fun Wong Fong."

"No, Fong Fu Fun Wong, Mister Guwah Hadi Abbabba."

"No—"

"Yes."

"But—"

"Fong Fu Fun Wong, sir."

"Oui. My name is Hadi Abbabba Guwah, not Abbabba Hadi Guwah, or Guwah Hadi Abbabba, or Guwah Abbabba Hadi, or Hadi Guwah Abbabba."

"Precisely."

"Thank you."

"It is my pleasure, and welcome to my humble house, Monsieur Guwah. Now, may I see your maps and charts."

"Yes, O Mighty Excellency." I salaamed profoundly. He bowed. "Lab es dilla!" I said. "May you be spared from all trouble. I say to all, may Allah increase your paunch, O Mighty Lord and Master. I—"

"May I see, please, your maps and charts? If it is not too much trouble?"

"Yes-yes." I, Hadi Guwah Abbabba, reverently dug for my maps and charts and stood to present them to him.

"No, please, Mister Abbabba, you give the maps and charts to my servant. She will bring them to me. I can understand what you want without explanation from you. There is always Ubanmasifa to help me. Secondly, you must take a bath immediately. You have got the sand fleas, yes?" He clapped his hands.

"Yes, O Grand Master."

One of the Bedouin girls appeared immediately and led me to the bathhouse. At once three other Bedouins appeared, and as I was scratching, stripped me of my clothes which they did dump upon the floor as rags. Then I was soaped on the head and my little hair cut off. Then the hair round that which makes babies, then urged to the pool quickly. Ayam-maaaa, it was hot. I was rubbed, soaped, and scrubbed all over my body in a matter of twenty-five clicks of the tongue. So much busy activity. After my bath I was invited to visit an adjoining room where one could rest after the bath, and I did begin to recline on a silk-covered divan but was urged to a table to lie flat upon. Here the girls rubbed into my body all over a purple liquid that they did say would rid me of my fleas. I did see there was a latticed balcony just above the many divans.

It was explained to me by one of the tattooed girls seeing me look how that one musician always sat on the balcony and did play sweet music while the naked Sultana and her naked courtesans rested on their divans after their baths. And then she hastily added, "But of course, master, the musician was blind so as not to gaze down on the naked Sultana."

"Where is the Sultana now?" I did ask.

"She is presumed dead, master."

"Who once did own this house?"

"This was the first villa of the Sultan Mograb, master." Then she added, "You will have to keep this purple fluid on your body for the night and one day." Thereupon I was dressed in a robe designed the way Monsieur Fong's robe was, then taken and led back into the large guest room with Ubanmasifa and Fong. Looking purple all over for twenty-four hours. Wo-ye.

"I am sorry, Mister Abbabba," he bowed to me while sitting. "It was all necessary to your health and mine. Be seated, please." He clapped his hands.

Immediately the two girls brought in trays on which there were bowls. In these were soup, by the name called roast pork yatka mein, which was delicious. Long, thin noodles spiced with long, thin pork strips and Chinese cabbage as they call it, in a yellow chicken broth. Also barbecued spare ribs with plates of dim sum, an assortment of flower-like-looking objects resembling roses, but were truly chopped pork balls cooked in boiling water and wrapped in broad noodles with carrot slices on top and poured over with a delicate dark sauce made of pork fat. And there was now as I was sitting down the sound of much tinkling and I did look round wondering what made this strange, yet charming sound.

"Those are Chinese wind bells, Mister Guwah Hadi. I hope they do not disturb you." He spooned in his soup in a loud slushy fashion. "As to your maps and charts, Mister Guwah—" Later I was to learn loud slurp sounds were for the cook to hear. These were compliments. "Where did you get this information?"

"From the charts and maps of Mograb's library, Excellency—"

"I see. You were in Mograb's library—?"

"Yes, as you say, your Excellency. The Sultan doesn't read— the library is for prestige only. For his—"

"Does he" (now attacking the barbequed spare ribs) "know you have these?"

"No. They are copies I made, Excellency."

"And these—" (He clapped his hands as he did finish his roast port yatka mein, the spare ribs, and the dim sum. Next were rushed

in trays of paper bag chicken with extra plates of roast pork strips.)
"—drawings of Sicily ships, can you do better?"

I salaamed profoundly, spreading my hands. Then drank and
finished my soup. Gobbled up all the spare ribs and swallowed down
the dim sum all of each one piece. Quickly. Not to be impolite.
Ai-yaaa.

"This astrolabe," he said; crackle-crackle went the chicken, "I
can have this made. You with these Sicily ships, these Italani ships
with deep keels made; three of them, yes?"

I, chomping on the chicken: "Yes!"

"What else do you require?" He pointed to the girl that I needed
more of the roast pork strips, which were instantly brought.

"I need Egyptian dhows, your Excellency Lord Master for
transport of the spices from here to France and Italy. The Sicily ships
will go west from here to Cairo, then go right as you look on the map,
south to Aden. I will—"

"You will not." He had finished. He clapped his hands. In was
brought a seafood plate of shrimp with lobster sauce, and two plates
each of butterfly shrimp and a large bowl of sweet and sour shrimp.
These he did eat not with fingers but with long wooden sticks.
"Ubanmasifa will be captain of your fleet and in charge of all trading.
Is that understood? He will also be in charge of all transport to
France. Is that understood?"

"Yes, as you say, your Excellency Master Lord. What will I be
in charge of, O mighty swayer of the world?"

"You will be the bookkeeper of monies and arrange all cargoes.
You can write. What comes in and goes out you will note. You will
decide all cargoes. Here to the Isles of Spice and here to France. You
can write. Ubanmasifa can't. He has two arms. You do not. You are
paperwork for the rest of your life. If you live that long. That and
to prevent you from drinking. You drink too much due to your
Samonama. So to protect my business interest I will get you a wife.
Which will take your mind off Samonama. In turn, you will get me
two wives with your Sicily ships." He exuberantly clapped his hands.
More food.

The girls brought in that which I was to discover later was moo
goo gai pan, with secondary plates of fried Hawaiian chicken wings
and pork cha shu ding.

Then there were the plates of crabmeat soong with sizzling
seafood Cantonese style. After that, and in Mandarin style, lobster

with secondary plates of shredded beef with Hoi Sin sauce. Such extravagance! And not to think me a savage, I had to and forced myself to eat everything.

You could tell Fong was not a lazy mouth. He did yabber incessantly. He would have built for me three Viking ships. Everything from me was yes, yes, yes. Then at the end of eating he ordered his girls to buy a goat, cut off its head, then throw its black face out the door. "It's good luck," he said.

I betook my sack sans Saadia and my purple body in its colorful Chinois costume from this confrontation with the China food, and followed the Bedouin girl to the room that was assigned to me. I had saved my bottles of Pinard. Voilà! Here in my room, as he did instruct, I was to draw delicately and with precision outlines and details of the Sicily ships that were to go easterly.

In time I took muchly drinks of my Pinard. I did see within me that as my own bookkeeper there was much to be done. Or I would be sold to the Turks and be laid on by their army. Or, I would starve to death and be a heap of teeth in the dust. I was, I did cry out, no better off now than when I was heretofore a bandit in the desert with the Tebu of Gandoga. I did weep I was no better off now than when I was heretofore a scribe with La Brave Legion. To better the circumstances of Hadi I must still succeed in pleasing. Now this émigré Chinois would get seventy percent of the profits from our first voyage. This was to pay him back his monies put forth in Sicily shipbuilding and barter money for trade goods. After this the scale of profit for him would descend. I must plan and act accordingly.

Fong did instruct me to ring the tiny bell beside my knee table if I did need anything. I did ring in a wild way for I did require much, much paper, inks, calabashes, reed pens, Pinard. I wanted a Hausa cat, no, two Hausa cats, and lots of birds of many colors in cages for the cats to be excited about and lots of flowers to surround me in my room.

Entered my giggling mademoiselle du chambre, yet another delectable Bedouin, but this time only of about fifteen years of age, small and thin. Charming, charming. As you would say, English, she had that aspect and smile and manner that could make one want to drool all over one's Chinois roast pork strips.

Mademoiselle du chambre's name, she announced, was Amandii. She smiled sweetly, Aay-Yammaa, and did hold her full, ripe legs close together and twisting her full-breasted body with lowered chin. A classic pose, isn't it, English?

She did giggle and say she would attend me. In all things and in every way she had a penchant, she said. She did say especially at night. "Indeed," I did say. She did smile. I, purple Hadi of the fleas, did smile, hoping I did not have camel breath.

I, Hadi the melted, decreed my orders and clapped my hands as did Sung Fu Fum Fong. Amandii did stop and turn around. I did look. "Your more orders, master?" "No," I said. "You clapped," she said. She did dash away to fulfill my orders.

I, Hadi the bourgeois, would come to desire books empty of writing which I would fill with my writing and my plans. Firstly I would have a company named The Fong Guwah Ubanmasifa Trading Company Limited. Voilà, très bien. I drank my Pinard. Monsieur Fong has treated me well and shown me much favor. I would cease to frame my distressful lies, I think. I would succeed in pleasing my émigré with his money bags and perhaps there would be joy for Hadi for the rest of his life.

With my empty books, blank papers, colored inks, calabashes, pens, Pinard brought to me by Amandii, now I did begin to build an empire for The Fong Guwah Ubanmasifa Trading Company Limited. As you say, the first task was the first voyage map for my three Viking keel ships. For barter, most importantly, nails, then fishhooks, rifles and pistols, powder, small cannon, and cotton woven fabrics, cooking metal pots and pans, metal knives, forks, spoons, tin mugs, plates, bowls. Powders, perfumes, and grease for the women, and toys for the children.

The map I did draw for this first sea journey of Ubanmasifa, considering the danger and seventy percent profits to Wong Fu Fong Fun, would be easterly along the coast, hugging the land and not to lose the land; and sailing in and out of bays and rivers. And indications of stops for the nights' rest. To Cairo. Down southeast to Aden, then the single crossing of the Arabian Sea northeasterly to arrive at the Malabar coast with its capital of Bombay. Then trade and cheerio and southeasterly to the Island of Ceylon and the capital Columbo. Trade and there directly easterly to the Moluccas. After trade here it was northwesterly to the port of Kanton for Fong's wives.

Lists of competent and reliable crews would be Ubanmasifa's task. And fighting men. I did want Ubanmasifa to give me charts of areas where corsairs did work. Risk, further risk. But I would design a demon pennant to corsairs that would say there is no gold or monies on Hadi's ships, but only trade goods as I have mentioned, which are completely useless and unsalable for corsairs who would dump them into the sea in a fury, so said Mograb's journals. Corsairs wanted gold, silver, and hostages and spices which easterly traders never carried on the sea route in Viking keel ships but rode the overland sand route to Cairo.

The return trip would be more dangerous, as the corsairs would note in their logs. Spices from the first port of call in Bombay, then Columbo, the Moluccas, and two Chinois wives would make a profit that would last for twenty-five years. This the corsairs knew. Pennants would be useless. The Sicily ships were now a fortune to them. Goods pillaged be all sold by corsairs to confederates in Italani's Genova and Naples. With a safe return passage westerly, spices from the east would be transferred to dhows for Ubanmasifa's passage across to France.

To draw and write sea charts, lists, instructions were Hadi the trader's Christian crosses to bear. I did labor overmuch and obtained little sleep. I did drink Pinard due to again burning eyes and the pounding in my head. I began not to see clearly my instructions and lists. But in this paper endeavor I was loath to quit. No faux pas. All through the night and a Buon Giorno to my Amandii bringing me trays of Szechuan hot and sour soup with rice, fried wonton with rice, shrimp and lobster lo mein Cantonese with rice, chow har kew with rice, green pepper steak with rice, sweet and sour pork; no rice. I had rice, koon poo chicken, black bean gai kew and bowls and bowls of biscotti, or as you call "cookies," at my little table.

What other employment could I do, moreover? Hadi was a good man. Not a slave. Not a pagan. For obvious reasons not a savage. Not a barbarian. Not one pubic hair. Not good for Turks to lay on. I don't drink too much. I did drink. I took some Pinard. Only too much feel for Samonama. One does not find ever again Samonama.

Hadi a good Hadi. Hadi a good man. Not a slave. Not a slushy. Only too much feel for Samonama. After another mouthful of Pinard, Hadi fell to sleeping.

I did at last make it to the end of my writing lists for this trip to please Fong and get me a bride to replace my only Samonama and thus stop me drinking Pinard to soothe my passions.

Fong said, "This will be your lucky day because you were born in the year of the dragon," which, he said, "was the sign of the king and that you should have a wife born under the sign of the cow. Cows are faithful, loyal, and good wives."

I made more lists, as Fong was innocent of the desert and its travel. Fong did provide for me a guide of the name Fong Wong Soo Poo Chang, number eight son of money lender Fong himself, who did bring to show me a map—in Chinois writing—as to where this caravan was departing for. It was south and easterly a great way to a village which was most famous for what is named "The Brides Market." This burg was a mountain town of Aithadidou, called after that Berber tribe. Girls for marriage were taken by their families each month to be sold.

New lists submitted included a bodyguard of twenty men who eventually turned out to be marines who were from Fong's Spanish trade ships and who had defended them loyally by fighting off corsairs through the many years. Baggage for the caravan which I imparted to Chang would be tents, blankets, kerosene lamps and oil for them, cooking stoves, fire fuel, twelve score tea pots, my bottles of Pinard for I still did not have a wife, and my heavy English volume of William Shakespeare, who I have been studying to speak good English. Hark—forsooth, yon ahead is the evil time of the desert while I read this sower who scatters diamonds to this coming mummied desert. Alas, alack, this prince of braggarts, this prince of hearts and O magnificent sultan of words to me a pilgrimaging ant in this dull, savage desert, in your infidel tongue, your words of flame . . . you see what I mean, English?

All of which I would tediously and rigorously study on this journey to the Brides Market. Also too, Fong gave me red birds in cages as presents. Now, I implore you, English, what would I do with birds in cages in the desert?

The teacher that I requested and that Fong did provide me coolly announced he was a captain, and the Count Alexandrovitch Elia Puozkajlerovana Badarjewska. This statement was in an overbearing way, but I did salaam and spread my hands and did answer politely and quietly that I could not with my Afrique tongue pronounce his ridiculous name.

He waggled his head like a cow and replied, "Call me anything you want to call me, old man." He grinned amiably. "What about Smith? I think I'd like that. I've always wondered what it must be like to be called Smith. Can you pronounce Smith, old man?"

"Smith," I said.

"Splendid."

Smith could read and write and was much learned in English, and French which I did request of Fong as a master to teach me. He was employed for this journey to constantly teach me better the English language and French vocabulary, and primarily verbs. Also to better improve me exercising on paper the practice of the square-limbed, angled, and round Roman letters.

I had resolved, since I thought only for my improvement, that soon all my lists, books, maps, charts would be written in perfect square-limbed, angled, and round Roman letters and in perfect English and also I resolved to speak like the mighty Monsieur William Shakespeare. This English was the latest and most important of new trade languages.

Smith was Fong's Master-at-Arms for his Spanish fleet. He was also to be master of my bodyguards. Then, too, Smith was of the Polski royal family and at one time ago a cavalry master at the military academy of Stunsk, and at the moment in disguise in this land of legend. He was one secret agent. He did say to me with furtive flamboyance that his motherland wished to control by intrigue the Middle Sea Mediterranean and steal all the power from what he did call the Frogs and the Spaghettis. That he had been sent here to spy out whatever obstacles there could be as to this endeavor. No look of disquiet came to my face hearing this. I did not know where Poland was. I had never heard of a land called Poland. They did not trade in the Southlands.

But he had two arms and two ears. His face was forever frowning. Every night probably had nightmares that made him snore. The eyes of Captain Monsieur Le Count were proud and his voice blowing continually across my cheek was thunder. Also too, a thick, hairy neck, a body like bronze, and eyes like dirt. Dragon's eyes. Great long teeth and a disgusting underlip that hung wide. He would come to a bad end, this stately, stalking, meddling lordship with his Polski soul full of Mediterranean receipts. He had no honest mind, and his mad talk raped all the commonplace of my Samonama's land. This one could teach rats to squeal. And the Captain Polski Smith was also, to my mind, a drunkard.

The cameleers did load the baggage camels with camel rugs with the dangling tassels for the long-prepared necessities of the journey; many leather bags of Chinese food and condiments, thirty bags of well water, my bag of Caporal cigarettes, Pinard and rioja wine which turn the body into corruption.

And so on the morrow it was a misted early morning and it was cold. Soon the copper sun would turn into brass. Skies now thin blue would turn to yellow. There were leagues and kilometers to go. As the morning sun shone watered blood red upon Fong's rich silken clothes, I put on my green coat out of China with dragons worked upon it and my scarlet silk trousers because Hadi had to be svelte. Hadi the svelte.

As my splendid Mehari riding camel was saddled, I did deck myself in the clean robes of respect. Clothes to cover the scars of my life and the scars of my mind. A disguise, eh English?

Again to wear cotton trousers under my robes. Then the vertical blue-striped burnoose of the Berbers of Alger. That is the garment that is the first garment on the body instead of the white cotton taub of my Southern Popo, a sort of robe to the ankles. Then to be adorned if it is wished, with a Bedouin waistcoat with richly decorated gold embroidering. Then sashes. Then the Alger burnoose, and over this the low flowing garment called a gondourah, with a loose hood and not tailored as with your Christian monks. Then too, a cape, the white woolen garment that is the direct descendant of the Roman toga, these conquerors who ruled and collected taxes in this land centuries ago. Then for my yellow camel-colored curly toed slippers and my long white Kafiyeh headdress with its black-dyed coiled agal ropes of camel hair. Then I, Hadi the svelte, adorned myself with a chin cloth and cape of white cotton. Lastly, the silver hilt and guard of a huge, long, beautifully curved iron dagger one could kill a Turk with and which I stuck down through the front of the broad girdle sash about the long white burnoose over which is the gondourah.

Soon the day is on his wings. Chang guiding. After passing this town of Sidi-bel-Abbes, there was only the vast emptiness with universes beyond universes and the rhythmic fall of soft cloven feet on sand, the rhythmic swaying of my great camel's hot body and the world swaying the sun, swaying. To test my beast I raised the long camel stick that dangled from my wrist and my camel quickened its pace instantly.

Sun appears above the horizon giving warning time of heat and suffering has arrived. The bodyguard and the cameleers were tearing at strips of dried octopus as they rode, their new and shiny cartridge rifles were slung over their backs, and all carried sabres as well and had daggers thrust into their belts. While they also tore at tajin, which is dried camel meat, my captain Smith drank from his Harvey's Bristol Cream sherry bottle from England. Everything about him was so revoltingly English, eh English? I would become revoltingly English? We shall see.

The sun rose and we plowed on through the air which was a thick heat. The same red glare as far as I could see. I could feel my head swelling under the impact of the light. It pressed itself upon me trying to stop my progress. Each time I felt a hot blast strike my body, I gritted my teeth, tightened my hold on the reins, and used every resistance to fend off the sun and the dark befuddlement it was pouring into me. My jaws were set Legion hard. I was not going to be beaten and I rode steadily on.

To help me with my trial of the desert, I did drink some wanton soup and ate some powdered egg foo young, Cantonese style, but Samonama's face appears in my eyes even as light and shadows chide me. Tell me, my unruly Samonama, tell me where all my past cuddles are? Me, who can weep with spongy eyes and she who never cries. She—you—who has robbed me of my child and blinded me, and I, who am now a busy old fool not made for dramatic events like on the plain of Bal-al-Din. Let me go.

As I rode—hua—reading my Shakespeare to learn English more properly, alas, alack, over these long plains of abominations, it came to pass that my guide riding ahead of me, Chang, rolled and fell off his camel. This Chang, English, was a smoker of hashish. He did this all the day long while I ate my shrimp with bean sprouts. How would we ever reach the Brides Market?

Mister Shakespeare, you who have the witchery of an Epfumo, carpet this desert trail with your hymns of the whole of life and let your music bring all this broil of mine to ease. All that is in your book is mine. Allah in his mercy and not on the Christian cross murdered, "lab es dilla," may you be spared from all trouble, which isn't bloody likely.

And then it was struck into my heart that we were being tracked, as Chang fell off his camel again. Chang was picked up by two of the bodyguards at the orders from the rumbling throat of Count Smith, and beaten to wake him up so that we could continue on our way. Above, on a high dune, three men, perhaps tracking us into a bleaching grave, were dividing our shadows in the heavy sun. From their garments in color and crisscrossed leather bandoleers, I could tell they were of the Chamba Bedouin tribe of the Berber nation and no people to mess with.

All along the trail under this blast of yellow sky I saw the bodies of previous caravan cameleers, the picked meat ripped away by the buzzards here in this fool's forest, their bones with sometimes some brown dried meat on them, a dull prison in the dust.

Then I did spy the buzzards, cruising round and round on placid wings. I watched their full flight—waiting, waiting to devour death, keeping nature new. Was this an omen? Is Hadi to be dead?

And again the sun took charge. Waves of heat and light swept the desert day long and the sun stalked my caravan and struck like a sword blow. That night, the second night out of Sidi, I had a terrible dream, or vision, where I did see Ubanmasifa drowned and all his, our, cargo washed up on a beach.

The next day, working onwards on my camel, and reading my Shakespeare to pass the time and to learn well your speech, English, I am of a sudden startled by Chang, who gives an agitated cry and points. I did urge my camel along and topped the dune and came to a halt beside Chang. There, below the buzzards, were two men on foot, struggling arm on shoulders through the sands, dressed in raggling clothes, dragging, stumbling their feet. I quickly pushed my camel forward saying to myself, Ah-ha, the buzzards are for *them*. The bird carrion were not a bad omen for me or Ubanmasifa, but for these men they were above, waiting for them to fall down to die. Of course, I was lying to myself saying this. But it did soothe my dread of the time, that I and my caravan were doomed and the thought that nothing I would ever do would come to anything. I reached these men and furiously brought my camel to its knees. I ran to examine these people as Smith and the bodyguard rode up whirling all about sand dust.

The two men now standing still before me were white men, bearded, wore what was left of tattered European shirts and trousers which, on closer examination, did convince me was Legion cloth. They wore Legion boots and carried Legion cartridge rifles. Ha! Legionnaires! What, forsooth, were they doing here? Naturally, English, a dumb, stupid question for Hadi the scholar to ask myself.

Their lips and tongues were too swollen to speak. But one looked at me and I did manage to hear, "Chapeau Hadi." The other muttered, "Chap— Hadi." These clowns were at one time at Sidi and now in the field. "Chapeau Hadi" was famous in the legion.

The lolling heads of these thieves showed their minds were mostly on vacation for the moment. The Count, his great eyes shining bright like sparkling wine, with dust upon his nose, took out his revolver and intended to send them to the devil. I ordered an absolute "no" to the Count. These Legionnaires were good omens. I ordered these men to be given wonton soup. Then to be draped from the scorch of the sun and loaded up onto the baggage camels.

The ghostly Chamba riders to the right of me were now joined to the left of me with three others, both groups keeping their positions, hanging over us with sky aglare like fate. These true believers asquat their camels shuffled through the sand and stones, and they too bending to tighten their stirrup straps. Last sunlight glints on their rifles and makes them gold. And their desert dogs with them, tracking us also, at times barking as if to want to shake all the ground under our feet.

A sandstorm came upon us, and I did already burn my eyes by too long looking into all this egg whiteness and listening at times to my cameleers humming tuneless songs between their teeth and their sore cracked lips with the buzzards circling very high above, waiting for our deaths.

Then after this sudden low storm of sand did pass, we trekked toward the still slowly setting sun and I did watch the long blue shadows become little pools in the still hills' hollows. Then the light would stretch out and make flat all the dunes and hills in the distance until, slowly, the sun's last light would drop into the west.

We rode on by the light of the early moon, which was like a sweeping scimitar. And rode also during the night and thus avoided being tracked. At last we came to the Grove of a Hundred Palm Trees. Branching palms appeared to make the place an Allah heaven-sent garden of rest in this hot white land.

From a distance, the palms were like green-fronted feather dusters covering cool shaded gardens, whirling and swirling in the tumult of light. For weeks no palm trees on the desert's dunes, only the sun's come and go. At times like this I did like the smell of the wind among these palms. I brought my camel to its knees crying "Adar-Ya-Yam." The moon resumed all heaven now. White silence more than white. There would be a frost tonight.

Always and every night after Chang fell off his camel, the encampment was asleep before I finished my length of Pinard and

lo mein and dried subgum chicken. And I did watch those sleeping
rough seaboard men and did feel I was so alone. But, English, only
for a moment did I feel this, for I did see them so as slaves, as we
are slaves of someone or something. But I, Hadi the yearning, wanted
to be free of both love and hate and circumstance and to not waste
my time in the exercise of anything but survival. Which is also
slavery.

So I would take my lamp and go to bed but stay awake a little
longer to cover up some of the embers in the sand while practicing
my square-limbed Roman writing with a stick on the sand. At night,
with moonlight pouring and with my slowly reading *Macbeth* by the
lamp in the fireshine, and swallowing more wonton soup so as to not
waste it, and eating my sweet rice with raisins so as not to waste it
either, I would force my reading of *Macbeth* and write the lesson
words in the sand. Reading his blasts of passion that kept me awake,
reading his slow camel trump of doom that could whirl up this dust
of the desert but perhaps only actually hearing what my generous
Pinard wine says. Al-lah Yahmahrik; God be with you, Shakespeare.
Allah il Shakespeare. God is Shakespeare.

But now, sleep safe until tomorrow. Night would come again,
but again I would not sleep.

The desert passed by with my camel's steps and with my camel's
stomach rumbling to divert my attentions from Shakespeare who
had more words than there were grains of sand.

Then we came to this city, rising right out of the barren wastes
unexpectedly. The cliffs of Aithadidou are a geological phenomenon
of great interest. The main cliff is sheer to the height of nine hundred
feet, the most fantastique form of all these strange sandstone shapes
that still linger here. It has enchanted caves with deep crannies in the
tall vertical sides. In the wild valley above there are masses of green
bushes said to be brush that has lived there for more than a million
years.

Actually, Aithadidou is a city of walls, sloped and huge with six
main towers and more walls and lesser towers, then more massive
round towers of a fort and yet another smaller city built into the side
of the mountain, of stone-covered buildings with white mortar and
painted various shades of light to medium light blue. I did see steep
steps with their slippery cobblestones and sheep and goats and poul-
try wandering round the first and second stories of their buildings;

the women and children then above the men, and if a patriarch who was the grandfather was still alive, he lived at the very top of the house.

Inside the walls of the town were donkeys standing about with shopping baskets strapped over their sides and the gaudy awnings of tents and the open-bloused old men and tinkling women and squealing children and little Berber boys running in and out and about with their burr heads and their portmanteau of dirt. Tent poles and tent coverings, open shops of doorless tents with Berbers sitting round their goods. Tribesmen on horses dressed in rough homespun woolen cloaks which were without sleeves, and long hooded burnooses over jellabahs. In their brown robes with their brightly colored neck scarves at their throats, which told me these were of the ferocious Zowaia Bedouin tribe, amid the burnoosed Berbers of the Zaquig Bedouin tribe.

That night, after thinking of my Samonama, my whore of a thousand tents, and possessed by it, after the evening prayers had been said, the Count, each step sounding heavy in his insolent stride, and my two Legionnaires, now dressed in Berber clothes, walked with me to the classic Arab feast of an entire lamb stuffed with rice to absorb the lamb fat mixed in with almonds and raisins and all of it roasted whole over a large fire along with whole already stewed chickens to turn the chickens' skins crisp like thin wafers, and dwelling on that I would rid myself of this great lethargy and apathy in my heart and my dropping of tears, and not to think wearisomely of my Samonama.

Then white-clad servants brought pilafs of rice, nuts, and chopped meat kabobs of kid, and camel's milk curds to be eaten with bread, and with this, a pastelike macaroni cooked in butter, a heavy shortbread fried in oil and eaten with sugar, and between courses drank more bowls of lemon juice to aid our appetites, and we all needed aid as the hours wore on. And then, too, to dwell for relief on my Silver Bell and my cause of mourning, that until her loveliness had become unto me a thing of tears.

Then we had celery soup, two bowls of yogurt with lemon mint with a side plate of young pale green cucumbers and carrots, then dates, the dry yellow hard as acorns, greasy dates used for soap making that cleans the stomach out. Then chicken-cooked-in-with-lamb stew with hundreds of crushed walnuts with pomegranate juice served on a mound of Samonama—I mean, on a mound of a stewy sauced fluffy rice dipped in Iranian vodka and eaten with eggplant sauteed with yogurt, then yogurt soup with meatballs, while I thought of my distress, my throe, my ache, with that weak mouth so many men have kissed.

My bodyguards, the Legionnaires, were full to bursting and in a distended comatose situation. Then came the ceremonial drinking of mint tea after the rich coffee and we were finally offered very large cakes of very hard plain sugar all on a carpet round a red cotton cloth upon which was a vast brass tray laden with blue bowls of cakes filled to overflowing, and we ate with our fingers.

The next day, pondering on my Samonama of yesteryear, my ghostly flower, pondering my sorrows and my impassioned pain, I decided now I would leave off thinking of Samonama. I went to the bazaar to reckon with my competition and to rid myself of my thoughts. To tents offering my trade in spices, once from ships in sacks and now here in bowls: turmeric, dried olives, sesame seeds, cumin, mint, cinnamon, garlic, raisins, parsley, coriander, nutmeg, paprika, black pepper, ginger root, cloves, and bowls of sugar.

I came upon a tent that offered flaky pigeon pie and watched old sellers walking, staggering, offering mounds of freshly roasted pistachio nuts and wafer-shaped nougats sprinkled with rose water filled with pistachio nuts and almonds. Next past bland banks of cabbages, and grapes that hid their brightness under a sand dust, and piles of spicy plums and ill-shaped quinces. Here there were flutists with notes and whistles from fine enticing wood which could catch birds if the flutists played long enough, and whiffs of delectable fragrances among these vermilion tents, pots of steaming water for the quick food that is couscous, and snake charmers, magicians, and tribesmen offering for money games of checkers.

I should have been with Ubanmasifa. But then, what good would that have done? Being dead, that is. I am here to buy a precious bride while Ubanmasifa is in the shore surf with his belly full of crabs eating his stomach away.

I was going from one tent to another, sitting on black horseskin coverings and richly colored tribal rugs and cushions of Moroc leather and the shimmer of brass and copper that decorated these proud tents, tasting stewed lamb in assorted spices and salts, even though I was full to bursting.

Walking reflectively. I should weep no more nor sigh nor groan and no more be possessed prisoner in this cage of fire. I should find a love that is not like feeding your heart to the beak of a hawk.

At last I came to the end of the bazaar, and to the parade ground where I heard ancient Berber trumpets as the Romans had along with the sounded rapid boom of saddle drums, and there came a rush of horsemen onto this open place, waving swords and shrieking out in high voices. This meant the camel and horse races were due to start. Broad felt tents had been set up lining the parade ground on both sides and I heard the wild howling of Arab bagpipes and saw religious dancers, and acrobats leaping up and down at signals given by leaders in the center yelling the name of Allah in chorus and them also swaying and stomping and repeating the measures and invocations countless times until each dancer had lashed himself into a trance, a delirium that no longer felt exhaustion, only glory.

After the races came what you can call in English the fantasia, which is a wild superb group riding of desert tribe Berber horsemen in all their barbaric vitality. The best and most reckless riders had collected with their finest stallions for this performance. Wild riding is the national sport for these Berber people. For each maneuver, first-class horsemen line up at the end of the race course, some forty abreast in wave that will be coming and wave after wave. Each rider will strive to outdo his companions in brilliance of costume and trappings, saddles and bridles. Such a display of nincompoopery. They are dressed up in vivid hues and are leather studded with gold, stolen from the caravans, and covered with green and salmon silk, also stolen from the caravans. The linings of capes are aflame with color, and stallions mostly pearly white as Samonama was not. But like feeding your heart to the hawk. Samonama, oh I was your slave and you of a thousand loves, hard of heart; you who would never lie alone. Even now they rear and neigh and paw the ground in their impatience to be unleashed.

At a command, these marshaled warriors and caravan thieves drive their spurs into their horses' flanks. The beasts leap frantically forward in all this showmanship, and down the course they flash, goaded on into a terrific frenzy. The riders shout their tribal war cries, standing upright in their silver stirrups stolen from the caravans. All was white tails of stallions and flowing manes, white burnooses, capes lined with colored orange, then cloaks red and purple, sashes yellow and scarlet, draperies all loosened, turbans all streaming, a sweeping swirl behind them upon the wind storm from out of this infernal gallop of forty yelling demons, forty strong bronze arms stretch forth brandishing in the air forty copper muskets stolen from the caravans. Upon a signal at this mad career, they shout in unison and in unison twirl their guns, fire off a deafening fusillade, fling their gleaming smoking weapons into the air, leap out to catch them, and thunderously plunge on in a fury of dust and color.

Then this phalanx of men galloping on horses riding straight at you pull up short at the last moment as they again fire muskets into the air, then ride off to make room for the next phalanx.

Wave after wave of bandits, each worthy wave more abandoned, more warped and savage than the last wave, each superb rider fiercely handsome and graceful as a god. Saddles and bridles break, blood streams from the horses' flanks in their efforts, the ground is shattered by the pounding hooves. More muskets explode, the insane yelling and the smell of powder fill the air. The riders and the horses go wild and so do the spectators, but not I. My mind is elsewhere.

Then at sunset, after the evening prayers had been said, the drums drum a ghostly thud. For lust himself now leads me to the lasses; me, exhausted with the want of my Samonama. My trumpets will not let me rest. Now to the Brides Market itself, for it was considered très romantique to buy brides by torchlight.

It was another tent city, bell tents with their sides raised to admit air, with a large pavilion by the side of the cliff of Aithadidou. In front was a pool fed by an underground channel and baby rivers amid a little astounding forest of palm trees.

About the pool in this joyful gathering were merchant princes, stately men in fine raiment, sitting on their dyed camel hair rugs piled on carpets and puffing on their bubble-bubble pipes, their lances planted before themselves. Each one bore his flag and his ensign of territorial rule.

The prelude to buying the brides was the splendor and fanaticism of the girl folk dancers, and the music of the Berbers with their bagpipes and lute players wailing. They circled round the pool, vibrating and undulating, with much clinking of the tiny silver cymbals fastened to their fingertips. All through this performance I passed my time considering my lust, which was sharp, swift, and bright.

Then the bride sale began. And I waited in anticipation for a girl to shake my body and shake my bones. There would be three girls on the platform at one time, all dancing as their parents and their tribe taught them, and none would be dressed like tinselly gypsies, but richly decorated in low silken trousers clasped at the ankles.

All did start to do the traditional belly dance to the music, each revealing the ancient art as she had perfected it, her hips going up and down and round and forward and backward while her arms did weave the air, not clinking her silver finger bells which her family could not afford to buy for her, but only vibrating castanets, carefully carved in wood by her father when the girl was five years old and it was established she was destined for the Brides Market.

After one hundred clicks of the tongue, three more young girls came on, the others retiring behind the curtained platform. All lithe young creatures and how shining those great black eyes. One after another bride to be dancing, vibrating their undulations about their hips as they caressed their stomachs and buttocks and breasts. Then too, dancers gestured enticingly to the clapping of the merchant princes' hands and the beating of drums, and each girl sways and waves her arms rhythmically faster and faster until she is almost in a frenzy of motion, and the men in a frenzy of heat.

More girls came onto the platform. More triumphant ardor, quickening the blood to a heat, making it spread, changing men's voices that burst wildly out into the open. More stabbing eyes to you and curving bosoms that turn men grunting into swine. Even my own pools of passion began to clot. I watched my breath go in and out and gathered my lust in my fist, watching all these quickly rolling hips. The merchant princes were on their feet shouting, driving their fists into the air. The bride master had to mount the platform and beg for quiet.

I thought at that moment, brides are certainly a good business. This I must remember.

The music became languid. The men sat down. The music became a luxurious wailing. Try not to repeat the fervor of what has just happened. The new dancers had on veils, a precaution against the riot of desire. A disguise, eh English? But her disguise of a veil was unsuccessful.

This, my dancing love bride, was very subtle in swaying those quivering flanks of hers in time with her castanets' rattle. Keeping time and rhythm with her midriff gyrations, and the breasts crying against the embroidered cloth of her halter. Very elegant. I will buy this one heavy silver bangles and silver bells for round her neck and

wrists and for in the braids of her hair and for round her waist that
go cling, tinkle, ding, bing, ting.

Her dance quickly became lascivious and in three clicks of the
tongue, wanton. Then her veil did fall away. Besides silver bells, I
will buy her brass bells so that she will sound like a cow. Fong did
say my coming wife should be of the sign of the cow and cows make
good wives.

But this was no cow! This youth, scarcely fifteen years of age
and that I did know of a sudden that I knew this girl. There was
honey in her blood, which showed me a kingly danger. She had an
immediate fire. Then my brain said to me, I know what comes of
looking upon this damsel. Make soft her heart to me. So perhaps she
is my remedy against Silver Bell. My medicine. My love! With
Samonama's face, Samonama's mouth. Her name was Alik. She
couldn't read.

And so I bought for myself a wife at the Brides Market. Now
back to the north where the waters are, but first the gathering of
supplies from the bazaar and the purchase of raw sugar from Egypt
which I would make into a nearly black paste to put into a jar which
I learned about from a Legionnaire who had read about it in a book
on the Incas of the Andes. This mixture was fed to the best of the
Inca warriors. This raw sugar, mixed with barley flour and molasses
sugar that comes from the Sudan that makes another paste that could
be put on Fong's sweet rice with raisins in a stew of dried kid, whole
brown rice, and more raisins in a Berber couscous pot that could be
heated up with camel splat. Hence we gorged the camels with all the
shaft and barley pods they could fit in their stomachs.

Also purchased were cheaply priced sacks of tea to make the
thick Bedouin tea the consistency of my molasses sugar paste and
into which would be added small cups of raw sugar for energy to
survive this stinking desert. And yet more sacks of rice, essential
for living in the desert. Then comes flour for fresh, flat pita bread,
dried dates, fresh figs, twenty-five sacks of cooked Moroc platter bread, and fifty small sacks of goat cheese for eating in the
saddle.

But for me, the earth is gay for once, and I am happy to look
forward to a small house in Sidi-bel-Abbes of Nord Afrique with my
love, Alik. Now with Alik, all sullenness, uncomely sluggishness,
anger, grief, and haggardness away! Lo! Heigh-ho! Never a cloud I

could see with my fair love, Alik, to stain the shining days. Now is the coming of the fairest time of gentleness.

Eagerly I awaited the end of each day, then with the moon on my bed in silence of the night lust caught me by the hair and roused me. I will be the ram leaping. I will give to thee my love, Alik. I will stretch out my hand and give my love to thee.

One night, in our camp in the great desert, Alik did turn to me and say, "I am fertile now, and this night I will conceive and soon give birth to a child."

"That is wonderful, my love. A Little Hadi. . . ."

"No, it will be a girl," she said.

"That will be wonderful also, my great love," I said.

"I must tell you something. That it was necessary for me to let you lay on me to have this child. Women babies only come from men who are their husbands," she said.

"Yes, O love. Quite true . . . O love," I said.

"I wanted to have a child," she said. "A girl child."

"Yes, eternal love, good," I said breathlessly.

"But I must tell you something," she said.

"Yes, mistress of my universe?" I said.

"I am a girl who likes to lay on girls," she said.

"That is nice, love—what?" I yelled. I need only add, this reeked little of wit. Did she think me a savage? A pagan? What is this drivel? Now look at what I've got! Puh! Another rebuke meted out. Another laugh against Hadi, the scribe. Wo-ye. Living is dangerous for your life.

"I am a girl who likes to lay on girls. And therefore I find it repulsive and repugnant for you to lay on me ever again and I can never permit it again. I can only lay on women," she said again.

"Ohhhh . . .," I said.

"I want a girl child so that I can raise her and teach her as a woman to only want to lay on women," she said.

"Ohhh . . .," I said. This was really too much for a person to live with.

"Since you are my husband and rich," she said somewhat heatedly and in an aggravated way, "I want you to buy me more girl children so that I can train them to lay on girl children. Thus one day have a whole tribe of women laying on women, just as it is a right to have men who like to lay on men and train men to do so as with the Turks," she said.

Barefoot, ungirt, I did raise me up as in a dream and go to another tent; I lay down. I alone of all men could not sleep. My thoughts mocked me with their flitting illusions that come not from the temples of my God Allah. Of all the blows on blood-sodden battlefields, this is Hadi's worst. What would I be if I had not known Alik, I did ask. Better off, I say. Here is the body of Alik beside Samonama, to hang another black wreath upon. Wo-ye.

From that day on, I did not look at Alik riding upon her camel, but only at the endless sand. Eventually we came again to Sidi-bel-Abbes, and then we were in front of Fong's house, and Chung at last fell off his camel with his too much hashish. I, Hadi Abbabba Guwah, the ex-lover and non-merchant, was in no frame of mind to enter Fong's house only to tell him that I had bought a lesbian with Fong's money and a woman who didn't want to be my wife and wouldn't permit me to lay on her anymore. I was indeed wretched, more so than ever in my life. The Chinois had displayed faith in me, yet at the moment, look at the result. Everything is black. Now I have a lesbian. Ubanmasifa and my ships drowned dead, according to my dream. Fong will of course beat me like the true slave I am; beat me about my head and shoulders and all of my body in his wrath. I deserve it.

I did see a new bistro in the town, the Cafe de Paris. I would retire there to suffer. I told the Count, that dimwitted but likable chap, pursuing a Polski kingdom in the Mediterranean, that I was stupid. But then, he is so stupid even an ox wouldn't lend him his brains. I ordered the Count to take Alik into Fong's house and to dismiss his ridiculous bodyguard.

"Jawohl, mein führer!" he did shout.

I did walk. Heard footsteps here and there. The evening shades and silence descended on the town. The cafe inside had a meek and lowly grace, though you would not call it a tranquil place. It was full of Legionnaires, and the corners of the large room held spots of darkness as a blue tablecloth holds its purple stains. It had a nicely sanded gray flagstone floor. The floor ran wet with Pinard. And at a table with my one candle flickering, I would brood over my un-shaped dreams, laden with my beginnings. Is there hope in me? Or only bitter acid as if there were blood in my mouth.

The waiter brought me five mugs of Pinard. I did wonder, what was this? I did not order five mugs of Pinard. Then I heard about me, "To Hadi, the chapeau, the good fellow. Drinks on us!"

Then I looked to the Legionnaires about, all raising their mugs up in salut to their chapeau Hadi. I was almost in tears.

I did drink and ponder. I will ask to work for Fong, myself resolving against myself, which will in turn resolve into nothing. I will be crying into the dead black of my new clothing, which I will buy. What has my brain that it hopes to last longer?

Chapeau Hadi. He's dilly but not too clever. I had my Pinard. One mug. Two mugs. I've made a beastly rum go at everything. Right. We'll move along now and dwell on something else. If I had been with Ubanmasifa I would be dead now. That solves nothing. Then downed another mug of chapeau vin. We have but this one life and it is gone. Gnat-like thoughts and thoughts like gnats. Will I with sorrow become beautiful and wise? Since Allah has seen fit to make Alik lay on girls, it's his will. He's God, not me. Another mug of wine went down. And another. My fifth mug was gulped. Life hath quicksands, Hadi sayeth. More than flesh and blood can bear. Then five more mugs did arrive via a waiter for Hadi chapeau. I drank one mug down. I try to make myself worthy to succeed in pleasing everybody. Manners maketh a man.

I did look up just in time to see him shuffling into the darkened cafe. Him. The smear of a smile on his ugly, one-eyed, pockmarked face; his face smiling. Ah-ha! The ghost of Ubanmasifa. Come to shake my body and shake my bones. He came at me, squeezing through the tables, to tell me of his catastrophe, and remind me that I wasn't there in his unclean but vigorous sea. Closer, his one eye a little oval mirror like a tiny pool. I crooked my finger beckoning him toward me. A smile curls back loosely from his teeth. He slowly sat down, smiling, smiling, like the puppets in the marketplace at sunrise, the smell of salt spray still about him. Then he hisses at me, his words are dry and faint as in a dream.

"You are a rich man."

He said this to harass me.

"Oui, oui, absolument," I did reply.

"Your Sicily ships worked wonderfully well. Your charts and maps were perfect. All that you wrote was exact. Your instructions all correct. I picked up all the trade you asked me to pick up. Hence you are a rich man," he said.

"This has become ridiculous," I said. "Don't give me your ghostly jests."

"Ghostly jests?" he said.

"Ghostly jests. You are a ghost," I said.

"I am not a ghost," he said.

"You are a ghost," I said. "You are dead."

"I am not dead," he said.

"You are," I said.

"I'm not," he said.

"I saw it. I saw you die. In a storm. All my ships died. Sank."

"Where did you see this?"

"In my dream."

"Dream!" Then he kicked me in the shins very hard. "Wake up and see if your pain is a dream, you old goat."

"Old goat!" Of a second I reached and pulled his beard. He did scream and quickly slapped my face shouting loudly, "You insolent slave dog!"

Five, six, seven Legionnaires got to their feet immediately. Big men. Powerful. One man of them alone could have knotted up Ubanmasifa's legs and arms and head and rolled him out the door as if he were a bowling ball. No one slaps chapeau Hadi in a Legion cafe. I motioned to them it was très bien and to sit down. They did so. Hadi the führer.

I looked at Ubanmasifa. I did not understand. "My dream, my vision, it was so clear . . . so vivid."

"But only a dream. I hope you have no more of them. Our profit this journey was enormous. With the speed of the journey and the costs we made a nine hundred percent profit, more than any other trader before. Fong is very pleased. This is far better than our days of caravan raiding. And safer. And cooler. I have now been bitten by the sea. Once, I never wanted to return to the desert. Now, I do not want to return to the land."

I then did ask of the details of the journey and he related to me all of the wondrous sights he had seen, and how my work as a cartographer and map maker had worked so well, and the sea instruments I had Fong's craftsmen make had worked perfectly. Indeed, better than anything they had for travel on the Mediterranean, which was mostly a matter of guessing and a lifetime of the knowledge of currents. In sum, a matter of time and memory. And that all the information I had obtained from Sultan Mograb's library was absolutely accurate and far more detailed than even what the Hollanders had, but not as detailed as what the Portogee had, which was truly perfect. These sailors were the sultans of the East India trade. However, they did not have my Sicily ships, but the traditionally fat and clumsy and slow sailing ships that could only sail deep water and could never be brought upon a beach as my Sicily ships could.

I asked many questions of Ubanmasifa, and interrupted him often for more detailed knowledge of his experience. I instructed that he must learn to gather more information and also this alone should be paid for to whoever gave him good information. On this he did agree with great excitement, while I was thinking we must build more Sicily ships, hence more profit, if not on one island then another. And my fleet could disperse, according to quantities on hand of whatever spice that had been farmed. Every journey must show a great profit.

Ubanmasifa informed me that he had brought back much silk from Cathay, plus two brides for Fong. Silk? No, I said to him. No more silk. It is heavy for the Sicily ships and not that much of a profit, not with the number of traders who deal in it. He would confine his trade to spices.

We talked until the dawn crawled upon the yellow walls entering like an aimless moth and eventually on the blurred face of Ubanmasifa. It was time to go to Fong's house.

Due to my free Pinard, I rested my one arm on Ubanmasifa's arm and he strongly led me with his one blinking eye to Fong's house and through the gate to my old room, which Ubanmasifa said Fong had readied for me knowing from the Count of my return. Ubanmasifa led me to my mat. Alik was asleep there. I kicked her awake. Ubanmasifa left. Startled, she started up, pulling the covers about her.

"Out!" I said. "Get out! You obnoxious les-bian!"

Without noise she did rise and taking her clothes, and wrapped in a blanket, left the room.

I fell to the mat to dream of my success. Dwell on my success. Think of the future. I dream-thought I was so happy. I dream-thought that I would not dream any longer of Ubanmasifa dying in the sea and my valuable Sicily ships going to the bottom. I did sleep.

Who to wake me after the noon hour but Amandii. My Amandii. My one little victory. I had tried to make myself worthy of Samonama. But life is full of tricks, and joy is a cobweb, a flower in the dust. With Alik the dream storms breathed. With her, I strained toward heaven and lay hold of hell.

Amandii, tears forming beneath her eyelids, soft cheeks perfumed by winds. Smiles more light than petals. Her beauty is kind. My heart gave a palpitating flutter for this moth of a girl.

I did couple again quickly with this girl of cloud, with this body tawnier than wheat, and her bosoms as yellow as butter, her blue-black hair mussed over her eyes. . . . She did go mad with passion for me, Hadi, the ancient, the one-armed.

Then her hormones so suddenly were rioting, going berserk, popping out all over the floor. What were we doing on the floor? Where was the mat? Oh, it was over in the corner, rumpled, half against the wall. Her hormones were all over the floor, wet; we sliding around in her hormones, or she on her back sliding round the room on her hormones. The floor was wet and the heels of her feet could not get a proper grip on the floor. So we did slide from wall to wall, a beast with two backs. Slippery sticky wet. Grotesque! Then more hormones came from her, and again more and more; the floor an ocean of her hormones and she was yelling, "Don't stop! Don't stop!" Squeezing me, digging her nails into my skin; me not stopping. Then we slid over and I slammed my head into the wall.

"Don't stop! Don't stop!" The wall lacquer was all cracked. "Harder! Harder!" she yelled. Then, "More-more-more!" Her hands were about my throat. "More—harder! Don't stop!" I slammed into a knee table breaking one of its legs. The Chinois vase on it banged my head, then rolled onto the floor and made a sound as if it had dropped into water. I did look at my arm and shoulders. They were covered in blood. My blood. "More," she did choke. "In the name of Allah!"

"In the name of Allah?" I did breathe.

"Allah," she breathed.

"Is this for Allah?" I did pant.

"Yes. I haven't said my prayers today."

"This is praying?"

"Yes it is. You are Allah, my Allah, my wonderful, beloved, adored, blessed Allah and I will (oh!) give you (grunt) a prophet. Just more—more—more!"

Then the door panel slammed open. "What is this crashing and noise?" Fong stepped in, rather he slid in, and sliding toward the other wall. But before he struck, crashing it to pieces, yelling, "What is this?" he fell to his backside. He tried to get up, but slipped again. Then on his hands and knees, he crawled toward us, we still coupled. "I see, I see," he kept saying. Then over her face, stuck his down close into hers and said, "Young lady, get this room cleaned up and bring us some food. Is that clear? First take a bath."

Amandii groaned.

Then he said to me, "We will eat, and we will talk. There is much to discuss. I will wait for you in my chambers. You will remember your clothes?"

On his hands and knees Fong crawled out of the room. All I do say, English, is believe me, laying on her with one arm was no easy thing.

We un-coupled. She said, "I must get to work." I nodded. My Amandii. My one little victory. Contentment, though it went with Alik, it is that it came back now with Amandii. Now I would leave off thinking of Alik, it would seem. I had bought Amandii a present in Aithadidou, a braid for her long hair of heavy silver coins, in the center of which was a silver medallion which would hang down on her forehead.

As soon as I had composed myself, and found my clothes where they lay scattered about the room, I tried to go marching off to Fong. Or perhaps truly, lagged to Fong. Yes, lagged I think. He was sitting, as usual, on his many pillows. He seemed pleased, yet his eyes did seem to bore through me.

"This is more seemly," he said, motioning me to the pillows, "but you are fatigued, doubtless from your long journey. Sit down, I pray you."

I sat down, stinking, as you will remember, of hormones.

"Firstly," he said, "congratulations. Your work was well done. I am a richer man for it and so are you and Ubanmasifa. Now you must plan for the next journey. I want you off speedily. So, my bookkeeper, it's back to your charts, graphs, maps, instructions, and above all your marvellous lists. And take a bath to get rid of that smell. Do you have any more suggestions?"

"Yes. I want more Sicily ships. This will mean—"

"They are building them now. Ten to be exact. Does this satisfy you?"

"Indeed."

"Now, any other suggestions? Before you take a bath?"

"I must return to my papers. I will have some suggestions I am sure."

"I will wait for only two days. Then Ubanmasifa is off again. He is very eager. He is a good man. How was your trip? I see your bride. Are you satisfied?" At this point we were interrupted by the arrival of Amandii, bearing trays of mu shu pork with side platters of shredded beef in Hoi Sin sauce, and also fantail shrimp and crispy chicken wings. Our eyes met for the briefest moment.

"My gallant," she did impart with her eyes and rapid breathing, as she laid before me a platter of Happy Family lobster.

"My sweet," I as you say it, gulped, nearly soundlessly.

Fong perceived. Immediately he laid his hand intimately on Amandii, my flower, and then withdrew it, saying to her: "Your bath was insufficient, for the smell is still upon you. Please now to bathe again. Now!"

Then he did say to me, "I believe you were telling me of the Brides Market?"

"Yes, my bride . . . well it is terrible, a fate I could not have imagined. She, I discover, is a girl who likes to lay on girls . . ."

At this, he erupted in belly-shaking laughter, and pointing his stubby finger at me, said, "You tell me I spent all that money and you purchased a lesbian!" His laugh lost all control, his bowl of shredded beef in Hoi Sin sauce spilled into his lap, with more laughter the bowl itself fell. I was totally embarrassed.

"I did not know. I did not know. . . ."

"Do not be sad. It is a part of life. And you do entertain me. All you went through for a lesbian. Do not fret. I will give you the money to buy another bride—do not protest. I insist. But this is too much amusement for me to even eat by." He started to laugh again.

"I would like to purchase Amandii instead of going back to the Brides Market . . ."

Fong's laughter subsided. His countenance became serious, and he said, "Certainly not. Amandii is mine. You are not the only one Amandii lays on. I could never let her go."

"But Amandii . . . and I . . . we, I am trying to say I, Hadi Abbabba Guwah, would ask this one little favor of you, you who have so many wives and serving girls that you would not even miss . . ."

"Enough!" Fong cut my pathetic babbling short, for in truth I sounded like a man who has lost his reason. "I have spoken, and so it will be. From this day forth you will not see Amandii again, for I see the two of you are not to be trusted. I have many eyes in this town. And if you disobey me in this, I will practice on you the arts of the Tebu, and on the girl as well, and you will wish you were dead."

I sat there looking as numb as a stupid, wounded baggage camel. Wo-ye. This was the worst pain Hadi has truly ever had to bear. My heart made me feel honestly that I was one pubic hair.

"Listen to me," continued Fong harshly. "I think you are not lucky in this matter of women, and so I advise you to put them out of your head. You are a businessman, and with my help you will grow rich. I will build you a villa, with your own library for your researches. But do not cross me in this one particular matter!"

After I had eaten I returned to my room, with the laughter of Fong still ringing in my ears. I would bury myself in this work.

I crossed to the chest and took out my papers. Seated myself at my knee desk with quills and inks. I did my food supply list, giving each man a bigger ration this time of everything. List of trading goods to leave Arzeu would be the same. List of the monies to be spent and on what. I consulted my maps, rereading my original notes to myself. The silk from Cathay would be replaced by . . . by . . . something else lighter than the heavy silk. I will go to the docks this coming next day and talk with the traders . . . they will know something.

One of Fong's servant girls brought me food; no more Amandii. Well, Puh!, I thought. Then I asked her for eight jars of rice wine. She returned, and went to a cushion to play studious music. I put her out of my mind. No more wives for Hadi. I was between subgum wonton and Mongolian beef and rice wine when reading a report copied from Mograb's library. Something I had overlooked. A report on the small pearls from Oman.

All this talk of business is tiring, English, but you will see for yourself whether I have done well in following the advice of Fong. It is a long way to the port, and so I think we will not walk there. It is a pity that I am no longer a young man, or I would take you aboard all my ships tied up with their lateen sails drying and flapping in the Mediterranean breeze and also show you the inside of my storehouses. The waterfront bustles with carts drawn by donkeys, and there is close down there everywhere the scent of fragrant spices, my spices, then also the smells of oakum, pitch, tar, resin, and pieces of newly cut canvas, palm oil, or what you call copra oil.

But come, come this way to my house, English. You see, a cool nice wind comes always as we walk this road which twirls round into the grass that I have planted along this, my road, to make it beautiful, and the fig trees I've planted in between pomegranate trees lining my road which I call Boulevard de la Marne and I like to watch the wind with all its fragrant odors that come in from the Middle Sea bending each blade of grass north, east, south, west as it swirls off the cliffs of this harbor.

You see that my hills surrounding my house are covered with pepper trees that I myself did plant of a time ago as I heard my head once did say to me to do, and the clouds come of a day in the winter and drop their water here. There in the distance are my twelve thousand sheep which give my workers the coarse wool which is much suited to carpet manufacture. Look there, below that hill, those are my Angora goats that I have bought from the Turks, and which give me the material to make mohair cloth which I sell to the gentlemen merchants of Paris. And see there westerly, those are my grinding mills in which the spice stems and seeds and whole pods are grilled to dust.

And over there easterly, although you can't see them, are my salt pans, where Middle Sea water is let into the shallows and evaporated. The salt is heaped into pyramids and shipped in sailing vessels to various ports of the New World in my Hadi ships. My fine salt farms are of a large profit. I have many salt pans in the east. In the bad heat of summer evaporation is rapid and the salt left in the ponds can be quickly bagged and I can employ and pay many more free women; women to rake my salt into huge conical mounds which are then hand poured into heavy fiber bags I get from the French and all my beautiful salt is shipped to the Uruguayan and Argentine meat-packing plants, also to Paraguay plants where they salt up much beef which is named "bully" and then sent all the way back to England as "bully beef" and distributed to all of the men of the British Royal Navy and to all the infantry and artillery regiments and to all the Royal Highland Regiments of Scotland.

Then too, I have my white grape roots which I got from Jerez in Spain, and which now grow well in my white soil and I employ and pay many young girls and women as free girls and women and not as slaves to set out in flat baskets the pale grapes to dry. These I export to England where they use them in the town of Bristol to make sherry, which name you English use due to a corruption of your mispronunciation of Jerez; hence, sherry.

Come, here is my house . . . here is my property. As you can see, this is not a mud house with a flat roof made of palm wood. Come, here is one of my gardens which is a favorite of the Minister of Punitive Actions, who is my frequent guest at my many dinners, who is always uttering, "Oh, this is quite respectable!" You see here in my garden courts, marble statues from the Roman cities and villas, amid my masses of bougainvilleas and my vines and my geraniums over all of the walls surrounding all of my gardens, each with fluted columns and each wall a different color and every mosaic floor a different pattern. These here come from Emperor Caracalla's baths at Carthage A.D. 41. And here is where I do most of my work as Regional Consultant to the Minister of Finance. Of course, only upon decorating my person to become suave, to become Hadi the eleganti: taub, neckcloth, slippers, and turban. I now have many clothes to cover and hide my body that shows so well that I was once a slave. I have long taubs of kano, leather sandals, and slippers not made of beaten hemp.

Look, my wonderful marble fountain with all its water shooting into the air, and that with fixtures that I have devised; they can be arranged to shoot over there into my pomegranate trees and into my lemon trees and my orange trees. Here is where I hold most of my conferences, because I am now District Attaché to the Bureau de Commerce. More camel burbul-burbul can be heard here than in all of Afrique du Nord and, naturally, it's all devious French mind's sweating doubloons. Then too, what you call gossip, and rumors and continually, "Did you hear?" Or, "Is it true that—?" Or, "What do you think of this shocking—?" In between all this mischievous, unsavory, not too clever pandemonium of yabber-yacketty-yak, I stuff them with beef with oyster sauce, Hawaiian duck, sea dragon, Happy Family lobster, steak kew, beef Samoan, and a dish I discovered in New York City called chop suey. But I make it with goat meat. I also discovered the New York Stock Exchange. Then I went to seedy London, then to Oxford-of-the-bells, where I lectured at the School of Geography down by that bookshop named Blackwell's. I did a series of lectures, actually, on the flora and fauna and topography of North, Central, and the South Sahara Desert. For this I received a diploma from the Oxford School of Geography. Hadi the graduate. Have you been to Oxford, English? Cambridge, you say. Oh, well, we will drop the subject.

As I say, a cornucopia of burbul-burbul. And I must spend vast sums of these French louis to hold and live through these undelightful, unamusing bureaucratic parties, which as you say, can get on your wick. But I have been three times Mayor of this town of Arzeu, and it is a custom that I remain Mayor, old, dapper, and debonair, at a handsome salary. Yet I must be very aware of the Frank's political interventions, also advise them on how to secure redress for crimes committed by the beastly Berbers and how to quell revolutions and how to protect military property and diplomatic missions and business interests, so that we can all pull oar together.

Right. We'll move along now. That's a good chap.

Here is my own famous pool for swimming with its deep sandy bottom and with a rock four foot high at one end for a diving platform. The main pool is, as you say it, forty yards in circumference. Then there are the smaller pools for the children. All are built with marble and with three faucets from America, one hot, one cold, one with smelly Arab perfume, which of course, I make now.

What happened to Alik, you ask? Oh, she died because of childbirth. She produced twins. Two male children. A seemly sort of joke, don't you think?

In one garden I have exercise. I have my water wheel designed exactly as that of the one of the farmer Sidi-Bu-Khamsa's when I was with him as a slave long ago.

All of what I did see in the rich houses of the Arabs, I do now have: fountains with flowers in the water and statues, cypress and plane trees, attendants and servants, Rabat carpets of all designs, Roman columns that uphold my roofs, and thousands of pillows and cushions. I have my own Mosque of the Olive Tree. I collect birds in cages. I have thirty Angora cats from the Persians, not like the Hausa cats, and must watch their diet or they get too fat. And I have sixteen monkeys from Gibraltar who are good for the cats because they drive the cats to madness with monkey amusement, and at times, I have trained them to be good servants.

I have European tables and chairs and stools of ebony, all from Nubia, which I designed, for my European guests of honor. Also I must have receptions after weddings and for the long festivities that follow. Then too, I give to the bride Egyptian glass and Egyptian jewelry against misfortune. I myself prefer the look of my wine in crystal now. Not as from Legion days in a tin cup. Now mostly I wear a white taub, black ear and chin cloth and cape, and bright gold chains and my silver curved dagger, leather slippers, and at last the Gandurah over the taub.

Sometimes I try to think of how much riyalat am I worth now? Once I was worth only two silver riyalat. A horrendous nothing, which in your money, English, is seven shillings and sixpence. Before this I was worth fifty Kauri shells. That is one shilling and sixpence. Now I am worth millions and millions of Kauri shells. At times I do think, still, can I be sold to the Turks? Then I think of a sudden, I can live without fear of that now. Also, I no longer think of the sights of Kroo Lagoon in my land of Popo. Do you remember, English, the days when I was one pubic hair? Remember? Now I have got a freedom of a sort but obtained with much pain and great storms, but I, one pubic hair, have got fortunes, fruitful ground, a quiet mind, no grudge, no strife, no change of rule, no Turks. And I swell in wealth.

Come, see the cumulus clouds, see now the sunset reddens the walls and makes them orange. Soon yellow. Una atmosfera deliziosa. Come and follow me into this garden of my villa heavily scented with cedar, sandal and thuya woods. See, there, down there, the Port of Arzeu and way beyond, Oran. Just below, the ships with their noses to the docks and warping up and down in the tides and swells of the water. Those are my ships, English, being loaded and all those ships leaving the docks for the sea. Those ships there on the shore half built are mine also, my new additions to my Atalantika fleet. Those ships over there on the land are for repair. See the old, old sailors who are now sail menders and with their needles and string always mending and yet dwelling always on the memories of their Eastern voyages.

I have ships that come to me from Baltimore, America, because I do not have enough ships to go to service Baltimore or Philadelphia. Only my ships serve Boston and New York City. In Baltimore the McCormick Company which, do you know, has the largest spice mills in all of that land. Then too, here come ships from Salem, Massachusetts, who represent traders in Chicago, Illinois. My best trader is Chicago, Illinois, over Baltimore, but there is where most all of my best spices go; all the rubbish goes to Chicago. Nonetheless, they pay the best prices and want me to stop selling to Baltimore, and sell only to Chicago. This I will do for the moment. Considering their prices and also that I have traveled and charted the St. Lawrence River and my Sicily ships can navigate this river and dock in Chicago. This city, I am told, is the biggest meat makers in all that land for sausages of pork and beef. They use and pay well for my white pepper, coriander, sage, and nutmeg, all to make their sausages taste better.

Smell the oranges, English, and the olives, then all mixed up with the smell of oakum that is the caulking, and hear the sounds of the hawsers and the sounds of saws and smell the fresh-cut wood and listen to the pounding of mallets of the men building my new ships.

Now it is time for us to go down to my seashore. Come, the beach is not far from my house. One has only to cross a patch of high dune, a sort of plateau which overlooks the sea and shelves down steeply to the sands. The ground here is covered with yellowish pebbles and wild lilies that show snow white against the blue of the sky, which has already the hard metal glint it gets on very hot days.

I have no more mischiefs descend upon me. No more chides or rebukes meted out, not any other laugh against Hadi. My life is bearable. I am no longer tormented, confused, or have turmoil in my heart. My own library contains books in English, French, German, Italian, and Spanish. I can read them all. Novels, poetry, biography, travel, history. Do you like your Dickens? Cathy in *Wuthering Heights* is my Samonama. Mind like a cul-de-sac.

True, my beard is gray now, but I do have good skin and it is true that the teeth in my mouth do not wobble. And at times even now I find I think in the language of the Hausa and at another time in the words of the Fullani, and then in M'bum, Juku, then also those of the Francswari, Germani, Italani. But mostly I enjoy and rejoice that I have pleasure still in feeling the hard bodies of young women.

See, the aspect of the sea has changed. Its dark blue translucency has gone and see, there beyond the rock irises, under the lowering sky, it has silvery glints that hurt the eyes to look at. The damp heat of this spring made me long for the coming of the dry, clean summer heat. Which actually is quite disgusting. But I am always good-humored, always ready with a smile. I seem an addict of all normal pleasures, without being their slave.

You ask of Ubanmasifa. He was completely blinded on an Eastern run and now lives with me in my villa and has many servants and is quite fat. I will not have him a blind beggar in the streets. He is safe with me forever, never to know want or fear for a roof over his head.

There. The sun is gone now. You ask of Amandii? Well, Fong was dying and called me to his pillows. There he said I should take Amandii, not only that, but all his servants, if I wanted them. Plus his wives. I did the honorable thing, I took all his wives and all his servants. His children got his house. I made Amandii my first wife and told her to take what servants she wanted, which were all of them. Fong also told me I also had all his empire, all his ships, his stations, his merchants, his records, his docks, his storehouses.

And this is the end of my life, English, wives and children. But it is not yet the end of Hadi. True, I no longer go to the bazaars. However, perhaps next year I will go back to Paris and Berlin and live in the big hotels, because, after all, even the beauty which is all about me becomes tedious to the spirit of Hadi. So there must be change. But for now, look at the wild, wonderful sea, where the rushing water comes to the shore to all crumble up to look like torn paper, then it all disappears into spray and floats and glides its way to the sea as froth. Froth. Isn't life lovely?